YOUR FAVOURITE AUTHORS HAVE FALLEN FOR
THE START OF SOMETHING

"This is Miranda Dickinson at her very best"
Sarah Morgan

"A wonderfully romantic story about
the healing powers of love"
Milly Johnson

"Miranda is such a big-hearted, generous
writer, full of warmth and love"
Jenny Colgan

"Charming, quirky and properly romantic"
Mike Gayle

"A truly heart-warming novel, [it] will move anyone
who's ever taken a chance on love. A magical read"
Holly Miller

"Charming, relatable and sweet – I was fully
invested in the heartwarming love story"
Laura Jane Williams

"The perfect story to remind us all to reconnect: insightful,
clever, and with a gentle humour that left me wanting more"
Penny Parkes

Miranda is the author of twelve books, including six *Sunday Times* bestsellers. Her books have been translated into seven languages and have made the bestseller charts in four countries. She has been shortlisted twice for the RNA awards (for Novel of the Year in 2010 with *Fairytale of New York* and again in 2012 for Contemporary Novel of the Year for *It Started With a Kiss*). She has now sold over a million copies of her books worldwide. Miranda lives in the Black Country with her husband and daughter.

The Start of Something

Miranda
DICKINSON

ONE PLACE. MANY STORIES

HQ
An imprint of HarperCollins*Publishers* Ltd
1 London Bridge Street
London SE1 9GF

www.harpercollins.co.uk

HarperCollins*Publishers*
1st Floor, Watermarque Building, Ringsend Road
Dublin 4, Ireland

This edition 2022

1
First published in Great Britain by
HQ, an imprint of HarperCollins*Publishers* Ltd 2022

ISBN: 978-0-00-844075-6
US/CA: 978-0-00-848549-8

MIX
Paper from
responsible sources
FSC™ C007454

This book is produced from independently certified FSC™ paper
to ensure responsible forest management.

For more information visit: www.harpercollins.co.uk/green

This book is set in 11/15.5 pt. Caslon

Printed and bound in Great Britain by
CPI Group (UK) Ltd, Croydon, CR0 4YY

This book is dedicated to the amazing staff of the NHS, the emergency services, teachers, key workers and carers, who kept going when everything else ceased.
You're incredible. Thank you x

Live as though life was created for you
Maya Angelou

You'll never do a whole lot
unless you're brave enough to try.
Dolly Parton

Chapter One

LACHLAN

'Try to stay focused.'

'I *am* focused.'

I'm not. But I won't tell *her* that. What does she know about me, other than I'm the grumpy sod she has to wrestle into shape four times a week?

'You're forgetting I know you, Lachie. I can see you sneaking glances out of the window.'

'I'm not.'

I am, but only because the world out there is far more appealing than being pummelled by a self-righteous physiotherapist. I drag my gaze away and let her see it.

'That's it. Good. Try and lift that leg a little higher.'

She says it like it's easy. Like I haven't been trying for the last eight weeks. Easy for you, Tanya, walking in with that hip swing I thought was cute the first time I met you. Now it's just another kick to me: another thing your body can do that my body's forgotten.

I know what she's thinking: it's what I'm thinking, too. There should be more progress by now. Back when we started, the plan was ten to twelve weeks to regain at least 80 per cent mobility in my left leg. Doctors and surgeons, the hospital physios, they were all so sure of it. It was their job to be pessimistic, my doctor told me; whatever they'd told me about how long it will take was supposed to be worst-case scenario. But I'm eight weeks in and nothing's changed for a fortnight.

Tanya's smile is as annoyingly bright as ever, but recently a crease between her eyebrows has joined it. No amount of grinning is shifting it. That worries me.

I push harder and the pain forces a yelp from my lips. *Damn it.* Normally I can do this in silence, but now Tanya knows.

'Don't force it. Let's take a break. I'll get you some water.'

I can't tell which of us is more relieved as she hurries into the kitchen.

Shit.

Next time, I'll have to bite my tongue.

I let my gaze drift to the window again, to the building opposite. There's something going on in the flat directly over the hedge from mine. Its windows have been dark for a month now, ever since the old lady who lived there moved out. But last night, lights were blazing in it well past midnight. And today, all the windows facing my building have been opened. From time to time a carrier bag or a box will appear on the windowsill, only to be removed a few minutes later. Now the window is empty again, save for a pair of very worn gardening gloves resting against the glass. Looking closer, I can see a single naked light bulb burning in the ceiling. Something that looks like it could be a stepladder edges into view at one side, but it's draped in white – a dustsheet, maybe?

I look back just as Tanya returns with the glass of water. As she hands it to me, the chirpy dance tune of her mobile begins. She raises an apologetic hand, pointing towards the front door. She'll take it on the landing outside the flat as she always does. Judging by her tone as she answers the call hurrying out of the room, I reckon I have a couple of minutes at least.

Taking my chance, I push myself off the dining-table chair I've been doing my exercises on and hop to the window. My favourite spot. Funny, when I bought this place an age ago it never occurred to me to look outside. Now it's my lifeline. My safe place.

Standing by the glass, I can see the corner of the building next door and the wide sweep of communal garden that separates it from the main road. Two people are chatting on the pavement, their dogs making an enthusiastic appraisal of each other's behinds. I wonder if they might be connected with the activity in the opposite flat, but then they wave and go their separate ways. There's no decorator's van in the curving driveway, which is where I've seen tradespeople park their vehicles before. I glance at the car park at the rear of the building, but there's no van there, either, as far as I can see.

Yes, I know it's sad.

I never expected to become an expert in my nearest neighbours' lives, but here we are. I'm not proud of it – and I would be mortified if anyone spotted me. But – it helps. It helps to know the world is spinning on beyond these four walls. It's a promise that I'll see it again – that my own life waits there, just out of reach.

It's done more for my head than eight weeks of physio, that's for sure.

I look up from the road to the window of the flat opposite. My

3

breath catches. Someone is standing there. They have their back to the window, but I can see a dark ponytail and a paint-splattered T-shirt that might once have been a souvenir from a rock gig. Two hands appear at the small of their back, the shoulders rolling in a stretch. I imagine the satisfying crack of vertebrae coaxed back into line and I'm instantly jealous.

Turn around.

I want to see their face. I'm ashamed and fascinated at once: it is none of my business who owns the ponytail and tour T-shirt, and yet I want to know. I'm guessing it's a woman, but from this angle it's impossible to tell. Whoever they are, they look tired. I see it in the heavy lock of the shoulders, the slow progress of the stretch. I know how that feels...

'I thought we said no looking out of the window.'

When I turn, Tanya is standing in the room, hands on hips, like my mother does when she's about to deliver a bollocking. Better knuckle down, then, until it's done and she goes away.

When I look back an hour later, the flat is dark and the windows closed.

Chapter Two

BETHAN

It's done.

I nearly broke my back in the process and I don't think I'll shift the smell of paint from my nostrils any time soon, but the flat is decorated and I can start to consider it ours.

Gwych. Excellent.

Now I just need to make it feel like home.

Everything is white. Boring, maybe, but better than the weird magnolia-beige the previous tenant had. Utterly disgusting it was, like the colour of tinned rice pudding – and I can't stand that, either. This way I can buy some cheap colourful curtains, bedding and cushions and get all my colour from that. Noah adores colour. He told me last week he'd like to live in a rainbow. So I'm going to give my boy the closest thing to his heart's desire and paint a rainbow around him.

The thought of that makes me smile.

I check my watch: thirty minutes until I'm due to pick him up from Michelle's. Thank heaven she stepped in and had him to stay last night. Without her help I don't know what I would have done. And thank goodness my new landlord was okay with me redecorating the place before we moved in. I think he was relieved, to be honest. That yucky beige and the last tenant's gross mid-wall floral borders I think they used superglue to stick up were a nightmare to get rid of, so I saved him the trouble. Landlord brownie points are important, in my experience.

Now the space is closer to the potential I saw the first day I viewed this flat. The light is incredible, and being on the end of the building means three corners of windows. No more having to put lights on in the daytime, trying not to think about whether we could afford it. It's dry, too. No telltale black spots or heavy smell in any of the rooms. We might even save on heating bills, if the way the sun has warmed the living area is anything to go by.

Any way you look at it, this is a step up.

And thirty minutes to myself? Now *that's* a luxury.

I refill the kettle and set it to boil, fishing out the remnants from the Hobnobs packet that's been dinner, breakfast and lunch for me while I've been working. While I wait to make tea, I wander over to the window at the side of the kitchen area. It looks directly into the identical building next door. There's a large grey cat spread across the windowsill in the flat opposite mine. One of its front paws is pushed up against the glass, little pink paw pads a spot of colour against the steel-grey fluff. Noah will be overjoyed if he can see a cat from his new home.

Catttttttttt!

He's never lived in Wales, but he says that word in a pure Cardiff accent. A long *t* – almost an *s* by the time it ends. Mam would be proud. If she ever looked up from her own dramas long enough to notice, that is. I should call her. It's been too long. Once we're settled in, we'll attempt a FaceTime call. I'll have to get Emrys to go over and show her how it's done – again – but I know my big brother won't mind. When Noah starts chatting to them, everything else is unimportant.

Secretly, I'm proud of Noah's assumed accent. Last time I spoke to Mam she accused me of losing mine. Which proves she doesn't know me at all. Since I ended up in North Yorkshire, my accent has strengthened. Like a shield I hold in front of me. It's a confidence thing: that and the conversation starter it always provides. *Oh, you're Welsh?* Makes me laugh when people say that. I'm always tempted to feign shock and reply, 'Bloody hell, you're right!'

I keep that hidden, too, from most people. The cheeky side of me. Strange how people think they have the measure of you the first time they meet you and then never bother to revise it when they know you better. So they see a meek Welsh single mum who'd never dare crack a joke? Suits me.

Noah knows, though. That's all that counts.

When we're together, we have all the fun in the world. With him in my arms I can forget everything else. The worries, the circumstances I didn't choose, the list of demands on my time – none of them come from us. In our team of two we are strong. Defiant dreamers. Life-lovers. And in this flat, we're finally going to find our feet.

The kettle's click echoes in the empty space, an unfamiliar sound I will soon take for granted. Drowning the teabag in a mug, I smile. One more night in that awful bedsit and tomorrow Noah and me claim our new kingdom.

Outside the wind has picked up, sending wispy white clouds dancing across the sun. I watch the pools of light and shadow sail across the building next door and the tall beech hedge that separates us. The cat in the window opposite is sitting upright now, staring at me. Well, not *at* me. It probably doesn't even realise I'm here. Without thinking, I wave. It's such a daft thing to do, but this is my first encounter with anyone in our new neighbourhood and it feels right.

'Hello, cat.' My breath fogs the glass for a second as I speak.

The cat gives a long, slow blink. There's a moment of connection – and then it jumps out of sight.

Fifteen minutes left.

I move the paint-splattered dustsheet from the rickety old stepladder the landlord left for me and perch on a step to drink my last cuppa before we officially move in. I'm so tired it hurts to blink and I don't think my body will love me in the morning, but I don't care. I did it. Painting walls is another thing to add to my list of dubious new skills.

I glance at the now cat-less window and wonder who it shares its space with. Who its *slave* is, as my boss, Hattie, would say. She's got four of them at home and when she returns from a long day at work running the garden centre she owns she's totally at their furry beck and call. What does Grey Fluffy Mog's human look like? Older, like the previous tenant here, or younger, like me? There are so many questions in my new neighbourhood I've yet to find answers to. Even that will be a change – where we're living now it's best not to know anything about the others who share your space.

I saw signs of other younger people in the building when I came to view the flat, a month ago. A baby buggy by the communal entrance; folded toy boxes in the blue recycling bags inside the door, small muddy welly-boot prints along the vinyl in the corridor to the stairs. The landlord said it was a popular area for new families. It's around the corner from Noah's preschool, so I hope some of the mums I see there might live nearby.

Does the cat have a little human living there, too?

I guess I'll find out eventually. Maybe not about the cat. But about the rest. I like how that makes me feel. Possibility, after a long line of slammed doors.

Crap, I need to get going.

I rinse my mug and dash around my new home, closing windows and turning off lights. Then I grab my coat, hefting my overnight bag onto my shoulder that I used as a pillow last night when I snatched two hours' sleep on the floor. At the door, I turn back.

'See you, flat,' I smile. 'Back soon.'

I don't think my feet meet the stairs once as I hurry out.

Chapter Three

LACHLAN

There's a removal van parked next door.

It's a tiny Transit – not like the huge trucks they usually send out – but I recognise the logo from the removal company on the trading estate near the garrison. Until three months ago I passed their unit every day.

I stop my brain before it careers down a familiar road, turning my attention back to the flat opposite. The lights are on again, a couple of windows open. I can see movement inside, but can't make out any figures.

Not much to move in, then. Looks like mostly cardboard boxes and bundles of wood that I suspect are part of a flat-pack bed frame. Student? Single person? Someone with not much stuff, that's for sure.

My phone rings, making my heart crash against my chest. Will I ever stop being jumpy? Honestly, it's pathetic. I'm like a kangaroo most days. I accept the call, shifting to lean my weight against the wall. I didn't plan on staring at my new neighbour for as long as I have and my leg is yelling obscenities at me. At least when it heals I can get my life back and stop being a human CCTV.

'You haven't called me for a week.'

This is basically my life now. Hardly seeing anyone in real life but being yelled at by everyone via phone. And Skype. And FaceTime. And Zoom. If any of them had carrier pigeons they'd probably train them to deliver yells, too. I glance down at Ernie, my large grey cat, who has been head butting my shin for the last five minutes because he wants more food. I imagine what he'd gleefully do to any angry pigeon messengers. Surprisingly, it lifts my mood.

'I've been busy, Sal.'

'Doing what? Inspecting the walls? Bingeing Netflix? Staring out of the window?'

My cheeks burn a little at her last suggestion and I turn away from my vantage point, just in case she can see me. I don't think my sister is likely to have driven two hundred miles with her binoculars to spy on me, but I wouldn't put it past her. 'Physio,' I stab back, far too defensively.

There's a bruised pause before she replies and I instantly hate myself for using the injury as a weapon. Nobody deserves that.

'Right. Well, if you don't want me adding to your pain, call me once a week, yeah? Like you promised.'

'Okay. Sorry.'

Her sigh buzzes against my ear. 'We're all just trying to help, Lachie.'

'Yeah, I know.' I wish they could all help by *not* helping. Just let me get on with it. I know they want to do stuff, but it makes it worse. If I don't make progress with physio, I'll feel like I've failed everyone, not just me. I couldn't take that.

Also, I don't deserve their help. The knowledge of that sits heavy with me.

'I'm going to send you some things to keep you occupied while you're at home,' my sister says. Like I'm an unruly kid that needs entertaining. It doesn't matter how old I am, I'll always be Sally's annoying kid brother.

'Really, I'm fine.'

'It's either the box in the post or me on your doorstep,' she says. Her voice is pure exasperation but I can hear the smallest note of fun hidden behind it. 'And I'd have to stay for at least two days because of the journey...'

'Okay, okay, post is fine.'

'Good boy.'

Sal launches into a round-up of her latest news – my two nieces who are inexplicably at secondary school now; my brother-in-law Isaac and his dodgy session musician work; Sal's work in my parents' holiday let business, including her never-ending feud with Dad over how the business should operate in the twenty-first century, unlike his 'It was good enough for us in the 1990s' stance. I try to listen – honestly, I do – but soon it becomes soothing white noise while my brain considers other stuff. It isn't that I don't love my family. Of course I love them. It's just easier not being with them right now.

I move back to the window and glance across at the flat opposite. I can see a stack of boxes at one side of the window, a large bottle of water on the windowsill, half-drunk. I remember the rush of moving into this place, when I started my new post as Learning and Development Officer in the army's Educational and Training Service Unit and finally moved off-site at the garrison. It felt like a big step then. It was. Where has the new resident come from? I wonder.

A low growl calls my attention from behind me. When I turn, I see my other housemate, Bert, engaged in a sudden high-noon standoff with Ernie. Between them is Bert's favourite toy – a knotted sock he's had since I brought him home from the animal shelter three years ago. It's frayed and always damp and no amount of washing removes its stink, but my dog adores it. And who am I to stand in the way of true love?

I glare at Ernie, who lifts his chin as if impervious to guilt, one stealthy paw reaching out to rest, oh-so-gently, on Sock.

Uh-oh. Now it's war.

'Sorry, sis, I've got to go,' I say quickly as Bert rushes Ernie. 'World War Three is breaking out here.'

'Call me when you…' Sal begins, but the rest of her words are lost as my phone spins abandoned on the dining table.

I make a lurch for Ernie, just as he's raising his claws to swipe Bert's nose, scooping the spitting, hissing ball of feline fury onto my shoulder. The movement sends a shock of pain burning along my leg and I yell as it hits. Kicking against it, I turn and shuffle to my bedroom, depositing Ernie on the bed.

'Time out, fella,' I say. 'Cool it or else.'

My cat's look of utter disgust as he starts to wash his ears is the last thing I see before I close the door.

When I return to the living room, Bert is on the sofa, Sock safely cradled between his paws. He shouldn't be on there, of course, and he knows it. But rules in this place have become less important lately. I sit slowly beside him and close my eyes, breathing out the last of the pain. It has to get better soon – I can't function until it does.

A warm weight slides onto my good knee and I smile without

looking. There are very few things that can't be made better by a well-placed canine chin.

'Cheers, dude.' When I look down, Bert's chocolate eyes moon up at me, his tail thumping against the sofa cushions.

I love this dog. Never thought I'd be a dog person until I found this odd mix of uncertain breeds at the local rescue centre. I think Bert is the result of a dalliance between a border collie and a much smaller dog, possibly a corgi or a Westie. My mate Riggsy calls him a 'sawn-off sheepdog', which, while a bit cruel, sums him up. A black-and-white collie-shaped dog with little stumpy legs. Cute, in an oddly uneven way. I feel bad about not being able to walk him properly at the moment. I manage to get him downstairs to the communal garden for a bit in the morning and just before bed, but I'm no use beyond that. If he minds, he doesn't let on. But it's another aspect of my life on hiatus until my leg is sorted.

Everything is on hold. I feel I've been holding my breath for three months.

I don't want to think about what happens if the physio fails.

'Come on,' I say to Bert, pushing my body upright. 'Let's get you a treat.'

On the way to the kitchen, I glance out of the window and stop. Someone is perched on the windowsill in the flat opposite. The dark ponytail is now one of those gravity-defying hair scoops women do, all piled up in a way that looks messy and arty at the same time. The way my ex used to have hers when she'd just had a bath.

I balk at the thought. That is *not* Jenny.

But it's definitely a woman. She's drinking tea from a large blue-and-red mug that might be a Spider-Man head and she looks like she's talking to someone in the room, although I can't see anyone else from here.

I don't know why, but I feel relieved. For her – that she isn't in there alone.

Now that *is* crazy.

Embarrassed with myself, I head into the kitchen.

Chapter Four

BETHAN

'Is my bed staying?'

'Of course it is.'

'And my toys?'

'Those too.'

'And we don't have to go home and leave them?'

'No, silly. They're staying and so are we. This is our home now.'

Noah's eyes are filled with the wide whiteness of our new flat as he gazes around. 'Really truly?'

I grin at my boy from my windowsill perch. 'Really truly. What do you think?'

My son throws his arms open and spins across the newly cleaned carpet. 'I think… *wheee!*'

That's how I feel, too. Proper *wheee*. We're here and we made it and now my little boy is only just realising this place is ours. It makes my heart burst seeing it happen.

I'm so bloody proud of us.

All the crap of the last two years, all the scrimping and saving, clawing our way back from the place we were dumped in – it's worth it now to see Noah spinning and wheeling around our new living room that still smells of paint and is guarded by a line of box-stack sentries around its walls.

Later, when Noah is tucked up in bed in his very first bedroom of his own, I sit with a glass of wine and let it all sink in. I'm buzzing, even though I'm so knackered I can hardly string a sentence together. We have such a long way to go, but being here feels like reaching the best base camp to prepare for the long climb.

It's getting light when I bump awake, finding myself in the haphazard crumple of cushions on my sofa. The first blues of morning are flooding in through still curtainless windows, casting unfamiliar shadows in the new space we're going to get to know. I have just over two hours until I'm due to be up and out but I take a moment, in the strange stillness, listening to the new clicks and creaks of the building, the echoes of other flats below us and around us, the waking sounds of the street beyond. A dog barking somewhere. The rumble of a milk truck. A shudder of wind through the leaves of the beech hedge between us and the building next door. Soon, I won't even think to listen to them, so I listen now. It feels like a privilege.

When I finally rouse my aching body from the cosy grip of the sofa, I rescue my empty wine glass from the rug and walk slowly towards the kitchen. I'm about to pass the window when I notice a light on in the flat opposite. The large grey cat is there on the windowsill again, fast asleep this time. Its nose is pressed against the window, two little fogs appearing and disappearing on the glass as it breathes. Right now, I feel as content as that cat, even if my body is complaining. Does its owner feel as content? Are they a happy cat, too?

I laugh at myself, slapping a hand to my mouth too late to

catch the sound. I listen, heart thumping, praying it hasn't woken Noah. Ten seconds... twenty... thirty... Then I hear the faint chimes of Harry, his beloved musical seahorse toy, and know I'm safe. If Harry's playing, Noah's drifting back to sleep.

And then I see something beyond the sleeping cat. A shadow at first, glancing across the light source. Then, a hand, appearing at the cat's head and making a slow, gentle sweep along its furry spine. A man's hand.

I should move, but I can't. I'm fascinated by the hand, and the length of forearm that follows. There's a curl of a tattoo snaking around it from the crook of the arm to just above the wrist. From this distance and with the limited light available, I can't tell what it's supposed to be. But the tenderness of the stroking hand and the strength of the ink above it is a striking combination. I find myself hoping to see more of him, then step back from the window, my cheeks flushed from more than the wine I drank hours ago. It's wrong to be spying on someone. I don't know how I'd feel if somebody were watching me.

I hurry to the kitchen and rinse out my glass, taking my Spidey mug from the draining board and filling it with water to take to bed. I need sleep and I don't have much time to grab it. When I glance at the window, the cat has shifted position but is still sleeping, the hand and the tattoo gone.

I shouldn't have looked.

I know this, but I'm glad I did.

I won't do it again, obviously. I mean, that wouldn't be right, would it?

When I climb into bed and shut my eyes, I'm smiling.

*

'My life, lass, how are you still functioning?' Michelle Gartside takes Noah's coat and ushers him into her living room, where her youngest daughter Maisie and two other children are already playing.

'Adrenalin and tea,' I laugh, putting Noah's sandwich box onto the kitchen counter.

'You're made of stronger stuff than me. I'd be out for the count if I'd had to do half of what you have.'

I smile despite the thundering ache pounding my skull. 'It's all good. We're in now. I just need to get through the extra work shifts this week and then I can rest.'

Michelle folds her arms. 'Bethy, I've known you two years and in all that time I've never seen you rest once.'

I have to concede that point. 'What can I say? I grab life by the scruff of the neck…'

'Even when it kicks you in the balls…' My childminder chuckles, then grimaces and lowers her voice. 'Sorry. If Noah comes home saying that word you can chalk it up to me, okay?'

'I will. Seriously, Chel, thanks for this. I know it's short notice.'

'Ah, forget it. Consider it my housewarming present to you.' She does that odd reaching-out-but-not-touching gesture she's always done. That's her equivalent of a hug and it means the same to me. 'I'm just glad you're happy. Borderline comatose, but happy.'

I grin at her. She isn't a friend as such, but she's the closest thing I have. 'Thanks. I might be a bit late back…'

'Just pop me a text when you know. Noah likes fish fingers and beans, doesn't he?'

'Loves them.'

'So let me know by, say, four thirty, and if you're going to be late I'll just give him his tea with Maisie.'

'You're a star.'

'Don't I know it! Now go, before you fall asleep in my hallway.'

Driving through the slow morning traffic, I count my blessings. Noah has a safe place to be with Michelle while I'm working, a new home near his preschool for the days he goes there and a whole lot more potential for a happy life than where we were before.

More space too, that's for certain. Inside and out.

Yesterday we checked out the communal garden that runs from the side of the building along the beech hedge to a little rectangle of grass at the back. It's more green space than we've ever had and more than enough for my sports-mad little man to kick a ball around and have running races. Or fly like a dragon, which is his other great love. I asked the landlord about the garden when we moved in and it turns out he has a chap who mows the lawn twice a month but there's no gardening beyond that. I was thinking I might ask him if I can plant some flowers along the beech border. Nothing fancy, just some bedding plants to give a bit of colour to the space. I'm sure Hattie at work would let me have some for cost price if I tell her what it's for.

I like that I'm thinking this way. Where we were before we raced inside and shut the door as fast as we could – it never occurred to us to do anything to the place or its surroundings because it just wasn't an option. Here, we've put our mark on the inside of our new home, so why not the outside? A little bit of lovely for everyone.

By the time I arrive at the garden centre, I've made my plan. This is going to be *brilliant*.

Chapter Five

LACHLAN

'*No.*'

'Oh come on, Wallace, it's what you need.'

'Really?' I glare at my best mate and stab a finger at my injured leg. '*This* is what I need. I need this to get better.'

'Yeah, yeah, change the record, bud.'

'Remind me why you're here again?'

'Can't a mate visit a mate?' Riggsy clamps a hand to his heart as if I've mortally wounded him. 'Besides, someone needs to drag you out of this dump and stop you becoming a porn-surfing hermit.'

'If that's your idea of a joke you can get lost now.'

He looks at me like I've just sprouted an extra head. 'You used to be fun.'

'I used to be able to go to work every day, too.'

He reaches into my fridge and pulls out two bottles of beer. Uninvited, of course. Maybe I should stop buying beer altogether. I make a mental note to amend my online supermarket order when he's gone.

'And you will again. All the more reason to come out with the lads. Remind them who you are. Blow off some steam. Might unknot your undercrackers, give those balls of yours room to breathe.'

He lobs a bottle at me and I only just manage to catch it. My leg spasms but I bite the urge to yell. I might acknowledge pain to my physio, but I'm not giving Riggsy the satisfaction. He smirks like he's scored a point, then strides across the living room like he's always done.

Why can you still do that when I can't?

I can't ignore the voice in my head. I should be glad he's okay. But I'm not. It's his fault I'm stuck in here entertaining his sorry ass and not out there living my life. If I could say it to his face it might make me feel better. But so far, the words have eluded me.

It's a mystery to most people why Adam Riggs is my friend. To me too, a lot of the time. But he was there for me, many years back, hauling me out of a mess that could have ended my army career. We were on manoeuvres on our first tour in Iraq, barely a year after passing out, and I took a wrong turn. I'd been mouthing off about our commander and was already on a warning. Thinking I knew better I took a different route and almost walked straight into a local militia ambush. Riggsy found me, terrified and backed into a corner of a bomb-scarred building. He grabbed me and got me out, then convinced our commander that we'd just fallen behind instead of disobeying orders. He could have shopped me, but he didn't. Even years later, when I went on to command a unit of my own and Riggsy had to work for me, he never used my past mistake as a reason to discredit me. I can't forget that. You could argue I've repaid the favour a thousand times in the years since – and he's always been quick to remind me of it when he wants something – but I'll always be grateful. Besides, he's amusing, in a mostly offensive way. He's not much of a mate, but he's the best I've got.

Annoyed, I reach for the bottle opener on the coffee table and ease the metal top off my beer. At least I can drink what I like without thinking about how I'll get home. Maybe if I'd done that three months ago…

'So, this physio of yours.' He flops down on the sofa beside me, sending Ernie scooting for cover under the dining table.

'What about her?'

'Barlow reckons she's fit.' Mischief sparkles in his eyes as he swigs his beer.

'Barlow's talking out of his backside.'

'So she *is* fit? You're a sly one, Wallace. A fit bird running her hands all over you four times a week? I bet you love it. Probably slip her an extra twenty for a bit of after-hours relief…'

'Sod off.' I glance at my cat, who is eyeballing my friend in disgust. *Too right, mate*, I think. If Ernie's appalled, there's no hope for Riggsy. 'She's a professional. Someone who deserves respect.'

Riggsy sniffs. 'Is that what you call it?' Seeing my expression he holds up his bottle in surrender. 'Okay, I get it. I'll shut up.'

I nod and we drink. But if I think he's changing tack, I'm wrong.

'I'm just saying…'

'Well, *don't*.'

'Been a while since Jenny. Nobody would blame you for getting back on the horse.'

'Thank you for your concern, Cupid. You're fired.'

He groans into his beer.

He's way off about my love life but maybe he's right about

23

getting out more. I've not seen the lads since I came out of hospital and most of them didn't visit me when I was in there. I get copied into group messages on WhatsApp and occasionally one of them will call, but most of the time they're not around. Easy to forget someone you don't see every day. Part of me doesn't blame them – I mean, what would they say? It was different when we lived in the garrison together. If you didn't see them at work you'd meet them at the bar afterwards. Then you all talked about work anyway – the only thing any of us had in common besides maybe football, but even that was divisive. What would we talk about now? Once I moved off-site, things changed. They were bound to. We still worked together, still met up for drinks, but there was an invisible wall there. I'd become an *off-siter*, the same but different.

I'm not sure I miss them, other than the familiar banter and the feeling of belonging to something.

But how can I walk into a pub like this? How could I hobble in and sit with them and this *not* be the only thing they see?

I know I'm lucky to be walking at all. I don't take that for granted. But in the army you're your body first. That's what people see. It's part of the gig: physical strength, vitality, stamina, those are the tools of the trade. They know me as I was: to see this current version of me would be worse than not being there at all. At least staying here means they might still think of me how I was before.

It's stupid, I know. I'm more than my appearance. But this is the thing I can't get over, the thing I'm terrified to address.

What if this is me for good?

Three hours, several bottles of beer and an ill-advised takeaway later, I'm finally alone again. Well, the lads and me. Bert and

Ernie flank me on either side on the sofa as I flick aimlessly through Netflix looking for something to watch. Not for the entertainment, more for the noise. Riggsy is hardly perfect company, but the void his constant chatter leaves when he goes cuts deeper than it used to. It underlines my incarceration here.

No, not incarceration. This is my home, not a prison. But I feel its confines sometimes. These walls can be security and safety, or proof that I'm stuck.

It's a dangerous time right now. Too early for bed, too late to call anyone. Not that I have anyone to call. Too much time to think.

Riggsy will be back at the garrison now, drunk and loud with the rest of them. I wonder if they're talking about me, if he's repeating his filthy jokes about what I'm doing at home all day, or if I'm not even on the radar. I don't want them talking about me, but if they are it means I still exist somewhere.

Stuff this. I need to get out of here.

'Come on,' I say, pulling my body upright.

Bert is off the sofa and by the door, tail whacking the laminate, before I'm on my feet.

It's fresher in the garden than I was expecting. I was vaguely aware of rain earlier when Riggsy was regaling me with his dodgy anecdotes, but I didn't look out of the window. The grass is damp when Bert and I edge the building and head to the back garden, imprinting lines of moisture on the suede toes of my trainers. It reminds me of my time training up in the Lakes – that rush of cool petrichor that meets you after a heavy rain shower. Earth and air, water and stone.

I pause to rest against the still-warm brick of our building as Bert goes hoofing off into the too-long grass. The guy who usually comes to cut the lawn is on holiday, according to a neighbour I met out here this morning. It seems like weeks since he was last here, but all time seems elongated for me.

My dog is a fan of the messy green wilderness at least. In the deepening dusk I can just make out the waving white tip of his tail. When I'm sorted, I'll find long walks to take him on. It's a promise I make every morning and evening as we tread this path. He looks happy enough now, inspecting all the new smells in the grass. Getting all the neighbourhood gossip. I'm glad I've got him. And his bolshie mate upstairs, even if they are two paws away from war most of the time. I don't know where I would be without them.

Man, my leg is stiff tonight. I should have moved around more when Riggsy was here. Tanya won't be happy with me tomorrow. I brace my back against the side wall of the building and push my leg into the wet ground, pulsing it back and forth. Not much of a resistance exercise and it hurts, but after a few reps it seems to ease the stiffness in my thigh a bit. As I work the muscles slowly, my gaze drifts up to a lit window in the building next door.

There's a vase of flowers now where I saw the woman sitting yesterday. I don't know what they are, but they're pretty. Round heads, almost perfect circles like Sal's girls used to draw flowers when they were little; bright yellows, oranges and reds, on vivid green stems. I wonder if they smell good, too. They look like they should.

They *fit* her, I think, the woman in the window with the Spider-Man mug. Bright, bold, hopeful...

Wait. What am I doing?

26

I laugh under my breath at myself, answered by a muffled woof from Bert somewhere in the grass. Good job Riggsy and the lads at the garrison can't see me. I think I'd rather them imagine I surf porn all day than stand in my garden admiring flowers in someone else's window.

They're just – hopeful. Simple. Like Lake District air after the rain.

And I don't know why, but my eyes suddenly flood, the reds and oranges, yellows and greens dancing in the water as I blink.

Where did that come from?

I swiftly dismiss the tears with the heels of my hands, ashamed by their appearance, kicking my heels into the wet earth as I go to fetch my dog. It's time we were back inside.

27

Chapter Six

BETHAN

Bright Hill Nurseries is not what you would call a modern garden centre, but I love it.

Mind you, this morning, it isn't loving us back.

The rain yesterday sneaked into the cracks and gaps in the sixty-year-old glass-panelled roof and now the whole building is filled with the ominous sound of dripping. I've spent the first hour at work this morning dashing around with Patrick, our nineteen-year-old apprentice plantsman, putting buckets underneath the leaks. I'm still not convinced we've caught them all.

'That's the trouble when you work in a chuffin' great greenhouse,' he grins at me as we make a final circuit of the main building to check for more sneaky drips. 'Stupid hot in the summer, a fridge in the winter and basically a massive glass sieve when it rains.'

He ducks when another drip falls from the roof but it lands with a splat on his forest-green Bright Hill staff polo shirt. His nonplussed expression is so funny it sets me off again. We're dreadful for giggling when we're together and if our Head of Section catches us it'll earn us another rant about professionalism.

Which is rich, considering Darren Gifford isn't even in yet. Third time he's been late this week and still Hattie's said nothing. Patrick reckons he has dirt on Hattie's love life and that's why she won't sack him. It's daft, of course, but with all Darren's misdemeanours Hattie turns a blind eye to, I'm starting to wonder if Pat's right.

I put a bucket underneath the offending leak and we step back.

'That had better be the lot or we're going to have to start raiding the café kitchen for saucepans.'

Our entire stock of galvanised buckets is being employed, as are all the cleaners' mop buckets and the metal litter bins from the staff room and offices. I haven't seen it this bad for a long time and I've been here for two years.

'I thought Hattie was getting the roof fixed,' Patrick says, brushing roof moss from his shoulder that the drip brought down with it.

'She was. She *is*.' I glance up at the greening panes above our heads. They need a clean before anyone can think of fixing them. 'Business is tough right now.'

'No joke. It's like a ghost town in here today. Except no self-respecting ghost would grace this place in the rain.'

We look around at the starkly empty aisles of seeds, garden ornaments, banks of artificial flowers and stacks of planters. A symphony of drips fills the space where customer chatter should be. It's still early in the season, the weather too unsettled for barbecues and thoughts of outdoor entertaining yet.

'Once we get into June it'll pick up,' I say, determined not to consider what happens if it doesn't. I'm not going to get down today. 'Come on, I think we're done on Drip Duty. Let's unpack that delivery.'

It's a relief to emerge from the main centre into the yard at the back. At least out here with the waiting pallet stacks of new plants we can pretend Bright Hill is thriving. I love delivery days the most. The way everyone (except Darren) pulls together to unload the pallets, the quick-fire banter that passes between us as we move between the yard and the garden beds beyond the staff gate. I'm not one to call my work colleagues a family, but this is the time I feel most like I belong.

Eric Atkinson, our senior nurseryman, who has been here forever, brings in his legendary homemade coconut buns on delivery days and we all take our tea break together, sitting on piles of compost bags under the ageing Perspex canopy if it isn't raining, or squeezed into his shed at the far end of the site if it's pouring. Trust me, the best antidote to aching muscles is tea in a mismatched mug and sugary coconut snow-topped treats from two old Quality Street tins.

He's just arriving now, his lolloping gait unmistakeable as he puffs through the gate, a precious tin tucked under each arm.

'Let me help you with those,' Patrick offers, but Eric's wise to his scheme.

'Nice try, sunshine,' he grins. 'I wasn't born yesterday.'

Patrick shrugs. 'Can't blame a guy for trying.'

I give an upturned planter behind the compost stacks a gentle nudge round to the front with my foot, just as Eric ambles over. He won't ever ask for a seat, but with his hip as troublesome as it is he won't pass up the chance to sit.

'How's our little Welsh daff, then?' He is absolutely the only person allowed to call me that. He sits unsteadily and taps his brow. 'Now, what was it? *Sut dych chi*, Bethan?'

I can't hide my surprise. '*Da iawn, diolch!* Get you with the lingo, Eric.'

'Got a new app for my phone – *Lingo-Jingo* or something,' he informs me, cheeks flushed with pride. 'I told you I was going to learn.'

Bless him, that's so sweet. I never hear my home language here and barely use it myself these days, but it means a lot that anyone would try to speak it for me. It's also a constant source of amusement to me that Eric has the most up-to-date phone of any of us. He's a total whizz with his shiny apps, a poster boy for not judging people by what you see. Maybe that's why he's one of my favourite people.

For the next hour we lug bags of compost, unpack pallets of plants and tag-team to roll giant potted mature apple, plum and willow trees from the yard out to their areas in the nursery. It's hard work but worth it for the laughter, chat and, quite frankly, *filthy* jokes. I love every minute, even if the tiny amount of sleep I had last night makes every move a double effort.

'How's the flat?' Patrick puffs as we pick up a large potted apple tree between us and crab-walk it across the nursery.

'Better now it's painted,' I say. 'Noah adores it.'

'I'll bet. Probably misses the riot vans from your old place, though.'

I give him a look that makes him chuckle. 'That is someone else's delight now. I just have birds and neighbourhood cats.'

And intriguingly tattooed arms, I think to myself, the thrill of what I saw in the early hours returning. I'm really going to stop looking now. I think maybe I've seen enough. Of course, I could always say I was just admiring the cat…

'Sounds proper boring.'

'I'll take boring. Boring is good. Boring is *heaven*, actually.'

We swing the potted tree into line with the others in the fruit tree section. Patrick groans as he straightens his back. 'Glad you're in and happy.' He shields his eyes from the sudden burst of sunlight that's broken the cloud cover and yells over to the other side of the site. 'Eric! We done?'

From the gate to the yard, Eric raises a thumb.

'Yes!' Patrick taps me on the shoulder. 'Last one there misses the buns.'

I watch him sprint away and give chase, ignoring the knots in my calves, the loud objections of my body. All of us can find energy when a tea break is calling.

We've only just divvied up the buns and tea when we're rudely interrupted.

'Time to kill, have we?' Darren Gifford blocks the single ray of sunshine when he looms over us. Which at five feet two he can only do because we're all sitting down.

'Just finished unloading the pallets,' Eric says, never once raising his eyes from his coconut bun. 'Nice of you to join us.'

Our Head of Section bristles. You can practically hear the spikes of irritation rising across his shoulders. 'Good job I came when I did. Tea break's over. Back to your sections. Bethan, my office, now.'

All the weariness of the past forty-eight hours returns to my body. I'm about to stand when Eric raises a hand to stop me.

'We get a fifteen-minute break, lad. Ten minutes of which are still outstanding. That's the rule. Unless you want me to take it up with Miss Rowse?'

As one we all duck to hide our smiles behind our half-eaten elevenses. Darren Gifford might be able to call the shots with rest of us, but not Eric Atkinson. He's worked here longer than most of us have been breathing, taken on as a fifteen-year-old

32

apprentice by Hattie's father, who established Bright Hill. Nobody crosses him. Especially not Darren.

I don't dare look as Darren mutters something murderous under his breath and storms off. We wait until the yard door has slammed before we loudly congratulate our senior plantsman. I'll probably cop the flak later, but right now I don't care. Right now, I belong. Eric said so – and Pat and the team agree.

Later, I surprise Noah with the extra buns Eric gave me in a zip-lock bag as I was heading home. Noah's sticky-faced smile is the best reward at the end of the day. I bought a bunch of red, orange and yellow ranunculus on the way home, too, because why not? Nobody is going to buy me flowers and these beauties are my favourites. You can't look at them and *not* smile. Just like my son.

Reasons to be cheerful at the end of a long day. Since it's just been my boy and me I've made a point of noticing something good every day, however small it is. Finding them means I can forget the piles of paperwork Darren had me needlessly checking this afternoon, or the plant display he demanded dismantling and rebuilding three times. In our new home, money earned for the day, happy flowers in the window, dinner made and the lazy evening stretching out ahead of us, I can finally relax.

In the end I'm in my bed half an hour after I've tucked my son into his, too tired to consider looking out of the window tonight. But a large grey cat and its owner's tender hand weave through my dreams.

Chapter Seven

LACHLAN

My physiotherapist hates me.

I'm sure of it. I can't blame her, either. If our roles were reversed I'd have punched my lights out by now.

'Okay, stop, Lachie. *Stop.*' Tanya pauses, pinching the bridge of her nose as if the squeeze will evict the words she really wants to say to me. She has more patience than I've ever seen in anyone, but I think we may have just found its limit.

'I am trying...' I begin, but that's a lie, isn't it? Every atom of me is resisting today. I am a one-man protest for a pointless cause.

'I know.' She keeps her eyes closed, the pinch still in place. 'Just... give me a minute, okay?'

Why can't I let her help me? Even I don't understand my attitude anymore. Why does everything have to be a battle? I want to reach out, apologise, but that would be a mark of surrender, wouldn't it? Admitting I need her – that I can't do this on my own.

I know what it is: I'm scared. I'm scared if I ask for help it'll be game over. I'll stay like this forever and the old Lachie Wallace will be lost.

I want *him* back. Even if he was a dick sometimes; even if he spent more time thinking of himself than anyone else. He was happy, mostly. Happily blasé about life. I want to get up in the morning and not have to consider *every damn thing*. I want to get to the end of the day and not be able to say what I did because everything was so bloody automatic and easy.

'Lachie, I think maybe you need someone else.'

My heart stops. My words desert me.

'I've been thinking about it for a while now. You're not making progress and I think I may be the problem.' She holds up a hand to silence me. 'No, hear me out, okay? Part of this working is *us* working and – it's just not, is it? I think you'd benefit from a different approach, from another of my colleagues, maybe. A male one...'

That's worse than anything. Now she thinks I'm crap *and* a misogynist. Way to go, Lachie. Already sunk and now crashing through the base of the pit.

'It's not you...' I splutter, instantly taken back to another conversation in this place, only now I'm speaking the lines Jenny threw at me:

It's not you, Lachie. I just don't want this anymore...

I had no words then. I have to find them now.

'My mind's made up, I'm sorry. I'll talk to my supervisor this afternoon, get you reassigned...'

The door buzzer blasts away the end of her sentence. I jump – of course – and stare at the door.

'You should probably get that.' She's turning away towards the corner of the room where her coat is folded over the rucksack she brings to every session.

'Stay there, yeah?' I jut my hand out as I edge towards the door. 'Let me get this first. Don't go anywhere.'

35

Tanya nods, arms folded tight across her chest, eyes trained on the floor.

I reach the intercom and press the answer button. 'Yes?'

'Package for Mr Wallace?'

Talk about timing. 'Sure, come up.' I buzz him through, open my door and wait, not sure whether to look back at my physio or just block her escape route until I can sort this.

It takes an age until the red-faced delivery guy arrives on my doorstep, a large box gratefully dropped on the mat as he hands me a sweaty PDU to sign. He doesn't stop to check if I need help bringing the box in, legging it down the stairs now the bulky parcel is no longer his responsibility.

It should annoy me. But strangely, it gives me hope. Because he didn't for a moment consider I wasn't capable. He saw my defined arms, the tatts, my build, and figured I was okay. Like the old me would have been.

Maybe old Lachie Wallace isn't a goner yet.

Of course, that doesn't mean getting this enormous box into my home is going to be easy. I bend to pick it up but the weight makes my head swim and turns the muscle in my thigh into white-hot lava. At close quarters I recognise my sister's no-nonsense letters stabbed in Sharpie on the address panel. What has she packed in here, one of my nieces?

'Don't try and lift that by yourself. Here.' Tanya slips past me and grabs one side of the box, not quite making eye contact. It's not even a raised flag but she can't leave until the box is on the table. I have between the doormat and the opposite side of the room to say what I should have said weeks ago.

'I'm a git,' I say, as we begin the slow shuffle across the floor.

'An utter arse. You should ask for overtime for mental anguish incurred in rehabilitating me.'

She still won't look at me. But she isn't arguing back.

'Please don't leave. Not until you've made me really suffer.'

Still nothing. The table is steps away and I have one volley left. Last-ditch effort. Here goes nothing…

'I'm terrified I can't do it.'

My words hang in the air like a clay pigeon awaiting a shot. Fear constricts my belly. My eyes prickle. That's it: the moment I admit I need help. I feel old Lachie break free of my grip and drift into the ether.

It's said. And I bloody hate it.

But she's looking at me now.

'You shouldn't be.'

I feel sick. 'But the fact remains.'

We've reached the table, just one final swing required to deposit the box. The jerk sends diamond-sharp spears coursing down my leg. I swallow the pain; keep my eyes on her.

'Lachie, I still think…'

'Give it another month. Two weeks? I'll do whatever you tell me and I'll stop complaining.' I bite back the word before I let it fly: *'Please.'*

Tanya gives me a look like even being here is against her better judgement. 'Two weeks. And I think we're done for today.'

I nod because what else can I say?

We part with unsure smiles, but it's a fragile truce. Next time I have to give it everything.

I'm shaken when she leaves.

Releasing Bert and Ernie from their personal holding cells in my room and the spare room respectively – and feeling the rush of their energy as they dash into the space – unleashes it all in me. I crash onto a dining chair by the window and kick out the shame and fear. It exits my body in huge hacks of emotion that rattle my chest and burn my throat. I grip the edge of the table as it takes me.

I have done everything I could and it wasn't enough. I was so determined to do this alone but those days are gone. That person is gone. I don't know what's left in his place.

I am *broken*.

I am *finished*.

And I have nobody to hold me.

I haven't wanted anyone to touch me since the accident. But now the ache of its absence rips the breath from me.

It hits like a tsunami.

I have no one.

It's not you, Lachie…

Except it is, isn't it?

I lean my arms on the cool wood of the table and drop my head onto them. The darkness welcomes me, my eyes aching behind closed lids. I breathe out, conscious of the blood pumping at my temples, the scream of stress in my ears, the low rumble of my heart. The first things I was aware of when I came around in the hospital, weeks ago. My vital signs. Before the pain hit. For a moment, I am right back there, confused but not yet aware that my life had changed.

And then I feel something that wasn't there then: the insistent push of a warm nose at my elbow. I lift my head just as Bert jumps, our skulls meeting in a painful display of affection. But a shower of licks and scratches rewards me as he scrambles up into my lap. The ridiculousness of it makes me laugh, my damp hands leaving salt streaks on the soft fur between his ears as I stroke his head.

Ernie blesses me with a grumble of affection from the windowsill behind me, which is the closest to a display of love he's prepared to give. It's what I need, dragging me back from the brink before I tumble.

Maybe not completely alone, then.

The moment has passed, so I ward off any return by busying myself with unpacking the box on the table. I push myself to my feet and as I do so I turn involuntarily towards the window. The flowers in the window next door instantly catch my attention – their colours even more vivid in daylight than they were last night. It's only a splash of colour, but it feels significant.

I look back at the box, ripping open one side and wondering again what Sally has considered essential for my recovery.

Inside is an Aladdin's cave of oddities. Four craft kits, six Sudoku books, three jigsaws, two running magazines, which are in bloody poor taste if you ask me, a corner shop's worth of chocolate, which I'll forgive her for, that weird iron pedal machine Dad used to stick by the sofa and cycle when he was watching the Masters (which explains the weight of the box), an ancient pair of binoculars and a threadbare bird-watching book. And the last thing I pull out is an A3 sketchpad and a pack of Berol coloured-barrel felt-tip pens, the kind we used to get as kids at Christmas and guard jealously from each other. What the hell am I supposed to do with those? I am about as good at drawing as Bert is at hurdling.

I glance back at the flowers in my neighbour's window, consider using the vintage binoculars to get a better view of them, but quickly rethink it, because how much of a stalker would that make me?

But then I have another idea.

It's crazy. And possibly dangerous.

It might be the worst idea I've ever had.

But I'm going to do it.

Chapter Eight

BETHAN

Darren Gifford is on the warpath. He's been a nightmare since that dressing-down Eric gave him and there's no sign of his bad mood abating any time soon. He might not be able to carry more than one paving slab at a time, but my Head of Section can heft a grudge far longer than any of us.

It's hanging over the whole team today, a rain-heavy storm-cloud waiting to break. It's not helped that it's Eric's day off. He only works four days a week now, overseeing the polytunnels of Bright Hill hybrid plants. Eventually, Patrick will take over the day-to-day operations there with Eric acting as consultant. That's a way off, though. Today we feel his absence – our knight errant off on his travels while the Dragon of Bright Hill roars.

No, I can't call him that. It's unfair to dragons.

As usual, I'm the closest target for his ire. And today, he's surpassing his usual depths of horrendousness.

'No, I said the *heucheras* under the canopy and the *hostas* in the bins,' he growls as we do our daily check of the plant area.

I trail after him, my boots feeling like they're stuffed with sharp sand. Everything aches today, and I don't think it has anything to do with the flat and the move. I slept the sleep of dreams last night – a full ten hours, practically unheard of for me. Noah was so fast asleep this morning that I'd showered, dressed and made his breakfast before I tiptoed into his new bedroom to wake him. The thought of his ruffled hair with its warm-biscuit smell as I snuggled him awake brings a much-needed smile. I'm here for Noah, not for Arse-face Gifford.

'French lavender? In the English lavender row?'

'It happens. The customers move things...'

He swings round, jabbing a finger at me that stops just shy of my nose. Unfortunately for him, we're on the downward slope of the plant area so I have even more of a height advantage than normal. He gives hobbits a bad name, honestly. All my family are tiny, apart from Great-Uncle Bleddyn and me, two seeming Gullivers in a sea of West Welsh Lilliputians. And most of them are lovely. Bit rubbish at life, but sweethearts with it. Darren was the first proper nasty shorter person I've met and it was a bit of a shock, to be honest.

I pull myself up. I shouldn't hold Darren's appearance against him. It makes me no better than he is. Because you can guarantee there's one thing about my life he'll throw at me whenever he wants to score a point.

'Blaming customers? What's next, *the plants moved themselves*? It's always blame with you lot, isn't it? Never your fault. Always everyone else's.'

And there it is.

My lot. Not Welsh, as you might think. My lot, aka single mothers. I didn't know hating lone parents was even a thing until I became one. Now I know different. It's all anyone sees when they know you're on your own with a kid. Never mind that it wasn't my choice. Never mind that my life has been one long battle to be seen for who I am ever since. Gifford is wrong – *so* wrong. But I don't tell anyone about my past and I sure as hell won't give him the satisfaction.

It burns though. The injustice. Calling my son a bastard because it somehow makes people like Darren Gifford feel clever. It's a wonder I have any tongue left, I have to bite it that often.

'Ask Eric,' I reply, before he can ramp up any more insults. 'He knows.'

That shuts him up.

We walk on in silence, Darren spitting out his impotent fury in a series of tuts and loudly sucked-in breaths. I know he'll explode again but in this temporary ceasefire I make myself focus on the good stuff as I follow him into the lines of roses.

The sun is out today.

I get to work with Patrick this afternoon.

Noah and me are making cookies tonight for pudding.

The roses smell amazing, too. I love this section of the nursery, the rows of standard teas and climbers, a heady rush of colour and scent that lifts you whether you want to be lifted or not.

Darren can't smell roses.

That's something I have that he doesn't.

Eric told me that last week and it's a nugget of knowledge I tuck in my pocket for mornings like these. You have to find your strength wherever you can. A snippet here, a pebble there, pinpricks of power to draw strength from.

If it were up to Darren, I would never have been promoted to Assistant Head of Section – or the plant section at all. I'm a constant thorn in his side, it seems, and he won't let me forget it.

'Bethan!' a voice singsongs behind us. When I turn, my smile is instant.

Hattie Rowse is standing by the water features at the top of the path we've just walked down, waving madly like she's flagging down a bus. She's the reason I have this job at all, not still working three days a week in the gift and homewares section in the main building for a minimum wage.

The groan from my boss is unmistakable. Another glint of power for my collection. Hattie is on my side and Darren knows it. For as long as she's with us me and *my lot* can rest easy.

She's out of breath when she reaches us. Or at least, that's what she wants us to think. I reckon she's fitter than anyone. She ran a marathon last year, though she swore me to secrecy when I found out.

'It's best everyone doesn't know,' she'd grinned at me, pulling the medal from the top drawer of her desk and wiggling it so it sparkled in the light. 'Better they think I'm just pottering around, eh?'

See, that's what I love about Hattie. She's the kind of person who is open and warm and lovely but who also knows her power and chooses what she wants people to see. I aspire to that. Although with idiots like Darren around, it might never happen.

'Lovely day, isn't it?' Hattie says.

'So lovely,' I smile, ignoring our Head of Section's pointed silence. 'Everything okay?'

'Fine, fine, perfectly fine,' she chirps. But I catch the flicker of something in her bright smile. *Too many fines.* Something's going on. She regroups quickly. 'I need to borrow you, Bethan. Darren, I hope that's not a problem?'

Her question is diamond-edged, her tone a warning not to disagree. Beside me Darren visibly shrinks.

'Of course not. I need her back before lunch.'

'Perfect.' Hattie stares at him until he takes the hint and slouches off. She turns to me and I swear she glows with triumph. 'Walk this way, Bethy.'

We turn back up the hill past the roses, the shrubs and the fruit trees, passing the rows of stone benches and stacks of terracotta pots and on to the scar of waste ground at the farthest edge of the site. Eric's shed is here, the sole remaining wooden building in the section that used to be filled with garden offices, summerhouses and play sheds. We lost the contract with the shed company eight months ago and the empty hard-standing bases where the demonstration buildings once stood are stark reminders of what once was.

It's not a good sign being here.

Usually we are drinking tea in the comfort of Hattie's office, the portrait of her late father beaming down on us from the bank of primulas painted around him. We only ever venture this far from the main building when there's something Hattie doesn't want anyone else to hear.

Her smile fades as soon as we're standing by Eric's empty shed.

'What's up?' I ask, not really wanting to know. The leaking roof earlier this week, the lack of footfall in the place, the rumours that are never far away when I'm talking with the plant team – and now this?

'I need ideas,' Hattie says. It's strange to see her face without a smile. 'Big ideas. Pretty soon.'

'Are things as bad as that?'

Her gaze drifts from me. 'Could be. We need something to

give us a boost. Maybe a lot of things working together. I don't know.' She leans against the sun-bleached wood of the shed. 'Fact is, we can't compete with the modern places. Grocutts, Hartley's, Gardenworld – they're all owned by huge companies with enormous budgets and expensive marketing. We have a shoestring budget and Derek, who's just about worked out Word Art.'

I have to laugh at that. Derek is our maintenance guy who does a nifty sideline in hand-painted posters on luminous paper and home-printed flyers. 'That last lot of leaflets he made were pretty good, though.'

'Apart from spelling "nurseries" wrong: N-U-R-S-E-R-Y-apostrophe-S, I ask you.' Hattie sighs. 'He tries his best. I'd never part with him. But the fact is, unless we find ways of bringing in business, we might all be out of a job.'

No. *No*, this can't happen. Not when we've just settled into the flat. I'll never find a job that pays as generously as this at short notice and I have no savings to fall back on. 'Oh man…'

Hattie's eyes fill with concern and she places a hand on my arm. 'My lovely girl, I am so sorry to put this on you now. But I know you think outside the box. I know you've had to… Anything you can come up with would be a huge help. I don't need an answer immediately and we aren't at crunch-time yet, but please, take some time and think of something for me?'

'Of course I will.' I force a smile, but all of my carefully curated positives spill from my pockets as we walk slowly back across the site.

My head is banging when I finally get home. Noah had a falling-out with Maisie this afternoon so Michelle and I had to stage a peace summit in her tiny lounge before we could leave. I have no ideas for Hattie and trying to force my brain into action is useless. I'm scared again. I haven't felt that fear since we moved here.

I watch Noah now from the kitchen as I wait for the kettle to boil, biting my thumbnail as he plays on the rug with his cuddly dragons. He's got them lined up like draconic soldiers and is chattering away to them, the cutest general you've ever seen. He loves it here. So do I. We can't lose this place, not now we've made it ours.

I swallow the tears that want to run, kicking my heels into the tile-marked lino. I hate not being in control. It scares me more than anything.

And I feel so alone.

At work I have allies, people to chat and joke with. Outside of work there are people I know, like Michelle, but here there's just Noah and me. Nobody else. I can't call Mam because she'll fret and it'll become another drama for her to feast on. She has too much of her own stuff to deal with, anyway. My brother is too wrapped up in his own disasters to have room for mine. I know Mam and Emrys love me and I love them back, but I know what they can and can't deal with. If Dad were still alive he would have understood – the original oil on troubled waters of my family before I inherited the mantle. But he's been gone six years.

I haven't wanted to admit it until now, but I'm lonely. I'd love a friend, you know? Someone who listens. Or someone who rocks up with a bottle of wine and talks bollocks with me for hours. Someone who wraps their arms around me when words won't work.

Someone just for me.

I need to snap out of this. I need to think, and I can't do that if I'm obsessing about what I don't have. That road leads nowhere.

Rattled, I wander over to the window. I don't know why. I think I just need to move, a physical shift to cause a mind-shift. I turn my attention from Noah and his dragon army to the deep red brick of the building opposite...

... And that's when I see it.

A sheet of paper, stuck to the window of the flat with the cat. On it, written in large red, orange and green letters, is a message.

A message for me.

HI, FLAT OPPOSITE MINE.
WHAT ARE THOSE FLOWERS CALLED?

My hand flies to my mouth. A sob of surprise escapes.

'What's up, Mummy?' Noah is staring over at me, deep brown eyes like chocolate moons.

I smile, not sure whether I'm laughing or crying. 'Nothing, *bach*. Mummy's okay.'

I turn back to the window. It's got to be for me. I'm the flat opposite.

Did the hand I saw the other night write this? Or is it someone else living there? I try to imagine the hand and the tattooed arm above it moving over a sheet of paper with bright felt-tip pens. It's so crazy it makes me laugh out loud.

The kettle's click sounds behind me, but I don't go to the kitchen. Instead, I move to the leather-effect chest that masquerades as our coffee table and lift off the lid, reaching inside where Noah's craft things are kept.

Tea can wait. There's something I need to do first.

48

Chapter Nine

LACHLAN

Come on…

It's hours since I put the sign up. Still nothing. Have they even noticed?

What was a blinding idea at 2 p.m. now looks like an A3-sized white elephant stuck in the window. There's no pretending it didn't happen. I am such a dick.

I push away from the window and shuffle into the kitchen. I'd told myself I wasn't going to check, but like a loser I've travelled back there every ten minutes. It's 6 p.m. now. Four hours of pointless vigil – and for what? What did I hope to achieve?

It's only now as I lever the cap off a bottle of beer that I realise how stupid I've been. How would I feel if someone sent me a crazy message like that? I have neighbours in this building I've never met in five years of living here. Why would anyone in the building opposite be interested in my questions? If I'd seen a message asking me about something in my flat I'd have run a mile. Back when I *could* run.

I blame this bloody leg. I've blamed it for a lot lately. If I still had my old life I wouldn't have gone anywhere near my stupid window, let alone decided to send invasive messages to a complete stranger from it.

I drink, but pretty soon I'm bored: the bottle is left to go flat beside the sink as I limp back to the sofa. Ernie glances at me from the cushion he shouldn't be on, weighing up the potential for my arrival meaning food for him, realising it doesn't, and going back to sleep. From his basket beside the TV, Bert raises his head, ears alert and twitching. He's warm and reluctant to move, but wants me to know he's got my back if I need canine assistance.

'You're okay, boy,' I say. 'Snuggle up.'

My dog gives a cheek-puffed *oof* of understanding and settles back down, his nose buried in the dubious depths of Sock. I pick up the Sudoku book I've been trying to start for hours, but two minutes later it's back on the arm of the chair. My gaze rests on the bookcase, where five new novels await my attention. But it's no use: I couldn't focus on a story if I tried. I'm restless and annoyed that I am. It's not a winning combination.

Thing is, I hoped she'd see the fun in it. As I was drawing the ridiculous letters on my doomed message, I kept thinking about the Spider-Man mug, the rock tour T-shirt, the happy flowers. They all seemed to point to someone who appreciated the lighter things of life.

She might have a fella.

I didn't think of that.

He might be on his way over to punch my lights out.

I glance at Bert and Ernie. I don't reckon they'd be much cop as wingmen in a fistfight.

It would be an answer, though. Right now, I'd take that over radio silence.

I look at the paper stuck to the window, the words in reverse visible where the felt-pen ink has bled through. *Hi, flat opposite mine*... How lame is that?

Okay, that settles it: I'm taking it down. If she's not seen it, I can just forget it ever happened. And even if she has seen it and is now thinking I'm a crazed stalker with a cut-flower fetish, the chances of us actually meeting after this embarrassing episode are zero.

Mind made up, I struggle upright and make my way over. I reach up and peel back the masking tape strip to release the top right corner of the message. The paper edge rolls back...

... and my heart slams against my chest.

There's a sheet of paper stuck in her window beside the flowers. Across it, bright rainbow-coloured bubble letters form a reply:

RANUNCULUS.
WHAT'S YOUR CAT'S NAME?

I blink hard and look again, in case it's a trick of the light or my mind playing games. It's *real*. A message back – and she's noticed Ernie, too. Which means I haven't been the only person looking out across the hedge.

I can't explain what that means.

Leaning my weight against the edge of the window frame, I read the message again. It's perfect. I *knew* she would get it.

I swing my body on to a chair at the table and grab the sketch-pad and pens. My hand shakes as I try to pull out a colour that won't budge from the felt-pen pack. Impatient to reply, I shake them all out instead, a clattering rainbow explosion skidding

51

and spinning across the dining table. Bert gives a loud bark and appears beside my chair, ready to defend me from the noisy invasion. I reach down to ruffle his fur and he licks my hand before I bring it back to the table. I have to resist the urge to rip a sheet from the pad, instead taking my time to carefully detach it. Then I set to work.

I should calm down, remember I'm a grown man and not an overexcited kid. But screw propriety: nobody is watching, except for my concerned furry housemates. And this is the most exciting thing that's happened in months. It might turn out to be nothing but a daft diversion. She might not reply again. But it's my turn to respond.

So I do.

HIS NAME IS ERNIE.

I glance down at my feet, where Bert is watching me with concern. I know she hasn't seen him in the window, but I can't leave him out of the roll call. Smiling, I add another line:

I HAVE A DOG CALLED BERT, TOO.

And then what do I say? Should I mention my name yet? Or ask another question first? I look at my message. What question would I ask? *HOW'S YOUR NEW FLAT?* Far too stalkery. She'd know I'd been watching her painting it and moving in. *WHAT'S YOUR NAME?* Too forward. Too pushy.

It's such a surprise she replied at all. And a shock that I wrote the message in the first place. The old Lachie Wallace would never have thought to do that. The thing Jenny complained about the most was how I kept myself to myself. In the end I think that's what made her leave me.

'You're such a closed book all the time. Sometimes I wonder if you want to let me in at all.'

There's nothing wrong with being a private person. People don't need to know your every waking thought in order to care about you. I told Jenny what I wanted her to know: that I loved her, that I wanted her in my life. Everything else was window dressing.

What changed today? I don't know. But that aloneness I experienced when Tanya left this afternoon was stronger than it's ever been before and… it scared me. Looking at my neighbour's window this past week has made me feel I'm still part of the world. That I still have a place in it, beyond these four walls. I don't know who the woman is, but the things she surrounds herself with make me think she could be someone who understands the need for belonging and bright things.

Could she be lonely, too?

I'm still not sure why I'm doing this, but for the first time since my accident, I'm hopeful. It's like discovering I can breathe after months underwater.

She might not be a friend. It might be two messages in a game that gets me through a tough day. But I'm going to enjoy it while it lasts.

I add a final line, smoothing out the paper with my hands, willing the words to be the right ones. Then I take down the original message from the window and replace it with the new one.

As I fix the last piece of tape in place, I peer around the edge of the paper at the window opposite. I can't see anyone between the flowers and her message. But knowing she's there makes my heart work faster.

I step back from the window, reading the words in reverse.

HIS NAME IS ERNIE.
I HAVE A DOG CALLED BERT, TOO.
AND I'M LACHLAN.

Chapter Ten

BETHAN

Bert and Ernie? That's *brilliant*.

And it's weird, but knowing that reassures me. Would a crazy stalker have a cat and a dog with such cute names? Well, okay, they might. But I don't think my message-sending neighbour is like that.

Lachlan.

That's a good name. Bit different. Mysterious. I'm not sure I'd be this excited if he'd been a Steve, or a Tom, or a Bill. Or, God forbid, a *Darren*. That would have been cause to get a blind for the window immediately and keep it permanently drawn. I know that's a daft position to take but discovering he's a *Lachlan* seems to make a difference.

I love where we live now. But apart from the landlord, who I'm unlikely to see often, Lachlan is the first person to say hello. The first name I've encountered in our new neighbourhood. Like the thrill I felt when I saw his cat on my first day here – *Ernie*, now – this is another hint of welcome, a newly opened door. Like this is where we should be.

Properly introduced, Mam calls it. For someone so generally unfussed with propriety, she's a firm fan of some archaic conventions. Like always starting any new association properly. 'Your

55

name is the first thing you give anyone. It's polite. Once you're properly introduced you can talk about what you like.'

I should return the favour, then. Can't disappoint my mam.

I grab a piece of paper from the stack on the edge of the kitchen counter and pull the top off a blue felt-pen with my teeth, ready to write...

'What are you doing, Mummy?'

Noah is standing beside me, his arms wrapping around my knees.

'Love you, baby. I've just got to do this and then we'll make the cookies, okay?'

'Cookies for tea!' My son claps his hands. 'Love you lots-a-jelly-tots,' he says, his version of what I say to him about a thousand times a day. He grins the widest smile, proud of himself, making my heart swell ten times bigger. Then, his face becomes very stern. 'Now I need a POO.'

I instantly drop the pad and the pen, scooping him into my arms and dashing to the bathroom. We're only just out of the woods with potty training, but while he's mastered weeing with enthusiastic flair, poos remain a tricky area. When my son needs to go, he needs to *go* – in the middle of a supermarket, walking down the street, sitting in a café. There's no time to check if facilities are available. A Noah Gwynne Code Brown waits for nobody.

We make the toilet in time – mostly – but he needs a wash and a change afterwards and I quickly revise my plans to make cookies today. We have cake in the cupboard, which he'll be happy with. I don't think I could face eating anything we'd been quite so *hands-on* baking tonight.

By the time we're done, I need to get Noah's tea ready. The peace effort with Maisie earlier and all the excitement with Lachlan's note just now have pushed everything later. He's usually fed, bathed and in bed by 7.30 p.m. – there's no chance of that happening tonight.

I throw tea together, clumsy in my anxiousness to get it all done. I keep passing the sheet of paper and pen and fluffy penguin pencil case that stare accusingly at me from the kitchen counter, but I don't have time to write my reply yet. The next hour and a half passes in a blur of bedtime routine, but I swear my heart is beating twice as fast through it all.

When Noah's finally tucked up, two bedtime stories read and a lullaby sung, it's almost 9 p.m. He'll be a right old grump in the morning, but I'll deal with that when it comes.

I hurry into the living room, finally free to send my message back to Lachlan. But when I reach for the stack of paper, I stop.

What do I say to him?

I should tell him my name. But then what? *What's the tattoo on your arm?* is what I really want to ask but then he'd know I'd been looking more closely than just noticing his cat.

I'm not going to mention Noah. Not yet. I never tell anyone about him until I'm sure of them. It's become a thing for me, a defence mechanism that clicks into place. I'd like to say it's totally because I want to protect my son, but if I'm really honest it's about 90 per cent of the reason. The other quiet 10 per cent is a selfish need to have a bit of time in someone's mind where it's just me. Once they know about Noah I'm never quite sure whether their reactions to me are because I'm a single mum or not. I don't ever trust them fully after they know.

I shouldn't care what anyone thinks. I love my son. He's my life. And it makes no sense, but I want Lachlan to know me, just for who I am.

It might not matter anyway because he shared his name with

me and I ignored it for almost three hours. He might have just given up waiting because he thinks I'm rude.

I glance over.

His message is still there.

AND I'M LACHLAN.

It's like a beacon. I breathe in the hope it gives me.

And then I go and grab the open bottle of wine from the fridge and pour a glass. Because this suddenly doesn't feel like a frivolous thing and I'm worried I'll stuff it up.

I clear a space on the kitchen worktop and brush toast crumbs from the surface. After a large gulp of wine, I brandish the felt-pen and begin.

HI, LACHLAN. I'M BETHAN.

The tip of my pen hovers over the paper. Now what?

I run through more possibilities – *nice weather we're having … how are you? … what do you do for a job? … how do you like living here?* – but none of them are what I really want to say. I don't know Lachlan, beyond his nice name and the pets he lives with. I know he has a tender-looking hand and an intriguing tattoo on his rather nice arm, but I can't mention that yet.

I stare at the paper.

What do you say to someone you've never met or fully seen, who's just said hello? How do you reply without sounding like a strange voyeur or an utter bore?

I don't even know if he'll reply again. It might just be a two-message kind of thing. Which, you know, is better than nothing.

I drink more wine.

Okay, so if this is the last message I send Lachlan, what do I want to leave him with? My great-uncle Bleddyn believes the most important words you'll ever say to someone are the last ones you voice before you leave the room. He's nutty as a box of pecans most of the time but I was always struck by the wisdom of this theory. 'What you leave people with colours their memory of you. You can make it a parting gift or a lingering curse. That's the power you have.'

What do I want Lachlan to be left with of me?

Heart thumping, I write the next lines:

YOUR MESSAGE MADE MY DAY.
THANK YOU ☺

It feels really personal. But it's the thing I want to say.

Before I have a chance to talk myself out of it, I grab the sticky tape and set about replacing my first message with the new one.

It's done now. Step away, Bethan.

I look at the first message in my hand, then glance at the kitchen bin. No, I'm not going to throw it away. If this is the last time, I want to remember how the window messages made me feel. I take it into my room, pull out a large flat plastic box meant for shoes from the bottom of my wardrobe and store the paper carefully inside.

I'm smiling when I return to the living room.

Against all odds, today was a good day. Whatever happens – or doesn't happen – tomorrow, tonight I'll sleep knowing someone else in the world knows I'm here.

That's enough.

Chapter Eleven

LACHLAN

Last night in bed I decided it didn't matter whether she replied or not. It was enough of a moment to restore my faith in good things, in the possibility of being surprised in a good way.

This morning I don't wake until after 9 a.m., only coaxed from the deepest of sleeps by a pair of righteously angry grey paws pummelling my face. Ernie is *not* impressed. I'll be in his bad books till at least lunchtime. Bert, on the other hand, forgives me as soon as I get out of bed. Dogs are like that. *You exist! Wow! I love you!*

Be more dog, that's what I reckon.

To avoid any further disgust from my feline housemate, I decide to feed them both first before I take a shower. Tanya isn't coming today – probably a good thing given yesterday's scare – and I just have a video call with my superior this afternoon to be ready for. Until then I have time to do things at my own pace.

My body is as mad at me as my cat this morning as I make the slow, aching walk from my bedroom to the living area. The heavy strapping on my left leg runs from my pelvis to just below the knee, great ugly red scars hidden beneath layers of black padding. I don't have to see them to know they are there. My doctor reckons it's all healing well, but I'll be heavily scarred for life. The battalion insignia tattoo on the top of my thigh – the one I got with the rest of my squadron mates when we passed out of Catterick eighteen years ago – is sliced in two, the damage irreversible. There was talk of skin grafts, but I'm not willingly signing up for more time in recovery. It's too early to think of any of that, anyway. I need to get my leg back in action first.

The strapping is usually hidden but I sleep in shorts at night because they're more comfortable, so now it's on display. I glare at it as I move. That's where the scarring is worst, but above my waist more damage is visible. The heavy bruising I sustained across my ribs and abdomen has been slowly fading through purples and blues to greens and yellows. Colours on my body that I didn't choose: unlike my inks, which are finally looking more vivid than the bruises now. My hand bears a thick red scar and while the airbag burns on my face have mostly disappeared, I feel their scars pull tight beneath my skin.

I'm a mess.

But I feel lighter this morning. Yesterday helped.

Breathing against the now-familiar kick of pain as I put down Bert and Ernie's food bowls, I look up at the window. My message is still there, one edge of masking tape curling away from the glass. I smile at the memory of yesterday's game and move over to sort the errant tape.

When I glance outside, I can't believe it.

She's replied.

Bethan. I like that.

'Hi, Bethan,' I say, the laugh of surprise that follows momentarily hiding her bright letters as my breath meets the cold glass. Bethan – you can't say it without making an involuntary smile. It sounds Welsh. I wonder if she is? Mind you, with a name like mine most people expect a Scot when they first meet me. And my family *were* Scottish – about four generations ago. Like me, Bethan could hail from anywhere.

Maybe I could ask her that next time. Or later, if we carry on the game, which, given I have a reply I'd pretty much talked myself out of expecting, is now a real possibility.

So, Bethan-across-the-hedge, what shall we discuss today?

From the time she responded yesterday I reckon she works during the day, so I'm going to think about what to say next and put my reply up around 5 p.m. There's no way I want to repeat my idiotic four-hour window-watching exercise of yesterday. It will only be our fifth shared message, but already the fear of her not responding is gone. We've shared names now, and she knows Bert and Ernie, so I reckon we're past the formalities.

She's no longer the stranger in the flat opposite mine. She's Bethan.

And yesterday, I made her day.

My superior officer is not a Zoom natural.

It's 3.40 p.m. and I'm sitting at the dining table, staring at

Major Tom Archer scowling at me and mouthing what are no doubt obscenities at the screen.

'Still can't hear you,' I say, bored of this now.

He gestures at the screen like he's under fire from a battalion of angry wasps.

'Ask Lieutenant Daimler,' I suggest, knowing it will annoy him but also aware that without help this conference call could run indefinitely. I need to write my reply to Bethan before she gets back from work. I wish I could be thinking about that now and not what my superior officer might say.

DAIMLER? he mouths, followed by a lot more muted words I don't have to hear to understand. Since they've been in an office together, sparks have flown between him and my colleague Kim. She's forever bailing him out when technology gets the better of him and he detests it. He's meant to have been on a course to learn all this stuff, but Riggsy reckons he fudged the paperwork to bunk off it.

Kim's familiar weary smile appears on-screen and moments later Major Archer's voice booms into my flat.

'Bloody nonsense. Whoever invented this piece of crap should be shot.'

You have to thank your lucky stars Archer's in the Educational and Training Service Unit now and no longer on active duty. It's safer for everyone.

'Good to see you, sir.'

'Likewise. So, I read the report from your doctor. Rehab going well?'

He makes it sound like I'm booked into the Betty Ford Clinic, not engaged in a punishing physical regime to coax life back into my damaged body.

'I think so.'

'No word of a return date, but I expect you know that.'

I nod, not trusting my reply. My superior clocks it and looks uncomfortable.

'Right. Well, carry on as you're doing. I know you'll be working hard, Wallace. Always have, always will.'

'Sir.'

'Now. I need to discuss a delicate matter with you and I...' his words are lost in a loud rustle of papers as he sorts them too close to the microphone, '... not want to answer, but I'm afraid it's imperative you do.'

'Sorry, sir, I didn't catch all of that?' I may not have heard the words, but I can tell from his expression what's coming. I knew it would, sooner or later.

'Ah. Right. Bloody microphone. To recap, there's to be a formal inquiry into the crash. Military police, Special Investigations Branch. Initial accident investigations from the civilian police have been completed and were as we expected. However, some – *information* – has come to light that Command wishes to address.'

Shit.

Since the crash, Riggsy's maintained this wouldn't happen. So what information do they have? And more importantly, where has it come from?

'Information, sir?'

There's a moment before he replies, as if he's picking his words from between lines of landmines. 'I don't know what it is. But I can assure you, Wallace, I have your back on this. Most likely it's the high-ups playing Big Boss again. But you should be aware it's going to happen. And – be very clear about the answers you give. You owe it to yourself, to the successful continuance of your career, to do this correctly. Do you understand?'

My guts knot. 'I do, sir.'

'Excellent.' Archer claps his hands together, the crack of it loud as a gunshot. Behind me there's a skittering of paws as Bert and Ernie dash for cover. I wish I could join them. 'So, I will call next week and update you. In the meantime, rest up. Try to stay positive, yes?'

For him, that's the equivalent of a bear hug. I manage a smile. 'I will, sir. Don't have too much fun without me.'

A glint of mischief sparkles in my superior's eyes. 'Parties every day, Wallace. Be a bloody bore when you're back.'

The silence is welcome when I close my laptop. I wasn't expecting it to happen so soon. It was inevitable, whatever Riggsy said. I'm just annoyed I believed him the other day. I know what we agreed our story would be, if we ever had to account for it. I just didn't think I'd ever have to say it aloud, like it was what really happened. Like it was the truth. Military police, a formal inquiry – that's a much bigger deal. We'll need to agree far more detail to make our version of events stick. More lies…

Stiff from sitting too long, I haul my body off the chair and make a slow circuit of the room. I can't think about the investigation now. Today began with a good surprise: I'm going to focus on that rather than the bad one I've just been dealt. I make coffee and fetch the sketchpad and pens from the kitchen drawer where I stowed them last night.

Then I return to the table, take out a sheet and write my next message to Bethan.

Chapter Twelve

BETHAN

'How did you do that?'

Patrick stares at me as we hurry past the herb area, racing to get away from the main building and the Head of Section, who has just had an utter meltdown in front of the plant section team, much of which was directed at me.

'Do what?'

'Stay calm while he was chucking abuse at you? I would have lamped the bastard. I nearly did.'

'Well, I'm glad you didn't.' I know what Darren was trying to do and not letting him succeed was the absolute best feeling. The calmer I stayed, the more furious he became. And the more power I felt. It hurt, of course it did. But standing my ground, poker face in place, was the best form of retaliation.

Besides, nothing can dampen my mood today. I keep wondering if Lachlan's seen my reply yet. His flat was dark when I left this morning, with no sign of Ernie, either. I guess he might go to work earlier than I do. What will he think when he sees it?

He might have given up. But my gut feeling is he hasn't. I know hardly anything about Lachlan, but I know he reached out and

66

that means he was looking for a reply. Why go to all that trouble if a delay would put him off?

I might be laying too much store by this. I'm lonely and at the exact moment I needed a friend, Lachlan sent me the message. I don't know if I believe in fate, but I do believe life can chuck you nice surprises as well as crap ones.

I think Lachlan might just be one of the nice things.

It's made me smile since I woke up. Noah noticed first, pausing at breakfast to reach across his toast and jam and place his sticky little hand on my face. 'You have a happy face, Mummy. It's lovely now.' It pretty much made me grow an extra inch when he did that. He's seen the opposite too many times in his three years.

Michelle clocked my mood too, the moment she met us at her door. 'Okay, what happened to you?'

'Nothing, why?'

'See – *that* – what you're doing right now. You can't stop smiling. What's going on?'

'Can't I just be in a good mood?'

I could tell she wasn't buying it as she helped Noah off with his coat. 'All right, who is he?'

I fended off her question but it still gave me a shot of joy. It's not like *that*, of course, but I love having something good only I know about. Someone who might become a friend.

Patrick and I reach the relative safety of the polytunnels where Bright Hill's signature plants are grown. I love it in here – row upon row of Hattie's father's favourite plants. It's the past and the present merging in long lines of verdant life. And as this is Eric's kingdom, Darren is highly unlikely to come in.

There's no sign of our resident Lancelot, but that doesn't

mean he isn't here somewhere, crouched down beside the rows of seedlings, tending to them with all the care of a mother hen. It amazes me that Eric has personally coaxed every plant that leaves this tunnel into life. I wonder how many plants he cultivated are now growing in gardens across the country.

The polytunnels' plant rows are green for now, but soon they'll become a riotous rainbow of colour. It's all from Bright Hill's signature plants: *Primula auricula* – known as bear's ear primulas because the brightly coloured overlapping petals on each flower head are small and round and resemble teddy bear ears. When Hattie's father, Hector Rowse, started his nursery business the bear's ear primulas were the plant he chose. They won him fifteen Chelsea Golds – which are all still proudly displayed behind the tills – and huge popularity in the 70s, 80s and early 90s. A little out of fashion now, sadly, and not so in demand. But I think they're wonderful.

I love the power of growing things. It's hopeful. The promise of brand-new life. It's always calmed me working with plants – that's why Hattie promoted me from gifts and homewares to the plant section a year ago. I happened to let slip that I kept a window box in the horrible bedsit and had plants around the cramped space. When we talked about it more, she created this job for me. I'm so glad she did.

'Seriously, B, the guy is a dick.' Patrick is still fuming beside me. 'You should tell Hattie.'

I'm touched he's gunning on my side. But getting angry is pointless – and exactly what Darren Gifford wants. 'And what would she do? She wouldn't sack him, Pat, you know she wouldn't. He's done worse than be vile to me and he's still here. It would only give him ammunition. If it comes down to a choice between him and me, who do you think would keep their job?'

Patrick kicks a stone with the scuffed toe of his boot. 'It sucks.'

'It does. But thanks for having my back.'

He bumps his shoulder against mine. 'Always. Reckon Eric's got any home baking with him today?'

'Ha, you wish.'

'Hey, I can dream, can't I?' His smile fades just a little. 'You sure you're okay?'

I think of the window messages from yesterday, the thrill of connecting with someone in my new neighbourhood, the promise of what might happen next. 'I'm more than okay,' I smile.

Darren Gifford can throw his worst at me today. I'm happy and he can't touch that.

It takes an age to get home. I'm impatient behind the wheel of my car as traffic blocks my view stretching away to red lights in the distance. Noah will be waiting for me at Michelle's, his preschool afternoon session finished an hour ago. He'll be extra grouchy after his long day because of his late bedtime last night. I plan to settle him with an early tea as soon as we get in so I have ten minutes in peace to see if Lachlan has replied. The traffic may not be moving yet, but my brain is already hurrying through every detail of the evening ahead.

I can't wait to see if I have another message.

I switch the radio on, flooding the car with music to take my mind off not moving. The song ends and another begins: 'Shine' by Years & Years. It makes my heart contract – not because I don't love it, but because when I loved it first I was living a different life, a different version of me. A Bethan Gwynne who thought she was safe; who never saw the sledgehammer about to smash it all. She's so far from me now it's almost as if I never lived as her. I'm tempted to turn the song off, but like so many aspects of my life I'm determined to claw back what I lost. I didn't run then. I won't run now. Instead, I crank up the volume and sing loud against the pain, the heel of my hand beating out the rhythm and the memory on the steering wheel. Tears appear, making the long line of red brake lights snaking ahead of me dance in my vision.

All of this – all of where I find myself now – is proving I can do it. I'm growing: firmly planting my boots in the earth and reclaiming my life. Today's meeting was hard, but I got through it. I held my ground and Darren looked like an idiot because of it. Every tiny triumph matters. Growth is my ultimate revenge on those that wanted me to fail.

Finally, the traffic eases and I make it back to Michelle's just before 5 p.m. Half an hour later, with a very grouchy little boy in tow, I unlock our door into the golden sunlit welcome of our flat. I want to run to the window, but I make myself go straight to the kitchen. And actually, making tea with the window constantly calling to me from my peripheral vision makes it all a hundred times more exciting.

I let Noah eat tea in the company of his cuddly dragon chums, with the promise of watching the CBeebies bedtime hour if he clears his plate, which pacifies him. I'll eat later, when he's in bed. My stomach is too crowded with butterflies to consider eating now.

When I'm certain Noah is settled, I turn to the window.

I don't know why I'm so nervous when this is what I've looked forward to all day. The tea in my Spidey mug trembles as I carry it to the window. I take a breath – and look over at Lachlan's flat.

There's a new message!

I swallow my squeal of delight, feeling it travel all the way down from my throat to my happy curling toes inside my Wonder Woman socks.

HI, BETHAN
GLAD YOU LIKED IT ☺
HOW WAS YOUR DAY?

I can't remember the last time anyone asked me how my day was. It's such a simple question, but when nobody ever asks it, it becomes a rare gift. One tiny point of human contact lost the moment you're on your own.

Heart so full it might just pop, I take a sheet of paper and write my reply.

Chapter Thirteen

LACHLAN

LONG AND BUSY,
BUT GOOD.
HOW WAS YOURS? ☺

Bethan might just be the best thing to happen to me this week.

She's fast today: one hour after I stuck the new message in the window, I noticed her reply. And, next to the vase of ranunculus flowers, the red-and-blue mug I saw her holding last week.

I was right, it is Spider-Man. I can see it clearer now, the unmistakable spider web mask with the black-outlined white eyes across the body of the mug and the bright blue of Spidey's suit forming the chunky handle. That is one cool mug. And another reason to like my new neighbour.

I could wait until tomorrow to send back a reply, but the mug is an invitation I can't ignore. So I write a new message:

NOT TOO BAD.
GREAT SPIDEY MUG, BTW.
SO YOU'RE A MARVEL GIRL?

Smiling at my cheekiness, I swap it for yesterday's reply in the window. Then I busy myself in the kitchen making dinner.

'I'm not going to look until I've eaten,' I say to Bert, who is gazing up at me, willing scraps of beef to fall from the chopping board like manna from heaven into his waiting jaws. 'And maybe I won't even look until after I've watched TV.'

Bert cocks his head to one side, ears twitching, clearly unconvinced.

He knows me too well.

In the end, I only last an hour until I check. I can't explain the thrill when I see a new message in her window:

MARVEL AND DC
I'M BILINGUAL IN SUPERHEROES!
HOW ABOUT YOU? ☺

Bilingual in superheroes – how cute is that? I like her. I want to reply immediately, but I don't want to push my luck. This is already more than I ever thought would happen when I posted the first message yesterday.

Was it really only yesterday this began?

Yesterday, I didn't even know her name. It was crazy to even think she might respond to my message. But now there isn't just a polite reply, there's the beginning of a connection. I could never have predicted that. The air around me fizzes with possibility. What if this becomes a regular part of our days? Already Bethan has a place in my thoughts. I couldn't stop thinking about the window notes today, even when Archer dropped the bombshell about the investigation.

Without realising, Bethan's reply kept my head above water today.

Yesterday, when I almost lost my physio and suffered the crushing defeat of asking for help, I felt so alone. Today, what could have sent me back under *didn't* – because of her.

I knew she would understand. Even before the messages. I've had a feeling about this girl since I first saw her framed in her window, the weariness and toll of work visible in the way she moved. I can't explain why it mattered but it did. And maybe I'm insane to even think she might care about what I think, but I *like* her…

Whoa.

Hang on.

I jump into the path of my veering train of thought to make it halt.

Stop, Lachie. Don't get ahead of yourself. It's still a game.

It's not even twenty-four hours since the first message. I can't read anything into it. I can't get carried away or I could screw it all up.

It's just new. And I don't do this – I never just open myself up immediately. I might like Bethan's attitude and cute humour, but I don't know who she is. And she doesn't know me. It's fun to exchange messages but would we get on if we were in the same room? It's shocked me how fast all this has happened, but it would be so easy to run away with it. I sense the danger waiting down the line.

It should make me back off the gas.

But I want to keep talking to her.

So I write another message:

DC TILL I DIE ☺
BUT I HAVE A SOFT SPOT FOR SPIDEY.
WHO'S YOUR FAVOURITE?

I've just put it in the window when my phone rings. I take one last look across at Bethan's window and head to the sofa to answer the call.

'How's my gorgeous boy doing?'

I have to smile. Eighteen years in the army, tours of duty in Germany, Iraq and Afghanistan, a body of muscles and ink, but to my mum I'll always be three years old with hair that won't lie flat, trailing after her with Hovis, my old battered bear. 'I'm good. How's the nuthouse?'

Her laugh is warm against my ear. For the smallest moment I wish myself closer to her. 'Your father is driving Sally round the bend. If he crosses one more line with her she'll go stratospheric.'

'Same as ever then. How are you?'

The slight hesitation before her reply tells me all I need to know. 'Oh, you know, plodding on.' Mum's answer to everything. It sounds breezy but it masks a defence stronger than steel. If Jenny thought I was a closed book, she should have met the Master. You just don't ask my mother how she is and expect an honest answer. I keep asking, though, because there's comfort in the enquiry. She knows it and she knows I know it, too.

'You couldn't plod if your life depended on it. Exocet Wallace they call you in Bourton-on-the-Water. Advances towards her targets with devastating speed...'

'Shush, you.' Despite the rebuke I can sense her smile. 'Listen, I want to talk to you. About the future.'

Bloody hell, pull no punches, Mum. 'Well, I reckon we'll have lunar tourism within twenty years and personal VR capabilities but I still don't think flying cars are viable,' I say, knowing this is only delaying the inevitable.

'Lachlan John Wallace, if you think that's likely to deter me you can think again.'

'Sorry.' I lean back into the sofa and close my eyes. Bert wriggles across the cushions to thump his chin on my stomach, huffing warm breath against my T-shirt.

'Have you thought any more about what you'll do?'

'Get back on my feet, go back to work.'

'But your leg is…'

'… On the mend. I spoke to Archer today and he's keen for me to get back.' She doesn't need to know the rest.

Her long sigh sets my hackles rising. 'Is he looking at the same doctor's report we saw? It's been two months, Lachie, and how close are you really to full mobility?'

'Cheers for the vote of confidence, Mum.'

'Don't do that. Don't be flippant. I just want you to actually consider what happens if things don't improve.'

'I will – if they don't.'

'Lachie…'

'Mum, I'm working hard. I'm doing everything I can. I get that you're concerned, I understand that, but this is my battle. You don't have to fight it for me.'

She goes quiet but I won't backtrack. I love her but she needs to let me do this my way. I've seen the knots my sister ties herself in to fit into Mum's expectations and I'm just not doing it.

And then she drops the bomb.

'I want you back here. With us. There's a two-bed cottage on the farm you could move into immediately. If you get the worst news about your injuries we can have the place adapted to make it easier for you. You can work with Dad and Sal and we can get you proper help with rehabilitation.'

Proper help. As if my doctors and medical team aren't doing enough. As if my parents chucking money at my body will heal it any quicker. And a granny flat on their farm? Constantly under their surveillance? No thank you.

'You make it sound so attractive.'

'It's better than being stuck in that poky flat of yours, struggling...'

'I'm not struggling.'

She doesn't even acknowledge what I said. '... harbouring ridiculous thoughts of still being employed by the army. I love you, my darling, but you're deluding yourself if you think your life can go back to how it was before. Let us help you.'

'We're not going to agree, Mum. Just leave it.'

'So I just stop worrying about you? Sorry, son, that's a lifelong job.'

I take a breath as she does, letting my gaze rest on the new message in my window. Bethan knows nothing about my leg, or any of the baggage that comes along with it. She's the only living soul in my life that just sees me, not what happened to me. As far as my family is concerned, that's all they see.

And I think: if I'd had this conversation with Mum yesterday, when I was at the edge of myself, totally lost, I might have been tempted to run back home.

Bethan has no idea what she's done for me in just a few hours.

'What happened on that road, Lachie?'

I stare at my sleeping dog, wishing I hadn't heard it. 'We hit a hidden dip in the rain and skidded off the road.'

'That's not what I meant. Your friend should have been paying attention. Why wasn't he? Why was he driving and not you? Why were you even there?'

'Mum, leave it.' I cut her off, not wanting to go any further down this line.

'I can see I'm wasting my time. This won't go away, not until you face facts. Your dad and I will be here when you decide to be an adult about it. That's all I wanted to say.' I picture her stuffing her questions and her irritation away in her bag, ready for a swift exit, like she always did when we fought at home. 'I expect Sally will call you later this week.'

'I expect she will.'

'Right. We do love you, Lachlan.'

Her words cut with a bittersweet edge. 'I know. I love you, too.'

I throw the phone to the cushions when the call ends, met with a look of pure disgust from my cat perching on the arm above them. I reach up to rub my eyes. I'm never going to make her understand me. But her questions about the crash were too close for comfort. That and the news of the inquiry cause a rush of cold dread. I'll call Riggsy tomorrow, tell him to come over. We need to get our stories straight. Watertight.

Because if we don't, I could lose so much more than just my career.

I slide free of Bert's chin and shuffle to the window, needing reassurance, praying for a reply. Something happening in the here and now. No ties to the past. No weight of responsibility. No fear of the truth.

And, like a brave single flame in the deepening darkness, there it is.

> HOW LONG HAVE YOU GOT?!
> MIGHT TAKE MONTHS
> TO ANSWER THAT.

☺ ☺ ☺

It's the best answer. And a wide-open door.
My reply is the easiest yet.

CHALLENGE ACCEPTED.
TALK AGAIN TOMORROW?
☺

Chapter Fourteen

BETHAN

Do I want to chat with someone who wants to listen? Hmm, Lachlan, let me just think about that for a moment…

What a daft question!

I'm still smiling about it this morning, driving into work. My cheeks ache when I do, making me wonder if I was smiling in my sleep all night. I wouldn't be surprised if I was. And of course I replied to him before sleep won the battle for my head.

YES PLEASE.
NIGHT–NIGHT, LACHLAN ☺

It gave me a thrill writing his name at the end. Like I've known him forever. My friend next door. It might not last and I know only too well what can go wrong when you trust someone. He could still be a serial killer, although I'm not sure a psycho would admit to a secret love of Spidey. Maybe it will peter out when one of us gets bored. All I know is that I needed those messages this week and Lachlan was there to send them. It's the loveliest thing and I'm in, for as long as it lasts.

It's worryingly quiet at Bright Hill again today. When I first started working here, we were still getting groups descending on us for day trips out – ladies from the local WIs coming for afternoon tea and a wander around the gift shop, a Knit'n'Natter club on a Wednesday, a church craft group that used a section of the café for their activities on the first Thursday of every month, and an army of mums and toddlers who came for a chat while their kids played on the rickety old wooden canal boat-shaped play place, until it finally bit the dust and was condemned last year. There are five coach spaces marked out in the car park, but the only people who park there now are the car drivers who sit having a cheeky smoke they don't want their other halves pottering around the nursery to see.

I've been thinking about that as I've been trying to summon potential ideas to help boost business. Maybe we could offer a deal to any community groups who want to visit? Give them use of a dedicated area in the café, perhaps? It's not like it's ever rammed in there these days, not even at Christmas.

We can't compete with the chain-owned nurseries in scope and marketing, but we have something they don't have: personality. We used to be a vital part of the local area, before the big guys moved in on our patch. Could we become that again?

I've been looking for Hattie all morning to discuss this, but so far there's no sign of her. Come to think of it, I didn't notice her car in its space when I arrived. Although my mind wasn't really concerned with identifying staff cars, so I might have missed it.

Do I tell Lachlan where I work, if he asks?

The thought pops into my head without warning. I shouldn't be thinking about this now, but the shiver of excitement it causes is addictive. Like tiny shiny pebbles of joy appearing in my path...

'*Bethan.*'

... Unlike the bark of my boss, that is. I stifle a groan as I turn back.

Darren is high-speed striding across the sales area like a tiny tornado, his neck buried so far into his shoulders that his collar appears to be attached to his ears.

'What are you doing out here?'

I keep my face expressionless. 'I just delivered the shift sheets to the cash office, like you asked, and now I'm on my way back.'

'Shouldn't trust you with money,' he snaps, completely unnecessarily considering I'm doing what he told me to do twenty minutes ago – and how does taking a list of agreed shifts for next week constitute cash handling?

'Why's that?'

'Can't keep a bloke so you bludge off the state. That's what you do, isn't it? Have a kid for the money it brings in.'

Bastard. I shine a smile of pure middle-fingered joy at him. 'Ah, but it's not what I do, is it, Darren? I work and pay my tax, so I benefit the state, not the other way around. Ask the cash office, they have my P60.'

I shouldn't answer back and normally I wouldn't, but I'm not willing to take his rubbish today. I recall the thrill of Lachlan's last message and let it flood my bones with strength.

CHALLENGE ACCEPTED.

Darren seethes, but he's wrongfooted by my reply and too slow to recover. 'The Alpines need restocking. I want it done by the time I come back.'

'Where are you going?'

His brow knots. 'None of your business. Get to work.'

I walk away as steady and defiant as I dare.

The Alpine section was the first one I worked on when I started on the plant team, so it holds a special magic for me. I love that these tiny, fragile little plants that look like they'd disintegrate in a breeze can survive in some of the most inhospitable places in the world. Our Alpine display is in the shadow of the temperate house, sheltered from the path of the wind that gusts between the greenhouses. I fetch the new plants from the delivery area in one of Bright Hill's squeaky yellow carts and make my way through the A-to-Z (what we call the general plant area because that's the system they are arranged in) and round the topical enclosure filled with plants in season. It's like a tour of every plant you can grow in the UK and a reminder of how amazing horticulture is.

If the day ever comes where I don't embrace my inner garden geek, I'll be finished. I love my job, even if nobody in my life has ever shared that passion.

'Plants? What do you want to bother with them for?' Mam's reaction to me being promoted to the plant team was a classic example. I smile, remembering it as I put each tiny potted plant in place on the gravel-covered banks of the Alpine display. 'They grow, don't they? You just let 'em get on with it. Hardly a job in that, is there?'

Mind you, what passes for a garden in her house is testament to Mam's love of plastic flower-filled hanging baskets, and a strip of knock-off Astroturf she got off Llew the Dodge, her local dubious goods procurer. Says it all, really.

Michelle's only interest in gardening is her favourite daydream of bedding Monty Don, so she doesn't ask me about my job, either.

I won't tell Lachlan where I work. But I might tell him what I do. It would be so good to share it with someone who's interested. I wonder what he would think? I have a good feeling he'd want to know more. He started all this asking about flowers, after all.

The final pot in place, I stand and brush the soil from my work trousers. I'm pleased with the display. It's more tabletop gravel hummock than craggy Alpine slope, but the Alpines are so beautiful they speak for themselves.

As I stretch out the knotted muscles at the base of my spine I see Hattie hurrying between the lines of fruit trees. I raise my hand but her head is ducked down so she doesn't see me. Before I can call, she's gone.

Oh well, it can keep.

I take my lunch to the delivery yard, not wanting to risk meeting Darren on the way to the cramped staff room. I'm better when I'm outside. Even though it's resolutely overcast and there's a chill in the air when the wind picks up, the open space is good for my mind.

Over behind the main delivery area is a motley collection of ex-display furniture, weather-beaten and more than past their prime. Patrick calls it the Bright Hill Retirement Village – the place old benches and picnic tables go to while away their twilight years. I love the rickety, faded wonkiness of them. They feel like old friends. Unless it's chucking it down, this is where most of us take our breaks.

Today only one of my colleagues is there, carefully packed sandwich box open and mini pork pie slices arranged on a small white square-folded serviette beside it. Murray Hope nods at me as I sit.

'Bethan.'

'Murray. How's the lunch?'

'Identical, as always.' He almost unleashes a smile, the bare hint of it itching the corners of his mouth. One day, I'll actually make him laugh and see how wide his smile gets. Patrick's been trying for a year, but Deadpan Hope is the master of poker faces. He's also a purveyor of the most devastating jokes, which he wields like a cutlass. His trademark lack of a smile when he's reduced the rest of us to tears is the stuff of Bright Hill legend. I love Murray. He's the quiet giant in our midst, the backbone of the plant team. By rights, he should be doing Darren's job – everyone thinks so. But Murray is a man of simple desires: he likes doing what he does, no fuss or ridiculous expectation. Give him a list of jobs to do and he's content. Ask him to want more and you're wasting your breath.

'Looks good though,' I smile.

'S'alright. You seen Hattie today?'

'Not to talk to. She was in a hurry.'

Murray takes a slow, deliberate bite into his ham and cheese sandwich, his bushy eyebrows lifting like my answer was what he expected. 'Not surprised.'

'Why?'

'Meeting with the bank this morning.' He reaches for his Thermos cup and takes a sip.

My heart hits the tarpaulin-covered ground. 'Bad meeting?'

'Could be. Did she tell you we're in trouble?'

I don't want to break a confidence, but if Murray knows does that mean everyone else does, too? 'I – wondered.'

My colleague sniffs. 'Long time coming. Hector left this place in a heck of a state when he handed it over. Did you know she had an offer from Wyldacre, couple of months ago?'

My appetite vanishes. I stare at my lunch, not knowing how to respond. Wyldacre owns several large chains of garden centres, including Grocutts, two miles up the road from Bright Hill. 'I didn't.'

'Turned them down.' Murray finishes the final slice of pork pie, picking up the serviette to wipe his hands. 'But it was the closest she'd come to offing this place.'

'What were they offering?'

'Not as much as they should. And it turned out they wanted to flatten the place to sell for houses. Remove the competition from Grocutts, earn a shedload of dosh in the bargain.'

'Gits.'

'Right enough.' Murray nods. 'That's how it works now. Tradition counts for nowt. We need to up our game or...' He doesn't need to finish that sentence. I don't want to hear what those words would be.

My stomach is in knots by the time I get home. I can't just offer vague ideas to Hattie: we're past the point for that. I need to come up with a solid plan – and soon.

While Noah has tea and gabbles on about all the things he did at preschool this afternoon, I stand at the kitchen counter with my notebook, willing my brain to keep working. I'm so tired but this won't wait. There has to be something we can do to turn the tide, even if it's just for a few months to boost business. The question is, what?

I'm so caught up in it that I almost miss the thing I've looked forward to all day.

'Mummy! It's a cat!'

Startled, I look up. 'What?'

'A cat, over there! A big grey one. Come and see!' Noah yanks my sleeve, dragging me over to the window. What I see makes every concern of the day vanish.

Ernie is curled on the windowsill in a pose identical to the first time I saw him. But above his head, a new message glows. My message from my friend.

HEY, BETHAN
WHAT SHOULD I WATCH
ON TV TONIGHT? ☺

'Can you see the cat?' Noah's hand is at my sleeve again.

Heart full, I beam down at my son. 'I can. That's Ernie.'

My son gazes up at me, astonished by my mystical neighbourhood-cat-identification skills. 'How do you know that?'

'Can you keep a secret?'

He nods, wide-eyed. I crouch beside him, feeling the warmth of his little back against my arm as I lean towards his ear to whisper. 'He told me.'

Noah frowns. 'No he didn't.'

'He did.'

I never realised a three-and-a-half-year-old could wield

world-weary sighs until my boy became one. 'Don't be silly. Cat's don't talk.'

I grin and tap my temple. 'Maybe I know the secret cat language.'

'You're weird, Mum. *Cat language...*' He returns to the TV, chuckling his little head off.

I turn back to the window and smile. It wasn't the message I was expecting, but it's so much more personal than the options I'd considered. It isn't just a *What's your favourite...?* or *This show or that show...?* He's asking my opinion. Strangers don't do that. Friends who care about the answer do.

There's just one problem: until Noah goes to bed our television is strictly the domain of CBeebies – and I've been so knackered since we moved in I haven't watched any grown-up TV. I can't really suggest Lachlan watches *Mister Maker*, *Hey Duggee* or *Bedtime Stories*, even if the rather lovely Tom Hardy is reading them all this week.

A stab of guilt hits from nowhere.

I can't mention those shows because it would reveal I have a kid and I don't want Lachlan to know about Noah yet. That's the real reason. It could be the perfect opportunity to mention my son, but I don't want to. I glance back at Noah, but he's gazing happily at Maddie Moate on *Do You Know?*, who is bouncing around a factory explaining how tractors are made.

I need to keep this just for me, for now.

I also need to find out what's on TV tonight...

Chapter Fifteen

LACHLAN

'Information? What information?'

Riggsy asks it like it's the most ridiculous thing, his face a picture of amusement on the FaceTime screen. So why doesn't it reassure me?

'Archer says he doesn't know. But I think he might have an idea.'

'It's bollocks. High-ups throwing their weight around. Come on, Wallace, you know what they're like.'

'Hmm.'

'They just want to yell about the crash. *Setting a bad example for the garrison*, that kind of stuff. Maybe one of the locals complained. They're always looking for reasons to slag us off.'

'An overturned car and a smashed ancient yew tree are pretty solid reasons.'

'Will you just chill? It'll be nothing.'

He's probably right. It doesn't help that I was annoyed with him when I answered. I called several times today but this is the first time I've got hold of him. For someone supposedly on sick leave with whiplash and trauma-related stress, he's awfully busy.

'You're right, sorry. Occupational hazard of being stuck indoors all day.'

My friend rolls his eyes. 'Which is *why* I was trying to kick your arse out of there the other day. You stay in that flat all the time and you'll start eating cat food and chatting to imaginary friends.' He scowls at the screen. 'What?'

I realise I'm grinning at the thought of my new, definitely-not-imaginary friend and quickly stuff my smile away. 'Eating cat food? Have you ever smelled it?'

Riggsy's eyes narrow. 'Something's happened.'

'Eh?'

'With you. What is it?'

'I don't know what you mean.'

'Bollocks you don't.' His face brightens. 'You got your leg over with that physio bird, didn't you?'

'Shut up.'

'You did! I knew it.'

'Hey, don't project your sexual frustrations on me. Just 'cos you can't find anyone insane enough to have you.'

Riggsy shakes his head. 'I'm not buying it, Wallace. That face you have on is pure shag energy.'

'You're gross.'

He has to concede that. 'Yeah, but you're my friend, so what does that make you?' His wry smile returns. 'Order a pizza, I'll be over in an hour.'

I glance at the window, where my message for Bethan is still awaiting an answer. I wanted to have this talk with Riggsy much earlier in the day, not this close to the time Bethan is back. If he comes round now I'll have to take the message down and what happens if Bethan thinks I've given up on the conversation? I can't let that happen.

'Not tonight, mate.'

'Why? Fit bird coming over?'

'No. I'm beat, man. Need to turn in early.'

I will weariness into my expression, hoping it's enough. Riggsy peers closer to the screen, then shakes his head. 'All right, Grandpa, suit yourself.'

'How about lunch on Saturday? Pub down the road?'

He nods and makes a winding motion with his hand, clearly needing more for the bargain.

I sigh. 'My shout?'

'*That's* more like it. I'll come to yours for eleven.'

Relief washes over me, grateful that he bought my excuse and that I'll soon be rid of him. I can't keep Bethan waiting. 'I'll meet you downstairs, then.'

'Later, loser.' My mate flicks the V-sign as the call ends.

I breathe out the tension my body has involuntarily knotted itself into and glance at the clock over the kitchen hob. It's 7 p.m. Enough time for a reply to have arrived?

My leg protests as I push up from the sofa, my route to the window complicated by the enthusiastic weaving of a large grey cat around my ankles.

'Ern, do you mind?'

My cat replies with an accusatory yowl.

'I'll get your food in a minute.'

At the sound of the magic F-word, Bert thumps off the sofa and skitters across the floor. Ernie hisses between my feet.

'Enough! Bert, back in your bed.'

I watch my dog slink sullenly back to his basket and try not to notice my cat's triumphant paw-washing beneath the dining table.

Honestly, it's worse than having kids.

But when I look over at Bethan's flat, I forget my irritation.

Instead of a single large sheet of paper, there are three smaller sheets, with a large red arrow pointing to the middle one.

IF YOU NEED TO LAUGH ☺
DERRY GIRLS
ON NETFLIX

THRILLS & SHOCKS!!
EYE, SPY
ON BBC ONE

LOVELY OLD FRIEND ☺
AVENGERS ASSEMBLE
ON FILM 4

Written along the length of the arrow, she's written:

PICK ME! PICK ME!

That's my decision made, then.

But first I need to reply.

I think for a while about what to say, helped in this delay by Bert and Ernie who are at fever-pitch levels of food anticipation. If I wait to feed them until I've written a new message I'll cause a furry Armageddon in my flat. So technically, feeding my pets and therefore averting certain disaster makes me a superhero.

But would I make Bethan's list of favourites?

I can't help my smile as I deliver Bert and Ernie's food.

My dinner can wait, though. I write the next message and put it up, looking again at Bethan's brilliant reply to my last question in her window. She did all the work with that conversation. Time to roll up my sleeves and return the compliment...

THANK YOU ☺
YOUR TURN...
ASK ME ANYTHING

... Even if it scares me.

Maybe being scared isn't always a bad thing. I've thought a lot about that today.

I used to be able to channel fear into action. People assume that, being a serving soldier, I was never scared, that I'd had that impulse pummelled out of me by my army years. But the truth is, you just learn which box to shove it in to deal with later. Except the boxes get stacked on top of each other, towering cardboard skyscrapers in the dusty recesses of your mind. And you never deal with them at all because where would you even start?

My accident upended so many of those boxes, spilling old terrors and sending demons screeching for freedom. They clustered, ten-deep, around my hospital bed, leaching their fear and darkness into every waking thought. I've heard people talk about getting a wake-up call, but I always thought it was attention-seeking rhetoric. I was wrong. The experience of emerging into a world devoid of the controls, constraints and defences I'd relied on was terrifying.

It's why I jump at the slightest sound. Why I can only sleep with headphones in and music playing. Why, try as I might, I can't face the prospect that my leg won't heal.

But I sent a message to a complete stranger at my lowest ebb.

And I've just offered her the answer to anything she wants to ask.

Some fears are okay, it seems.

Chapter Sixteen

BETHAN

*A*sk *him about the tattoo.*

I can't. He'd know I'd seen him. *Bits* of him, anyway. Nice bits…

I snigger into my tea. Thank goodness Noah's just gone down. There's no way his mam could explain that joke.

Bethan Nia Gwynne, you should be ashamed of yourself…

Perhaps I should, but what the heck. The world seems to think I was a one-time hussy, so why not actually be one?

It's that inference I hate the most: that I played around and got my son as a result. My son is a gift, not a punishment. The absolute best thing to ever happen to me. It wouldn't matter if he came from a long-term love or a one-night stand, I would never have wished it any different. People have asked. They ask all the time. Let them: it's none of their business and my right not to answer.

I glance out at Lachlan's message.

YOUR TURN.

Is it my turn for something good to happen? I don't mean that nothing good has ever happened to me – my son, my job, this place, they are all wonderful things I couldn't have imagined for my life. But when is it my turn to have my own good thing? I've spent so long shoring up our lives to keep us safe from storms that I've forgotten what it feels like to think about *me*.

I look back at our new flat, at this space that's so quickly become our home and not just a box we're renting. There are so many blessings packed in here it's a wonder Noah and I can squeeze inside. Bright, sparkling found treasures, jammed up to the ceiling. I don't need anything else, do I?

ASK ME ANYTHING

… Except maybe this.

So, what *do* I want to know about Lachlan?

I mull over the possibilities as I wander into the kitchen. Beyond the tattoo, what do I know about him? Not much. For all I know, he could be pushing sixty and be an avid collector of snails… Okay, not snails. Not with Bert and Ernie around. Maybe I should ask about what kind of dog Bert is. Dog owners like talking about that kind of thing.

Can you just stand in the window with your dog, so I can see him?

Nope, not advisable.

So, what else?

On the kitchen counter are four bumpy lumps of air-dry clay Noah brought home from Michelle's this afternoon. Each one is decorated with exuberant gold glitter paint strokes. They are supposed to be recently excavated pirate treasure, which my son is an undisputed authority on at the moment. Dragons hide pirate treasure, apparently. That's why Noah brought some home for his draconic chums to guard.

'It's so the pirates don't spend it all at once,' he informed me earlier. 'They have to learn to save it. And pirates are too scared of the dragons to get it back, so they have to wait.'

Pirate pocket money. I like it. Part of me is glad my son is learning the importance of saving, but the other part feels guilty that he's had to learn by watching me. I have savings jars hidden in the cupboards, every penny we get distributed between them before we ever think of spending any of it.

I see Michelle's little girl with so many new toys they form a mountain in the conservatory she uses as a playroom; and then I bring Noah home to his toys that are never new and always from a charity shop.

Like his dragons. A nice lady called Doreen who volunteered in the Sue Ryder shop across the street from our old place gave us a bag of them for 50p. I strongly suspect the biggest dragon she gave him – a funky black one flecked with iridescent rainbow spots – wasn't donated at all. Doreen insisted it was, but her smile told another story. Tiny acts of kindness like that keep you going.

I think of the imaginary nuggets of positivity I stow as treasure and weapons when my days are tough – and right then I know what I want to ask Lachlan.

Not about movies, or pets, or tattoos.

Instead, a question of dragon-guarded treasure…

TELL ME SOMETHING
THAT MAKES YOU SMILE

I change the old message for the new and hurry back to the safety of my sofa, heart thumping hard.

Switching the television on for distraction, I scroll through the options on iPlayer and find the latest episode of *Eye, Spy*. It's getting near the end of the second series and everything is happening. As the battle between the heroine Laura Eye and her nemesis Anya Soren reaches boiling point, I think of Lachlan watching the same thing. Separated by brick walls, two strips of garden and a beech hedge, tender connections are being made between our windows. I imagine them, delicate as gossamer, spider-silks traversing the space. Each message makes a new one appear; each thread joins another, strengthening the link...

I'm probably reading too much into it. I mean, it's still a game, isn't it?

He might be flippant with his answer. I already know he's a bit cheeky, so it won't be a surprise if that's what he does. But if he gives me an honest answer? That could shift the game into a new gear.

I should be wary by now.

But I want to see where this goes.

An hour later, *Eye, Spy* reaches its jaw-dropping cliffhanger and I flop back against the cushions. I've loved it, but I'm exhausted. Has Lachlan loved it, too? I wait for my heart rate to slow, until I realise the reason for it hammering has nothing to do with an industrial spy and her enemy on TV.

Right, I'm going to look...

...

... ...

... ... Oh.

Disappointment thuds to the pit of my stomach when I see the same message in the window. Ah well. It's getting late – I need to think about bed so I'm not a gawping zombie in the morning. I smile over at my neighbour's home.

'Night-night, Lachlan. Speak soon.'

I can't be disappointed. He's taking his time, which means his answer is less likely to be a jokey deflection. I can sleep happy tonight, knowing I have a nugget of sparkly treasure to unearth tomorrow.

Does that make me the dragon? I laugh at my own joke. Maybe it does. I mean, it's been said in the past...

Suddenly, my laughter vanishes as if someone has reached into the air and snatched it away.

Lachlan's message is *moving*.

And then I see his arm, the tattoo I so want a closer view of pressed against the window as he takes his message down, strong fingers curling around the top edge, pulling the paper away from the glass...

I duck to the side, flattening my back against the wall; my breath coming in short, shaky bursts.

He's *there*, feet away.

I could just turn back and wave...

No. That's a step too far. Too intrusive. Too risky. What if he sees me and never sends another message?

I'm torn between curiosity and self-preservation. I want to know and I want to hide. So I creep a little closer to the window's edge, inclining my head until I can see a sliver of light. I risk a little more, peering around the frame...

His head is bowed, a roll of tape in his hand, most of his body hidden behind the new message balanced between his hip and the glass. Both arms have inks, I see now, of differing lengths and shapes and colour. His hair looks dark from here, close-cropped at the sides, longer and mussed-up on the top. I watch him slowly lift a strip of tape to his mouth and tear it with his teeth. It's a moment I shouldn't see, which makes it feel even more intimate. Then his fingers take the corner of the paper and his head begins to lift as he raises the new message into place...

I roll away from the window before he sees me. But I'm buzzing.

It's a full ten minutes until I dare to look back. When I do, it's the most perfect reply:

FREEDOM.
FRESH AIR.
AND YOU ☺

Chapter Seventeen

LACHLAN

Was it too much?

Last night I was proud of my answer. This morning, I'm not so sure.

Her question threw me, I'll admit. I thought I was the one being brave and then Bethan blew me out of the water. I considered chucking something cheeky back at first – I would have got away with it, I reckon. She's lovely and clearly enjoys a laugh. I think she would have taken it in the spirit it was intended. But what would that have achieved? It might have made her smile, but it would have been a warning shot, signalling deeper questions were off the table. I want us to keep talking. I want this to continue. But it has to be allowed to grow.

So I had to meet her brave words with my own.

I took my time thinking about my reply because, honestly, I don't think anyone's ever asked me what makes me smile before. People see me smiling and that's their answer. And I've never challenged it because, unless they ask, why would I tell them? It's a hell of a lot safer doing it that way.

I have no such restraints here. It should terrify me, famous

Alcatraz of Emotion that I am, infamous closed book. But it's Bethan asking. So I asked myself the question – and when I really looked, the answers were there.

FREEDOM.

It's what I crave the most, its absence worse than the pain or the necessary hiatus it's imposed on my life. I miss taking it for granted. I miss jumping in the car and driving anywhere just for the hell of it. I miss my car, full stop. I miss moving my body without it reminding me it hurts. Freedom, when I find it, will make me smile. For now, I smile at the thought of finding it again. I don't want to think what happens if it never comes back…

FRESH AIR.

This is about so much more than getting outside. I never expected having space to breathe to be a privilege, but now I know it is. I miss long walks with Bert, the kind I carried him most of the way for, his grateful bulk snuggled against me as we adventured on. My morning and evening visits to the garden with him have been the highlights of my day until recently. Fresh air is defiance, proving to myself I still own the right to breathe it in.

AND YOU.

I wasn't going to add that last line. But I can't think about the first two without thinking about her. They're inextricably linked. I've smiled more this week than I have in years. Even before – with my career and relationships and everything good I've achieved. It's crazy, but it's true.

Maybe it's because this started the exact moment I needed hope. In the middle of the constraints and meticulously planned regimes to get me back on both feet, the thing that has meant the most is the one thing I didn't plan. I never planned to find a friend.

I never planned for Bethan.

And it scares me, you know, because even as I was writing those two words, I was shocked by them. It's moving too fast, not in our messages but in my head. The way I've been thinking about her is dangerous. I don't want to be so desperate for positivity that I make her into some kind of deity. I can't pin all that on her; however sweet she is, it isn't her responsibility to make everything right in my life.

Should I break protocol and post a new message? A question that pulls us back a little? Or do I wait for her reply?

The sharp blast of the door buzzer answers this for me.

'You took your time, sunshine,' Riggsy says as I reach the bottom step. 'I could've come up.'

No you couldn't, I think, picturing last night's message in the window, its predecessors piled on the table. 'I'm meant to be working this leg,' I reply.

Riggsy accepts this but I know I won't be let off the hook that easily. Sure enough – 'Want me to phone ahead, get our drink orders in? At your pace we'll be lucky to get there before closing time.'

'Sod off.'

Our progress is frustratingly slow but for once I'm glad of it. I need time to sort my head out and being away from the flat will be good for me. I'm using my single crutch I'm supposed to use at home but never do. I want to get used to walking unaided from the off – it's a matter of pride. Tanya knows and doesn't challenge me on it, although I suspect she thinks I'm putting too much pressure on myself that way.

Riggsy gasses on about the latest gossip from the garrison, careful to avoid any mention of Archer or the investigation. To hear him talk, you'd think it was all pranks and taking the piss. Is he not worried at all? Or is this bluster to mask something else?

I watch him as we walk. Does Adam Riggs have any levels to him beyond the surface? That's a mystery I've yet to solve. I've known him since we met on basic training as bloody annoying sixteen-year-olds and he hasn't really changed. Can handle his beer a bit better, works out more and has more ink than me. But emotionally? No different, as far as I can tell.

I used to think I was like that – what you see is what you get, ask me a deep question at your peril, and so on, but I'm not. It's not just the accident, either – the first cracks appeared when Jenny left. When she left because I didn't let her in like I should have...

Angry I've let her name slip back, I stuff it away again, like the evidence of a bad habit I want no one to see. If I'm not thinking about Bethan this afternoon, I sure as hell am not letting Jenny sneak in.

When we reach the pub, I'm sweating and too conscious of my leg to ignore side-glances of passers-by. I have to get over the panic of being outdoors. Run towards the enemy instead of retreating. If I don't, I'll never get my life back.

My mate doesn't even notice, already at the bar with a tenner raised as I struggle through the door. At least with Riggsy around I can pretend everything is normal. No special treatment or fussing from him. It helps, especially as the rest of the pub appears to have lowered their drinks to watch me walk in like a gunslinger entering a Wild West bar. I'm imagining it worse than it is, I know, but every sideways look hits a nerve. Even the blasting music system seems to fade to silence as I move, the distance from the door to the table stretching longer than a football field. The moment I reach the table and swing myself onto the padded bench seat, the sound returns, everyone is drinking and nobody is looking at me.

'I got you an old man's beer to match the stick,' Riggsy states with zero tact, pushing a glass tankard at me. It's the kind you always see on Father's Day cards – glass handle and a criss-cross of raised glass squares around the body, the creamy head of beer neatly sitting on a pint marker line at the top. Beside Riggsy's sleek German Pilsner glass it looks like a relic.

'Cheers.'

He grins, the joke at my expense another point scored for him. 'Never thought you'd be the one hobbled by the job.'

'Hardly the job.'

He concedes this with a nod to his lager. 'But it's getting better, yeah?'

'Slowly. I think I…'

'Mate, you should have heard the shit Summers was giving everyone yesterday. Anyone would think he'd been promoted. Thinks he's commander material…'

'He's a git with a God complex, always has been. Soon as this leg heals I'll have words with him. I'm getting there, I think. It's just…'

'And Cooper got his leg over at last. Gross. Some poor cow from the catering civvies. We're all hoping he stuffs up. Him gobbing off about their down and dirty sessions is enough to put you right off your scran…'

I stare at him, irrationally irritated. I don't expect deep thoughts from Riggsy but I expect him to listen when I speak.

That's what mates should do, isn't it? It's never going to be equal with us and I would be a fool to think it could be – but surely I should be somewhere in the equation? I let him gabble on while I silently simmer behind my beer. A full five minutes of utter guff later, he stops.

'You're quiet.'

Oh, you noticed? 'I'm just listening.'

He shrugs it off. 'So, have you stopped stressing about the inquiry yet?'

Unbelievable. Except it's Riggsy, so I do believe it. 'I hoped you might have *started* stressing about it.'

He fixes me with disdain. 'What do I have to stress about? We went for a drive to blow off steam, hit water in a hidden dip, skidded off the road and turned the car.'

'And the rest...'

His glass meets the table with more force than necessary. A slop of lager crosses the rim, flooding golden liquid and white froth down the elegant contour of the glass, pooling on the dark wood beneath. 'There is no *rest*, mate. Is there?'

'Not according to you, no.' I can't help my eyes straying to his perfectly good leg stretched casually across the floor from my useless one. According to Riggsy we got out so we're good. *He's* good, is what he means. *He's* okay.

'Not according to the coppers. Not according to the incident investigation.' He leans over the lager-stained table. 'We're sorted, Wallace. It'll be sweet.'

Then why don't I feel like it is? 'Archer said I have to be very clear on what I tell the inquiry.'

Riggsy shrugs. 'So be clear. Because it is. We hit a dip and crashed. End of.'

'It was a warning, Riggs.'

'Bollocks was it. More like Archer playing big scary boss. Relax – it's all good.'

I don't reply. I can't – the words I need have deserted me. If we have nothing to worry about then why do I feel so much guilt? And why do my injuries feel like my punishment for what happened before?

When Riggsy visited me in the hospital, he'd made it all seem so easy. 'You've got enough to deal with, mate. No need to tell them everything. Besides, we have an understanding. We look out for each other.' He'd given me a look that rendered words unnecessary. *Like in Iraq*, it said. *Like when I got you out of that dead-end*. So many years have passed since that event it's become a silent point between us.

Maybe he is right. When the inquiry's over and we're exonerated I can put it all behind me. I'm doing myself no favours obsessing over it 24/7. Needing a break from thinking, I shelve my concern, easing back in my seat as Riggsy launches into another tale of squaddie misdemeanours – late-night drunken shenanigans in the mess kitchen that earned several mates disciplinary warnings, practical jokes played on the staff sergeant, a staffer's car wrapped in loo roll after they complained about a waste of resources. The same old stories we've traded for eighteen years.

I watch him, so completely unaffected by any of it. He's not worried about anything. As far as he's concerned, it's business as usual. The accident is nothing more than an inconvenience, destined one day to become another close-to-the-knuckle story of army mischief. He can do that because his leg isn't held together by more pins than bones and he isn't reminded of it every time he moves.

According to Adam Riggs, we're safe.

But what if we aren't as safe as we believe?

Chapter Eighteen

BETHAN

'*No.*'

'Noah…'

My son scowls until his face becomes a scarlet-flushed gargoyle, furious fists pumped onto hips, staring me down. 'I said, *no!*'

I used to love Saturdays.

It's the first battle we've had in the new flat and it's a humdinger. A full fifty minutes so far, and no sign of surrender. To be honest, we've done well to be here as long as we have without a Noah Gwynne Strop. In our last place they happened almost every day. I'd put his calmer mood down to having his own space at last, more light and colour around him and his mam less scared to be in the place alone with a kid. I should've known it wouldn't last.

I force breath into my lungs, slowly counting to five – a coping mechanism for toddler strops I learned during the terrible twos (or in Noah's case, terrible-one-and-a-half-to-just-turned-three). Wait. Give yourself air. Find your footing. Stand your ground. If I just yell back he ramps up a gear and before we know it we're screeching at each other like Formula 1 cars around a racetrack.

He eyes me while I breathe, wise to my game. Yeah, *bach*, just you wait. Your mam's going to win.

When I'm ready, I use my softest voice, fixing his big blue eyes with mine.

'You need your pants on. Otherwise your bum will freeze and drop off.'

There's a flicker in the stare. I've got him. Must keep my face steady – if I laugh like I want to I could throw this match.

I exact an overblown sigh. 'And then where will all your poo go?'

The frown wobbles.

Victory lap is on its way, *cariad*.

I seal the deal by miming an explosion, throwing my hands wide and pushing air from my cheeks for the sound effect.

His eyes sparkle and then he's giggling like a trouper. Standoff forgotten, friendship restored, and me the undisputed champion of the world. Or the flat. But this is our world, so it's as good as a global title – only instead of a champion's belt, my prize is a pair of red and white striped pirate pants on a small bottom.

It's only nine thirty and I'm exhausted. He's been up since six, rousing me from sleep by singing the opening bars of *The Lion King* song loudly in his brand-new big boy bed. Nobody has explained to my son about the weekend lie-in rule, so here we are. I settle my thankfully now fully clothed boy in front of CBeebies and drag my aching carcass into the kitchen to make his strop-delayed breakfast.

It doesn't help that I'm rattled because of Lachlan's message – and what I saw last night. I can't stop thinking about it. And how close I came to being seen. What would I have done if he'd looked up earlier? Styled it out, most probably. I mean, what else could I have done? But I don't know now if I'm disappointed he didn't look up.

Do I want Lachlan to see me?

The thought prickles across my shoulders.

What if I do?

I need to think about this. It's all very well playing a game and having fun but if it's moving this quickly I have to watch where I let it take me. Because it isn't just me, whether Lachlan knows about Noah or not. I am loving being the unexpected centre of someone's attention, but I can't let it cloud my thinking. I have to stay in control and not get carried away.

Plus, there's a far more pressing matter to deal with this morning: how do I reply to his damn near-perfect words?

I chop banana and rescue toast from the toaster before it burns, blowing on my fingertips as the heat stings them. The kettle boils for my cuppa and the microwave warms Noah's morning milk, and all the time my head is a tumble of words and images, inks and heartbeats, questions needing answers and thoughts I shouldn't indulge.

My son fed and happy, I decide to grasp the nettle.

I take down the old message and spread a brand-new sheet across the kitchen counter. I just need to be honest, follow my gut on this. Thinking about it too much will drive me insane.

Keep it simple. Real.

I take a breath, find my footing, claim this new ground.

YOU MAKE ME SMILE, TOO.
SO WHAT DO YOU WANT
TO KNOW ABOUT ME?

If he asks about kids, I'll tell him. If he asks about me, I'll answer. The glimpse of him I saw last night settles my nerves. He was taking so much care over the message for me, like it mattered to him. Like *I* mattered. I haven't felt like I mattered to anyone for a long time.

And I don't mean in *that* way, although it's been two and a half of Noah's three and a half years since anything like that. And even then, it wasn't perfect.

Mam thinks I'm too independent. Which is ironic, considering that's what's saved me. I didn't have a choice in the beginning, but I think I'm learning to embrace it. Being scared and on your own and totally responsible for keeping a small human alive leaves no time for lamenting how hard done by you are.

I don't need looking after. But I'd like to matter to someone.

I stick the message up, a little shaky but excited. What will Lachlan ask me?

The sun comes out at twelve, so I decide to take Noah into town. It's a short bus ride from the stop a few doors down from our building and usually a double-decker, which he adores far more than being strapped into his car seat while I'm battling traffic. I reckon we both need a break after this morning's fisticuffs. I can grab a few bits of shopping and Noah can go and play with the toys in the small play spot at the back of the Market Hall. We can wave at the castle or go for a blast around Friary Gardens if the sun stays out. A bit of breathing space. A bit of fun.

And it stops me being tempted to check the window. There was no answer from Lachlan when we left – although I didn't expect there to be.

Sitting at the front of the top deck with Noah pretending to drive the bus, I let my gaze drift along the still unfamiliar route. I like it here. People are friendly, like the lady sitting behind us who cooed over Noah and never once went for the *I bet he has his Daddy's eyes* or *where is Daddy today* comments I'm so used to hearing. That's double lovely.

We reach the bus station and walk the short distance into the town centre. It's busy today, the whole of Richmond apparently out doing their shopping. Noah skips alongside me, his little head whipping left and right in that way he does, like his eyes are cameras and he's trying to capture every detail, everywhere. His hand is warm in mine and he's chattering away. I catch roughly a third of it as his head turns away and back, away and back. But that's fine: it's a tiny little monologue that doesn't need replies.

The Market Hall is crowded when we arrive, the farmers' market in full flow. There are bags and backs and sharp elbows and groups of stationary chatterers everywhere. Noah drags me on towards the back, where his favourite place is. The hardware stall – and the box of toys the owner keeps stashed between clusters of faded floor cushions beside it. It's not a crèche really, more of a respite stop for parent-weary kids who need time out of the mêlée.

As we make our way over, I'm suddenly aware that any one of the bodies we're squeezing past might be Lachlan. I might bump into him anywhere – on the bus, in the street, inside a shop… I didn't get a full view of his face last night, so would I recognise him if he were here? The thought causes a butterfly flutter in my stomach. What if he is here? What if he's the next person I see?

'Mum! Come on!'

My right arm almost yanks out of my socket as Noah strains towards his prize. The angle he's leaning at reminds me of Tegan, the Welsh Collie dog we had as kids, who would walk happily by your heel when off the lead but dragged at a permanent 45-degree angle whenever she was on it.

'Okay, okay, slow down!'

'I *can't* slow down,' he retorts over his shoulder, pulling harder still. 'My legs won't go slowish!'

Slowish. I keep thinking I ought to start a notebook to record his Noah-isms before they disappear. He's growing up so fast and before I know it they will be gone. *Mink* for milk, *I puspose* for I suppose, *microquave* for microwave. Already words he used constantly are fading away – and when I quote them back to him he shoots me pitying looks like I'm making them up.

In honour of his *not-slowish* legs we push on until the hardware stall comes into view. The older couple that run it look up and grin when Noah emerges and heads for them.

'Look sharp, it's the Dragon Master!' the man says, pushing his reading specs up onto his head.

I smile as I reach the stall. 'Say hi to Chuck and Jean, Noah.'

My son, who is already on the floor cushions, shoes kicked off and hands in the toy box, looks up briefly. 'Hi, ChuckaJean.'

'Hello, poppet,' Jean says, handing a white-paper-bagged purchase to a customer and rummaging in the dark blue money pouch she's wearing for change. 'Gracious, you're getting big. What's your mum been feeding you, eh?'

'Toast,' Noah replies, from somewhere inside the toy box.

Jean laughs. 'Good job, Mum.'

'Well, I like to try, you know. How are you both? It's busy today.'

Chuck nods approvingly at the crowd. 'Aye. 'Bout time, too. I were beginning to think folks had forgotten we were here.'

'Forget you? Never?' I reply, but I can't help thinking about Bright Hill's worrying quietness.

'Let's hope, eh?' Jean leans a little closer, her tone dipping beneath the crowd noise. 'We've had four stalls close in the last month. Can't get the new people in, you see. Lots of them just doing online these days. Ebay shops and that.' She shrugs and I recognise the weary acceptance. I see it from everyone at work.

'But we're not dwelling on it, are we?' Chuck says, his hand resting lightly on Jean's shoulder. 'Sun's out, people are in and we have our favourite customers here.'

'Aye. So how's work your end, lass?'

'Quiet, but it's still early.'

'It'll pick up.' Chuck nods. 'Weather's going to be nice next few weeks, they reckon. Which reminds me, I want to pick your brains, young lady.' His bushy eyebrows lower over still-twinkling eyes. 'Slugs.'

'Ah.'

'What do I do to stop the beggars munching my courgettes?'

Jean rolls her eyes. 'He's obsessed with them. I swear he'd be out there in the garden patrolling all night if I didn't lock the doors.'

I can just imagine Chuck stalking the vegetable beds armed with a torch. 'Eggshells. Grit. Coffee grounds if you have them.'

He doesn't look convinced. 'That works?'

'Mm-hmm. Too sharp for them to crawl over so it keeps them

off. And if that fails, beer traps. They go for the beer, rather than the plant, and drown.'

'What a way to go, eh, Jean?'

'If we put beer in the garden this one'd be sneaking out there with a straw.' She gives her husband a playful nudge and they share smiles.

I like seeing that. I glance over at Noah, who's slotting scuffed plastic shapes into a wooden cube I suspect is Chuck's handiwork, surrounded by piles of much-loved cuddly toys. There was a time I thought he'd see me as part of a partnership like theirs – a mum and a dad, always together. I kick the stab of pain away. *He's happy*, I tell myself. *Much happier now.*

We arrive home just after 5 p.m., Noah in my arms after falling asleep on the bus. I jam the entrance door open with my foot as I manoeuvre a sleepy boy and my shopping bags through. I stop beside the stairs and unlock my postbox, finding a handful of envelopes inside. I set up a redirect with the Post Office when I moved but this is the first batch of mail that's reached us. Stuffing them in one of the shopping bags I head up to our flat.

I lay Noah on the sofa surrounded by cushions and fetch Tân the dragon from his room. He'll be tough to put down later but I'm glad of the respite. I go to unpack the bags in the kitchen and pull out the stack of post. Mostly junk mail, a confirmation of my new electricity and gas accounts for this place and a letter from our old health centre confirming we've left them. But the last one makes my heart plummet to the empty canvas bags at my feet.

I know what it is before I open it, but I need to see what I'm up against.

Guts twisting, I tear open the envelope, read the single sheet of paper inside.

ARREARS OUTSTANDING...

The figure has hardly moved. All that work, all our sacrifices, for a drop in the ocean. The injustice burns. I cover my eyes, my fingers damp where they meet tears. Two and a half years and it's still not over. The number on the statement screams *years* to pay back, not months. How old will Noah be when the letters stop arriving? Secondary school? College? Later still?

All the lightness I've gathered around us today pales in the looming shadow of the towering figure on the page. Hopelessness and pain crowd in...

No.

Stop this.

I fill my lungs with air, force strength into my body.

It's better than it was.

I start to scrabble for scraps of scattered positives. It *is* better – the extra money from my job on the plant team is helping. Being here is helping. I'm not scared like I was. I can live with the betrayal if I'm not terrified we're going under again. It was always going to be a long haul, I knew that. It won't always be this hard.

I just wish I had one day without this. One day without feeling I'm the only person scaling a lonely cliff-face.

Noah stirs on the sofa and I go to check he's okay, but he's curled up again before I reach him. Halfway between my son and the letter on the kitchen counter I'm adrift.

And then I look out of the window.

Lachlan's words are waiting.
A question from a friend who cares.

IF YOU COULD HAVE
ANYTHING IN THE WORLD
WHAT WOULD IT BE?

Chapter Nineteen

LACHLAN

I thought of the question I wanted to ask her as I waved Riggsy off at the end of the painful walk home yesterday. I'd told myself I wasn't going to think about Bethan, but who am I kidding? She's been on my mind all the time.

I finally worked it out – why what's happening with us matters. It sparked during the night and began to smoulder, a slow-burn realisation that I can't believe I've only just noticed. She matters because she *listens*. And that stands out because nobody else in my life does.

All that crap in the pub with Riggsy started it yesterday, his railroading my every attempt to speak. I put it down to his bullish mood, his determination to ignore any talk of the crash. But once I'd clocked it, I couldn't ignore what he was doing.

And the worst thing? He didn't even realise he was doing it. Which means his expectation of me as the silent sounding board for whatever crap he spouts is so ingrained in his thinking that he's no longer aware it's happening.

He's supposed to be my best friend. So why do I feel like I'm just serving his ego these days?

And then I started to look at every relationship in my life, like I'd been given new lenses to view the world. The more I looked, the worse it became.

Tanya doesn't listen to me. She asks questions and she tells me what to do, but the only time she responded to anything I said was when I practically begged for her help. Even then she resorted to her old approach as if embarrassed she'd heard me, badly plastering the Lachie Wallace she expected back over the real version. When she returns on Monday, it'll be business as usual, my past indiscretion stuffed away in that rucksack of hers with her weights and resistance bands and papers.

My family aren't listening to me. Sal adopts her *big sister knows best* attitude whenever she isn't winning the argument. Dad is too concerned with the business to hear me. And Mum won't hear me because that's not the deal. When I was away from home, serving abroad for months at a time, my own life firmly established, none of them needed to listen to me because I didn't need them to hear me. The accident changed everything. It made me an entity to take care of, my misdemeanour reason enough to surrender control over my own life.

Archer won't hear me because he's doing his job. And I don't know what to say to him, because despite what Riggsy says, I feel responsible. I didn't cause the crash, but it's my fault we were on the road…

It's pointless going over it because the only person listening is me. And I haven't listened to what I really want since it happened because I can't see past the guilt.

There's only one person in the world right now listening because they want to hear:

SO WHAT DO YOU WANT
TO KNOW ABOUT ME?

Bethan has no agenda, no expectation of what my answers should be. She isn't trying to fit me into an assumed version of who I am. She isn't assuming she knows best. She isn't using my answer to draw breath for her next statement. She knows nothing about me and doesn't need to listen. But I feel like she wants to hear me.

I was all for pulling back. But now I know I need her. I need to know someone is listening.

IF YOU COULD HAVE
ANYTHING IN THE WORLD
WHAT WOULD IT BE?

I asked because however she answers will reveal something fundamental about her. If it's material stuff – a nice car, a million pounds, an exotic holiday – that'll be cool and I'll know how to steer our conversation. If it's something more personal, I'll know where we stand. Secretly I'm hoping for the latter. I want to know her, discover what motivates her and shapes her world. If she retreats, I'll follow. If she goes deeper, I'll dare to go there, too.

It's half past five and I'm just allowing Ernie out of my room after another set-to with Bert when I see her reply. I don't know why, but I wait a moment before I read it. We're at a crossroads: whatever Bethan says next will determine the way ahead. When I'm ready, I look:

'Perfect answer,' I say, laughing when Bert woofs in reply. 'She's cool, boy. I reckon you'd like her.'

I know I do.

Half an hour later, I post my reply. I haven't stopped smiling and it feels good. Scratch that: it feels amazing. Like finding something precious you've been searching for.

I'LL SEE WHAT I CAN DO.
QUESTION IS,
WHICH BISCUITS?

What I want to say is that I'm here for as long as she wants me. But there's not enough room on the paper to write that large enough for her to see across the hedge. And even knowing what I do about why it matters to me, I'm not brave enough yet to say it.

I just hope she understands.

Despite Sundays usually being my rest days, I attempt some of my exercises after dinner. My injured leg is unimpressed by my epic hike to the pub and back yesterday and the muscles are knotting in my good leg, too. But Tanya will be here at nine tomorrow morning so I need to prove I'm serious about my rehab. Ernie jumps onto the dining table and stares at me like I've lost the plot. Bert watches with concern from his basket. They're useless as training buddies or motivational coaches, but having them here lightens the experience. That, and the thought of my friend across the way.

I manage half an hour before I admit defeat. Tomorrow will be better, I tell myself. New week, new challenge. I have to accept it's going to take time. And from tomorrow, I'm officially not doing it alone.

My mobile buzzes on the table beside me and I wipe sweat from my hands onto my T-shirt before I reach to answer it.

'What have you said to Mum?'

Hello to you, too, big sis. 'What kind of a greeting is that?' I say, knowing I'm pushing my luck but unable to resist its call. 'Do you use that tone with *Cotswold and Beyond* customers? Because you really need to work on it...'

'Mum's in bits, Lach.'

'What are you talking about? Mum's never *in bits* about anything. She's carved from granite.'

'Yeah, you keep telling yourself that. But you don't see her every day. I do. What did you say to her?'

I stretch my leg out as far as I dare, a stubborn knot in the small of my back refusing to budge. 'I didn't say anything to her.'

'Try again.'

I groan and stare at the ceiling. 'What do you want me to say, Sal? She wanted me to go home, I refused. I don't see what the problem is.'

'Did she tell you she's already renovated the stable cottage for you?' I feel her glare down the line in the pointed silence that follows. My chest tightens. 'I'm guessing she didn't.'

'She told me she *could* renovate it. She didn't say it was a done deal...' My head hurts. I should have seen that coming, shouldn't I? Mum doesn't consult, she *informs*. 'How much has she done?'

'The whole place. In three weeks. I swear the builders didn't dare breathe until it was finished.'

Bollocks. 'I never asked her to.'

'Of course you didn't. Because you never do.'

Okay, I'm not having that. 'I'm thirty-four years old, Sal. My life is here. Why would I ask to come home?'

My sister's voice quietens. 'Because your life is different now…'

'Get stuffed!'

'See? This is what I'm talking about, Lachie. You're so – bloody pig-headed all the time. And refusing to see this for what it is won't make it go away.'

'What *this is* is an injury I'm recovering from. I'm getting better.'

'You nearly died, Lachie! We nearly lost you. The police said you were lucky to get out alive. And you stopped breathing in the ambulance…'

I can feel doors slam around me, shutters draw, defences lock. I don't need to be reminded how close I came to not being here. Does my sister think I haven't constantly lived with that reality ever since? 'I am *fine*. And Mum should've told me what she was planning before she steamrollered ahead. I'm sure she can let it out like the other properties on the farm…'

'It's adapted.'

I can't tell if Sally is defiant or embarrassed by this. I know it's not her fault and she's trying to peace-make like she always does, but that word makes me go cold.

'What?'

'Rails. Hoists. Chairs that lift you to standing.'

'I don't need any of that.'

'You might…'

'I am living in a first-floor flat in a building that doesn't have a lift. I take my dog for a walk twice a day. Yesterday I walked a quarter of a mile to a pub and back. I do not need assistance, Sal. I am making my own way.'

'And it's a valiant effort.'

'Oh, patronising much?'

'I'm trying, Lachie. I just don't want you to burn bridges you might need.'

I'm not going to yell at her. But this conversation is over. 'My physio is confident I can make a good recovery. My doctor is confident, too. I will be staying in my own home, and will go back to my job when I'm allowed to. I would appreciate it if you would let me get on with that.'

'You know this isn't over,' she says. The call ends without goodbye.

What did she expect me to do? Surrender and go home like a good boy because Mum's decided she knows my life better than I do? So, she's upset. Not as upset as I am that my own family have decided I need an adapted room under their constant guard. *If* I needed those things – if my medical team had said that's what I should have – then perhaps I might have been touched by my family wanting to provide it for me. *If* they'd asked me, instead of making the decision over my head. But at no point has anyone said I won't be able to regain my independence. Even the worst projection where my hip and leg are permanently damaged and I need a stick to walk never mentioned rails and hoists. I've spent eighteen years in the army and even though I've worked the last eight as a mostly classroom-based trainer, I'm physically fit. I have to be to keep up with the students under my care. My doctor told me my fitness is a reason I've made the progress I've achieved already. She says that stands me in good stead for recovery.

But Sal wasn't listening to her, was she? The revelation I had in the pub yesterday has thus been proved. My mother doesn't hear me. My sister isn't listening either. The only way I'm going to be heard is by proving them wrong...

I glance at the window, my heart lifting.

... And by speaking to the only person who will listen.

DANGEROUS QUESTION!
HOBNOBS, FOR STARTERS.
HOW ABOUT YOU? ☺

Chapter Twenty

BETHAN

HOBNOBS? BORING!
GIVE ME A BOURBON ANY DAY
☺

Oh, like that, is it?

I knew this topic was dangerous. But I love his reply.

Right, Lachlan, you diss my Hobnobs, you're asking for it. Prepare for a Biscuit War!

BOURBONS ARE FOR WIMPS.
I'D RATHER HAVE A
CUSTARD CREAM ☺

Who knew a biscuit battle could be so thrilling? I sit on my sofa after posting my reply, the urge to giggle overwhelming. Every muscle in my body is itching to bounce over to the window to check if he's responded. I'm happy we have a new direction and a little relieved, too. Don't get me wrong, I loved what Lachlan said about what makes him smile and I was touched that he asked what I wanted out of life. But I was letting my head be carried away with it and that's dangerous for me.

An hour later, there's a new message in his window, a very sleepy Ernie stretched along the sill beneath it.

CUSTARD CREAMS? WOW.
DON'T TELL ME YOU
LOVE PARTY RINGS TOO? ☺

Oh *now* it's on...

My eyelids are starting to ache, the toll of a busy Sunday bearing heavy on me. I don't want to go to bed just yet but my body appears to be outvoting my head. I have such an early start tomorrow because it's Noah's first full day at preschool and I've got to get him to Michelle's early with everything he needs. I want to stay and mock Lachlan for his biscuit choices, but I can't afford to lose any more sleep. But just so he doesn't think I'm mortally offended by his blatant party rings prejudice, I write one more message and put it in the window.

PARTY RINGS ROCK!
CLEARLY, YOU NEED EDUCATING.
NIGHT–NIGHT x

Then I blow a kiss to Ernie across the hedge.

And if Lachlan happens to be anywhere near the window and happens to catch the kiss, all the better...

'So, you'll be okay taking him into preschool and picking him up?' I ask Michelle, not sure whether I've already asked this question or if it's just on a loop in my mind with everything else I'm meant to remember.

Michelle takes Noah's coat. 'Of course, lass. Like I said.'

I offer a sheepish smile. 'Sorry. It's his first double-session, is all.'

'So you said.' She laughs. 'You need sleep, lady.'

'Tell that to my son.' Noah gazes up at me, toast crumbs dancing at the corners of his mouth as he grins. 'Because a certain little chap decided 2 a.m. was a good time to demand to watch *Hey Duggee*.'

Michelle grimaces. 'Ouch. No wonder you're comatose this morning.'

'Good job your mam loves that show too, eh?' I wrap Noah in my arms and kiss his forehead. He giggles, wriggling free to join Maisie in Michelle's living room. I look up at Michelle. 'Waking nightmare.'

'No! Another one?'

I nod. I know what's causing it; we're coming up to a change. He goes through spates of them and they're nearly always linked to something changing, either physically or emotionally. Teething started it, in the darkest days when we found ourselves alone and broke, living in a strange bedsit; then when he started potty training; when he started at preschool; the first week Michelle had him for me. This one was definitely a precursor to his first full day at preschool. I should be used to them now, but they're terrifying. My gorgeous little boy, kicking and flailing, eyes wide open but not seeing, a rising temper tantrum that nothing fixes. He punched me during one really bad one and I had to wrestle him with one hand while holding a tissue to my bleeding nose with the other.

Last night's wasn't bad by his standards, just unexpected and disorienting when his yelling had shocked me out of sleep. I don't care how ace a parent you are, nobody is able to fully function at 2 a.m. The only way I've found to calm Noah when he's in a waking nightmare is to distract him – showing him an episode of his favourite kids' TV show on my phone. I don't know what it is that works – the colour, the sound, the sudden appearance of a familiar thing – but it calms him enough to come around properly and then he can be settled.

All the same, I wish it hadn't happened last night.

'Want me to make you a coffee to have on the way to work?' Michelle asks, her almost-touch on my arm soothing this morning.

'You angel! Yes please.' I smile at her kindness, thanking my lucky stars for the millionth time that I found her to child-mind Noah.

She bustles into the kitchen to make my drink. 'Actually, Bethy, I wanted to ask you something. Now, feel free to say no, if you want, but I thought it might help.'

I wish my defences didn't immediately jump into action whenever anyone offers to help. I push the Mama Bear urge away and make myself listen. 'Okay.'

Michelle turns from the still-boiling kettle to face me. 'I don't know if I've mentioned it, but my sister Cass is starting a kids fun club on Thursdays, after preschool. She's doing structured play, dance, craft things – I reckon Noah would love it.'

'Sounds good. How much are the sessions?' It's automatic, that question. I hate how quickly I ask it. But the fact is, so many things for kids cost and I have nothing spare.

My childminder dismisses this. 'Oh, it wouldn't cost Noah

a thing.' She holds up her hand. 'Okay, cards on the table: Maisie wants to go but she won't know anybody there and it's likely to put her off. She would love to go with Noah. And then I could give them both tea before you pick him up. What do you reckon?'

I glance down the hallway to the living room, where Noah and Maisie are currently promenading, hand in hand. I know he adores her and I'm conscious that being an only child means all his friendships have to be out of the flat. 'That's so kind of you...'

'It isn't, but thanks.' She pours boiling water into a travel cup and puts a heaped teaspoon of sugar in it without asking. It'll be too sweet but I'll take any energy I can this morning. 'So, what do you say?'

Of course I accept – why wouldn't I? It would definitely help to have one day a week where I didn't have to dash home from work. If Michelle does his tea, it might even mean I get an hour at home before I have to fetch him. It's unexpected – and I still have the shadow of guilt over being helped – but it's a good surprise.

Michelle's rocket-fuelled, thunderously sweet coffee must be working because nobody at Bright Hill comments on my tiredness, only how happy I look.

'You found a tenner in the street.'

'No.'

'You've booked a holiday.'

'Hardly.'

'You've won the lottery.'

'You think I'd still be here if I had?'

Patrick jogs to keep up with me as we head to the plant tunnels. 'Knowing you, yes.'

I laugh. 'Fair point.'

He's been bugging me with this since we started our shift. The inquisition isn't annoying when it comes from him, though. I find it endearing – although I'd never be daft enough to tell him that. Patrick Metcalfe thinks he's Jason Momoa in training when in reality he's a gangly nineteen-year-old who just started using weights. He's like a kid brother in the best sense and my happiest days at Bright Hill are when we get to work together.

We're almost at Eric's polytunnel kingdom when Patrick stops and claps his hands. 'Got it! You. Got. Laid.'

I burst out laughing. Patrick frowns and trails after me as I head inside. 'What? *What?*'

'Best laugh I've had in ages,' I say, over my shoulder.

'Come on, B! People aren't just happy for no reason. Not your kind of happy, any road.'

'My kind of happy? What's that?'

He reaches my side by the long beds of juvenile plants. 'The kind that makes you fizz like a bath bomb.'

It's not the metaphor I or anyone else on the planet was expecting but I love it. 'What do you know about bath bombs, Patrick?'

'I don't… I mean I…' He gives me a look like he'd like to bury himself beneath the rows of tiny green shoots in the bed beside him.

Luckily for my colleague, at that moment our senior plants-man Eric emerges from the tiny wooden lean-to office tacked onto the end of the polytunnel. And he isn't alone.

'Well, isn't this a sight that does your heart good?' Hattie beams at us both, then at Eric, who has noticed a wayward brown leaf on one of his charges and is bending over the bed to remove it.

'Takes one to know one, Miss Rowse,' Patrick replies, every inch the charmer again.

'Oh, you are sweet, Pat. Bethan, you've been teaching him well.'

'She hasn't...' My young colleague rubs the back of his neck as if Hattie's gentle mocking has sneaked beneath his collar like a midge and taken a bite.

'Actually, I'm glad I caught you, Bethy. Can you help me with something in the office?'

My mood dampens a little bit as we head back into the main building, passing through the STAFF ONLY door to the warren of tiny corridors and box offices that run along one side of the main building. Most of the offices are now storerooms for the gift and homewares stock, so I am familiar with the well-trodden path. At the end, tucked away from view, is Hattie's office.

Hector Rowse and his sunny bear's ear primulas look down with pride as we sit either side of the great oak desk that only just fits in the small space. When Hattie's father established Bright Hill his office was a large timber-framed barn he inherited with the purchase of the land. I've seen grainy black-and-white photos of the young entrepreneur sitting in a palatial space, his crossed feet up on the desk we're sitting at now, looking like he ruled the world. I can't help thinking it would've suited Hattie, too. But the original barn office was lost in a fire when summer lightning hit it. Eric reckons the desk still bears the smell of smoke, if you get close enough to it. His tales of shattering greenhouse glass and Hector's uninsured business going up in smoke are legendary at Bright Hill.

'We called him the Phoenix for years after,' he says, whenever we get him chatting over tea and buns on delivery days. 'Risen from the ashes. Dragged that great big desk out of the flaming barn with his own two hands, the daft beggar. Almost lost his life. But that was Hector: everything at full tilt.'

I wonder what Hector would make of things here now. I glance up at his soft smile in the portrait as Hattie takes her seat.

'I wondered if you'd had a chance to think of anything to help us?' Hattie asks, her bright smile betrayed by eyes heavy with concern.

The problem is, I don't have anything concrete. I've been thinking about this since she asked me for ideas and I have notebook pages filled with possibilities, but not the big project I know she's hoping for.

'I'm still working on it,' I say, wishing I didn't see the telling sag of her shoulders. 'But I think we need to make Bright Hill a key part of the community again. I'm just not sure how yet.'

Hattie places both hands on the smooth oak of the desktop. 'Well, I've had an idea.'

'What?'

'How would you like to have a whole day to work on this?' She observes me carefully before continuing. 'You work so hard and I know it isn't always… *ideal* here…'

Is she talking about Darren?

'… and with your little one at home, too. I mean, it can't be easy.'

'We're fine.'

'Oh, I know you are. This is what I'm thinking: take one day a week and work from home for me.'

'But I work in the plant section.'

'Yes, I know, but…' Hattie blinks, floundering for a moment.

'Truth is, my love: we are in dire straits. If we don't find something very, *very* soon, there won't be a plant section for you to manage. So... One day a week, work from home, use the time to contact people, look at marketing Bright Hill, pursue any route you can think of to find ways of bringing funds in.'

It's a huge act of faith in me, but what do I know about that stuff? Is Hattie pinning her hopes on me being able to save the nursery? What if I let her down? 'It's very generous, but wouldn't it be better to bring someone else in? Someone with experience?'

My manager seems to shrink in her director's chair. 'That isn't an option. Financially...' Her voice trails away and I see what this means to her.

'Let's trial it,' I suggest, torn between helping this lovely lady who has done so much for me and being terrified of failing her. 'Give me three weeks. If it works and we need longer, we can talk then.'

She brightens. 'Yes. Excellent. Do you have broadband at home?'

I nod.

'Bethan, I know you can do this. I have faith in you. Now, is there a particular day you'd like to do it on?'

Tiny pebbles of positivity, lining up in my path, pointing the way...

'Thursday,' I say, heart hammering hard. 'Thursday would be good.'

Chapter Twenty-One

LACHLAN

Tanya keeps stealing glances at me as I work through my exercises. Her eyes flick to my face over the top of my knee as she eases it into my chest for me to push back. It's like she's checking I'm still her grumpy patient and haven't been replaced by a cheery clone. Only the pain from my leg stops me laughing.

Yes, Tanya, I am different.

My attitude is different. Maybe asking for her help last week broke the stalemate. Or maybe it's sheer bloody-mindedness aimed squarely at my family. If it hurts too much, I picture the rails and the hoists and it makes me push harder.

It's Bethan, too.

I took down my message from last night before Tanya came. Bethan won't be back until this evening and by then I'll be alone with a brand-new message in place. The Great Biscuit Rumble, back for round two...

'Good. Really good, Lachie.'

I grin back, more of a teeth-gritted grimace than a smile. But she seems to appreciate it. She moves onto the next exercise and I obediently follow, my thoughts far away from this room.

The fun is back between Bethan and me and I like it. Layer upon layer of trust being slowly constructed between our windows. Even if her taste in biscuits is *woeful*.

Party rings and custard creams, I ask you.

'Everything okay?' Tanya looks up from placing my foot against a foam block.

'Yes. Why?'

'You looked like you were in pain.'

I grab a towel and wipe a layer of sweat from my forehead. 'Actually, that was a smile. Wow, I must have been grumpy before.'

She reddens and goes back to the block.

I'm exhausted and hurting like hell when we finish the session, but I keep my smile in place. I need Tanya to believe I'm committed to this. So far, so good.

'Great job today,' she says, handing me a bottle of water. 'Thanks for working so hard.'

I nod, taking a long swig. It's so cold it sends needles down my throat, but today it might as well be a trophy. Proving my family wrong is the best motivator. 'It's going to be like this next time, too.'

'Careful, Mr Wallace,' Tanya smiles as she swings her rucksack on her shoulder, car keys jangling in hand. 'I might start thinking you're enjoying this official torture.'

I hold up my hands. 'Never.'

She's at the door now, my ordeal almost done for today. 'Rest now, please. And no tripping off to the pub later, okay?'

I really wish I hadn't told her that...

I sit in the silence of the room for a moment, letting the day so far sink in. That session was hard this morning, but I felt the first easing of my thigh muscles. Barely perceptible, but there. I know it's too early to say if this will make a difference or not, but for the first time I *feel* like it might.

I let Bert and Ernie back into the room and am treated to a hero's welcome by both of them. This has more to do with their hope that treats may be imminent than their desire to support me, but that's okay. I reckon I've earned a treat, too. I reach into the cupboard and find an unopened packet of bourbon biscuits.

Bourbons are for wimps.

For wimps are they, Bethan? I open the packet and stuff two in my mouth, turning towards the window and doing a mad, hand-waving victory dance in my neighbour's direction, which of course she can't see.

Bert and Ernie observe me in sudden, ear-pricked shock from the sofa.

My hip jars and I stop, halfway between pain and laughter. The combination of gasps for air and sharp-edged biscuit crumbs is not the best and I lean against the kitchen counter, coughing. Inexplicably, it feels like a release.

She made that happen. Not the coughing fit, but the dance. *You used to be fun…*

Riggsy is right: I used to be. I've lost sight of him lately, that lad who likes a laugh, who made everyone else laugh along with him. It wasn't the accident that made me forget fun. It started long before that, before Jenny, right back to when I transferred to the Educational and Training Service Unit and stepped away from active duty. In my squadron I was the joker – the one who plagued his Staff Sergeant with accurate impressions of the senior officers, the one copping flak for practical jokes and cracking up during drills. All those tales Riggsy was spinning at the pub the other day could have been about me eight years ago.

I miss him. *That* Lachie.

I want to be respected and taken seriously. I want to take responsibility for my own life. I don't want to be like Riggsy, strolling along, never thinking of anyone but himself. But I want some fun back in my life.

The biscuit messages are the first attempt at daftness I've made for years. And Bethan accepted them immediately. Is that how she sees me? Not serious Lachlan Wallace, him of the solemn responsibilities and battered self-confidence, holed up in his flat alone with a shattered body, which is all anyone else sees since the crash. Is she slowly piecing together a picture of what her message-exchanging neighbour is like, like I'm doing with her?

If she sees me as someone who loves life, who isn't afraid of honesty and who loves a laugh, maybe I can be that man for her.

And if I channel everything into making my body work again, might I be able to see her for real? Face to face?

Because I've been thinking about that, too. More than I should. We can't keep sticking messages in our windows for ever. I don't want to lose this new *thing* we've discovered. One day, we'll have to find another way to talk or it will end.

I don't want this to end.

If my leg heals, I want to see her.

I pull a new page from the sketchpad, ease my aching frame onto the chair, open the coloured pens and start to write:

READY TO BE EDUCATED, MA'AM.
WHAT'S MY FIRST LESSON?

I make lunch and take it to the sofa, two very willing volunteers arriving immediately to offer their assistance. Finding a film on a movie channel, I ease my left leg onto the sofa, pushing Ernie off as he tries to claim my stomach as his premium cinema seat, piling cushions behind my head until my spine can relax. Warmth surrounds me, my body revelling in rest. Colours dance on the screen as the afternoon sun pools in from the window, the shadow of a paper rectangle stretching across the floor. Thoughts of Bethan swim in my mind as my eyes begin to close, sleep calling me to a far distant place…

When I wake, summoned back to consciousness by the snuffle of Bert's bristly snout against my cheek, I realise I've slept for five hours. I ache all over and lifting my head from the cushions takes a significant effort. Dizziness makes me pause on the edge of the sofa before I can attempt to stand. I wait until it passes, the familiar clanging of tinnitus in my ears. Then I push myself to my feet.

It takes an age to make it across the room and when I get there I have to grip the windowsill with both hands to steady myself. But my sleep-blurred eyes receive the best reward:

BISCUIT #101

Around a small sheet of paper bearing the lesson name, Bethan has stuck four hand-drawn biscuits, each one labelled with her verdict:

HOBNOBS = GOOD   PARTY RINGS = COOL
CUSTARD CREAMS = ACCEPTABLE

BOURBONS = COULD DO BETTER

By the bourbon biscuit verdict, there's an extra sign:

> * BUT IF YOU LIKE THEM
> THAT'S OKAY ☺

She's just talking about biscuits, I tell myself. It's a bit of fun we're having a mock battle over. A little bit flirty, maybe, but it's just fun.

So why do I feel like she's saying so much more?

Chapter Twenty-Two

BETHAN

I wasn't expecting a final message last night, so I went to bed chuffed with myself for my, quite frankly, awesome biscuit montage sign. Took ages to draw those biscuits and my face ached from smiling by the time I stuck them up.

I was tired, too. Noah had come home from his first full day at preschool so whacked that I just about managed to get some tea into him before he crashed out on the sofa. He went to bed in his pants, vest and socks because the only layers I could remove were his preschool T-shirt and trousers as he curled up in a tight little ball in his bed.

My dreams when they happened were laced with the sound of Lachlan's voice – which, I know, is nuts because I've never heard him. But the more I read his messages, the stronger I *hear* him in my head.

I might be completely wrong, mind. He could be squeakier than Joe Pasquale or deeper than Idris Elba – how do I know?

And that's the problem. I *want* to know.

'Penny for 'em?'

I look up from the stack of growbags I loaded onto the Bright

Hill trolley five minutes ago and give Patrick a guilty smile. 'Sorry. I was miles away.'

'It looked like a nice place. Are you running tours?'

I take the brake off the trolley and wheel it around. 'You couldn't afford it.'

'Story of my chuffin' life.'

I grin at him. 'Grab that stack of pots for me, would you?'

'Sure.' Patrick swings the four large stacked terracotta planters onto his shoulder. That weight training is paying off. I'm pretty strong, but the most I can lift is two of those and then I'd need both hands to carry them. 'Where are these going?'

'Offer bins by the entrance,' I say, giving the trolley a shove and setting off towards the main building. 'Nice weather's coming, so we're aiming for impulse buys.'

Walking alongside me, Patrick doesn't look convinced. 'Impulse buys by the entrance? Who's going to heft a planter or a growbag around this place while they shop?'

'Well, we are.'

'Ha ha. We're paid to do this. I wouldn't do it for free.'

'Ah, but think of the money you'd save in gym fees if you did.'

'Yeah, but significantly less chance of pulling... Morning, ladies,' Patrick turns on his brightest smile as he skirts the jutted-out baskets of two older ladies rummaging in the discounted plant bins. He waits until he's out of their earshot to continue. '... considering the average age of our customers is 103.'

'They love you,' I say, glancing back at the ladies, who are clearly enjoying the sight of Patrick's retreating behind. 'You could corner the market.'

He has a point, though. Most of the customers visiting Bright Hill are older. It's a place they feel welcome when all of the big garden centres in this area are aggressively pushing for the younger market. But is there a way to appeal to both?

I keep thinking about what Hattie's asked me to do. It's such a mammoth responsibility – what happens if I can't make it work?

But I like the idea of having a whole day on Thursdays to work on it. With everything else going on around me at the moment it's impossible to give it enough brain time after work. All the same, Thursday will be *strange*.

Although, it's got me thinking. There was a surprise message waiting for me this morning from Lachlan. I keep going back to it in my head.

YES, O BISCUIT MASTER! WE SHOULD DO TEA AND BISCUITS ONE DAY ☺

Does he want to meet me, too?

After my dreams last night and my thoughts of late I can't get away from the question. It might just be another bit of cheekiness, right? I mean *one day* could be *one day in the vague, unspecified future* rather than *one day soon*. But what if it's a test shot? Throw it out there and see how I respond?

I wish I knew.

But I was thinking: if I'm going to be home on Thursdays – without Noah – might that be an opportunity to say hello?

No. Hang on, that's ridiculous. I don't know the guy and I'm planning clandestine meetings?

'Earth to Bethan? Colleague about to succumb to planter stack crush.'

I realise I've stopped pushing the trolley and Patrick is steps ahead of me, holding the door open to the main building.

'Man, I'm sorry,' I rush, heading quickly inside.

'What is with you today?'

'I'm just tired,' I lie. Thankfully, Patrick is too concerned with his aching shoulder to notice. 'Are you okay there?'

He winces. 'It was a good idea five minutes ago.'

I laugh and pat the stack of growbags. 'Pop them on here and just keep your hand on them to stop them toppling off.'

'You are my saviour, Bethan Gwynne!' He gratefully relinquishes the planters and casts a furtive glance around the empty building. 'You won't tell anyone, will you?'

'Your secret's safe with me, He-Man.'

'Who?'

Rolling my eyes, I head for the entrance.

'... And then we did 'nastics on the beamy line and roly-polys on the mats and then we had juice and fruit and then we did numbers and ay-bee-*cees* and then we had carpet-time story and then we went home!'

I beam at my son who's just managed to relay his entire day at preschool to my mam and Emrys on FaceTime without drawing breath.

Mam, who is mostly chin on the screen because she hasn't quite mastered the art of where to look on a video message, smiles back. At least, I *think* she's smiling.

'Get you all grown up, Noah! What's your teacher like, then?'

'A lady,' my son replies, waving Tân the dragon at the screen.

'She's called Mrs Guest and she's lovely, isn't she?' I prompt. Noah continues making Tân roar at his mam-gu and Uncle Em.

My brother's big daft face looms into view. 'Is she fit?'

'You're dreadful.'

'I know, but is she?'

I grin back at him. In small doses, my family are wonderful. And in the miracle that is getting Mam on a video call, they're even more so. I know they adore my son and the positivity of their conversation does us all good. And with Noah here, it means they don't have to mention anything *else*. I can feel their relief through the phone screen.

'Good to see you both happy,' Mam says, finally cottoning on and bringing her full face into view. 'And you're settling in okay?'

'We are. This place is amazing, Mam. I love it.' And not just because of these four walls, I think to myself. My cheeks flush at the thought of my secret friend I *definitely* won't tell my mother about.

'And – um – no news on…?' Emrys ventures. I see the swift elbow jab Mam gives him.

'There won't be,' I reply, my steady smile a shield.

'Ah, *sori*. For the best, yeah?' He doesn't expect an answer and I don't give one. The conversation moves back to safer ground and I can't hide my relief. Today, I want to celebrate all the good stuff. Find the positives, fix on them.

An hour later, call over and tea made, Noah is still jabbering on about his school day. I'm suddenly aware of how grown-up he's getting. Gymnastics and beams and numbers and stories – not to mention all the dramas of his friends, which are a mini soap opera in themselves. It's a whole society that belongs to him and not me, an entire world I'm not part of. Before I know it he'll be moving to primary school and Reception. I thought I'd be gutted to see him striding off into the world but actually I'm just so proud of him. And relieved. It's been just us for as long as he can remember and I want him to have his own friends, his own interests, his own life.

I remember a health visitor telling me once that your job as a parent is to prepare your kids for leaving you – that's always stuck with me. Noah will always know I'm here for him but he'll also know I won't prevent him from discovering his world.

All the same, I don't know if my heart is ready for him to leave me yet.

'That's so cool, *cariad*. You still like it, then?'

Noah grins a tomato-sauce smile at me. 'I love it! Can I do it tomorrow, too?'

'Of course you can. Every day in the week now, big man.' I reach to rescue a dangle of spaghetti making a bid for freedom from one corner of his mouth. 'Want some chocolate milk as a treat?'

Daft question.

I haven't looked out at Lachlan's window since we got home, partly because of the FaceTime call and because I wanted to hear every detail of Noah's day now he's awake enough to share it, but also because I was too scared to look.

I thought about his last message so much at work I ended up tying myself in knots. Of course I'm tempted to meet him for real, but I can't just hurry into things. It took so long to find this flat and we're only just settling in: if I rush a meeting with Lachlan and it doesn't go well, how safe will this place feel knowing he's so close?

I don't know him. I have to protect Noah. And me – because I know my heart and it's already hiking up mountains it shouldn't climb.

I give Noah his milkshake and stand awkwardly halfway

between him and the window. I don't know what to do with my hands all of a sudden, my feet not sure where they should travel next.

What am I doing?

Okay, I just need to write a reply and stick it up. Then it can be me and Noah and none of *this* in my head.

Checking he's happy with his treat, I bite the bullet.

NOT UNTIL YOU
GRADUATE
BISCUIT SCHOOL ☺

It isn't a *no*, just a breather. I hope he'll take it the right way. But if he doesn't, that's my answer, I suppose. Either way, I'm not going to think about it again tonight. I'm going to hang out with the main man in my life and stop thinking about the man across the hedge.

Chapter Twenty-Three

LACHLAN

It's a relief when she answers.

I'd talked myself into a corner waiting for her reply, convinced I'd stuffed everything up with my not-so-subtle hint about us meeting. In the end I'd taken myself for a lie down – mainly to get away from the glaring accusation of my note, blocking light in my window – and ended up sleeping right through till dawn.

I shouldn't have said it. But I'd been thinking about what could be next for us. She could get bored any day now and then what? We just stop? Pretend it never happened? I got carried away. I won't make that mistake again.

At least she answered. I'd all but resigned myself to it being over.

It's a sweet reply, still playful and written in the spirit of our recent messages, but it's a definite rebuttal. I'm lucky. I have to reel this in now, make it last for as long as I can and keep it fun. This time was a warning: next time I might blow it for good.

I don't answer immediately. I'm still shaky after convincing myself everything was over yesterday. Instead I do my session with Tanya, take a very grateful Bert down to the garden for a stroll, hunker down with my latest book for a couple of hours and then, when evening comes, order takeaway pizza and settle in for the night with a box set. Despite my mammoth sleeping session last night, my eyelids droop as I wait for my dinner to arrive. Within minutes, I doze off.

The rasp of the door buzzer jolts me back. I make my way over to answer.

'Pizza for Wallace?'

'Cheers, mate. Flat 4, straight up the stairs and second door on the left.'

I grab a twenty from my wallet on the counter and am about to open the door when I suddenly remember my sign is still in the window. My leg burns as I try to hurry across the floor, my hip jarring when I slam against the window and pull the sign away. I scoop up the pens and the sketchpad and shove them in a kitchen cupboard, slamming it shut as my doorbell rings. It takes a huge effort to reach the door, just as a loud knock sounds.

'Yeah, okay, one second.'

I open the door and freeze, folded note in hand.

'Any longer and I would have scoffed this,' Riggsy grins, balancing a large pizza box and a smaller box of garlic bread on one hand like a waiter in a high-class Parisian restaurant. 'I paid the fella at the door, so I'll have that, ta.' He swipes the twenty from my fingers as he strolls in.

Bert goes full-on wannabe guard dog, rushing at Riggsy, teeth bared and snarling. It doesn't help that all four stumpy paws leave the ground simultaneously with every bark, but I appreciate the gesture.

'Call off your Rotty, would you?' my mate yells, and for a horrible moment I think he'll kick my dog.

'Bert,' I snap, secretly wanting to scoop him clear of Riggsy's boot. 'In your bed.'

He stalks to his basket, eyeballing Riggsy over his shoulder the whole way. Once in, he pulls Sock to his side like a locked and loaded weapon – the ultimate Bert warning move.

'Just passing, were you?'

'Charming, that is. How about I was just checking up on a mate?' He's already on the sofa, opening the box to appraise my dinner. 'You know, I heard pain meds make you paranoid. You want to watch yourself, amount you're on.'

I let that pass and pull the chair from the dining table over to the sofa to sit. 'I'm guessing you're staying, then?'

My mate grins from the middle of the slice he's just started eating. 'Very kind. Beer would be good.'

'I'm all out. Cup of tea?'

He doesn't even rise to it. 'Shut up. Get the beer.'

I leave him to scoff my dinner and take the bottle I was saving for myself from the fridge. As I do, I glance over at Bethan's apartment. Her kind decline is still there and it looks like the main light is off. Probably for the best. I'll put a message up tonight for her to read tomorrow.

If I can work out what to say, that is…

We sit and eat – him considerably more than me, of course – while the TV plays an episode I've lost the thread of now. After ten minutes, Riggsy grabs the remote and switches to Sky Sports.

'I was watching that,' I protest, not that he's likely to hear it.

'The match is on.'

'Your telly not working?'

'It's not as big as yours, Lachlan,' he says, batting his eyelids at me. 'Anyway. I have news.'

My stomach knots. 'About what?'

'Not the inquiry. Mate, your face...' He shakes his head, folding another pizza slice in half before ramming it in his gob. 'About Byrne.'

Any hunger I had left disappears.

Sergeant Cathal Byrne, arch-nemesis of my best mate. It started at basic training when Riggsy and Byrne got in a fight over a girl that ended with a broken nose for Riggsy and four cracked ribs for Byrne. They've been engaged in a bitter battle ever since. It doesn't help that they're cut from the same cloth: both hotheads, their fists quicker than their brains. But it's no longer fistfights between them. Riggsy accused Byrne of conducting illegal business using army transport – when their superiors cleared Byrne of wrongdoing, he got promoted to sergeant over my mate, pushing Riggsy's nose firmly out of joint.

And then the threats began. Real threats, not just mouthing off. Riggsy got wind of an after-hours gambling racket Byrne was operating and threatened to shop him. Then word came back to Riggsy that Byrne was planning to get him arrested for intimidation and bullying, alleging he was bribing others in the garrison to testify against him. Setting him up for a fall. It could all be bollocks, but knowing Cathal Byrne, I wouldn't be so quick to dismiss it. The hate he and Riggs harbour for each other could take them both over the edge.

Nearly has, already. Has he forgotten that?

'What about him?' I ask.

'Got him this time, mate. Good and proper.'

'You are kidding me.'

'Nope. Bastard lined himself up in front of the target and...'

he cocks his fingers into a gun shape, taking aim at the television, '... *BOOM*.'

Not this. Not now. Has he any brain cells left? 'What have you done?'

'Nothing. It's what I'm thinking of doing that's important...'

'Stop it, now.' I swing onto the sofa, almost sending the open box of garlic bread flying.

'What?'

'Whatever thick-ass scheme you've got in your head, drop it.'

'Okay, *matron*. Did they do a sense-of-humour bypass when they stitched up your leg?'

'I mean it, Riggs. We are in enough crap already. Leave Cathal Byrne alone.'

'On whose orders?'

'It's not an order. It's a warning.'

'Yeah? You pulling rank on me now, *Captain*?'

'Have you learned nothing? What do you think Byrne wants to do? Tie you up in knots so you do something stupid. It's how he works – you know this, mate. He gobs off and riles everyone up, then walks away from the fallout. The best thing you can do is report him. Official channels. He can't fight that...'

He's not smiling now. Eyes glaring in the shadow of his scowl, he's suddenly inches from my face. 'Ain't your place to preach, *mate*. If you hadn't stopped me sorting this before, I wouldn't have to deal with him now, would I?'

'We are here, *now*, because I stopped you. I'm like *this* because of it.'

He ignores my accusation and gives a hollow laugh, the beer-stained breath right in my face. 'You haven't a clue, have you? Holed up here like a bloody plaster saint, far away from...

that. What do you know about how it is on the garrison right now? It's worse than before. I should have sorted it that night. Removed the threat. Instead of getting wrapped around a tree in a car with you. You didn't help me by taking me away from Byrne: you made it worse. That bastard is planning something and he's going to take me down. So damn right I'm going to get him before he gets me…'

I can't believe what I'm hearing. 'Do you want to go to prison?'

'Oh, *spare me*…'

'That's where you would have ended up if I hadn't stopped you. And then Byrne would have won. Is that what you want? And what about the inquiry we're about to go into? Now is not the time to act on a grudge.'

He raises his chin, staring me down like a prizefighter. 'No time like the present, I reckon.'

'Are you really that stupid? You know why we were on the road that night and it wasn't because you fancied a drive.'

'Way I remember it, you were the one shoving me into the driver's seat.'

'Because I had no option.'

'Because you wanted to pull rank.'

'I was saving your skin!'

My shout reverberates around the walls. Bert flies from his basket in an apoplexy of barks. Ernie shoots down the corridor and into my room. Riggs stares at me.

'That's what you think you did. So give yourself that medal, soldier.' He takes the last slice of pizza and the box of garlic bread and calmly walks past me to the door. 'And keep your mouth shut. Don't go backing down on what we agreed.'

I hate that his words sting but they do and he sees it.

The shadow of a smirk appears. 'I had your back once: now it's your turn. We'll talk when you've grown a pair, yeah?'

Disgusted, I watch him leave.

My flat recedes to quietness once more but the air is thick with gun smoke. How did he imagine I'd take the news? I thought the crash might have knocked some sense into him but that was never going to happen, was it? Once again Adam Riggs got out of his mess unscathed, unlike me.

I should report it to Archer, let the top brass deal with them. But this inquiry is so finely balanced anything could tip the scales against me. Because it'll be me that comes off worse: always has been; always will be.

I can't do anything, except hope that Riggsy is just sabre-rattling and spouting bollocks as usual. When we come up before the inquiry, I have to stick to the story we agreed – if I don't, I could lose everything...

A warm bump against my shin makes me look down. Bert needs his evening visit to the garden. He has the right idea: I need fresh air, too. And I need to think. I can't do that in here.

I grab Bert's lead and glance back towards Bethan's window.

No, I'll send her a message tomorrow morning. Tonight is not the right time.

'Come on, dude.' I say to my dog, my spirits lifting at the sight of his utter delight.

If only life was a simple as a handful of dog biscuits and a mooch in long grass...

Chapter Twenty-Four

BETHAN

Dropping Noah at Michelle's was weird this morning.

Driving back home afterwards was worse.

Now I'm questioning the wisdom of sending him to Michelle's sister's kids club straight after his fourth full day at preschool and letting Michelle give him tea afterwards. I won't see him till 6 p.m. and that's *nine hours* away. The time we're apart stretches out impossibly long in front of me.

I don't like it.

At work I'm busy enough to not think about Noah – or not worry about him, at any rate. Here, I'm – what *am* I doing, exactly? Staring at my ancient laptop screen as if suggestions will just jump to my aid and type themselves into the search bar?

This was a bad idea.

I'll talk to Hattie tomorrow. Suggest she finds someone else. I am clearly not up to the job.

I leave the laptop on the sofa, its whirring fan inexplicably loud in the room. I've had three coffees already since 6 a.m. but each one has been a distraction. I need to trick my mind into working somehow.

Toast. Toast will work.

For a bit, at least.

My foot taps involuntarily against the vinyl floor as I wait for the toaster to do its stuff. I'm restless this morning, a bundle of excess energy despite not sleeping well last night. I kept bumping awake, thinking I'd heard Noah cry. He was fine – slept the sleep of the righteous from the moment I put him down. By rights I should be dragging myself around the flat this morning, but I can't keep still. Of course, that might be something to do with all the caffeine.

There's a click behind me and I turn to find the toaster is offering me two pale slices. Basically just warm bread. Bloody thing. It's on its way out, you can bet your life. I risk another go in the toaster, my finger hovering by the 'cancel' button in a kind of deranged bread-based game of Chicken.

I watch the second hand tick around the Peter Andre clock someone bought me years ago as a joke on a day trip to Aberystwyth, counting slowly along with it. Peter Andre smoulders cheekily at me as I count. I've never been able to part with that clock. Turns out I like the chap watching over us from the kitchen wall. He's been the most consistent and useful bloke in our lives. And he doesn't stick when his batteries are getting low...

At forty seconds I slam the 'cancel' button just in time to receive two slices of slightly singed toast. Pretty much a metaphor for my day, I think, and then laugh at myself for being so melodramatic.

It's just toast.

It's just a job.

It's just looking for possibilities.

Hattie asked me to do this because she believes in me. I owe it to her to give it a shot. I can't back away just because I don't know where to start.

Mind made up, I allow myself a moment to eat toast and think. As I do, my eyes naturally stray to the window, and the building beyond.

Lachlan's latest message is still there. He must have put it up last night after I'd gone to bed, or very early this morning. After my 'no thanks, not yet' reply to his suggestion of meeting one day, I wasn't sure what his next volley would be.

As it turns out, it's a sweet one:

DEAL. DO I GET
A CERTIFICATE WHEN
I PASS? ☺

Maybe I'll just reply to him first. A little bit of creativity might kick the old grey cells into action…

… Oh, who am I kidding? I want to reply to him and I'm not going to wait until Noah's in bed this evening. It can be my first perk of working from home.

I'm guessing Lachlan's at work today so he won't see it till later but that will be fun, too, getting my message sent first. I think of him coming home from a boring Thursday and finding a surprise message to welcome him back. I think he'll like it. I reckon it will make him smile…

What does Lachlan's smile look like?

I've been wondering about that.

I feel like I know him. I hear his voice in the messages he sends; I sense his humour and his thoughts on stuff. But I don't know his face. That's just weird, isn't it?

I think I know the problem. You can't invest in something like this without there being some kind of progression. It *moves*. It has to. You don't talk to someone every day for a week and not end up further down the road than where you began.

What are we, exactly?

Friends? Neighbours? Strangers who send each other window messages?

I sense that restlessness in Lachlan, too, but am I imagining it?

I put the finishing touches to my new message and stand back to look at it. The side of my hand is stained in rainbow blotches where it's passed across the felt-tip pen lines. I remember Mam playing merry hell with me for that when I was a kid: 'No skin on your knees and half a rainbow up your arm.' Until I had Noah I'd all but forgotten the thrill of drawing. It's good to welcome it back.

And I must say, my latest work is pretty good. I reckon he'll like this: a large certificate with a rainbow border, bearing his name and newly bestowed honour, complete with a red felt-pen seal:

THIS IS TO CERTIFY
LACHLAN
IS NOW A MEMBER OF
BETHAN'S BISCUIT ACADEMY.
~ Go forth and dunk ~

The sun has been strengthening all morning and now long stretches of golden light fill the flat. I'm not used to seeing these mid-morning shadows yet – on the days I have been here at this time there was hardly any sun before midday or just constant rain. It makes me stop what I'm doing to take it in.

And I am arrested by its beauty and positivity.

Every new discovery here is bright and exciting. It's a world away from where we were before. In the bedsit, I came to dread new developments because they were never good. New mould patches and damp stains, new scary neighbours and unwelcome late-night disturbances. I heard fights in the street, domestics in the rooms around ours, a lady who got drunk and cried every night for a month before she moved somewhere else. I would lie in bed with Noah in my arms, willing him to sleep through it when I couldn't. And now he sleeps all night in a warm, safe place of his own which even waking nightmares can't tarnish.

And Lachlan is part of that.

I have to stop worrying about this and go back to enjoying our window conversations. They are lovely in themselves. That's what counts.

Sunlight is streaming between our buildings as I glance out, a soft-focus golden sheen washing everything. I've never seen it do that before. Smiling, I reach up to pull the masking-taped edges of my last message down, gently easing the paper away, taking care not to tear it. It's destined for the box in the wardrobe where all my other signs now live. Carefully, I lay it on the kitchen counter and pick up Lachlan's certificate and the roll of tape.

I turn back to the window and…

Lachlan is standing there.

Staring at me.

The message he's just removed from his window still in his hand, his eyes wide with surprise.

And then, he smiles.

It's a smile I could never have imagined. The most wonderful smile I've ever seen.

I smile back, lifting my hand to give the smallest wave. Because right now my body doesn't know what else to do. The light between the buildings mists my view of him but finally we're face to face.

'Hi,' I say, even though he can't hear me.

He says something back, but I can't tell what it is. It doesn't matter: I *see* him now. Not a stranger posting funny signs. Not an acquaintance I hardly know.

He's Lachlan: my new friend with the loveliest smile.

Chapter Twenty-Five

LACHLAN

She's beautiful.

Really, remarkably, steal-your-breath *beautiful*.

And I'm just stood here, like a great lumping oaf, unable to move.

At least I'm smiling back at her, although from her point of view it probably looks more inane than alluring.

'It's you,' I say to the glass. 'Wow. Hi, Bethan.'

She smiles and waves back, mouthing, 'Hi.'

And then we both just stand there, not knowing what to do.

It's a shock. I thought she worked during the day. I was just taking down the old message because Ernie managed to rip it when he pushed his head up against the bottom edge and it tore away from the tape. I took it down – and there she was. The light is bright between us, making her image soft, like looking through sun-coloured glass. But I know enough to know this is the moment everything changes.

She's lovely. Shoulder-length dark hair that's loose today, a sweet heart-shaped face and a smile that feels like the biggest welcome when it's aimed at me. From here I can't tell what colour her eyes are but I can see them sparkle with surprise. She's wearing a yellow-and-white-striped T-shirt under a deep blue cardigan, the sleeves pushed up to her elbows like she means business, and at her neck is a silver necklace with some kind of drop that catches the sun as she moves.

I've tried not to imagine what Bethan looks like because I didn't think I'd ever see her for real. And while my mind always found a way to drift there, I couldn't have imagined *this*.

So what do we do now?

I want to stay here, taking in the sight of the woman I've come to depend on so much. But we can't keep idiotically grinning at each other from our windows. One of us has to break the moment – I just don't want it to be me.

I'm about to try some form of sign language to speak to her when she points to her new sign, then pats the window. She must have come to the same conclusion and has decided to make it easy for us to step away. My heart sinks a little, but she's right: this was a surprise interlude but we should return to business as usual. I send her a double-thumbs-up, which instantly makes me cringe.

And then she's sticking up the sign, stealing smiles at me as she does so. I should be wary of feeling too much but watching this is pretty adorable. I can see it properly now: a large certificate confirming my enrolment in her biscuit academy. Cute. I give her a small bow and see it instantly register. I've imagined her reaction to my messages every time I've put a new one in the window: to see it in real time is a gift.

When her sign is in place, she peers around it and raises her hand. I mirror her gesture, mouthing *Bye*—

—and then, she's gone.

I stare at the space where she was for a while, the ghost of her figure still imprinted on my vision and my pulse hammering at my throat, until my leg insists I sit.

Reluctantly, I shift my aching, shaking body to the dining-table chair. I don't know how long our exchange lasted – it could have been minutes or hours – but in that time the game changed.

I feel it, sudden like the swing of a weathervane, strong like the rush of air after a storm. I close my eyes and let it sink in.

The moment I do, Bert joins me, his warm nose pushing insistently against my hand where it rests on my knee. I ruffle the fur behind his ears just where he likes it, receiving a happy rumble of appreciation in return.

'Well, dude, I wasn't expecting that,' I say, watching his ears twitch at the sound of my voice. 'Bit of a game-changer.'

Because it is, isn't it? I can no longer say I don't know who I'm trading messages with. Bethan now has a face and a smile and she seemed as happy about us being face to face as I was.

Now what?

It's my turn to reply to the message and the pressure to get it right is suddenly magnified. How do you follow that? We didn't plan to see each other but what comes next falls to me to decide.

So, potential approaches for replying to a person you believed to be pretty special and have just unexpectedly had your thoughts on them confirmed... I line up the candidates one by one, like a motley crew of recruits on their first day of training.

I could joke about it – WHAT JUST HAPPENED?

Bit vague? Also, she might think I was complaining. I am *not* complaining.

Go for the cheeky approach – WELL, MY VIEW JUST IMPROVED...

163

Ugh, maybe not. I cringe about even thinking of that one.

Or just the straightforward, no-messing angle – GREAT TO SEE YOU.

I mean, it has potential, but is it a bit like *the thing you'd say when you're about to leave a party and you definitely don't want the other person following you out?*

Come on, Lachie, it shouldn't be this hard.

YOU'RE BEAUTIFUL.

No, *no*, way too forward.

HELLO, BISCUIT ACADEMY PROFESSOR…

Pathetic.

BIG SMILEY FACE EMOJI AND NO WORDS

… therefore completely passing the buck? Right now, it's tempting…

I wish I had more time to think about this, but I really need to reply soon. It isn't like I can leave it till 5 p.m. when she's back from work – because she's *there*, right now.

I'm stumped. Seeking any kind of inspiration because I am totally out of my depth with this, I turn to my faithful, loyal friend for advice.

'What should I say to Bethan, boy?' I ask Bert. 'What would you do?'

I look down at my dog, who is diligently licking my sock like an ice cream.

'Well, you're a great help.'

He ignores me and carries on, the warm dampness and hot puffs of his breath now reaching the skin of my toes.

'Bert,' I say.

Bert looks up, mid-lick, ears upright.

'You're fired.'

He blinks and returns his attention to the sock at hand.

The answer arrives an hour later, after I've exhausted every other possibility. And of course, as soon as I write it down it's the obvious reply. Simple, honest, not pushy or flippant or trying too hard. Something I would say if we'd met in real life and were becoming friends.

GOOD TO SEE YOU TODAY ☺
P.S. CALL ME LACHIE

I don't know why I haven't said about my preferred first name before. It's usually the way I introduce myself these days, unless it's something official or work-related. People only tend to use my full name if they're shouting at me – my mum, my sister, my superior officers. I like my name but I like my version of it better. Lachlan always feels like it has expectation attached to it, a deployed parachute dragging behind after a jump. Lachie is still allowed to have fun, be a little irreverent or make somebody belly-laugh with his jokes. That's who I want Bethan to know, not the formal, dry, solemn one.

Does she shorten her name? Or prefer another name entirely? Does she have a nickname or a pet name her family call her?

So many questions still to ask.

But the biggest is one I won't think about tonight – because I'm not ready to know the answer: what if us seeing each other isn't enough? What if Bethan wants to meet face to face?

Chapter Twenty-Six

BETHAN

I saw him. I can't believe it.

Lachlan. *Lachie*, now.

He's real, not just a half-seen, half-assumed entity. We exchanged waves and smiles and uncertain silent words. He was *gorgeous*, too. More than I expected. And I can't stop thinking about it.

The last twenty-four hours have passed in a mind-boggling daze. I woke this morning not sure if I'd dreamed the whole thing. It was just so unexpected. I mean, how are you supposed to prepare for something like that when it turns up out of nowhere?

LACHIE SUITS YOU.
LOVELY TO SEE YOU, TOO ☺

I posted my reply yesterday evening after putting my very sleepy boy to bed. The combination of almost a week of full-day pre-school sessions, plus the adrenalin-pumped experience of his first club with Maisie *and* one of Michelle's teas afterwards all but wiped Noah out. We came home with armfuls of weird and wonderful works of art, a zip-close bag of very flat-looking melting moments biscuits and a toilet-roll-stack sword for fending off pesky pirates, should any happen to arrive at our flat. Always handy, if you ask me.

Lachie does suit Lachlan, now I know what he looks like. Lachlan is a lovely name but always struck me as quite formal. Mind you, I'm not likely to ask him to call me Beth. That's the name Mam uses when I'm in trouble. Totally contrary, but that's her. My friends at school always found it hilarious that their mothers would yell their full names – first, middle and surname – up the street to get them home, where my mam used the shortest number of syllables to the greatest effect.

He could call me Bethy, maybe. I like it when Michelle and Hattie call me that, although it does make me sound like I'm nine years old and should be riding a sparkly Barbie bike.

'How did it go, B?'

Or B, like Patrick has decided is my official nickname.

I wait until we've smiled at and walked past Bhupinder and Kerry-Ann from the gift shop before I regale him with the details of my first day working from home. Which aren't many, unfortunately.

'Slow,' I say, keeping my voice low in case Darren is circling. I have been left in no doubt of what he thinks of my new Thursday responsibility.

'Define *slow*.'

I blow air from my cheeks. 'Glacial. I know it's early but it was tough going.'

'What were you doing?'

'Researching local community groups. Making endless lists. Sending emails to anyone who might be remotely interested in helping us.'

'Well, that all sounds good.'

'Yeah, except I've had zero replies. And without knowing who might help us, it's hard to plan anything. I just felt like I was grasping at straws, you know? Hattie needs options now, not in four weeks when we've emailed everyone in North Yorkshire.'

Patrick offers a grimace of solidarity and holds the door open for me to step out into the plant A-to-Z. Thick grey clouds, sweeping across the sky like wind-driven stubborn waves, have succeeded yesterday's sun. The wind has picked up considerably, too, buffeting the few hardy plant hunters walking the aisles. Careful comb-overs lift and flap like battle pennants, while perfect shampoo-and-sets are tempted out of their tight, pastel-washed curls.

Murray is kneeling by a wooden trough in the middle of the central aisle, planting up our annual display of wood anemones. The wind catches a stack of empty black plastic plant pots beside him and sends them skipping and skidding across the brick pavers towards us. Patrick leaps into their path, stopping each one with his boot, and grins at me as he scoops them up.

'Your juggling act needs work, Murray.'

Our colleague continues tipping plants out of pots and bedding them in. 'It's always going to beat your comedy, though.'

'Vicious, mate.' Patrick mimes being shot in the heart.

Murray almost smiles. 'You're welcome.'

'Hey, B, we could do a talent night,' Patrick says, beaming at his clearly genius idea.

'For what? To scare the customers away?'

'No. You wanted the local community to get involved – so, what's better than a talent show?'

'Corporate sponsorship, large chain buy-out, Deborah

Meaden rocking up in a limo and chucking us fifty grand,' Murray mutters, still planting.

Patrick rolls his eyes. 'No, think about it: *Bright Hill's Got Talent*! You're Welsh, so you could sing. Murray could do devastating stand-up, old Eric could get drunk and play the ukulele like he did at the Christmas works bash last year... Local paper would be all over it.'

I place a hand on his shoulder. 'And *that's* why ideas were slow coming yesterday.'

'It's a good suggestion.'

'We need money, Pat. We need schemes that bring in sustained income to support the nursery when business is lean, not gimmicks.'

I love him for trying to help, but any way I look at it, it's a tall order. I just have to keep thinking. The trouble is, something else is taking up space where my Bright Hill ideas should be.

Not something. *Someone.*

I've seen him. I know what his smile looks like. I know he's gorgeous. It's what I wanted to happen – so why do I feel so restless?

I know the answer: I want more.

So what happens next? Do we just go back to where we were before seeing each other yesterday? Or does it change the rules? I'm thrilled it happened, but it's an added complication to this *thing* we've been doing. It doesn't feel like a game anymore, but it *is*. If I just think about how those first messages made me feel, I'm okay: I'm right back there with the heart-in-mouth, breathless joy of it. But my brain is trying to find solutions and a way forward and that muddies the waters.

The thing is, the last two and a half years of my life have been ruled by the need to constantly assess what's in front of us, to keep focused on where we need to be. Stamping out fires in our path before they can take hold. Trying to predict what life may chuck at us next so I can defend our ground. I've learned not to trust my heart when it runs away with ideas – because listening to that is what got me in this mess.

It's what happens when you trust someone with your whole self, only to find they've been dragging you through the dirt all along.

It's what happened when I believed Kai Roberts.

I glance at Patrick and Murray, certain that the unwelcome thought of *that name* is showing on my face. But they're too busy ribbing one another about what their *Bright Hill's Got Talent* acts would be.

I move away from them a little and busy myself with righting a line of staked clematis plants that have tumbled over in the wind. My hands are clumsy as I pick up the pots. I wish I hadn't thought about Kai.

Nobody knows about him because they assume I have Noah due to an indiscretion of my own. And I don't tell them the truth because that assumption is offensive to anyone with a child and it's none of their business. But also because I don't want to hear that man's name associated with the life I have now. He's nothing to Noah – by choice. He's nothing to me – but the legacy of what he did to us remains in every brown envelope that lands at my door...

Hang on.

Stop it, Bethan. Lachie is not Kai.

He's *not* Kai.

'Is there any particular reason why a third of our plant team are bunched up in one section doing sod all?'

We turn as one to see a red-faced Head of Section glowering. 'Just doing the rounds, boss,' Patrick chirps.

'You appear to have stalled,' Darren replies, not blinking once. It's a skill I have to give him credit for. He could out-stare anyone in a non-blink war. Maybe he could turn that into a talent show act…

Patrick's smile disappears. 'I'll – er – carry on then.' He shoots me a daring look over his shoulder and then he's off, walking along the plant aisles like a man possessed.

'Murray, are you planning on devoting your entire morning to that display?'

'I was considering it.' Murray doesn't even flinch. That man is 100 per cent *rock*.

I can see the direct hit this has scored and keep my expression steady despite the urge to laugh. There is much I can learn from Murray Hope's approach to life.

Darren's mouth flaps like a beached goldfish and then he turns the full force of his ire on me. Of course he does, because Darren Gifford is a one-trick pony. He was probably the kind of kid that pulled the legs off spiders when he couldn't get his own way.

'I don't think you need to be here, either,' he says. 'There's a stack of jobs outstanding thanks to us being one staff member down yesterday.'

'Just give me a list and I'll get cracking,' I reply, back straight, eyes meeting his glare.

'I expect you're well rested after bunking off work,' he snaps. 'Probably dossed around all day on the company's time. Do you good to do some actual work for a change.'

'Unlike some people,' Murray mutters into the anemone display behind me.

'What was that?'

'Just talking to the anemones, Darren.'

Darren's eyes narrow and I imagine the processors in his brain desperately whirring to find an appropriate response. 'Well… Stop talking to inanimate plants and tell yourself to get a shift on. The topical section is a *pit*. Bethan? Still here?'

I nod and start walking, but I swear I see Murray wink at me as I leave…

Chapter Twenty-Seven

LACHLAN

The hospital waiting area is stickily warm and too bright. It's the third one I've sat in since the taxi dropped me at Darlington Memorial Hospital this morning – blood test, X-ray and now physiotherapy for my consultant review – and the only discernible difference between them is the range of terrifying NHS information posters on the noticeboards. Sit here for too long and you could leave with twice as many afflictions as you arrived with.

I'm purposefully not looking at them, but I need something to take my mind off the pain of sitting in three lots of highly uncomfortable plastic seats. My fellow patients look equally as uncomfortable as me – and in this waiting room most of them are as trussed up as I am. A variety of sticks, crutches, casts and walking frames surround the space and in each person I see the familiar weariness of weeks spent wrenching a body back to health, their lives on hold until movement returns.

We exchange brief smiles and grimaces when our eyes meet, followed by swift downward glances at our phones or books – because while we may all be in the same boat, none of us volunteered to be in it.

I look down at the book I've brought with me, having learned my lesson the last time I had these full-day rounds of blood tests, X-rays and progress consultations, when my phone battery died after too much use avoiding eye contact with other patients. It's a good book, too. A proper page-turner, with a great reformed con-artist-turned-lawyer protagonist who appears to be never more than three pages away from certain death. I like the guy. I'd like him on my side if I were wrongly accused, but I'm not sure he'd be relaxing to hang out with. Mind you, having Riggsy as a best mate is enough of a test in real life.

Reading is one unexpected bonus I'll walk away from the crash with. I never had much opportunity to read before: life and the demands of the army claimed most of my time. But since my accident I've read almost a book a week. I had to buy a bookcase a month into my enforced isolation at home because Ernie was intent on toppling the growing new book piles by the sofa at every opportunity. He perches protectively on top of it now, his latest favourite vantage point to taunt Bert from.

Does Bethan read? I bet she does. The thought of her warms me as I follow the fictional Eddie Flynn's exploits across the pages. Maybe I'll ask her with my next message.

My hospital appointment card holds my place in the book, as much to make sure I don't lose it as to act as a bookmark. One side is filled with dates and times already. Today's triple appointments encroach on the second side. Will I complete my rehabilitation before the card runs out of space or will it stretch beyond into multiple cards? The thought unnerves me.

I *am* making progress. Tanya said so. My GP called after my last session to say she'd checked in with my physio and was pleased with what I'd achieved. I've committed to it now and the daily exercises are beginning to feel different, as if my determination has unlocked a route to new muscles I couldn't access before.

I want it to work. For me, for proving to my family I'm still capable, and now, after what happened two days ago, for Bethan. Not *for* her, but so I can suggest we meet one day and be able to walk alongside her as easily as possible.

I resumed the Biscuit Academy conversation after our almost-meeting, figuring it was safer ground. She's joined in and hasn't referenced the meeting, either, but I know we're both aware of it.

WHAT ARE YOUR THOUGHTS
ON CHOCOLATE DIGESTIVES, PROFESSOR?

MORE THAN ACCEPTABLE.
GOOD WORK, STUDENT.

THANKS. SO, BIG QUESTION:
CHOCOLATE HOBNOB OR
CHOCOLATE DIGESTIVE?

THAT'S ADVANCED COURSE
STUFF! DON'T RUN BEFORE
YOU CAN WALK ☺

BEFORE YOU CAN WALK. If only she knew…

I know I shouldn't pin my hopes for recovery on Bethan, but something changed when I saw her. It was safe from the window – and I loved being able to stand face to face without worrying what she thought of my gait. But if she wanted to meet right now I couldn't do it, much as I want to. I need to heal, get stronger, so I can finally see myself as *me*, not my injury. Until I deal with that, I'm no use – to her or anybody else.

'Lachlan Wallace?'

I raise my hand and shove my book in my rucksack, grabbing my crutch and getting out of the plastic seat as fast as I can.

'No rush,' the physio smiles.

That isn't the encouraging phrase he thinks it is. I press on, breathing against the pain as I follow him.

'Stifling in here today, isn't it?' he says, pinching the front of his blue polo shirt and flapping it to make his point.

'Just a bit.'

'Problems with the air-con, apparently. Good job there isn't a heat wave happening outside or we'd all be toast.' He grins at me and leans in a little, as if he's about to bestow a pearl of secret wisdom. 'We've nicked all the fans in the department so our room is a haven of cool.'

Our shoes squeak as we walk along the shiny peach vinyl floor that seems to be endless; a high-pitched cacophony that sends my teeth on edge. The physio's shoes beat out a perfect march rhythm, the *schhlup-schhlup* of his steps achingly regular; while mine are discordant with a heavily accented second beat. It echoes as we walk and I imagine every head turning as we pass, every person aware of the misstep, judging my injury without even seeing me.

It's been happening all day: the turned heads, the looks. I've already had to refuse three offers of wheelchairs from well-meaning strangers judging my awkward progress through the main hospital concourse. Now I see pitying looks from the relatives of patients on the chairs that line the corridor. I know they mean well, that they're probably burned from watching a loved one going through recovery, but I hate every sad smile, every slight shake of the head aimed at me.

It's a relief to get into the room. And that has nothing to do with the six tall fans blasting cool air at us.

The consultant physiotherapist in charge of my programme grins beneath thick-rimmed glasses as she stands to greet me. Dr Fairbairn looks like a female Joe 90, an old Gerry Anderson TV show I was obsessed with as a kid when they showed reruns on Saturday mornings. The first time I met her this comparison alone kept my head above water.

Her accent is pure, broad Yorkshire. It's cheery, no matter how bad the news she's delivering. I almost wonder if that is her killer touch in this job, besides the years of training and personal vocation. Like the companies who employ call centre service staff in Newcastle or Swansea because it's so much easier to relax when those accents are soothing your complaint.

'Take a seat, Mr Wallace,' she offers, pulling a chair out a little from her desk to make it more accessible. 'We'll just go over your progress charts first and then we'll have a look at you in action.'

I sit, watching the three other physios preparing equipment in the rest of the large room. Parallel bars for walking reps, foam shapes for resistance work, a series of weights and bands laid out for weight-bearing tests. They chat amongst themselves in low tones, oblivious to me – and for once the normality that affords is a welcome change. They see my injuries but also my potential for recovery. It's taken me weeks to appreciate that.

'Right, we're still waiting on your X-rays so we'll get cracking on your review and hopefully by the time we're done with the physical checks they will have arrived.'

She opens a buff cardboard file and flicks through a series of sheets. I can't see what's written there and I push away the irritation of not knowing what she can see. I now know how my student soldiers feel when we're undergoing one-on-one reviews. The power wielded by a few sheets of paper in a file...

'Mm-hmm... Good,' she signs one sheet and continues to read.

I try to remain still and straight in my chair, which, while padded and more expensive than those in the waiting area, is no more comfortable. This is worse than an exam.

'Right.' She peers over the file at me. 'Excellent work, Mr Wallace. I'm very impressed.'

'There's been progress?' I ask, unable to contain the question any longer.

'Recently, yes. I was concerned the last time we saw you because the improvement had plateaued somewhat. But that's to be expected, to a certain extent. Muscles are tricky beggars, as I'm sure you're aware.'

I smile with her, my relief at the word *progress* beginning to break free.

'Then you think I'm on the road to recovery?'

Her smile tightens just a little. They're not supposed to let you see but I've learned to spot the signs. 'You're making progress and that's what we want to see. For now, that's what's we focus on, yes?'

I could leave it there, accept her firm deferment and focus on the task ahead. But if I don't ask, the question will ruminate and grow until it becomes a stumbling block. I don't want that: I'd rather know what I'm facing. 'What are my chances of full recovery as you see them now?'

'It's probably still too early to say…'

I'm not leaving this. I place my hand on my thigh and take a breath. I need her to understand how important this is to me. 'Knowing this will help me. I'm the kind of person that needs to know what the deal is. No surprises. I'm trained to identify the threat before I tackle it. Gather all relevant intel in order to know how to fight.'

'An army man.' Dr Fairbairn nods. 'My husband was at Catterick for twenty years, so I understand.' She closes the file and twists her office chair to face me. 'Things could change. They are changing, it would appear. Now, if you'd asked me the last time we met, I might have answered very differently, so – good sign. The fact is, we don't know. Your body has its own way of dealing with physical trauma: all we can do is work to strengthen your leg muscles to create the best framework for recovery. How much recovery and how far-reaching it is for the future are really down to your injuries and how your body responds.'

'So, what does that mean, practically?'

'Caveats thus established,' her smile is kind, 'I think you have a fighting chance. It may not be regaining full movement of your leg, so you should still prepare yourself for that. However, if the progress you've made can be sustained, I see no reason why you can't expect a return to almost normal gait.'

My eyes prickle, but I keep my head high, nodding my thanks.

Behind the thick frames, her eyes soften.

'You are doing a great job, Lachlan. Truly. And we are here to help you every step of the way, okay?'

'Okay,' I sniff. 'Thanks.'

She beams. 'Good. So, shall we see you do your stuff, soldier?'

Chapter Twenty-Eight

BETHAN

I've made up my mind. I'm going to ask Lachie if he wants to meet. I mean, it's the obvious next step, isn't it?

We've been sending Biscuit Academy messages for almost a week now and they're fun and lovely and all. But I can't help thinking we're both stalling for time. I like him. From his reaction last Thursday, it was pretty clear he likes me too. So what are we doing trying to chat with signs still? Something needs to change. And I think we both know it.

I wasn't going to say anything to anyone about this – because I never do. But it had become such an almighty mess in my head that if I didn't let it out it could engulf me. And when Patrick noticed, it was the push I needed.

He was helping me load a plant order for our delivery driver, Malcolm, when it happened. I'd noticed him sneaking glances at me when he thought I wasn't looking – forgetting that as a mum of a three-and-a-half-year-old I have already developed the peripheral vision of a warrior. It finally became too much when we were carrying a mature tree to the tail lift at the back of the truck.

'Okay, *what*?' I'd asked.

He'd feigned innocence, of course, but gave that up pretty sharpish when he saw my expression. 'Something's going on with you. And I don't think it has anything to do with working from home tomorrow.'

'Pat, I'm fine.'

'You're always fine, B. But this is different. You've been somewhere else in your head for days now. What's going on?'

So, I told him.

Well, not *everything*, I mean baby steps and that. But I told him a lot more than I would usually tell anyone, which for me was the ultimate confessional.

'Okay, suppose there was someone...'

'Someone?'

'*Someone* – who hadn't dated in a while and, you know, was fine with that. But then suppose they met somebody – not in person, just to exchange messages.'

The corners of his mouth began to twitch. 'Rude messages?'

Already out of my comfort zone and regretting ever mentioning it, I rolled my eyes as we travelled on the juddering tail lift up to the inside of the truck. 'No, not rude messages. What do you take this... *someone* for?'

'Obviously a lovely person who would never dream of sending anything rude. Apologies. Continue.'

I suspected he'd sussed me from the outset but, bless him, he still played along.

'Just messages,' I'd said, as we puffed our way over to the far end of the truck, pushing the tree into place. 'Jokey, friendly, saying hello, that kind of stuff.'

'Right.'

'And then, supposing they both came to the natural end of *those messages*,' I said, checking his reaction as we walked back to the tail lift and began our shaky descent down to the yard floor. 'Because, you know, there's only so much you can say – in a message.'

'Are you talking about Tinder?'

'*No*.'

'What then?'

I was tempted to say *Windows* but Patrick, who is far more tech savvy than I am, would've rumbled me immediately. 'Just bog-standard messages.'

We walked to the rest of the order on pallets awaiting loading. 'So, are you asking if they should stop messaging?'

'Yes. No. I don't mean stop altogether. Just change things up a bit?'

'You mean *meet*.' Patrick swung two bags of compost on his shoulder and I watched him as I collected a large box of perennials from the pallet stack.

'Maybe. I don't know. Would it be bad to ask?'

'To meet?'

'Yes. Hypothetically.'

'B, just tell me what's going on.'

'I'm trying to.'

And that's when he said it. The advice that made my decision: 'Okay, I get it. If this *someone* liked the other *someone* and the feeling was mutual, why wouldn't they want to meet? It's hard enough to find a friend these days. Finding someone willing to chat to you in messages shows a bit of commitment, maybe? That's what you need in a friend. That's what *you* need, B.'

And he's right, isn't he?

Why wouldn't we want to meet in real life?

I thought about it all last night, too awake to sleep. I've come to depend on hearing from Lachie and being able to talk back to him. I've loved having a friendship of my own, based on nothing more than words and stolen glimpses. Meeting him, talking in real time face to face, that would make sense.

I need a friend. I think Lachie does, too.

So what are we waiting for?

That's why I'm here, now, staring at a blank sheet of paper when I should be doing Bright Hill work on my second home-working Thursday. I know what I want to ask and why I want to ask it. So why are the words I need evading me?

Should I specify a time and place? Or float the possibility and hope he answers with specifics?

I have to be careful because we're still strangers beyond these windows. It would have to be somewhere public, like the front of our buildings, perhaps, or the little park down the road that always seems busy. It doesn't have to be a long meeting, just a little time to test it. I reckon I'll know within minutes if it's a non-starter.

But if I float the idea and he doesn't respond, how will I feel then? And does it matter?

I'm overthinking this. I just need to ask, don't I?

I grab my pens and write what feels right:

GOING FOR A WALK IN
THE PARK AT 1 P.M.
WANT TO COME? ☺

There. It's done. Now maybe I can get on with what I'm supposed to be doing. I stick the message in the window and walk resolutely back to my makeshift desk at the coffee table. I pick up my list of local community groups and start composing emails.

I won't look at his window till midday, I decide.

Midday is sensible.

I press 'send' on the first email, tick the box on my list. Move on to the next.

Midday gives him time to reply, right?

Right. Midday is perfect.

Five more emails sent. Five more boxes ticked.

I glance at my phone to check the time. *Three hours* until midday. Hmm. My pencil taps a triple-speed beat against my notepad. Three hours is a long time to wait...

I smooth out the list, which is now covered in tiny dots of pink from the eraser on the end of my pencil.

Would 11.30 a.m. be too early to check?

Or 11 a.m.?

Elevenses would be a natural time to stop, wouldn't it? And I'd have to pass the window to get to the kitchen. If I *happened* to glance out then, what harm would there be?

Eleven it is, then...

Chapter Twenty-Nine

LACHLAN

SHIT.

I rub my eyes in case sleep is still affecting them, and look again.

GOING FOR A WALK IN
THE PARK AT 1 P.M.
WANT TO COME? ☺

I didn't imagine it. It's real.

No, Bethan, why now?

How do I navigate this? If she'd asked if I wanted to meet *one day* I would know what to say. But we've already done that, haven't we? *I* did it with my 'we should do tea and biscuits one day' message before we saw each other. That time, she backed away – so what's changed?

And how do I pull back now?

I'm making progress and my review at the hospital has encouraged me. But she can't see me like I am now. My gait is so pronounced it takes me an age to walk a short distance. If

Bethan sees that, it's all she'll see, just like it's all everyone except my medical team saw at the hospital yesterday.

I don't want to feel like that with Bethan.

What the hell do I do? I can't refuse, because I was the one pushing the question last time. If I retreat, she'll take it personally. I would. Maybe she's a better person than I am – not difficult, to be honest. But what other conclusion could she reach?

What happened to this being easy?

I back away from the window. I need to think.

Ernie is sitting on the kitchen counter, which he's not supposed to do. I'm about to turf him off when he pulls his killer counter-move: stretching up from his front paws to bump his furry forehead under my chin. It's devastating and he knows it. Within seconds I'm stroking his back and Ernie is going for the full loving cat act. I shouldn't fall so easily for his schemes having been aware of them since he was a kitten, but this morning it's reassuring and familiar. I need that, even if it is an elaborate ploy to score food. So, I give in.

Bert, observing the scene from the pungent warmth of his basket, gives me the dog equivalent of an exasperated eye-roll and pushes his nose into the far more trustworthy depths of Sock.

The problem is, I want to meet Bethan.

I tickle Ernie's ears and he flicks them in happy reply.

If I try to be rational about it, I think she might be able to see past my injury. But there's no way I would know for certain until it was too late. I can't risk that.

But I haven't been able to get her out of my mind and seeing her in the window last week only confirmed what I already knew. I like her. I like the way that talking to her has altered how I see my days stuck at home. When I've been away from here, she's been with me in my head. I think she might just be the friend I've needed for a long time.

It's impossible.

Ernie is milking it now, promenading up and down the kitchen counter, purring like a pneumatic drill, his tail high and flicking under my nose as he passes.

If only I had a way of meeting Bethan without her seeing how I walk. Which is a complete non-starter because how would that work? We could open our windows and yell across the hedge at each other, I suppose, but that would be crazy.

My cat continues his swaggery walk until his paw hits the running magazines Sal sent me that are stacked by the hob, sending him skidding off the counter with a yowl. I jump and peer over the counter to check he's okay. He's ruffled but styles it out, the only hint at his ungraceful fall a row of raised hackles across his shoulders as he stalks away.

It's the jolt I needed. I let myself laugh, eliciting the filthiest look from my cat and the tail-wagging delight of my dog. The last time I saw Ernie fall from grace was when he tried to walk along the top of the hedge one morning when I was out with Bert and quickly discovered that beech hedges aren't as solid as fences. There's still a defined hole halfway down the hedge where I had to dig in to pull him out…

Hang on. The *hedge*.

Would that work?

I glance at the window.

The hole is about my chest height, running from my side of the hedge to Bethan's. Too low to crouch down? Maybe. But chest height to me means no view of my leg for her. How tall is Bethan? She didn't look as short as Jenny, who barely came up to my chest when I held her. But I'm six feet one and I don't think Bethan looked as tall as that when I saw her. My guess is around five feet six or seven?

I lean against the counter, mind whirring.

I've got a shooting stick thing Dad bought me a couple of years ago – a folded seat on a long walking stick with a spike that sticks in the ground. Could I sit on that and talk to Bethan through the Ernie-shaped gap in the hedge?

It's ridiculous. But it might work.

Just to begin with.

Just till I'm sure she sees me first.

I check my watch. 10.50 a.m. She'll be waiting for an answer. This is the best I have.

I move to the table, pull a fresh sheet of paper from the dwindling art pad, and write my invitation before I can think better of it.

PLAN B: MEET ME YOUR SIDE
OF THE HEDGE BY THE CAT-SIZED
HOLE, HALFWAY ALONG, 1 P.M. ☺

She'll think I'm insane. Or having a laugh.

But this is the only way it can happen.

Will Bethan agree?

I put the message up, peering around its side in the vain hope she might be looking over. But her window is empty.

She said 1 p.m., so I'll check back at noon. If there's no answer then, I'll check again at 12.30 p.m. And 12.45 p.m., if I have to.

Man, I hope she answers soon. Even if it's just to tell me where to get off.

This is worse than the first time I stuck the sign in my window. My palms leave damp imprints on the dining table when I lift them. My pulse is working harder than it did during the physical tests in the hospital. I have to consider every breath, purposefully slowing each inhale and exhale. I wasn't expecting a make-or-break situation with Bethan today, but when have our exchanges ever conformed to my expectations?

She is the most remarkable person to arrive in my life. I would be a fool not to try to meet her where she is.

All I can do now is wait.

Chapter Thirty

BETHAN

Meet him by the *hedge*?

What?

I look away from my window, and then back again because
– *what?*

So, Lachie doesn't want to go for a walk, but he wants us to
talk through a hedge?

That's crazy. And I don't even want to think about how he
knows the hole in it is cat-sized.

Right, let's look for positives. I start to make a mental list
but my thoughts are so all over the place it's like trying to pin
sticky notes on a spinning top. I take my message down from
the window, turn it over, and start to write.

> He replied.
> He didn't say NO.
> He wants to meet me.
> He wants to meet TODAY.
> If we meet, I'll know if this has potential or is a waste of time.
> First time I'll have arranged to meet by a hedge...

Okay, point 6 is a bit tenuous, but it could be fun.

Also – and I haven't wanted to listen to it, but – I've had a nagging doubt in my head since I posted that message. That perhaps I was a bit rash asking him to go for a walk with me. We might not get on, he might be creepy, I might not like him and a lap of the park is a long time to regret asking someone to walk with you.

I want to hear what his voice sounds like – and see if the humour and fun I imagined when I read his words exists in real life. I was brave in my messages, but I'm not a naturally confident person. What if I lose the power of rational speech when I'm with him? What if I'm overawed or can't think of anything to say?

This way of meeting is nuts. But I would be on my territory and Lachie would be on his. We could chat, get used to talking to each other instead of writing everything down.

It *might* work.

I tap my list with my pen.

If it does work and becomes the next thing we do, it also solves the issue of Noah.

I pull myself up. Noah is *not* an issue.

But it would mean I could tell Lachie about him when I was ready and if the conversation felt appropriate.

I take a swig of now very tepid tea from my Spidey mug.

I'm going to do this, aren't I?

I have to do this.

YOU'RE ON.

SEE YOU THERE ☺

I post the message and step back from the window, not sure whether to giggle like a schoolgirl or burst into tears. It's done now. This is happening.

So, next dilemma: what do you wear to meet a potential friend by a beech hedge?

I look down at my red-and-white-striped T-shirt that Noah calls my *pirate outfit*. There's a smear of strawberry red on my chest where he blessed me with an enthusiastic jam-covered breakfast snuggle this morning. I can't meet Lachie in this. He might not notice it, but I would forever associate our first meeting in person with having a jam-smeared right boob. I'm all for memorable, but that's not what I want to remember.

So I go into my bedroom and open the wardrobe. It's not the most inspiring view. Working in a garden centre means I'm in uniform all week; my clothes of choice at weekends are comfortable for me and colourful for Noah. I have a stack of old gig T-shirts from before I met Kai, many of which are more darn than material because I can't bear to part with them. And I have two dresses: one black one for evening soirees I never get invited to and a long floaty maxi dress I got in a Primark sale years ago to go to a wedding in. I can't meet Lachie in either of those – because I'm going to be standing by a hedge for at least twenty minutes.

Eventually, I find a pair of jeans without holes or paint-smears and a slightly faded Wonder Woman T-shirt that Emrys gave me for Christmas the year I had Noah. I put it on and don't hate it. I pull my red pretend-Converse supermarket trainers from the depths of my wardrobe and twist one half of my grown-out fringe into a plait across my head, tucking it behind my ear. It'll keep the strands out of my face while we're chatting and looks a bit cool, too.

That'll do. I'm talking to Lachie through a hole in a hedge, for heaven's sake. How much of my chosen outfit is he likely to see?

All the same, I might just add a little eyeliner, some mascara and a bit of lipstick. Just in case he can see my face through the cat-sized hole. Wouldn't hurt, would it?

I chuckle as I grab my make-up bag from the bedside table. *Cat-sized* hole.

I'm hoping he hasn't used Ernie to make it.

At two minutes to 1 p.m., I walk out of my building. Without thinking, I cast a furtive glance around me to check for prying eyes, before hurrying down the side along the strip of grass that links the front garden to the back.

What am I doing? This is barmy.

I follow the line of the hedge, my fingers brushing along the bright green leaves as I go. I don't remember seeing a hole in it when Noah and I have been out here before. Let alone one that could accommodate a cat. But Lachie said it was halfway along, so that's where I aim for.

As I reach the side of the building directly beneath my window, I see it: a dark indentation a little further along.

I stop. Take a breath.

This could be the most ridiculous thing I've ever done, or the start of something wonderful.

There's only one way to find out.

I walk towards the gap and stand by it.

'Hello?' I say, pushing away the embarrassment of talking to a hedge. 'Lachie? Are you there?'

What if this is a joke? What if he's up in his window right now, laughing his head off because I'm down here talking to a green hole? I didn't even consider that. Why didn't I think of that before?

'Bethan?'

My mouth goes dry. His voice is deep, the sound unfamiliar. But he says my name like he knows me.

'Um, hi.' Still self-conscious, I peer into the small space between branches and leaves.

And there he is.

His eyes are blue-green, the colour that sunshine turns the leaves of my favourite eucalyptus plant, *Eucalyptus pulverulenta* 'Baby Blue'. His smile up close is even lovelier than I remember from my window.

I wonder what he thinks of me, but at this moment it doesn't matter: we're here, our faces inches apart, hearing each other's voices for the first time. And Lachie is smiling like he's known me all his life.

'Hello.'

'Wow, it's – it's – you,' I say, taking it in.

'And it's you.' He rolls his eyes and gives a hesitant laugh. 'This is bloody weird, isn't it?'

'Completely. Why the hole in the hedge?'

'It seemed like a good idea at the time?' His eyes smile when he does, so that even if I couldn't see the rest of his face, I would know exactly what expression he was wearing. I like that. Eyes tell you a lot about a person.

'Please tell me you didn't use Ernie to make this happen.'

'Oh, Ernie made it happen. Just not specially for this occasion.'

'How?'

'He tried walking along the top and I had to rescue him from the middle.'

'Oh, poor thing. Was he okay?' I glance up at the top of the hedge. It must be seven feet high. That's a heck of a distance to fall.

Lachie laughs, and the sound is so delicious it makes my toes squidge up inside my trainers. 'He's fond of death-defying falls, so he was fine. A bit embarrassed, but nothing broken.'

'You sound like you really love him,' I say, instantly wishing I could take it back because how gushing was that?

'Yeah, can't help it.' He runs a hand through his hair and I catch a glimpse of the tattoo that sparked my curiosity in the beginning. It's strange, seeing those familiar details of him up close, while his voice and expressions are so different and new.

I'm tempted to ask about his tattoo right away, but this moment feels too fragile to rock just yet. So instead, I ask a question I've wondered about from the beginning. 'Why did you decide to post that message? The first one?'

He observes me for a while before he answers, his eyes still. The directness almost makes me forget we're looking at each other through a shrub. 'I had a tough day. I'd seen you move in and – I don't know, I thought you might understand.' He shakes his head. 'That came out creepy, didn't it? I wasn't stalking you, I wasn't trying to be weird…'

His self-conscious apology makes my heart swell – I couldn't be mad at him if I tried because I did the same thing too, didn't I?

'I saw you, too,' I say, stopping him mid-flow.

He blinks. 'You did?'

'Your cat, first. The day before I moved in, when I was decorating. And then when w— I moved in.' A furious flush burns my cheeks. Who sounds like the pervy stalker now? Too late to take it back. 'Not all of you, just your arm. You were stroking Ernie and I noticed…' Okay, time to ask. I've dug enough of a hole already. 'Your tattoo, you have a tattoo on your left arm. What is it?'

The eucalyptus eyes are smiling again. 'Which one?'

I'm as red as my trainers now. So much for playing this cool. 'The one that goes from your elbow round your forearm.'

I see him glance down at his left arm, twisting it to look as if he's forgotten what's inked there. 'It's part of a larger one – here—' He pulls up the sleeve of his white T-shirt to reveal a labyrinth of intricate patterns and lines covering his bicep.

'Oh, wow…'

'But the lower one is a quote. From Maya Angelou. It says…' He stops and peers through the gap at me as if working out if I'll approve or not. 'You can read it yourself.'

Suddenly, his arm is through the cat-sized hole in the hedge, his hand outstretched, his fingers curling a little over his palm.

And then, I'm touching his skin…

I don't even think about it: it just happens.

Live as though life was created for you – Maya Angelou,' I read, my voice a shaken whisper.

Lachie's skin is warm, so much warmer than I imagined.

I'm aware of my pulse in my fingertips and padding at my throat.

And then I am in two places at once. I'm standing behind myself, shocked to see my fingers tracing the gentle curls of the words inked around his forearm, formed by twists of dark-outlined ivy, each leaf coloured deep green and white, watching my lips mouth the words as I read them. And I'm in my body, feeling the softness of his skin beneath my fingers, the slight rise of the design, the sudden lack of breath in my lungs…

Chapter Thirty-One

LACHLAN

I can't speak.

I have to think about breathing.

I just watch… and feel… and wonder how the hell we got here.

I don't know what I was thinking giving Bethan my arm, only that it was easier for her to see the ink than me trying to describe it. Did I want her to touch me? I didn't even consider it at the time, but now…

Now it's like electricity fizzing across my skin.

I see her lips forming the shapes of the words but I can't hear her voice. I'm staring: I know I am. I can't stop watching her mouth.

I don't want to pull my arm away but I can't stay here indefinitely with it stuck through a hedge. My shoulder is pressed right up against the beech leaves, the prickle of twigs and branches scratching my forehead. I leaned further than I intended so she could get a good view of the tattoo but now my body is twisted at a strange angle, my leg beginning to burn as the shooting stick starts to sink into the damp grass.

'It's lovely,' she breathes. The syllables dance in that soft Welsh accent of hers. I thought her name was Welsh, but I'd pretty much decided she wasn't. It's perfect for her. When she speaks, laughter trips through the words. The humour woven through her messages is *there*, magnificently alive. It makes me smile even when she isn't making a joke.

'Thanks,' I reply, wondering if I sound like she'd imagined – if she had imagined my voice at all.

'You should probably take your hand back, sorry,' she says. She curls her fingers over mine to close them over my palm, as if she's hidden something precious beneath them, and gently pushes my arm back to me.

It's the gentlest, most tender act.

And if I weren't sitting down right now it would take my feet from under me.

'Why did you choose that quote?'

It's always a weird question when someone asks me about my inks. Why did I choose any of the words and images I carry on my skin? I've had some of them for so long I can hardly remember what inspired them, let alone why they mattered to me at the time. I don't mind Bethan asking, though. After what just happened she can ask whatever she wants. 'My mum gave me a book of Maya Angelou quotes. I liked the words of this one.'

'Did it hurt?'

Another question I'm used to. 'Well, yeah, a bit. You get used to it.'

She gives a laugh that sounds a bit shaky. I wonder if she's still reeling a little, like I am? 'I couldn't do it, but I love seeing other people's tattoos.'

'It's a personal thing. You either do it or you don't. Would you ever be tempted?'

'No. Fake ones, maybe. I had a friend in college who did these amazing henna tattoos. We'd all have them done before the holidays if we were going to summer gigs or festivals. But those don't hurt, so that's probably why I liked them.'

'So that was in Wales?'

'Yep. Back in the day.'

'I like your accent.'

'*Diolch.*'

I peer at her. 'What?'

She shakes her head and I see she's a little flushed. Heaven knows what I look like – my face feels as red as a stoplight. 'It's *thank you* in Welsh.'

'You speak Welsh?'

'Funnily enough. Do you speak English?'

I could kick myself if it were possible without face-planting in the grass. 'I'm sorry, that was a dumb question.'

She peers back at me and grins. 'That's not the worst I've heard. Usually it's *Do you keep sheep? Are you Charlotte Church's cousin? Can you say the place with the crazy long Welsh name?*'

It's too tempting. 'Can you?'

'Probably. Being Welsh. What's the longest English place name, eh? Can you say that?'

This is perfect. There are times in life where the exact random piece of information you've inexplicably stored away in your brain becomes the most important thing you know. This is one of those moments, sitting by a hedge in my communal garden, talking to a beautiful woman who thinks she has the upper hand. I thank the universe for one snippet of pub quiz trivia

I've known for years but never had the chance to use until right now. 'Hyphenated or not hyphenated?'

She stares at me. Her eyes are a bright blue, sparkling now. 'Does it make a difference?'

'Well, that depends if you live in Cottonshopeburnfoot in Northumberland, which is nineteen letters and no hyphen, or Sutton-under-Whitestonecliffe over near Thirsk, which has two hyphens and twenty-seven letters.'

'You are kidding me.'

'Look it up.'

Bethan laughs, a real belly laugh this time. 'How the hell do you know that?'

'Pub quiz question I learned in Germany, of all places.' Hang on: should I tell her I'm in the army? Will she want to know why I'm here and at home so much? It's too early to say, so I quickly add: 'I worked over there for a while.'

'Impressive.'

I feel the fun begin to sparkle around us again and decide to push my luck. 'Not as impressive as you saying yours.'

'Mine?'

'Yep.'

'Oh you mean Llanfair PG?'

'Nice try.'

Her face is the picture of innocence. 'Or Llanfairpwll. I mean, it's called both locally.'

'The full name. Unless you can't...'

That does it. 'I was practically born saying it.'

'Saying *what*?'

She rolls her eyes.

'Llanfairpwllgwyngyllgogerychwyrndrobwllllantysilio-gogogoch.'

Awesome. Bethan rocks. But I'm not done... 'Sorry, didn't catch that?'

She squares up to me, brows low over those stunning blue eyes, and repeats, slowly, '*Llanfairpwllgwyngyllgogerychwyrndrob-wllllantysiliogogogoch.*'

For a second, I forget to smile. Or breathe.

One of her eyebrows rises. 'That the one you wanted?'

Hell, yes.

'How many letters is that?'

'You're the King of the Pub Quiz, you tell me.'

Now she's got me. 'Um...'

'That'll be fifty-eight and a win for me, I think?'

We grin at each other through the hedge window.

'Could you teach me to say it?'

She shrugs. 'Depends.'

'On what?'

'On whether you want to do this again?'

Wow. There was I trying to work out how to broach the subject and Bethan just knocked it out of the park. 'Yes, I do. If you do?'

'Only if you bring biscuits next time.'

That cheekiness will be my undoing. 'Bourbons?'

'Get stuffed. Hobnobs or nothing.'

'Done. Shake on it?' I put my hand back through the hedge and she takes it. It's a perfect fit. I hold on for a moment longer than I dare. 'I'm so glad we met today.'

'Me too. Will you be here next Thursday? Same time?'

'Don't you work?' That was too forward, despite our hands being still linked. 'I'm sorry, I mean...'

'I work at a garden centre usually,' she rushes. 'But Thursdays I work from home.'

That explains the early message last week, our sudden sighting of each other – and why she's here now. 'Perfect. I work from home, too, so that would be good.'

Reluctantly, our hold releases and our fingers drift apart. 'Like this?'

Am I ready for her to see me without this barrier between us? I wish I were, but everything that's just happened – our confidence, our flirting, the playfulness of what we said – did so because I felt safe. I think Bethan felt safe, too.

'It could be fun, don't you think?'

Please say yes…

I watch her expression for signs of disappointment, but there aren't any. Her eyes are as bright, her smile as wide as before I asked.

'I think it could. I mean, it's weird, but kind of cool.'

'I'll take that.'

'Good. I should probably…' She nods towards her window.

'Yep. Me too.'

'So, you bring the Hobnobs, I'll bring the tea – coffee?'

'I'm happy with either.'

Bethan smiles. 'Okay.' She turns to leave, but then returns to the hedge window. 'What do we do about the window signs?'

I hadn't considered that. This has been great – *wonderful* – but her messages have meant so much, too. I don't know how I'd feel to be without them for the sake of another single meeting with her. 'I really like your messages.'

'I like yours. Love them, actually.' She brushes her fingers across her forehead. 'How about one message each, once a day? Say, evening time?'

'Perfect.'

'See you, Lachie.'

'See you soon, Bethan.'

I wait until she's gone before I try to move. I want to get back inside before she reaches her flat, so I don't run the risk of her seeing me from the window, but I can't move until I know she's inside her building. If she caught sight of my walk looking through gaps in the hedge, all my good work would be undone.

Everything aches as I put my weight on my good leg, folding up the seat of the shooting stick and pulling it up from where it had sunk into the grass. But I don't care.

I feel alive. As if Bethan has sent her energy powering through my veins. I thought we would get on, but I never expected this.

I hear the bang of her building door closing and take my cue to move. Using my seat gadget as a support, I walk stiffly back.

Two expectant faces greet me on the threshold when I enter my flat. The place itself seems to be waiting, too.

'It was good,' I say.

One tail wags, another flicks impatiently. My housemates couldn't care less what just happened. Unless whoever I was with sent food for them. I reach down and stroke them both.

'Thanks for asking.'

As they scuttle after me into the kitchen, I feel on top of the world. My leg remains to be impressed and I'll probably suffer for my extended garden sit later. But it doesn't matter. What could have been a total disaster and the end of the friendship I'd begun with Bethan has become the start of something brand new.

Real.

Vital.

Tangible.

The way she touched me… The laughter in her voice. Our unlikely flirting over biscuits and comically long place names. All of it, every moment, *perfect*.

I love it.

I catch sight of my reflection in the double oven door. I hardly recognise the man smiling back. Bethan did that.

I love that she did.

I could love *her*…

Chapter Thirty-Two

BETHAN

I'm still shaking.

It's Friday afternoon and Darren is being more of an arse than usual. But all I can think about is Lachie.

I thought we'd get on. I hoped it would be fun. But I never expected *him*.

Who am I kidding? I'm crazy about him.

'And another thing, while you were off farting about on the company's time, I was left to deal with bonkers old women asking for you.'

'For me?'

'Something about emails?'

Oh, result! 'Who were they? Did they say where they were from?'

Darren observes me like a sack of rotting manure. 'How the hell should I know?'

'Sorry. I've been contacting local community groups as part of this project for Hattie, asking if they'd like to get involved.'

The mention of Hattie and the project is a mistake. I know it the moment I see my manager's expression. 'Are you taking the pee? We need funding for this place, not bake sales and knitting.'

'Right, I mean we're working on that…'

'Oh, you are? Would that be you and your co-workers Sky TV and McDonald's?'

I let it slide. I am friends with a gorgeous neighbour who is cheeky as all get out but has the softest skin on his arms and the loveliest smile… Darren can say what he wants to me today and it won't matter. I am impervious. I am a duck in a mackintosh. It's all just going to *slide* right off me… 'So, did they leave their details?'

'They tried.'

Crap. 'What did you do?'

'I don't like this attitude, Bethan. I think maybe I should have a word with Hattie, tell her how your *extracurricular activities* are affecting your work.'

I keep my nerve steady. 'What did they look like?'

'Old. Female. Tits to their knees.'

'Okay, there's no need for that.'

He holds up both hands like I've just threatened to griddle them. 'Does nobody have a sense of humour these days? You can't joke about anything without some screaming liberal snowflake wagging her finger…' Seeing my stare, he relents a little. 'I think they said WI. I don't know which one.'

'Thank you, Darren.'

It's not much and it could be any one of eight WI groups I've emailed. It's a good development that someone responded, but moves me no further on.

I just have to hope they get back in touch.

The morning passes surprisingly quickly as I tackle the

ever-growing mountain of jobs Darren has given me. Most of them involve heavy lifting, it seems, or pointlessly moving one set of plants from one side of the nursery to the other. Patrick is busy helping Eric in the polytunnels today, continuing his education about propagating plants from cuttings and seeds. I miss our banter, but I like having my own space to work in, especially with my current frame of mind.

There are a few more people about, which is promising. The sun we've had over the last few days might just have got them all dreaming of barbecues and outside gatherings. Murray is building a 'barbecue garden' in one of our three tiny courtyard plots that face the café windows – plants and colours and shapes inspired by a summer barbecue. There's a row of russet red heucheras in a square of spiky *Ophiopogon planiscapus* black mondo grass to look like sausages on a grill over barbecue coals, a small cast-iron table with white gerberas to look like plates, and tiny potted blue, pink and lilac lobelia plants in plastic wine glasses to look like an alfresco tipple. It's a bit of a cheesy idea but he's made it look amazing.

I'd love to get my hands on one of those display gardens. No idea what I'd do with one, but it would be bright and wild and joyous, the way working with living things makes me feel.

I often catch myself wondering what the gardens of our customers look like. Are they all stripy lawns and immaculate flowerbeds, or are they more like Mam's with her crappy Astroturf and plastic flower displays? I don't reckon it matters as long as you like looking at it. So many people don't have gardens these days, so even if you have a square of green you'd have difficulty swinging a hamster around, let alone a cat, I think you should love it and enjoy it.

I look at the trays of bright, jewel-coloured bear's ear primulas in my trolley. If I put a row of these along the line of the hedge, it would transform that strip of shared garden. I'd thought about that when I moved in, I remember now, but like so many other things it got lost in the stack of jobs filling my head.

And then, the idea comes.

I could brighten my side of the hedge.

And maybe I could get Lachie to plant his side, too.

I stifle a little squeal that arrives. That would be perfect. There's only so long we can stand by a hedge talking about biscuits. But if we use that time to do something nice for our neighbours *while* we're talking, it then becomes something lasting and beautiful.

A gift from us to the gardens we share. Proof we were there…

Hattie, thankfully, loves the idea. I order what I think will be enough to run the length of the hedge with a few over in case my calculations are wrong. But when I discuss paying for them, Hattie won't hear of it.

'We have a fund for community projects that never gets used,' she tells me, later that afternoon, as we do our by now usual circuit, takeaway teas in hand. 'It can come from that.'

'But I'm supposed to be making Bright Hill money, not spending it.'

'We don't include that in the profits anyway. Besides, it's tax deductible if it's donated to good causes.'

'It's a hedge border in the garden by my building,' I smile. 'Hardly a good cause.'

'How many flats are there?'

'Six.'

'And, what, two people per flat?'

'Probably more. I know there's a family of four on the top floor.'

'Well, there you go, then. Your community will benefit,' she says, her hand making a wide sweep of the nursery beds as if she's displaying her entire kingdom. I picture her as Mufasa from Noah's favourite DVD of *The Lion King*, which I suppose makes me Simba.

'I'll take pictures of it, for the website.'

She beams. 'You do that. Actually, I was going to suggest that we invest a little in order to make a return.'

'I don't know what that means.'

'The project you're putting together for me – providing the costs aren't prohibitive, I thought maybe I could give you access to the Community Fund and you can dip into it if you need to do publicity, go and do a plant demonstration somewhere, that sort of thing.'

That's one heck of a responsibility. 'Oh, I don't know about that…'

'Run what you need past me. But it's best you have access to the funds directly, or else every decision will take a week just to jump through all the hoops of me, the accountant, the bank…'

We've reached the scar of derelict land beside Eric's shed now. I turn to look at the site and glance at Hattie who is clearly very pleased with her idea. My nerves are building, but I can't tell her why. 'But I can get your approval first? On everything?'

'Of course. I'll give you written confirmation if you want, so there's a paper trail.' Her mind is set, it seems.

'Okay. But I will check every little thing.'

Hattie laughs, a tinkling fountain of a sound that could charm a smile from a stone statue. 'I have no doubt you will. Just – find something soon, yes?'

There's no mistaking her meaning. Stomach twisting, I drink my tea.

Chapter Thirty-Three

LACHLAN

It's today.

I don't care that I'm ridiculously excited about sitting by a hedge. I've been looking forward to Thursday all week.

We've done the night-time, daytime sweet messages in our windows like we agreed – and they've been good as always. But it doesn't feel as thrilling as it did before. Not compared with what happened when we met.

I swear my arm is still tingling from where she touched it.

And yes, I know I said *tingling*, but that's what Bethan's done to me. What the memory of her touch is still doing to me…

Bert gives me a quizzical look from the sofa, Sock dangling between his paws. It's a good job dogs aren't mind readers. He'd be horrified with me. If Ernie senses anything, he's saying nothing. Let them think what they like. A woman hasn't had this effect on me for a long time, so I'm going to enjoy it.

It takes an age to reach lunchtime but finally it arrives. I make my way down to the garden ten minutes early, positioning my shooting stick seat close to the hedge in case Bethan looks out to check I'm there before she comes down. I'm nervous now, suddenly aware that I should have thought of things to talk to her about. Last time our conversation flowed effortlessly, but was that because of the shock of it? Or the novelty? Will a repeat performance lack the magic of last time?

Just before 1 p.m. I hear the bang of her building door closing and the *swoosh* of approaching feet through the grass. I don't know if the same chap who's meant to cut our building's grass is contracted to cut Bethan's side, but I reckon the building managers need to find someone new. It's damp today after last night's rain. The hems of my jeans are soaked already and my leather trainers catch the light where the moisture has gathered on the toes.

If this turns out to be as good as I hope, I will probably be sitting out here in snow, storms, hail and high winds – because to miss one chance to talk to Bethan would be worse than enduring anything the weather could throw at me. Maybe I should get one of those red-and-white-striped tents the telephone company workmen erect beside junction boxes. Perfect for all-weather hedge chatting.

'He-llo?' Her voice is a two-note melody that blows away every other thought in my mind.

'Hi,' I reply, peering through the hedge hole.

Her smile fills the space on the other side. My life, she's lovely. 'I'm a bit late, sorry.'

'You're not late,' I say. 'Now, important question…'

'So soon? You don't hang about.'

I grin and pick up the bag at my feet, lifting it so she can see. 'Coffee or tea?'

Two lines appear between her brows. 'That's the important question?'

The fun is there immediately, sparking between us. I needn't have worried: this *works*. 'Well, you're the biscuit guru, you tell me.'

'What are you going on about?'

'*Dunkability*. Key consideration in determining the perfect biscuit. Am I right?'

She laughs, her hair dancing about her face. She has a beautiful face… 'I stand corrected. Good work, student.'

I doff an imaginary cap. 'Thanks, Miss.'

She returns my smile but then it vanishes. 'I was supposed to bring the drinks, wasn't I?'

'I couldn't remember what we said, so I brought both.'

'Oh, *man*, I'm so sorry! I completely forgot!' Her hands cover her eyes.

'It's no problem, honestly. You can bring them next time, if you like.'

She peers at me through her fingers. 'I feel such an idiot. Remind me, okay?'

'Message in the window?'

That summons her smile back where it should be. 'Perfect.'

More than a little pleased with myself, I bring two flasks out of the bag. 'So, I have tea, coffee and Hobnobs. Chocolate ones, by the way.'

'Great work. You're hired. And coffee would be nice.'

'Coffee it is.'

I hook the carrier bag over one arm and unscrew the flask cap. It's a bit precarious doing this while balancing on a not-very-stable shooting stick in damp ground, but I pour it without causing myself a minor injury and pass the cup through the hedge to her.

Her fingers brush mine when they meet in the middle and I have to force my leg against the ground to stay upright.

'Milk?' I ask, aware of the slight tremor in my voice. This was a blinding idea. Any excuse for contact – and the reward of her touch on my skin.

She cradles her cup on the other side of the hedge as I twist the cap off a small bottle of milk and pass it through to her. This time, I swear she holds my fingers for a moment before she takes the bottle. I wait like an eager puppy for her to pass it back, heart thumping now.

'Sugar?'

'Please.'

I played safe with sugar packets for this but that touch is just as disconcerting. As we pull our hands back to our respective sides, we're both a little flushed. I think I can safely say that is the most exciting cup of coffee I've ever shared...

'I did bring something...' she says.

'You did?'

'Yep. Hang on...'

She ducks down and when she returns she's holding a small black plant pot. In it is a flowering plant I recognise from some of the ornamental flowerbeds in the local park. Couldn't tell you what it is, of course. The thought of my first ever question to her makes me warm inside. I picked the right person to ask about the flowers in her window, considering what she does for a living..

'Nice. Is that for me?' I ask, suddenly concerned. I've never really had any plants and my chances of keeping one alive are not promising. If she expects me to put it in my window and I kill it, that's not going to endear me to her.

'In a manner of speaking.' Her gaze holds mine for a moment

before she speaks, as if she's trying to see my answer behind my eyes first. 'Okay, feel free to say no, but I had an idea. I'd like to do something for my building – for everyone to enjoy. So I'm going to plant a line of these along the length of the hedge. Make a border, space them out, to give a bit of colour to anyone coming out here. It's so nice to have any kind of garden and I just want to make it lovely for everyone, if I can.'

'Wow, that's… I think that's great. Where do I come into it?'

Please don't ask me to come and join you on that side…

'I wondered if you'd like to join in… On your side,' she adds quickly, just as I'm braced for the worst. Not that it would be the worst to be closer to her, just not until my leg is better. I don't want anything to break the spell here and I need to be sure of her before she knows the truth.

All the same, it presents a problem. Planting means kneeling down, doesn't it? There's no way I can do that yet. I could sit on the ground and twist, but that might do more damage than kneeling.

'I'd love to,' I answer anyway. I'll cross that bridge when I come to it. She's clearly so excited by the idea and I don't want to say no to her. 'I don't have any tools or anything.'

'No problem, I brought you a trowel.'

I jump, as an ancient-looking garden implement appears my side of the hedge hole. 'Where did you get that from?'

'A friend at work. He's the oldest employee and totally rocks. You'd like him. Eric reckons the older the tool, the more wisdom it possesses.'

'Judging by the state of this I would say it's *very* wise.' I can't stop my laughter. This would be the most impossibly random conversation already if we were standing side by side. As it is – taking place through a cat-sized gap in a hedge – it's hilarious.

'Okay, maybe it has character, then.' She's peering at me through the gap and I wonder if I've offended her. 'But, you know, only do it if you fancy it.'

'I do,' I rush, because doing anything with Bethan is an instant *yes*, regardless of how logistically challenging it might be. I'm already thinking about how I could manage it. If I put my bad leg straight out and used the shooting stick to support me as I crouch down with the other, might that work? I can't very well lie flat in the grass, which is the other option. I'll just have to give it a go. I want to try for her.

'Great. Coffee first, though. Get our priorities straight. And where are those Hobnobs?'

As we talk and laugh and *definitely* flirt and share biscuits – okay, I admit, she might be right about chocolate Hobnobs – I know I'm signing up for everything with her. I should be worried about how fast this is progressing. I haven't been this invested in someone else before, not even Jenny, and I thought I was head over heels for her in the beginning. Is it too much, too soon? I don't think so. Should I be this thrilled by being with her? Why not?

It's like a long intake of fresh air after hours in a windowless room. I'm surprised by it, but it's as natural as breathing at the same time. How is that possible?

And yet I know how precarious it all is. One wrong move, one misunderstanding, one step taken too soon could have it crashing down around us.

That's what makes it so exciting – and dangerous. And why I'm determined to protect it, no matter what.

Now all I need to do is work out how the hell I'm going to plant a line of flowers along my side of the hedge…

Chapter Thirty-Four

BETHAN

I don't take sugar.

Can't stand it in drinks, actually.

But I wanted to touch his hand again.

Is that bad? Yeah, probably. But it was worth it...

'So you just push the soil around the base?'

'Yes. The way you're doing it is great.'

'You might want to ask the plant that.'

I laugh. 'It's fine. Make a nice hole, pop it in, tuck it up and it's happy.'

'You make it sound easy.'

'It is easy.'

'When it's you. I reckon you scare the plants to grow...'

'Oi, watch it!'

'See what I mean? Scary!' He chuckles, the sound warm by my ear as we start to plant the next. 'Okay, not scary. Authoritative.'

'Not sure that sounds much better.'

'Maybe I like authoritative. Maybe I enjoy you telling me what to do...'

Lachie has a very odd way of getting himself to the ground to plant the primulas, I notice. Quickly, I stop looking, in case he thinks I'm judging him. He's never done this before, so I guess he's working it out as he goes. And if the grass his side is longer than on mine it's not surprising he doesn't want to kneel in it.

I keep checking he's okay with each new plant I pass him though the gap, but he insists he's fine. All the same, I can hear him huffing and puffing the other side of the hedge so I've slowed down a little. I forget how easy this is for me.

'Have you ever done any gardening before?' I ask, pressing cold soil around the base of a bright red bear's ear primula. Through the knot of trunks and branches beneath the hedge, I can see his hand doing the same. There are no inks on his fingers, but I can see a long red scar across the knuckles of his left hand. It looks nasty and recent. I almost ask him how it happened but pull back at the last minute. It feels too personal a question.

'Never. I've always lived in places without gardens, or with communal gardens someone else looks after.'

'Even when you were a kid?'

He laughs. His hand turns into a fist and disappears into the long grass as he pushes himself upright. I hear a low grunt of effort and the tendons in his forearm tense, and then his arm lifts up out of sight. 'I was born on a farm, so we didn't have much call for gardening.'

I jump to my feet, clapping soil from my hands as I follow his voice slowly moving back to the hedge gap. Through the beech leaves I'm granted tantalising glimpses of him: the curve of his shoulder, the roll of his bicep where he's pushed the sleeve of his T-shirt up, the glimpse of a smile on his profiled face. I'm staring – of course I am. It's the most delicious view.

'Where were you born?' I ask. 'You don't sound like you come from Yorkshire.'

'Cotswolds. Near Bourton-on-the-Water. My folks own a holiday let company there.' His smile meets me at the hedge window. There's the loveliest flush across his cheeks now that makes his blue-green eyes sparkle.

'Nice part of the world, that.'

'It is. I've lived all over, though. But the last eight years have been here. How about you?'

As always, I edit my history to avoid unwanted questions. Except the difference this time is the pang of guilt that accompanies my well-rehearsed reply. Why is that there? I don't want to tell him everything. Do I?

'I grew up in Maentwrog in Gwynedd then my family moved near Cardiff when I was eleven. I came up here about five years ago. I like Yorkshire. It feels most like home now.'

'For me, too.'

'So, you wouldn't be tempted to go back to the Cotswolds?'

'Not really.' His eyes meet mine. 'I mean, who would teach me about biscuits if I left?'

Okay, Mr Cute Next Door Neighbour, you can have bonus points for that answer…

His smile could get me into all kinds of trouble. I wonder what he thinks of mine?

'Have you always done the gardening thing?'

'No, actually. I kind of fell into it.'

'Like Ernie did with the hedge.' He's too fast.

'I like to think I did it with a bit more dignity.'

He shrugs. 'He styled it out, eventually. Didn't go near the hedge for a good six months afterwards, though.'

'Poor Ernie.' I look along the line of primulas I've planted, stretching from the start of the hedge facing the main road and travelling all the way to my feet. Like a path of colour, leading to us. I misjudged the amount of plants we'd need so I'll have to continue next week, but what I've achieved looks striking. What *we've* achieved.

'So, what I want to know is, how do you work from home when you work in a garden centre?'

I'm not expecting this question, so it throws me for a moment. The pause extends longer than I want it to and I see Lachie's smile tighten.

'Sorry. That was really intrusive. You don't have to answer.'

'No, it's okay,' I reply, hoping the words I need will arrive in time. 'It's a new thing, so I'm still getting my head round it. My boss – Hattie, she owns the nursery – she's asked me to come up with ways of raising funds for the business.' I pause, unsure whether to say more. But it's Lachie, and the way he's watching me, like every word matters to him, makes up my mind. 'The business is in trouble. I'm supposed to be finding potential funding.'

'Sorry to hear that. It's tough for businesses right now.'

I nod, brushing a clod of earth from the back of my gardening glove. 'I'm still working out what to suggest.'

'You'll come up with something,' he says. And when he says it, I can believe it. 'I mean, you've got me planting flowers and I am the very last person anyone would expect to have a go at that.'

I like his faith in me. But then I like everything about Lachie. I grin back through the hedge hole.

'Thanks.'

'You're welcome.'

I remember something I picked up, when we were planting the first few primulas. 'I have something else for you,' I say, reaching into the back pocket of my jeans where I stowed it earlier. Lachie waits by the hedge window, his eyes intent on me. It's so delicious I'm tempted to string it out a bit, just to bask in that gaze...

'Give us your hand, then.' He does as he's told and I carefully place the small quartz pebble in the warmth of his palm.

He frowns when he pulls his hand back. 'A pebble. Um, thanks?'

So cheeky.

'It's not just a pebble. Well, it *is*, but to me it means a lot more.' When it's clear he doesn't follow, I press on. 'Every day, I look for something positive. Some days I can only find the smallest thing – like that pebble. So I hang onto it. Carry it with me. See it as a promise of bigger treasure up ahead.'

I can't read his expression.

'Thanks,' he says again, but this time it isn't mocking me. There's a depth to the word that I can't fathom yet. 'Can I keep this?'

'It's yours. To start your collection.'

We share smiles.

I want to stay right here, but I have to get back to the Bright Hill stuff. I'd said three weeks to Hattie to test working from home and this is my third week. Have I done enough? I wasn't sure in the beginning, but now I have Thursdays with Lachie, I don't want it to end. I have to get things moving for Hattie's project to protect my Lachie time.

Lachie time. I look down at the rows of newly planted flowers to hide my blush. 'That's all the plants for now. I'll get more for next week, if that's okay?'

Lachie raises an eyebrow. 'Oh, so we're meeting again next week?'

I match his impertinent grin with my own. 'Be a shame to leave a job half-finished, don't you think?'

'Very true.' He looks down for a moment and when his eyes return to me the cheekiness is gone. 'I've loved this. Planting stuff, I mean. It feels like an achievement.'

'It is an achievement. Planting living things always is.'

'That's what I'm trying to say, very badly. Do you ever wonder what mark you leave where you are? Like, if you disappeared tomorrow, what would remain to show people you existed? I've thought about that a lot, lately.' He rubs his forehead with his thumb. It leaves a light streak of soil across his brow. 'Sorry, far too deep.'

'No it isn't,' I say, because the air has suddenly stilled between us and his soft voice is speaking straight to my heart. 'I think about that a lot, too...'

Because I have a son...

I blink.

Because I have a son. His name is Noah...

No. Not yet. I can't risk it...

He's staring at me now. I can see the gentle rise of his collarbone beneath his T-shirt. 'Planting those flowers, it feels like I'm leaving something for the world to see. A legacy.'

'That's beautiful.'

'You stole my words.'

Now he's stolen mine.

It's only a moment. But there's a shift between us. Like we've moved closer, despite the distance.

It's broken abruptly by the loud bass thud of music as a car speeds by on the road. We share self-conscious laughter and I check my watch. 'I need to get back. Thanks – for helping.'

'Thanks for asking, Bethan. Hold on...' Eric's trusty trowel appears in the hedge hole. When I take it, Lachie's hand twists over mine, his thumb moving in a slow, deliberate stroke across my knuckle and down my fingers.

Bloody hell, I'm in trouble...

All afternoon I work on the Bright Hill project – more emails sent, calls to three local businesses gaining a spark of interest if not actual hard cash and my ever-growing list of potential avenues lengthening with the day's shadows that move across the floor.

Behind all my activity, an idea is forming. It began in that breathless moment when I felt Lachie opening up.

It feels like I'm leaving something for the world to see...

'A legacy,' I say aloud.

A legacy.

What if the project we established looked beyond the immediate future of the nursery? What if it forged links with the local community that became a way of life – a long-term commitment that binds Bright Hill with its nearest residents?

That's what Hector established the nursery for, sixty years ago. Hattie always refers to his original idea, scribbled on the back of an envelope that she still has, framed, in her office.

Not just a nursery.
A place that grows with its community.

What if the community grew with Bright Hill?

Adrenalin pumping, I open the search engine on my creaky laptop and search for 'community growing schemes', 'gardening co-operatives', 'community gardening projects' and even 'guerrilla gardeners'. Page after page of results light up the screen. I work through them, the memory of Lachie's voice and the stillness when he spoke weaving through photos of happy community gardeners, aerial shots of transformed village greens and city centre planters teeming with edible crops.

And then I find the perfect photo. It's in a school garden, but the proud gardeners posing with their homegrown carrots, tomatoes and armfuls of flowers are young and old, from many walks of life. And beside them is a line of four raised beds, each about eight feet long by four feet wide. Some have been painted with stripes of bright wood-stain; others bear the more traditional fence colours of brown and dark blue.

I print off the picture and furiously scribble notes down for fear that the brilliant new idea will fly straight out of my head if I don't record it.

What if we built a series of raised beds on the disused former shed and summerhouse plot and invited local schools and community groups to adopt one? We could grow through the summer and in the autumn have a big flower show, where friends and family could come to see the results of the gardens.

It's piecing together as I write and print and research. This could work! We could offer local businesses the chance to spon-sor a raised bed, with incentives if they pay for plants and maybe tool packs from the garden centre. We could put an advert on the side of each bed, so the gardeners know who has sponsored their plot – that could encourage business back to them, too. Everybody benefits. What's not to love about that?

It might not solve all Bright Hill's problems. But it would raise our profile in the area and link us with local groups and businesses, who may then prove to be more loyal to us as customers.

We could call it the Bright Hill Legacy – in honour of Hector's original dream. Taking the nursery back to its original vision. I think Hattie will love that.

None of the big, corporate-owned garden centres round here do anything for the local community, bar occasional 10 per cent discount vouchers in the free papers. We could buck the trend – be different.

It would be a hell of a lot of work.

It might bomb spectacularly.

But it's the best idea I'm going to have.

I spread out my notes across the kitchen counter, my heart going ten to the dozen. Time to call Hattie and tell her my plan.

I couldn't imagine ever dreaming up something like this before, or daring to believe myself capable of organising it. But as I've moulded this idea, I realise I haven't once questioned my own ability to lead it.

I feel like anything is possible.

And I have Lachie to thank for it.

Chapter Thirty-Five

LACHLAN

It's chucking it down today. We had a power cut this morning that lasted two hours. My date for testifying to the crash inquiry came through. And Bert and Ernie have been on the brink of war all day.

None of it touches me.

One glance out of the window makes everything all right.

My first flower border stretches towards me from the road and where it ends makes me smile more than all the tiny, brave flowers facing the onslaught of rain. Because that's where I meet Bethan. Next Thursday the border will be completed, an unbroken line of colour beneath my window to the car park beyond. But I like how it is now. Our place.

The place where she touched me...

Reluctantly, I drag my thoughts back to the flowers.

My flowers. That I planted. Who would have seen that coming? A month ago I'd have laughed away the suggestion. What do I know about gardening? Why should it interest me? I'm still not mentioning it to anyone else, though. Some secrets are worth keeping. And anyway, they wouldn't understand.

It was a challenge to make it possible and I'm certain Bethan noticed how long it took me to get down to the ground each time. But I found a way – a painful one, but still a way that worked. And it's got me thinking about what else I could achieve.

Tanya remarked on it this morning during our session. I've made good progress lately but today I managed three stretches I haven't been able to before.

'What's happened to you?'

'What do you mean?' I'd replied, my heart swelling.

'Did Popeye lend you some spinach?' she'd grinned back. 'Excellent work. Keep it up now, please.'

I intend to.

I can't stop thinking about Bethan – well, generally – but especially about how she dealt with my slowness when we were planting. She said nothing, but I noticed her slow her pace to mine. I watched her slim fingers wait patiently by the soil until I'd finished planting each flower; heard her voice rise to standing height only after I'd stood. Without making an issue of it, she accommodated me.

I love that she did that. But I don't want her to have to wait for me to move. So, I'm going to work until I can meet her pace. Until I can meet her where she is. No barriers. No secrets.

I have a focus now, strengthening with every day. I'm going to work until I can walk around the hedge and approach her. When the physio sessions are tough, I picture me walking to her side. And taking her in my arms. And never once thinking about how she sees me.

A notification bell sounds on my laptop and I move from the window to sit at the table. The video call connects and goes through its camera and microphone checks and then I am face to face with my commanding officer.

'Ah, afternoon, Wallace. We meet at last.'

'Apologies, sir. The power was out for two hours.'

'Same here. Power went about twenty minutes after you reported it. Bloody annoying. I don't know what the damn electricity bods are playing at. We've only just re-established power to the mess hall. Four hundred starving soldiers does not a happy garrison make.'

I can imagine. Two things you never get in the way of with a soldier: their food and their bunk. Multiply that by four hundred and you have a potential mutiny on your hands. 'All sorted now, though?'

Archer nods, taking a sip from the plain white mug on his desk. I know it will contain the strongest coffee in the Western World: five spoonfuls of instant coffee, two of sugar and a solitary drop of milk, a brew he lovingly refers to as 'mud'.

'Yes, for now. Got the back-up gennies on standby, just in case. Not risking blackout again. So, I expect you've had the summons?'

'It arrived this morning, sir.'

'Ah. Excellent. And how are you—' he tests the word warily on his tongue before deploying it, '—*feeling* about the process?'

I bury my smile. 'Good, sir.'

'Glad to hear it. I just thought it wise to mention that you will be asked about the accident in some detail. Uncomfortable detail. You should be aware of that.'

My stomach twists and I can't tell if it's the prospect of presenting our edited version of events or speaking about the accident for the first time. 'I am, sir. Thank you.'

'Don't mention it. Relying on you to do the right thing, Wallace.'

That pulls me up short. What does he mean? 'Sir.'

'Excellent. Right, I'll leave you to it. We've been fortunate enough to keep power thus far, best not push our luck today, eh?'

Pushing my luck. He doesn't know the half of it.

I wish I could talk to someone not connected to the crash before I have to give evidence to the inquiry team. But everyone has a vested interest already – apart from Bethan – and there the interest invested is mine. If I tell her about the crash, I'd have to tell her everything: my injury, what really happened, what Riggsy's decided is our best version of events. I suspect she'd take a dim view of me not giving the whole truth to the investigating officers. The more I consider it, the dimmer my own view becomes.

One day, when everything is out in the open, I'll go through it all with her. At least, that's what I should do. When the danger's passed will I want to revisit it? I wish the whole thing hadn't happened – the dangerous situation I hauled Riggsy out of; the real reason we crashed the car. I've tried not to think of it but since the argument with him it's played on my mind.

It isn't a surprise when he calls, an hour later. He'll have had his letter today, too. When he asks if he can come over I hesitate because I don't want a repeat performance of his last visit. But we need to talk again now we have a hearing date.

'I got two weeks on Wednesday,' he says, breezing through the door, ignoring the low growl from Bert at my feet. 'How about you?'

'A week on Monday.'

He settles himself on my sofa and opens the carrier bag he's brought with him. 'I brought beer, see?'

It's a surprise, I'll admit. But if he's thinking this absolves him for the scene he made on his last visit – and the radio silence since – he's got a long way to go. 'Cheap stuff, is it?'

He feigns injury. 'Proper expensive German stuff, actually. So you can shut up if you want one.'

'Too early for me,' I reply.

'I told you, staying here is turning you into a geriatric,' he shoots back, taking the cap off a bottle for me anyway and holding it out. I don't want to accept it because I don't trust this unexpected occurrence of hospitality. But beer is beer. He grins victoriously when I take it. 'That's the right response.'

I watch him for a while, Bert's constant growl reverberating against my good leg as my dog leans on it. Still not a care in the world, despite everything. Anyone else would have addressed what happened last time he was here, checked it wasn't a deal-breaker for the friendship, before making themselves at home. Not Adam Riggs.

'Any news from Byrne?' I keep my tone steady, my eyes on him.

There's the slightest flicker. 'Dickhead's not worth my time.'

'That so?'

'Yes. What? You wanted some salacious gossip about him?'

'No. I was thinking an apology would be better.'

He stares at me. 'From Byrne?'

'From you.'

He snorts and looks away, coming face to face with my highly judgemental cat, eyeing him from the sofa arm. 'I wasn't serious, was I? Thought you'd work that out.'

'Seemed pretty serious from where I was standing.'

'All right, princess.'

That's enough. I'm nervous already about the story we're

telling without worrying he'll go off on one again. I need to draw a line under this, now. 'Riggs, you've got to be straight with me, understand? If we're doing this, we have to be together on every detail. I have to know you've got my back in there.'

He turns back slowly, eyes resolutely trained on the floor. 'You know I have.'

I don't answer, keeping my silence until it becomes too uncomfortable for him.

Sure enough: 'All right, I was a dick last time I was here. Pressure getting to me, in't it? Stress, the doctor said.'

'That an apology?'

He shrugs.

Guess that's the closest I'll get.

Chapter Thirty-Six

BETHAN

'Raised beds?'

'Yes.'

'How many?'

'Fifteen?'

'*Fifteen?*'

I look at the rough sketch I'm holding and review my calculations. 'Ten, then?'

Murray, Eric, Patrick and Hattie stare at me, then at the scar of old hardstanding where the shed displays once stood. Can they see the potential like I can? I imagine the beds laid out across this unloved bit of Bright Hill, spaced apart so that groups of volunteer gardeners can reach all round to plant and tend to them. Fifteen is too ambitious: now I'm on the site it's blatantly obvious. But ten would work: it would look impressive and bring in a decent return while the project runs.

The team, however, remain to be convinced.

'What would they grow?'

'Anything they like.'

Eric sucks in air between his teeth. 'Wrong time of year for seeds, if you're after an autumn crop.'

'So, we offer more mature plants that are that bit further along. Like we do currently for our customers.'

'Could be expensive, that.'

'Not if a plant budget is part of the sponsorship deal. And if they choose to continue next year we could take them through the whole growing process, from seed to harvest.' Hattie and Murray exchange glances. They seem impressed, but I'm so nervous I probably wouldn't spot it if they were holding a six-foot banner supporting me. It's happening fast: my call to Hattie yesterday after seeing Lachie led to her immediately calling everyone in early today, practically unheard of on a Friday, which tends to be a slower day at Bright Hill. If they think it can work, we'll prepare today and start construction on Monday. This *has* to work. I don't have a Plan B...

'Would they bring their own tools?' Patrick asks. He's trying his hardest to be supportive but it's clearly a struggle.

'If they want to. But we also offer tool packs at a discount which they might just take up.'

'Might just?' Now it's Hattie's turn to frown.

'*Will do*,' I state, with as much confidence as I can muster. 'Imagine you're working on your plot with old tools, but every day you're here you see your fellow gardeners using their shiny new ones – tools we've made sure you've had to walk past in the main building in order to get out to the Legacy...'

Eric pats a hand against Murray's chest. 'Now that's clever. You've got to admit that.'

I grin at him, pleased I have an ally. 'Not to mention other customers who will see people working away on the community

233

beds. Maybe they'll come up for a chat and see all the lovely new tools they're using. And they might ask where they came from...' I *think* that's a point they can all concede...

It's difficult to tell, to be honest. I know Hattie loves the idea, broadly speaking, but now we're on site talking brass tacks, I can see her wavering a little.

'What if they can't afford new tools? Not everyone has a pot of money.'

I know that only too well. 'We encourage companies sponsoring the raised beds to include tool and plant packages in their sponsorship deal. That way it's a double-benefit for community groups taking part – an investment in the garden plot and the means to tend it, too.'

There are murmurs of assent between them. Then Murray raises his hand, which is completely unnecessary but rather sweet.

'Yes, Murray.'

'What are you thinking of making them out of?'

Ah. 'I was kind of hoping you guys might have an idea. Railway sleepers? Pallets? Wood we buy in?'

'Railway sleepers would be too heavy. Pallets too light. Can't afford the new wood to make ten.' He rubs his chin, looking across the empty site. We all wait, because Murray is like Yoda when it comes to logistics. Best to let him sort it out in his head first, and then blow us away with a completely random solution that always turns out to be brilliant. 'Scaffold boards,' he says, at last.

Patrick frowns. 'Scaffold boards? Er, I don't know how to break this to you, dude, but we don't have any scaffolding. Because we're a *garden centre*.'

'Nursery,' Hattie pipes up. 'Small point, big difference.'

Patrick's mirth fades. 'Right. Sorry.'

'We don't have any scaffolding, Patrick, but we do, as it happens, possess a large stack of scaffolding boards at the back of the loading bay.'

'Where?' I ask Murray, because we have lunch in the loading bay most days and I've never seen any.

'What do you think the Bright Hill Retirement Village is sitting on?'

As one, the penny drops.

I've only ever seen the tarpaulins that cover the ground beneath the old garden furniture. It never occurred to me to look underneath. Come to think of it, the furniture graveyard is a little raised from the rest of the yard, but Bright Hill is built on uneven ground, so nothing is the level you expect.

'Gracious me, that must have been there for five years,' Hattie says. 'We had a roofing contractor come to have a look at the roof but they went bust two days before they were due to collect the scaffolding stuff. We had all the poles, too, but we sold them to a scrap-metal dealer, as I recall.'

I turn to Murray, who has begun to slowly pace the former shed display area. 'Would they be in good enough condition?'

'Oh aye. Wrapped 'em up right before I put the tarps down. I had a notion I'd use them for turfing jobs but they just became part of the yard. They're sturdy, though. Make a great frame for the beds.'

'How many would they make?'

The chin rubbing recommences. 'I'll have to work that out.'

It's a start, at least. And I already have one local company pencilled in as sponsors – lovely Chuck and Jean from the hardware stall in Richmond have persuaded the owner of the Market Hall to sponsor two beds, one for a local primary school and one for a farmers' collective who meet to support each other once a month. I'm so glad I called them first. Jean reckons some of the other businesses in the town might follow suit.

'Leave it with me, poppet,' she'd said on the phone yesterday afternoon, after I'd called Hattie with my idea. 'I'll round 'em up for you. Chuck's a leading light in the local Chamber of Commerce, so I reckon he can persuade some, too.'

Everyone loves the project name, at least. Hattie welled up when I told her why I'd called it the Bright Hill Legacy. A worthy investment, a thing of value.

We spend the rest of Friday marking out the site and retrieving all the hidden former scaffold boards from beneath the furniture graveyard. We're lucky: we have enough for nine beds. Murray offered to source woodcuts from a mate of his who owns a reclaimed wood yard, but I think nine is close enough. Better if they all look the same to begin with. How the gardeners decide to personalise their beds is up to them.

Darren, of course, is the vociferous fly in the ointment.

'Never going to work. Bloody waste of time,' he says, tutting when Murray wordlessly hands him a saw and points at a large stack of scaffold boards that need cutting to size.

I wait for the tirade to continue, but Darren catches Hattie's stern look and joins in at last. Hattie stands over him, arms folded, watching his every move. Patrick and Eric hide their smiles as they fix a bed frame together and Murray gives me a wink. No worming your way out of this one, Darren Gifford.

He says nothing, but I can feel his disgust in every whack of the hammer.

Work recommences after the weekend, Monday a blur of activity as the Legacy begins to take shape. Five of the nine beds are built by the time I have to leave to pick up Noah from Michelle's. Murray and Patrick assure me they'll all be done when I return next day. And they are. We fill each one with soil and gravel for drainage, levelling them so they look identical. Eric brings in 'extraordinary buns', as he calls them, to celebrate the final bed going in and we toast the site with builders'-strength tea in chipped mugs from his shed.

With two beds already adopted – the primary school and the farmers' collective, the next community group to contact me are three ladies from the local WI. Constance, Thelma and Dot are *amazing*. They arrive in Dot's beaten-up Land Rover, emerging like Ascot ladies with flowing floral dresses, twinned incongruously with very un-glamorous shortie wellies. I love them the moment we meet in the café.

'We came in t'other week,' Constance says as I hand out cups of tea. 'Talked to a right grumpy sod. Said he were a manager, only he could barely manage a bit of common courtesy.'

No prizes for guessing who *that* delightful employee might have been...

'I'm sorry I missed you,' I say. 'I'm working from home on Thursdays to get this project off the ground.'

'No problem, love. We're just keen as brass, aren't we, girls?'

Thelma and Dot agree, the three of them then launching into anecdotes at once so I'm treated to a floral-clad wall of North Yorkshire sound. It takes a moment for them all to realise, descending into hearty laughter when they do.

'Forgive us, Bethan. We talk ten to the dozen when we're let out. You'll get used to it.'

'So, does that mean you'd like to sign up for a Legacy garden?' My pen hovers over my notepad as I dare to ask the question.

'Of course. That's why we're here!'

They mean business, too: within an hour of our conversation, they're already at work with spades they brought in the Land Rover, filling their newly adopted bed with compost.

And it continues into Tuesday afternoon. A team from a retired businessmen's group adopt one bed, an amateur dramatics company from Northallerton take another, a further education college takes one for its agriculture students, a charity working with kids who have been excluded from school adopts one, too. A firm of solicitors adopts a bed as a team-building exercise to work on at weekends and a mums-and-toddlers group from a small church in the nearby village take on the ninth bed. Murray – bless his heart – builds two tiny enclosures with off-cuts of scaffold board beside this bed so that the toddlers who accompany their mums have a sandpit and a little soft-play zone to keep themselves occupied. He even spends an evening sanding the boards down and sealing them with yacht varnish so there are no sharp edges. See, I knew he was a softie…

I watch it all coming together and it's like seeing a dream materialise before me. It's hard work and all hands on deck – and Darren *hates* having to help us – but we pull together and the Bright Hill Legacy slowly comes to life.

Patrick and I take turns to act as liaison for the volunteer gardeners already arriving to claim their beds, so that Darren doesn't lose two members of staff from his section. I quickly notice a bit of disappointment from the WI and the mums when they get my assistance and not Pat's. Those bodybuilding sessions are clearly working their magic.

'I reckon you're our secret weapon,' I tease him after he's returned from advising some very bright-eyed mums.

'Go away.'

'No, I mean it. One look from you and they'll buy anything.'

'You're just jealous.'

'You bet I am! And there was me thinking I had you all to myself.'

His eyes lift heavenwards, but he beams like a beacon as we walk back to the plant A-to-Z.

I'm shattered when I get home every evening, just about mustering enough energy to get Noah fed, washed, changed into his jammies and tucked into bed before I crash out, too. But it's a good tired. Days of solid work and so much to show for it.

And on Wednesday night, I have an extra reason to feel good: three trays of potted primula plants, keeping cool in the bathroom, ready for planting tomorrow.

By the hedge. With the man I haven't stopped thinking about...

Chapter Thirty-Seven

LACHLAN

I've almost got this planting thing down to an art now.

I *might* have been practising getting into my odd leg-outstretched-crouch position and back to my feet again in the seven days since I saw her. A little extra-curricular physio routine Tanya would probably be horrified by. It's all part of my plan to be able to meet Bethan. The thought of walking up to her is a powerful motivator, that's for sure.

After today, the hedge border will be complete. We'll have to find new ways to occupy ourselves on Thursdays, but I know we'll think of something. I just can't wait to see her.

The window messages have bridged the gap and I've loved sharing them with her. They are mostly wishing one another a good day or sweet dreams, but occasionally we stray into more flirtatious territory.

NIGHT–NIGHT, LACHIE.
P.S.
YOU SHOULD GET A BISCUIT TATTOO ☺

TWO Qs:
1. WHICH BISCUIT?
2. WHERE?
SWEET DREAMS, BETHAN ☺

MORNING ☺
1. SOMETHING TASTY
2. ANYWHERE YOU LIKE ☺

I love her cheekiness. It makes the days between when I see her the sweetest test. Most of all, I don't feel alone. And that's a huge deal right now.

I've been going over my statement, cross-referencing it with Riggsy's to make sure they tally. I'm not lying, I tell myself, just telling them what the police already know. Archer implied the inquiry is a formality, pushed through by the high-ups wanting to throw their weight around. I need to get on with my life, not have this hanging over me. Knowing that Bethan is waiting the other side gives me hope.

'You're getting good at this,' she says at lunchtime, handing me another plant through the hedge gap. Bear's ear primulas, they are. I'm proud of myself for learning two whole plant names since I met Bethan.

'I have a good teacher,' I grin back, embracing the cheesiness of my reply.

The way her face glows is worth it. 'Well, I have an excellent student.'

I wait until we're walking to the car park end of the hedge before I dare to say what I've wanted to all week. 'When this border is finished you'll have to think of something else to teach me.' I inhale against the ache as I move down to the ground.

'Well, it won't be cheeky comebacks. I think you've a degree in those.'

I smile at the glimpse of her hands beneath the hedge. 'Master's, actually.'

She snorts – a proper can't-stop-herself noise that's a joy. 'Not a PhD? I was about to call you Doctor Lachie.'

'I don't mind if you want to.'

Her hands stop at the base of the primula plant. 'Actually, what is your last name? I haven't asked.'

I stare at my own hands, caught off guard. It's such a simple request – and one that, had we met face to face at the start, I would have answered without thinking. But this feels significant, like everything I've shared with Bethan.

'I'll tell you at the cat-sized hole.' My heart picks up pace as I finish planting the flower and push myself back to my feet.

Her face is a picture of amusement when we meet by the hedge window. I love it.

I love you…

My breath catches. Did I say that out loud? It arrived so naturally I could have.

Bethan's eyebrows rise. 'So?'

'So what?'

'What's your surname, Doctor Lachie?'

I didn't say it. My cheeks burn as though I did. 'Wallace.' I offer my hand through the gap.

'Lachlan Wallace,' she repeats, slowly.

Watching her lips forming my name is *distracting…*

'And you are?' I manage, my voice several semitones higher than it should be.

'Gwynne.' Her fingers close around my hand. 'Bethan Nia Gwynne.'

'Nia? That's pretty.'

'Thanks.'

'Mine's John. Lachlan John Wallace.'

When she laughs, her hand squeezes mine. 'How are you not Scottish with a name like that?'

'Search me. Although I reckon my Caledonian ancestors would approve.'

Our hands let go. Bethan bends out of sight and returns with a pack of biscuits. 'Bourbon?'

'Hang on, I thought Bourbons were for wimps?'

'I don't mind being a wimp with you.' She bites a biscuit, her eyes lifting coyly to me. Once my leg is sorted, I am going to *march* round to hers... 'Can I ask you something?'

'Shoot.'

'How did you get the scar?'

My heart sinks to the cold ground. 'What scar?'

'The one on your hand? It looks nasty.'

'It was. Not now, though.' I try to wrestle my thoughts but they've gone into freefall. If I tell the truth, everything has to follow. I'm not ready for her to know that yet, even though we're closer. I've imagined telling her and it all being okay, but I can't shake the image of her seeing my leg and how I walk and that obliterating everything else she thinks about me. 'It was a glass cut.'

'That's awful. *How?*'

The truth is that the scar is where a large piece of twisted metal sliced into the back of my hand as I was covering my face when the car was rolling. It probably saved my eyes. Not that I've seen it like that. To me, it's another reminder of my stupidity for being on the road that night.

If I tell her how it happened, would she see the scar as a salvation or a sentence?

'Broken bottle,' I spit the words out, their taste bitter on my tongue. 'It fell – from a cupboard – smashed on the counter and a piece went into my hand.' I set my face like stone, but I hate every word I'm dealing her.

'Did it need stitches?'

I nod.

'Lachie, that's terrible.' Even her sympathetic frown is a burn to my skin.

'It's okay, though,' I say, holding my hand up for her to look. 'Healing well, see?' My brightness is forced and awkward. 'Anything else you want to know?'

Her smile returns and it's so welcome I forget everything for a moment. 'Do you want to do this again? Now the border's finished, I mean.'

'Yes. I love this. Um, I mean...'

'I love it too. So, let's think of questions we want to ask each other between now and then, okay?'

'Okay. Thank you.'

She peers at me from beneath the length of fringe that's worked loose from her plait. 'What for?'

For everything. For stealing my heart. For making me hope again.

'For being a friend,' I say. The word is nowhere near big enough.

*

All night, I'm restless. I lie awake, replaying my words from earlier, hating myself all over again. That was my chance to tell her. A wide-open door I just slammed shut. No matter what happens next, this will always be between us, won't it? If I get to walk to her side like I'm visualising every day, and she finally knows the truth, she'll come back to what I said this afternoon. The moment I lied to her. Until now it's been an omission: today, I lied.

I'm startled awake by the simultaneous ring of my phone and buzz of the door intercom. My head swims as I struggle out of bed, my bearings lost by the rude awakening. I stab my finger against the screen as I stumble through the living room.

'What?' I snap.

'Open the bloody door.'

Riggsy? What's he doing here? What time is it?

I stare at my screen: 4.28 a.m. Groaning, I push the entrance door release, leaning my aching forehead against the cool wood of my own front door before I open it.

What lurches up the stairs and towards me is horrific.

Riggsy sways as he staggers towards me, a three-quarters-empty bottle of Jack Daniels, in his hand, T-shirt stained with recent vomit and streaks of mud across one knee.

'What the hell? It's half four in the morning,' I hiss at him but he's already shouldering his way into my flat.

Bert goes apoplectic, barking and snarling and whimpering. Ernie is nowhere to be seen, most likely hiding somewhere. I grab Bert's collar and wrestle him into my bedroom, slamming the door. His yelps and scratches continue as I turn back to my friend.

'Byrne *knows*,' he growls, swaying in the middle of the room.

'Knows what?'

'That I took the car. That I had a knife. That I was threatening to slice the bastard, which is what you should have let me do...'

'Sit down.'

'I don't want to sit down! He's going to bury me, Wallace, do you hear? I'm *finished*...' He makes a strangled gasp – and that's when I see the fear.

I've seen him drunk, raging, goading someone into a fight, sorry for himself when he's been injured. But never scared. Ever. And between us we've witnessed our fair share of horrors. This is new and it chills me. Because I don't know what to do with a terrified Adam Riggs.

'Sit down,' I repeat, more gently, edging towards him. I'm wary of the bottle swinging in his hand, his fingers flexing around the neck. I've seen that look before... 'Mate. Sit down and we'll work it out.'

His knees buckle and the sofa catches his fall. Righting himself, he leans his head back against the cushions. 'It's all over the garrison. Everyone's saying Byrne's cashing in.'

'Who's saying it?'

He answers through gritted teeth, every muscle tense in his jaw. 'Everyone.'

'Has he been called to give a statement?'

'Word is, he volunteered.'

I take a seat beside him. 'Doesn't sound like Byrne.'

'Suits him, though, doesn't it? He knows I was out to get him, so he gets his punch in first. *That* sounds like Byrne. High-ups have been after him for years for all the shit he's swimming in – those dodgy deals, that business with the gambling racket he hid from them, all the blokes he's got dirt on jumping at his every word. They know it's happening but they can't get the witnesses to take him down. They've just been waiting for him to trip up and lately he's been sloppy. He knows they're on his tail.'

'That makes no sense. If he knows they're onto him, why go to them?'

'Trade-off. Simple as. He goes in, plays the model soldier, shops me, they're grateful, he gets off.'

Could Byrne do that? Would he risk his freedom to destroy Riggs? And if he knows about the car and the threat – and the knife I stopped Riggsy using that night – what else does he know?

I feel sick and not just because of the odour emanating from his clothing. This was supposed to be straightforward: we tell them we went for a drive because Riggsy needed to clear his head, that we hit water in a hidden dip and rolled the car; then they close the case and everything goes back to normal.

Except they already know something, don't they? Archer said it: some information came to light that Command wished to address. Was that Byrne's statement? Is he the reason we're facing a military police inquiry? Are we only just discovering it now?

'We stick to our story,' I say, wishing I believed it. 'Two of us against him. If we don't waver they can't get us.'

'What about the car?'

I swallow. 'I don't tell them where you got it. Because you didn't tell me until I came around in hospital. If I'd known it wasn't yours to take...'

'And if they ask why we were on the road?'

'I'll just say you needed some space.'

He's shaking his head now. 'No. You can't say that.'

'I have to. We agreed.'

Riggsy closes his eyes. 'They know, Wallace. There's no way round it. If you say I was stressed they'll link it with what Byrne's said.'

'Not necessarily. They know what it's like in the garrison. Sometimes the bullshit just gets too much...'

'No.'

'I have to say something!' I protest. 'Because that's the first question they're going to ask.' There's no other solution I can see. If I can answer that question clearly, they'll move on, I'm certain of it. If I can't – that's going to make them push harder. 'I have to tell them why we were on the road. Like we agreed: you'd got stressed, I suggested a drive. It's the only way we can explain why we were out there at that time of night. It'll be enough.'

'They'll make the link. If Byrne's said I threatened him and you tell them I was stressed out enough to need to get off the site, it'll be bloody obvious. I was relying on you – as an outranking officer. Good reputation, clean record. Who's going to listen to me, huh? They'll do me for intimidation. Or threatened assault. I've got previous cautions, Wallace. They ain't going to overlook those. They'll say I didn't have responsible control of the vehicle if I was aggravated – how is that going to go down on my record when I'm an army driver?'

He's staring at me now, bloodshot eyes brimming with tears. 'You owe me. I had your back, years ago. And I didn't go after Byrne because of you. I was on that road because of you. And in the ditch because you grabbed the wheel...'

'I had to! You were all over the road!'

'Because you hadn't let me do what I should've done!'

I want to kick him out of my house but we need to be unified when we go before the inquiry. I need him on side. I did the right thing – didn't I? State he was in that night he could have killed someone.

But if I hadn't intervened – if I'd come home like I was supposed to – I wouldn't have this injury and an uphill battle to get my life back.

I would have been able to tell Bethan I loved her today. Nothing between us, nothing stopping us taking this where we both know we want it to go. I've been stalling because of my injury, but I've known all along. I love her. And if I hadn't been on that road that night, she would be mine already.

If I don't say Riggs was stressed: if I omit that part and just say it was a late-night whim to go for a drive, the military police investigators can't make the link.

One lie.

I thought it was a courtesy car Riggsy had while his was in for repairs – and I didn't know the truth until days later, when he confessed at my hospital bedside that he'd taken it. *On the night* I didn't know, but I do now.

Two lies.

And they won't know for certain about the knife – because it wasn't in the car when I was cut out of it. There was no mention of it in the crash investigation report from the police. They can't make a link there, either.

Three lies. Just three. And then I can get my life back.

Riggs is waiting for an answer. I hate that he's asking me to lie more. I can't move on unless I do. Moving on means a chance to meet Bethan for real, my leg healed and my job restored.

But is being with Bethan worth risking everything for?

Chapter Thirty-Eight

BETHAN

MORNING, MISS G.
TELL ME SOMETHING
TO MAKE ME SMILE ☺

I wasn't expecting his window note this morning. Last night we shared our now usual single window message exchange, so I didn't think I'd hear from him again until this evening. Luckily, I got up early today to make sure I packed all the Bright Hill Legacy stuff – the folder of sponsor details and my lists of people I've still to contact, marketing plans and the community fund account details which I'm keeping with it all because I'm petrified of losing them. I promised Hattie I'd bring them in today for her to go over. I was a bit worried it wouldn't look like much when I collected it all together but the resulting stack in the folder is reassuringly thick. She's excited about the project and I want to keep it that way.

Lachie's message was the surprise I needed. Although I'm wondering now if that means he's had a tough night. I hope he hasn't. Anyway, I managed to reply before getting Noah up. I hope it helps…

MORNING, DOCTOR W.
THERE'S A SPECIES OF DAISY
IN THE USA CALLED
WALLACE'S WOOLLY DAISY ☺
(ERIOPHYLLUM WALLACEI)

Rather chuffed with that…

'You've got that smile again,' Michelle says, as Noah dashes in.

'Have I?' I reply, but my Belisha beacon of a face undoes all my good work.

She folds her arms. 'Okay, out with it.'

I never talk about personal stuff with anyone. Michelle doesn't even know about Noah's dad – she's never asked and I've never said. But today I find I need another person to hear it.

'I've met someone…'

Michelle shrieks, then apologises to Maisie and Noah who are staring at her. She reaches out and flaps her hand inches from my elbow – a big scoop of a hug in her body language. 'Yes! I was right, wasn't I? What's his name?' Her eyes widen. 'Or hers?'

I've really kept my cards close to my chest, haven't I? I love that she checked, though. 'His name is Lachie. He's just a friend…'

'… but not for long, you hope?'

I shrug but my smile says it all.

She clamps a hand to her mouth to muffle another squeal. 'Oh sweetheart, I am so pleased for you. Does Noah know?'

That sorts my smile. 'Not yet.'

'There's no rush. I dated Craig for seven months before I told him about Maisie.'

Now it's my turn to be surprised. 'I didn't realise. She looks just like him.'

'I know! Proper freaked me out when I met him. They were thick as thieves from the day they met. So, we're proof it works.'

'How did you know it was the right time to tell Craig?'

'Well, he were talking about us moving in together, so...' Michelle smirks. 'Listen, you'll know. And if he makes you smile as much as this chap does, I reckon Noah will love him. I'm made up for you, Bethy.'

It was good to tell someone about Lachie, but by the time I arrive at Bright Hill my head is already engaged in a standoff with my heart. I've always dealt with things by myself: sharing is an uncomfortable comfort.

I'm pleased to see the car park fuller than it has been for months. Lately the Bright Hill Legacy gardeners have been arriving earlier and earlier to work on their beds. Murray's taken to letting them in before we open, meaning they spend more time here. That's fine by me – if nothing else, it's a promising sign. I park, grab the Legacy stuff and my bag and hurry inside.

I spotted Darren's car by the entrance, which is a bit of a surprise considering he's rarely in work before ten most days. I was planning to stash my bag and coat in the cloakroom and then head over to Hattie's office before I started work, but if he's in already I need a rethink. Deciding to go straight to Hattie first, I make for the staff door. I'm just entering the door code when there's a shout from across the building.

'B! We need you!'

Patrick is over by the door to the plant section, waving

like a man possessed. He isn't smiling – and that's reason enough for concern. I hurry over.

'What's up?'

He's breathing hard when I reach him, despite me being the one who has been running. 'A kid… We've lost a kid!'

'What? Where?'

'The Legacy,' he rushes. 'Toddler got out of the soft-play bit by the mums and tods' bed. Little lass. Her mum's going spare, Murray's in bits…'

Panic rushes me. Every parent's worst nightmare – and in a nursery like ours there are untold dangers a child could encounter, which makes it a hundred times worse. Patrick is shaking by my side – he can't search for a kid in that state.

'Where's Darren?'

'Can't find him.'

Bloody typical. So much for him being in early. He's probably holed up in the staff room ignoring everyone. 'Right.' I push the project folder at him. 'Take this to Hattie for me, okay? I'll go and sort it.'

Relief floods his expression and he dashes off on his new, safer mission.

I push through the door and run.

Four groups of Legacy gardeners are in various stages of panic, everyone yelling at once. Murray is staring at the soft-play zone, shaking his head and worryingly on the verge of tears. The toddler's mum is pacing the plot, sobbing, while Connie, Thelma, Dot and two of the mums are trying their best to console her.

'Who's missing?' I demand, my voice barely audible over the din.

Connie looks up. 'Little girl. Lowenna.'

'Right. Murray, check the A-to-Z and temperate house.' He looks up, nods, and lumbers off. 'Thelma, you stay with Mum. Connie, Dot, you take the tree and rose sections.' I wave at the group of excluded kids and their support worker, who hurry over, eyes wide. 'Okay, guys, just do a sweep of the site, yeah? Backwards and forwards between the beds. Check the planters section and the paving too and when you've done that, check the hothouse where the cacti and greenhouse plants live. Understood? Off you go.'

I shrug off my coat and bag, stashing them by the Legacy beds, then scan the site for anywhere else a toddler might head for. Every avenue is frustratingly empty. I don't want to think about the towering bags of compost, the stacks of paving slabs that could easily fall...

Let me find her. Please...

I check around all the beds, including those whose teams have not yet arrived to tend them.

Nothing.

Where would Noah head if he had all of this to explore? I scan the site, around the perimeter fence at the back of the Legacy plot where low-hanging trees may look like inviting leafy dens.

Nothing.

And then I notice something.

The door to Eric's shed is just ajar. He's a stickler for security and insists we close the door if we use it on his day off, which today is. It's just an old rickety shed whose best years are far behind it. But to a toddler, a great big blue-painted palace...

I hurry to the door and peer inside.

Curled up in the ragged cushions on the seat of Eric's beloved armchair is a little girl, fast asleep, her toy rabbit clutched by one ear in her tight fist.

I breathe out my relief in the doorway. Not wanting to wake her, I turn back and wave to Thelma, who has her arm around the terrified mother. She grabs the woman's hand and they run across.

'Found her,' I smile as the mum bursts into tears and rushes in.

'We've got her!' Thelma yells. And then everyone is running to us from across the nursery. Old and young, strangers and friends, all arriving at the door to Eric's shed, out of breath and elated. They talk over each other, shaking hands, clutching hearts – and standing among them I'm struck by what we've created. It's so early for the Legacy project, but already we have a community of our own. Whatever happens in the future, we made *this*. I don't hold my own tears back as I accept backslaps and hugs. I'm so proud of everyone here.

'Bloody hell,' Murray says beside me. 'I thought... I was so worried the lass might...' His eyes glisten and I look away to spare his embarrassment, squeezing his arm instead.

'Best get that enclosure sorted, eh?' I say.

'Aye. Right away. I'll extend the height, add a trellis top and... and...'

'Sounds great,' I smile at him. 'And don't be hard on yourself. Kids are all expert escapologists.'

He shakes his head. 'If anything had happened...'

'It didn't. We just thank our stars, learn from it and move on. Okay?'

He nods and slips away as Patrick jogs over.

'I just heard, B – is the kid okay?'

'Fast asleep. Did you get the stuff to Hattie?'

'Yeah, no worries.'

I smile at him, then at the lovely bunch of people who

surround us. I want to enjoy this moment of togetherness in the project I dreamed into life.

And that's when I think of Lachie. Because I can't spend time in the Legacy without thinking about his remark that sparked the idea. Togetherness: it's what I love most about spending time with him. I want more of it. More of him. Could that feeling extend to my son? Might Lachie be for Noah what Craig is for Maisie? I've seen Michelle's husband and her daughter together and it's a beautiful thing – even more so now I know their story.

Could that be Lachie, Noah and me one day?

Does that mean I'm ready to find out?

Chapter Thirty-Nine

LACHLAN

'Wallace! Bloody relief to see your face.'

Archer strides across the office to shake my hand.

I smile, despite the knots twisting in my stomach. I won't show anyone I'm nervous, but a night of no sleep and pacing a groove across my living-room floor waiting for the taxi this morning attest to the fact. 'You missed me, sir?'

'Sanity, Wallace. I've missed sanity.' His nod is akin to a pat on my shoulder. 'You good?'

'Getting there.'

'Excellent. A word?'

I follow him into his office, hoping my racing heart isn't as loud for him as it is for me. Once the door has closed and I've accepted his invitation to sit, he relaxes a little. 'Straightforward one today. You have three investigators from SIB, one interview. They call it a hearing to make themselves feel important.' His smirk helps my nerves.

'Sir. Anything I should know?'

'You're first in. Riggs, I believe, is being seen next Wednesday. They'll likely want to go over the events in some detail, particularly the crash itself. There may be some uncomfortable questions.'

'I'm expecting them, sir.'

'Quite. Tell them what happened. You are not at fault as far as this office is concerned. I've read the crash investigation report from the civilian police and it all seems straightforward to me. The SIB's role is to confirm events, not condemn you.'

I risk a smile. 'Thank you, sir.'

'Good. The team are due here at eleven, which gives us—' he consults his watch, '—twenty-five minutes. Lieutenant Daimler has been commandeered as minute-taker so you'll have a familiar face in there.'

I'm not sure how I feel about that. I can guess what Kim Daimler's views are on the subject. Sure enough, when I leave Archer's office, my colleague's expression is pure thunder.

'He's basically making me a secretary,' she hisses under her breath as we stand in the small kitchen. 'Making coffee, taking notes. What's next, shagging the boss?'

Her instant horror at what she's said makes me laugh. 'Mate, I'm sorry.'

'It goes with the territory. You nervous?'

'Is Archer a raving misogynist?'

She smiles. 'That bad, huh?'

'Nah.' I shake it off. I know my story. I've rehearsed it so many times it's practically written on my skin. 'I just want to get it over with.'

The three Special Investigations Branch military police officers arrive and introduce themselves as Willoughby, Saunders and Jenkins. Willoughby is senior investigator in name, age and stature and takes her place at the centre of a pair of tables forming a bench, flanked either side by Saunders, who I guess to be around my age, and Jenkins whose grey-flecked temples suggest he's older.

When I sit facing them, the gravity of the interview hits me. I glance at Kim, sitting at a small desk in the corner, but her head is bowed over her notes.

'Captain Wallace, the purpose of this hearing is to establish the facts of the events surrounding the incident in question. We are not looking to apportion blame at this time. We have been apprised of the civilian police investigation and that will be taken into account. However, this is now an internal investigation under the jurisdiction of the military police. Do you understand?'

'Yes, ma'am.'

'Okay, we'll begin.' Willoughby nods to Kim first, then Saunders, who starts the tape.

'If you could confirm your rank, name and position, please.'

'My name is Captain Lachlan Wallace. I'm a Learning and Development Officer in this unit.'

Willoughby grants me a brief smile before she begins.

'Captain Wallace, if you could tell us, in your own words, what happened on the night in question.'

I calmly reel off my learned speech. I'd suggested a late-night drive as a way of letting off steam after a long day. Riggsy drove. It started raining as we left the garrison and our route took us on unlit country roads. Approaching the village we hit a pool of water in a hidden dip, causing the car to aquaplane and catch the kerb. The momentum was too much to keep us on the road – which is why the car rolled, coming to land on its passenger side, where I was trapped by my leg crushed in the wreckage.

I expect to feel some emotion because this is the first time I've spoken in detail about the crash. But I'm oddly numb. It's a blessing, I reassure myself. If I'd broken down I might have let slip something I shouldn't. All the same, it bothers me.

None of what I say is a lie. But it isn't the whole truth, either. Knowing that puts me at odds with myself. When I finish, I take a long sip of water from the glass Kim gave me.

Willoughby, Saunders and Jenkins make notes, then lean together to confer. I sit and wait.

My ordeal is over. They have their statement. It corroborates what the traffic police will have already told them in their report. I can walk away knowing I did what I could to assist the inquiry *and* protect Riggsy. I can go back home and focus all my energy on beating this injury – and moving closer to Bethan.

'Thank you, Captain Wallace. To recap on a couple of points...'

My heart sinks to my boots.

'Ma'am?'

'You stated that Lance-Corporal Riggs was driving.'

'Yes, ma'am.'

'Did the car belong to him?'

'Yes.' *Crap.* 'To the best of my knowledge on that night.' First lie.

She observes me for an uncomfortable minute. 'On that night.'

'Yes, ma'am.'

Silence. Notes taken. A shared look with Jenkins. The slightest nod. 'And in your opinion, when Lance-Corporal Riggs offered his car for your drive out, was he in a suitable frame of mind to be driving?'

No. He was screaming murder, on the edge of control. 'In my opinion, he was.' Second lie.

My stomach twists. I clench my teeth, willing my face to set like stone.

More notes.

'How fast was Lance-Corporal Riggs driving, prior to the accident, would you say?'

Like an idiot. I told him to slow down but he wasn't listening. 'It was a national speed limit road and I believe we were driving at the upper limit.'

'Speeding, would you say?'

'No, ma'am. We passed two speed cameras on that stretch of road and neither were activated.' Third lie.

A look between Willoughby and Saunders this time.

'The hidden dip where the water was, did you see any warning signs prior to hitting it?'

'No, ma'am. But I was in the passenger seat talking to Lance-Corporal Riggs at the time, so I wasn't paying full attention to the road.'

I was yelling at him to stay on our side of the road…

'I appreciate the next questions may be difficult, Captain Wallace, so please take your time and if you feel you need to stop at any point, just let us know.'

I'm shaky now. I thought what I'd already said would be enough. I wasn't expecting further questions. I nod back, not trusting my voice yet.

'You say that the first stage of the crash occurred when you hit the water in the dip. Can you elaborate on what you experienced, please?'

I take a breath. Picture Bethan's smile through the hedge

window – sunshine in human form. If I keep her there and not the confusion, the panic, the pain of that night, I can do this. I can do anything when she smiles at me.

'The car began to skid. It felt like it was being pushed from the driver's side towards the kerb. I yelled at Riggs to steer into it but he panicked. I reached my hand to steady the wheel and we righted but... There was a loud bang on my side and the next thing I knew we were lifting from the road and the car was rolling. After that...' I falter, the memory of the sound returning. Splintering, crunching, exploding, twisting, shattering all around me. It's woken me at night many times. I swallow hard.

'In your own time, Captain Wallace.'

I nod, wrenching control back. 'After that, I blacked out. I don't remember the impact, or being trapped. I only discovered those details later when I regained consciousness in hospital.'

It's all true, but it's little compensation for the lies that preceded it. The nagging doubt about not mentioning how stressed Riggsy was that night jabs hard against me. But I can't share that without incriminating him. I've said what needed to be said. So I sit straight and look Willoughby in the eye. Think of Bethan. Hold my nerve.

Think of her smile.

Forget the rest.

Think of the future – not the crash.

Outside the Educational and Training Service Unit building I fill my lungs with fresh Yorkshire air, letting the tension ease from my shoulders. It's done – my story given, boxes ticked, a line drawn. I push away the remnants of doubt. I'm going home to work on reclaiming my life, with this firmly behind me.

The still-fresh memory of the end of my interview plays out in my mind.

'Is that all you remember?'

'Yes.'

'And you're certain of the facts?'

'Yes.'

Yes. Yes. Yes, ma'am.

This is where I leave it. It's done.

Chapter Forty

BETHAN

I think I'm falling for him.

No. I know I am.

But knowing that presents a huge problem: I can't move on from where we are unless he knows about Noah. And if I tell him about Noah and it's a deal-breaker, I'll lose him. I don't want to lose him. But I don't want to lie to him anymore either.

It's early Saturday morning. Noah's been up since six, but it wouldn't have mattered if he'd woken at four or slept till eight – I didn't get any sleep last night going over everything.

Michelle said about being as sure as you can be before you leap. I am as certain of Lachie as it's possible to be. Being with him makes me happy; spending time with him makes me happy. *He* could make me happy. I never expected to need that again, but I do.

I think Noah would love him. Not that it's hard to impress my son. Just turn up and play dragons and he's in seventh heaven. I don't think he needs a dad, not in a way that suggests his life with me now is incomplete. But I suddenly don't want to be on my own. And maybe if I were with the right person, Noah would benefit.

I should have told Lachie when I had the chance. It's gone on for far too long without him knowing – first because I just wanted him to myself, and then because it was easier not to tell him. I don't know what his reaction will be. But I have to trust that if this is right, he'll be okay.

My brother Emrys has this theory about life, that it gives you celestial itching powder when it's time to make a move. He should know: he's never been one to stay in any job longer than three years and once one home is done up the way he likes it, he'll move onto the next renovation project and start all over again.

'You feel it coming, weeks before anything happens. Like, the air changes. The clothes you're wearing don't quite fit. The doors you're content with start sticking in their jambs. Then, the itching starts. Irritations, frustrations, things you've been content with for years suddenly make you angry. You can fight it all you like, but by then you've already left in your head: your body just needs to catch up.'

That's what's happening now, isn't it? I love our window messages. I can't wait for Thursdays to spend time with him. But the border is planted now and we've exhausted biscuit anecdotes. It isn't enough – and it scares me.

The truth is, I want more. I want him in my life. I can feel the moment coming, like it did before when the window messages started to not be enough. Everything that's happened with Lachie and me has been on this strange, unquestionable trajectory – nothing where I expect it to be, yet everything perfectly in place. The pull is there again – I know he feels it, too.

I don't have a choice, do I?

I stare across at Lachie's window and I make up my mind.

I'm going to tell him about Noah. Today. Do it first

with a hedge between us and then, if that goes well, ask him if he'd like to meet face to face. He said no before, but we're so much further now than we were back then.

If he can't deal with Noah, or this isn't what he wants, he can walk away. But if it is…

I pull a sheet of paper from Noah's craft box while he's engrossed in a picture book about odd dogs standing out. And I write the words I can't escape from:

CAN WE MEET TODAY?
11 A.M. BY THE HEDGE? x

I hesitate about adding the kiss, but write it anyway. No point in being cautious now. This is the moment I'm asking him into our lives.

An agonising hour later, his reply appears, next to a sleeping Ernie.

WOULD LOVE TO.
SEE YOU THEN x

That's it, then. It's happening.

'Where are we going?'

'I told you, out to the garden.'

Noah pauses three steps into the flight. 'Is there a football goal?'

What kind of a question is that? It's taken an age to make it this far out of the building and it's almost eleven now. 'No, but we can make one with our coats. We need to hurry.' I hold my hand out. 'Come on.'

I swear my son is doing this on purpose. Usually one mention of outdoors and it's all I can do to keep up with him as he races downstairs. Today, he insists on stepping on each stair with both feet before moving on.

Left, right.

Wait.

Left, right.

Wait.

I can't do this all the way down. Groaning, I scoop him up under one arm, his football cradled in my other, and haul him down the stairs. He whoops and giggles, throwing his arms wide like an aeroplane, which really doesn't help.

We make it to the ground floor in one piece and I hit the door release button to let us outside, managing to grab my son's hand before he dashes away. The last thing I need is Noah getting to Lachie first.

All I can hear is my breath and my heart as we round the corner and follow the line of brightly coloured flowers beneath the hedge.

What will Lachie say? Will he want me if it's not just me? I have to be prepared for that. But I'm crossing everything that he's the man I believe him to be.

We have reached and passed so many crunch points so far. He's always come through for me and we've always moved on. This one has the most riding on it – because if he accepts Noah, there's nothing stopping us moving forward together.

We're almost at the hedge window now. Noah is straining at my hand – so, confident we're far enough into the garden for him not to consider a dash to the main road, I let go. I kick the ball into the wider patch of grass that borders the car park at the rear and Noah races after it.

'Hello?'

He's there. I take a breath, run a hand over my hair, which I'm certain looks like I've gone through the hedge myself, and then walk to the gap.

'Hi.'

His smile is instant and familiar – and, at that moment, I don't want to tell him anything. Because this is perfect. The kisses we put at the end of our window messages are almost tangible between us. *We shared a kiss*, if only in the signs we wrote. That has to mean something.

I want him to mean something.

'This is a nice surprise. I was thinking I had another boring Saturday ahead and then *you* happened.'

It's perfect. He's perfect.

But I have to tell him.

'I need to say something,' I begin, careful to keep my gaze full on him.

His blue-green eyes flicker. 'Everything okay?'

'Yes – more than okay – I… Okay, here it is: I like you, Lachie. A lot. More than I've said. And I think you might feel the same…'

'I do…'

The next words in my planned speech vanish. I'm watching him as he watches me, our breath rising and falling together. It's the best news and the worst possible outcome at once – because what I say next could break it. And I *have* to say something next.

Noah is kicking the ball against the corner of the building. I want to stop him, but I can't look away from Lachie. Not yet. Not until I've said…

'But I need to tell you something first. I should have said it a long time ago and I'm so sorry I didn't...'

'Hey, it's okay. It's me you're talking to. You can trust me, whatever it is...'

The ball hits the corner of the building and crashes into the hedge. I tense but Lachie doesn't seem to notice. I have to say it, now.

'I was hoping you'd say that.'

'Come here...' He reaches his hand through the hedge window and I follow suit. His warm fingers hold mine then slowly, deliberately coax their way between them. I feel them lacing together, lost in the sensation and the deep draw of his eyes, taking me in, urging the words from my lips...

I don't hear the ball hit the building again, only the rush of air as it sails past my head; the rustle of beech leaves and cracking of tiny branches that fail to halt its path over the hedge...

... And then the shove of my son's shoulder as he barges past me towards the busy main road.

'*NOAH!*'

I forget everything and run.

'Bethan? What's happening?' Lachie is moving too, his voice just behind me.

'My son...' I gasp. 'He's heading for the road...'

'Your *what*?'

I'm sprinting now, but not close enough to grab him...

'Noah Gwynne! Come *back* here!'

The road seems to fill with speeding cars, my little boy running headlong towards the streaks of red, blue and silver...

'Who's Noah?'

I don't have time to think, or to find the right words. 'Lachie, stop him, please! *NOAH!* Come back! *Please*, Lachie, help me!'

At the last moment, Noah turns sharp left and rounds the hedge.

NO...

I round it two seconds later – arriving face to face with the man I'm falling for...

But he isn't the man I love.

His face is contorted in horror. Smile gone, eyes wild. *My* Lachie isn't here.

As Noah dashes past him, crushing the plants in the flower border, he turns to glare at my son, then back at me.

I want to explain, to find the humour in our sudden meeting after weeks of carefully avoiding it – but Lachlan Wallace is looking at me with utter disgust.

I can't believe it.

He's *judging* me.

Like everybody else.

My heart screeches to a halt like my feet have just done. I search his face for anything – any other flicker of emotion that isn't *this*. But I find nothing. I don't want my son to see that condemnation.

'Noah, come here *now*.' All of my shock and defeat registers in my voice, sending Noah scurrying to my side. I turn him into me, my hand stroking the back of his head as he starts to sniffle, the Mama Bear rising in my chest.

Lachie says *nothing*.

He just stares at me. Like I'm worthless. Like he doesn't know me at all.

And it all becomes clear. Everything I built on this man was a lie. Brave, gleaming glass towers of hope, belief and trust, resting on his shoulders. They implode one by one, shattering around me, so raw and sharp that I think if I looked down now shards of them would cover the grass around my feet.

I daren't look down. But I wish I didn't see what's ahead of me.

I should say something, but I have my answer, don't I? The worst possible outcome.

No words can alter that.

So I pick up my son and run.

Chapter Forty-One

LACHLAN

I call after her but she's gone.

I should follow but I can't move. I tried to run – and almost fell – but I heard the fear in her voice and I kept going. And now my stupid leg is on fire and I can't even think straight.

I was going to tell her – because when I saw her sign earlier I *knew*. We've been heading towards this for weeks and... She said she liked me. I saw it in her eyes, in the way she accepted my hand like she was accepting me...

But I met a different woman when she arrived.

She looked like my Bethan, but she wasn't.

She couldn't even look at me when she left.

She was disgusted with me, wasn't she?

I breathe against the flood of pain, internal and external forces assaulting me in a dual attack. How did we move from that moment when our hands joined to *this*?

I wasn't expecting a kid, but that wouldn't have made a difference.

Her reaction to me *did*.

Of all the people in the world, I wanted her to see past my

injury. I hate the way I had to move – the shooting stick too jammed into the ground to help me, so that I had no support except my good leg. She thought I'd outrun her: when I didn't and she saw why...

Her face...

I didn't think Bethan Gwynne was capable of an expression like that. Her light and positivity stole my heart. She was sunshine, always, even when her eyes looked tired or her body carried weariness, like the first time I saw her in her window. My Bethan would be smiling still. She'd be laughing as I took her in my arms and...

The worst thing is, I was finally ready to let her in.

As soon as she'd started to speak, I knew the time had come. My hand laced with hers was the first promise of us holding one another. I planned to walk around the hedge, even with my leg as it is today; ready to tell her I wanted her in my life.

I came so close to making the biggest mistake.

Her face when she saw me...

I know how I look now. Bent to one side, my shattered pelvis completely unaligned, the awkward roll of my gait as I move. I'd hoped she would see my heart, my love for her burning within me. But all she saw was a twisted shell, a body held tight in pain. She looked as though she'd slammed into a nightmare.

She couldn't have hurt me more if she'd shoved me back in that rolling car folding in on itself as it crushed my body. Only this was worse because the twisted metal and glass didn't reach my heart that night.

I follow the trail of devastation along the flower border where her son ran after his ball. Torn petals and shredded leaves beneath the hedge. Damage too devastating for small plants to withstand. I doubt they'll ever recover.

Everything I'd dared to hope – gone.

Her eyes when she saw me…

I have to get out of here.

In the safety of my home I rip the sign from the window, balling it up and launching it across the room. Only the corners remain, pathetic scraps stuck to the glass like a warning.

Bert and Ernie watch from the sofa, shocked into solidarity by the sight of me. They huddle together, eyes wide and ears back. I would never take it out on them, but it's best they leave me alone for now.

Fury pumping through me, I find the stack of window signs I've saved and spread them across the dining table. They were meant to be a record of our story – something we could revisit years from now, to remember where we began. Instead of hope, they scream delusion. How could I have thought anything good would come from this? My hands shake as I tear each one, ripping Bethan Gwynne piece by piece from my life. Stupid, meaningless bollocks. What have I let myself become?

I was looking for anything to pin my hope on when everything else was lost. So desperate I sent a message to a random stranger. How tragic is that? Bethan was never going to save me. Nobody can.

Nobody but me.

It shouldn't have taken me this long to work out. I was too weak to do the work for myself, so I found a convenient lie to hang it on. A story I told myself so I wouldn't have to face the truth. I'm here because of the choices I made: to intervene in my friend's crap, to stop him making a mistake that could cost his career, to grab the wheel on the road… Then I chose to focus on

Bethan instead of taking responsibility. I made her the reason for my recovery. That wasn't her role to play.

I stare at the ripped remains of an episode in my life I won't repeat. The signs mean nothing: just a pile of torn paper now. I see them for what they are, and I feel sick that I believed it. I grab the kitchen bin and sweep them in, slamming the lid.

It's done.

It's over.

It damned near took me under this time, but I won't let that happen. My recovery is my business, my reward. I don't need anybody else, whatever my heart thinks. Whatever anyone thinks.

Whatever Bethan thinks.

I love her. It hurts like hell. But I'll get over it.

It's *my* life now.

Chapter Forty-Two

BETHAN

I didn't sleep at all last night.

I can't think straight.

I can't get his expression out of my head. It loomed over me all night, that horror and condemnation directed at me. At my son.

The moment he became like everybody else.

He should have been mine today. He should have met Noah and fallen in love with him and told me he didn't care that I hadn't told him before because I love my son and Lachie loves me and that was all that mattered.

He has an injured leg and a stick – he didn't tell me that. But that makes no difference to how I feel about him. It's just an injury, not who he is.

I am the biggest fool. I trusted him, didn't I? I believed he could love me.

But here I am, hollowed out by the loss of him and the lack of sleep. And all the hopes I told myself I wasn't planting around his feet are as smashed as the plants Noah trampled yesterday.

I was going to tell him I loved him.

I had my heart gift-wrapped already.

At least I never got to say the words. If I'd bared my soul and then seen his face – I don't think I could have dealt with that. This way only I will ever know how stupid I've been. I'll bury it deep, like I have with everything else since Kai, and force myself forward.

Tomorrow.

Today, I think I need to feel it. To make sure I never make that mistake again.

Noah isn't up yet – a welcome blessing. For the next two hours or so I have the living room to myself. I grab the faded patchwork throw Mam made me years ago from my bed and tiptoe past his door into the living area, curling up as small as I can make myself on the sofa, the familiar old flowered patches soft friends around my face. I want to slip down behind the cushions like a forgotten penny and stay in the darkness, safe and warm.

I must fall to sleep because when I jolt awake, Noah is crying. Kicking the tangle of quilt and cushions from my feet, I scramble upright and hurry to his room.

'What's up, little man?' I say, kneeling by the bedside and stroking his hair. His face is wet with sweat and tears, his eyes tight shut. Tân the dragon is clutched in his hands, his knuckles white where he grips it to him.

He yowls again, louder and angrier.

'Noah, open your eyes.'

His headshake is violent.

'Open your eyes, lovely.' His hair slicks with sweat as I stroke it back from his face. 'Mummy's here. Do you want some water?'

Another furious shake of the head. When I try to straighten his bedclothes his fists ball around the fabric.

I don't need this, not now. It's a battle to keep my voice

steady and soft, when all I want to do is leave him to it. I know he doesn't realise it's happening but it's impossible to not feel the affront when he pushes me away. Nobody ever prepared me for this. The first time was terrifying and even though this is in daylight, the shock and tension of it is overwhelming.

'Okay,' I say, rising to leave.

'*No!*' His eyelids flick open and he yells, the strange non-seeing eyes trained on me. His sobs become wails, Tân Dragon flung across the room as he kicks and flails.

Quickly, I dash out of the room, pushing his pitiful screams away from my ears as I fetch my phone.

It always follows change. Has he picked up on my anger from yesterday? Or was he more aware of Lachie's response than I realised? Guilt rushes over me, stronger than I can withstand this morning. If I'd told Lachie when I had the chance – all those chances I let slip by because I wasn't ready to share him – yesterday would never have happened and my boy wouldn't have had to witness Lachie's disgust. Noah's screams meet my own tears as I hurry back into his room, the very last place I want to be right now because all of it is too much. Too unfair. I'm alone – more alone than I was before – with nothing but the incandescent anger of a still-sleeping child.

And I don't have *him*. Lachie abandoned me the moment I knew I needed him.

Noah is thrashing in the bed now, fists flying and feet kicking the covers into furious knots. I do the only thing I know to: I find his favourite TV cartoon on my mobile, turn the sound up and hold the screen in front of his face. I don't speak – because that can break the spell. I just wait, my arm outstretched, hand

278

shaking as I hold the phone, praying that it works, that this isn't the time the magic runs out.

I stand my ground, albeit on my knees, and face the storm head-on. Noah's crying drowns out the jolly narrator and cartoon dog that runs a club for other animals. The bright colours paint his face with a dancing rainbow. I breathe as best I can through the fear and the pain I have no strength left to fight.

Gradually, breath by breath, his sobbing fades. My son's eyes begin to focus; long, slow blinks punctuated by rhythmic shudders of breath. My arm aches where I hold the phone towards him but I daren't move. Duggee and his pals jump and sing and dance, their familiar voices and catchphrases comforting after the storm has passed.

But it hurts. Everything in me is bruised. And I'm too weary to see a time when it won't always be like this.

When I'm certain the waking nightmare has passed, I climb onto the edge of Noah's bed and feel a rush of relief when he curls his little frame into me. I take one of the large dragons from the shelf at the back of his bed and prop it behind my head, my eyes heavy. His breathing softens, his body snuggling into mine. I close my eyes, the storm navigated, only the dull ache remaining.

It's almost midday when we wake.

I must have turned my phone off at some point because I find it beside Noah's nightlight on his bedside table. When I squint at the screen, there's a missed call and a text message. When I open the text, my heart swells.

It's a picture message from Connie and Dot, a slightly blurry image of Connie pointing excitedly at a stake of pea plants in their Legacy bed. The caption, written in all caps as her messages always are, reads:

FIRST PEAS HAVE APPEARED! WE R V. CHUFFED. HOORAY FOR GARDEN MAGIC! (AND STARTING WITH MATURE PLANTS!) BUYING NEW TRUG FROM BH TO CELEBRATE. SEE YOU MONDAY, C&D XX (CONNIE AND DOT)

It feels good to smile. I love that Connie always clarifies 'C&D' after typing, as if I am regularly messaged by a raft of C&D candidates and might otherwise be confused.

'What's that, Mum?' Noah shifts upright, blinking away sleep to look at the photo.

'Connie and Dot have their first peas,' I say, the familiarity of it warming me from the inside out. 'That's the first harvest growing on the Legacy beds at my work. I told you about them.'

He strokes the screen. 'Can I see the Leggy beds?'

How can I refuse a request like that?

We wash and dress, grab a snack for Noah to eat in the car and a large coffee in a reusable travel mug for me, and head outside. The air is fresh, a hint of chill against the sun when the breeze picks up. I make myself walk on the garden side of the building rather than following the concrete drive to the car park at the back, my heart tearing as we pass the hedge and the border I planted with Lachie. But I have to face it today – if I don't it will become a towering phantom that robs me of this space I have every right to visit. I half-glance up at Lachlan's window as we pass. Just in case he's watching. Because if he *is* watching, I want him to see me and my son who I love more than the air in my lungs. I want him to see his mistake.

The sun dips behind wind-pushed clouds as we drive to Bright Hill, sending pockets of light and shadow chasing across the landscape and into the car. Noah gives a running commentary as he enjoys his 'car picnic', crisp and pastry crumbs flying as he speaks.

'... There's a big tree in that one. And poppies, too! That cloud looks like Tân Dragon, doesn't it? Doesn't it, Mummy? And in that field there are four sheep and, look, Mummy! Cows!'

I let it wash over me as the patches of shadow dance across the road ahead. It's good to be out. The fresh air is what we both need. I can't be at home today, knowing how close Lachie still is but barred from ever reaching him. We're on the hunt for lightness and positives. And the miles I'm putting between me and a man I thought I knew help my focus.

Murray is loading more growbags onto a stack by the entrance to the nursery and stops to greet us when we arrive.

'This is a surprise.'

'Noah wanted to see the Leggy beds,' I smile, the muscles in my face protesting like I haven't used them for a long time.

His mouth almost curls up at the corners. 'You have *got* to call them that from now on.' He looks down at Noah, eyes twinkling. 'Hey, Noah, how're you doing?'

'Good,' Noah beams up at him.

'I don't suppose you fancy a ride on my trolley to get to the Leggy beds, do you?' Murray glances at me. 'If your ma doesn't mind?'

Noah gasps and tugs on my hand. 'Can I, Mum?'

'Sure. You hold on tight now, okay?'

Thrilled, my son jumps into the empty yellow Bright Hill

trolley and grips the sides, giggling like a Munchkin. At least the drama of this morning hasn't dampened his spirits. Murray winks at me as he takes up the handles.

'Right-o, chappy, hang on now. Here we go-o-o-o-o-o-o-o!'

I follow them through the main glass building, passing the new summer seating displays, planted herb pots and barbecue sets, all framed by garlands of artificial sunflowers. Jenn and Judith, two of the café staff, grin at me as they head back from their break, while Claire from the outdoor clothing concession clamps a hand to her heart when she sees Noah.

'He's growing up so fast!'

'I know,' I smile back. 'And I think he's found a new best chum.'

Sounds of chatter and clinking crockery drift in from the café as I walk by; around the displays more people are mooching. It's not packed and nowhere near busy enough, but it's a relief to see anyone here. And the community I've helped create is all around me, too. Harriet and Charlotte, a couple of the gardeners from the farmers' collective, raise their hands when they cross my path and I notice both of them are carrying an armful of new tools. They look so proud of them and it gives me a huge shot of hope. It isn't enough to solve Bright Hill's troubles but it's a start. Little shoots breaking the ground.

Murray and Noah are flying ahead when I step out into the A-to-Z. I swear if anyone could ever make Murray crack a full smile it's my son. Maybe he is, right now, safely out of my eyeline. Perhaps Murray Hope has a stash of secret smiles for handing out when his Bright Hill colleagues aren't looking.

'What are you doing here?'

And just like that, the clouds cover the sun.

'Day out, Darren. My son wanted to see the Legacy beds.'

'Bit sad to be coming in on your day off,' he says, reaching my side. 'One of the many—'

No, I'm not rising to it today. I am not an employee, I'm a visitor. 'Busy day?'

'Usual weekend stuff. Not that you'd know.'

'Ooh, no, I gave up that peculiar pleasure a year ago.' That hits its target. But I don't need another fight, so I look at him and smile. 'Hattie said our tool and seed sales are up since the Legacy volunteers started.'

Darren blinks rapidly, the way he does when he's caught off-guard. Clearly, he doesn't know what to do with my sudden friendliness. Good. 'I heard that, yeah. So – I guess you were right on that one.'

Hang on. Is the great offensive grump known as Darren Gifford *complimenting* me? 'Cheers.'

He nods, his eyes fixed ahead. 'You've been good here. Useful. Whatever happens, I just want you to know that.'

And then he's off, walking like someone speeded up the shot.

I wasn't expecting that.

Five of the nine Legacy beds are being tended to when I catch up with Murray and Noah. The volunteers smile and point at their flourishing plots. It's a sight to gladden the weariest heart.

If I could just bring the sponsors down here, they would see how inspiring it is, how it's bringing people together who would never have met otherwise. The autumn show will help, I think, although we really need sponsorship in place before then. Hattie believes in me. When I see the Legacy volunteers coming back here day after day, I can believe in me, too.

I just wish I didn't see Lachie in every success. I wanted to share it all with him because I knew he'd understand.

But he doesn't understand, does he? About me or anyone else.

I take a deep breath and let the cool Yorkshire air in. This is what matters now. I built this: I have to make it work.

You make it sound so easy.

It is easy.

When it's you. I reckon you scare the plants to grow...

The memory of Lachie's voice stings my soul. I have to put him out of my mind.

'Mum! Look at the baby peas!'

Noah is over by Connie and Dot, Thelma waving beside them. Pushing Lachie from my mind, I hurry over to join them.

Chapter Forty-Three

LACHLAN

It's a late physio session today. Tanya's been on a training course in Northallerton for most of the day but she's keen to keep on with our current regime, so she agreed to come to mine for 6 p.m.

It feels strange to be running through my exercise programme so late. It doesn't help that I can see Bethan's window from where I'm currently working. It aches to see it empty of words. Or flowers. Since we stopped talking, the vase she usually keeps there has vanished.

I really need to hear from her. And that's the worst thing. I shouldn't miss her, after her reaction to me. But my heart didn't get the executive order.

'And again?'

I push against Tanya's hands and imagine myself pushing Bethan away. It's not the positive focus I need. My calf cramps and I grip it.

'Okay, okay, stop now.' Tanya stands, hand rubbing across her chin. 'It's probably the wrong time of day.'

'Sorry. I just need to get rid of this knot and we can go again.'

'Rest for a bit. I reckon we're both morning people, eh?'

I manage a smile. 'Reckon you're right. How was the training course?'

She leans against my kitchen counter with her water bottle. 'Long. Boring. I guess I'll use what I learned but I'm not sure they needed all day to teach me.'

The knot finally starts to budge. I keep massaging it. 'That's my job, you know – it was before… Delivering training.'

'In the army?'

I nod. 'We operate full-career training ops for soldiers and officers. So I've done my fair share of office training.'

'Bet yours wasn't as boring as mine,' she grins.

'Bet it was worse,' I smile back.

It's the first time I've had a conversation like this since Bethan and it makes me smile and hurt simultaneously. Tanya is cool, but she isn't Bethan.

'Listen, don't worry if things are slower today. You're tired now. Mornings are always going to be better.'

'But my progress has slowed.' I wasn't going to let on I'd noticed, but it's been bugging me.

Her head bows a little. She knows it, too. 'You reach plateaus. It doesn't mean the progress has stopped; just that we've reached the next stage in your body adapting. I can have a chat to my boss, if you like? See about changing things up a bit, developing your programme?'

'Would that help?'

'I've seen it work before.' She doesn't look as certain as I'd like.

'Yeah, okay. If you would.'

When she leaves I take a shower, leaning my head against the cold tiles in the hot steam. I'm weary today. But I don't think it has anything to do with my physio progress. It's been a week since I last saw Bethan and days have dragged without the window messages or the promise of our Thursdays. Everything needs double the effort and takes twice as long to happen. And nothing feels fulfilling like it did when I could tell her about it.

Why is she still in my head?

I know exactly where I stand with Bethan – which is exactly nowhere. What else is there to consider?

I only just catch the ringing of my phone on its last round. Turning off the water and grabbing a towel, I heave my body out of the shower and find my now silent mobile in the tumble of clothes on the tiled floor.

KIM DAIMLER
1 missed call

That's not who I was expecting a call from. Frowning at the screen, I head to my room and sit on the bed, rubbing my hair with a towel before I call her back. It's her personal number, so not an official call. And anyway, it wouldn't be her job to contact me. It's been so long since she last called me I'd forgotten I had her number in my phone. So, why now?

Ernie appears in the doorway, his tail curling up the architrave like a grey question mark.

'Yes, I know you need food,' I say, pushing up off the bed and following his delighted body back into the kitchen. I press call on Kim's number as I walk.

'Wallace, hi.'

'Sorry I missed your call. Everything okay?'

'Um, hang on a minute…' I hear footsteps and stabs of breath as she moves, the creak of a door opening and the distant hum of traffic. 'Right, sorry, not much signal here.'

Something in her answer feels off. I don't say anything, waiting for her to speak first.

'I need to see you.'

'Why?'

'There isn't time to… Can you meet me out somewhere? This evening?'

'Out? Where?'

'There's a pub just off the Yarm road, The Fleece? Do you know it?'

'Vaguely. I'd need to get a taxi, Kim. I can't drive yet.'

'Oh – crap – yeah. Sorry.'

'Or you could come here?'

'No. It needs to be somewhere we won't be recognised.' Her sigh is heavy on the line. 'It sounds weird I know, but it's important and I can't risk anyone finding out.'

Okay, *now* I'm concerned. She's called my mobile maybe a handful of times in all the years I've known her and now Kim wants a clandestine meeting in a country pub? I've never heard her like she is now. Jumpy. Uncertain. That's enough to convince me.

'I'll get a taxi. What time?'

'Eight?'

'Fine.'

'Good. I'll see you there. Get the taxi to pick you back up at 9.30 p.m. Book him before he drops you off or you'll never get a ride home. I'll give you the money when I see you.'

What the hell is going on?

*

The pub is a few miles off the main road, down a B road that snakes between endless hedgerows skirting large fields. The driver tells me he went there for his wife's birthday last year. I'm glad he knows where he's going: there's no way I would have found this place on my own.

It doesn't feel right. None of it does. But the only way I'll find out for certain is by meeting her.

The pub is old and low-ceilinged, half empty save for a handful of people eating at tables around the space and a valiant few casually propping up the bar. At some point someone has obviously tried to 'gastro-pub' the place – the telltale odd bits of vintage bric-a-brac stacked high on shelves and dark slate platters where plates should be – but it appears they gave up, judging by the old-school menu chalked up by the dartboard and the out-of-place hulk of a slot machine leaning at an angle on the flagstone floor.

I pick my way gingerly across the smooth stone slabs, still learning which surfaces are safe to put weight on with my crutch. When I transition to a stick, it will be easier, according to Tanya. Judging by the way the rubber foot of the crutch skids against stone, I'm not convinced a stick will give me any better support.

I expect all eyes to turn and watch my progression, but nobody seems bothered this evening. I glance around the tables until I see her, sitting at the far end of the pub.

Kim stands as I approach, hand outstretched to greet me. Formal handshakes, too? This can't be good. She looks different in civvies – younger, for one thing. Uniform can age you or take years off you, depending on your rank. All the guys in my unit when we served in Afghanistan looked like terrified kids. Kim's blonde hair is down, skimming the collar of the black leather jacket she wears. It's like meeting a member of her family who bears a striking resemblance to my work colleague. This, coupled with the choice of setting, is unnerving.

'Can I get you a pint?' she asks. Looks like she needs alcohol more than me. 'Bitter?'

'Cheers,' I say, because she's already halfway to the bar.

I shrug off my jacket and push the unoccupied chair from the next table further away to make room for my leg. The straighter it can be, the less it hates me next day, I've discovered. And as I'm here for the next hour and a half at least, according to the time Kim said I should book my ride home for, I need to get comfortable.

I'm not comfortable yet, but it has nothing to do with my leg. Beer will help. I hope.

When she returns she natters on for a while as I sip my pint – and I let her because I get the impression whatever she wants to say needs a long approach. She's definitely nervous, picking up a beer mat and turning it over and over in her hands as she speaks.

Finally, when a natural lull comes, I speak. 'So why am I here?'

Her face becomes flint. 'You need to know something. About – the inquiry.'

I'd hoped it wasn't that. But honestly, what else could it be? Kim didn't need to see me in a bland remote country pub to pass on the latest office gossip.

'Right.'

She takes a large draw of her IPA and sets the bottle down on the table, both hands around its base. 'You know Archer had me taking notes in the interviews? I thought it was a one-off that time you came, but it's been every one. You know how he is with consistency… Anyway, I was in one yesterday. With Adam Riggs.'

'What?' Alarm bells start ringing. This is illegal – anything said in the inquiry interviews has to remain confidential. 'You shouldn't be telling me anything, Daimler…'

She won't look me in the eye. Does she have any idea what she's doing? 'I know, but…'

'Mate – *Kim* – I appreciate the gesture but it's not your place to tell me.'

'Believe me, I wish I wasn't here, Wallace…'

'Then let's just have a drink and forget it.'

'I can't.'

What am I doing here? Why did I come? Everything about this screamed trouble from the outset. Why didn't I see it? 'You could lose your job.'

Her head snaps upright, her eyes fierce. 'And you could go to prison!'

I'm shocked into silence, my mouth useless as I stare at her.

'Just tell me one thing, okay? Did you tell the truth in your interview?'

'Yes – I… Why would you…?'

She glares at me. '*Off* the record, Wallace. Did you believe it was his car? Was he in a fit state to drive? Did you just hit a patch of water and leave the road? Or did you say all that to protect someone else?'

Now I can't look at her. Does the inquiry know? Have they worked it out? 'I don't know what you mean.'

'I need to know, Lachie.'

She *never* calls me that. 'Why?'

Her knuckles whiten around the bottle. 'Because Adam Riggs

says you knew. About the car being stolen. He said you were making threats against Cathal Byrne; it was his idea to get you off the garrison. Because you had a knife.'

The floor seems to drop away beneath my feet. I am suspended over a chasm, with nothing but the chair to hold me. I search her expression for anything to cling on to, any lifeline to respond to. But I find none.

'He said *what*?'

'He's pinning it on you.' Her eyes flicker a little. 'So *if* you lied to protect Adam Riggs, you need to change your story – and fast. Because the performance I witnessed would convince anyone that he was an innocent caught up in your crap.'

He set me up.

All that *I'm terrified, I'll lose my job, they'll believe you but not me* bollocks he chucked at me when he came over. And the way I believed him, like I've always believed him... Every word a lie. Setting me up to lie on several counts, to throw my testimony into doubt. And then he spins a tale that damns me.

I walked straight into his plan, didn't I?

I trusted him. I'm here, now, with everything I'm dealing with, because I was trying to do the right thing. I was trying to protect him – and Cathal Byrne. I've been bailing him out for years – so many times I can't even remember the details anymore. All because I couldn't get over my stupidity on that first tour of duty: how close I thought I'd come to losing the only career I've known. Riggs said he'd always have my back, but the truth is he helped me *once*. One solitary favour when I was too young and dumb to realise what I could lose. I've spent years trying to repay the favour but the price he set was never within my reach.

'He knew...'

'Knew what?'

I blink at her, aware I've spoken aloud. 'He said he was terrified he'd be arrested, that he'd lose his job if I said I knew about the car and the state he was in. I thought I was helping him, being a friend...'

She rubs her eyes. 'You trusted Adam Riggs? I don't know what to tell you, mate. He's been a selfish git as long as I've known him. It never made sense to me why the two of you were so tight. But I reckon he knew he was onto a winner, having you on side.'

I can't take it all in. Because now I'm reliving every instance he's asked for my help, every scrape we've navigated, every pile of crap we've come through. Was I so desperate for a friend that I blinkered myself to what was really going on?

'Bastard... He's setting me up.'

I jump as Kim's hand touches my arm. 'Riggs is a snake, mate. You should have seen him in the interview. Not an ounce of regret in anything. Said you bullied him and had done it for years. Said you used your position to keep him in line. Emotional blackmail, according to him.'

My head drops into my hands, the full horror slamming into my chest. 'He's going to bury me. I'm going to lose everything...' *Again*, my head screams.

'Not if you retract your statement.'

'I testified under oath. That's contempt...'

'I checked. With Archer.'

'*What?* He knows?'

She shakes her head. 'No, not specifics. I asked as a neutral bystander curious about the process. I think he thought I was referring to Riggs. Until a ruling is made, you have the right to amend, retract or remake your statement. But you don't have long. Riggsy's performance was pretty compelling and he was the last to be interviewed.'

Panicked, I look up at Kim. 'How can I do this? Can you help me?'

'Request another interview. Say you wish to amend your statement. I'll talk to Archer.'

'But he'll know you told me. You'll lose your job…'

'I'll say I took a call from you, first thing. He's not in till nine thirty tomorrow – meeting with the executive. I'll pass it on like a regular message. Just don't mention me when he calls.'

I stare at her, at my unlikeliest saviour, and wonder what I've done to deserve her as an ally. 'Thank you. I don't know how else to say it, but thank you.'

'You're a good lad, Lachie. Always knew you were. Kick that bastard to the kerb, where he belongs. That will be thanks enough for me.'

Chapter Forty-Four

BETHAN

I've put a blind up at the window.

It hurts too much to pass it every day, knowing he's there but his words aren't.

I picked the brightest, happiest yellow I could find. It filters the sunlight through the window, bathing the kitchen in warm honey. It should make me feel happier every time I see it. But all I see is a slammed door.

Noah likes it and that's what matters. He calls it our 'custard blind' and as very little in life makes my son happier than custard, I'm in no doubt how it makes him feel. It's his home and I want him to only find joy here.

I just wish I could see it without seeing Lachie.

I've been so swept up by everything that happened since that first sign in his window that I didn't see how much I was linking him to every aspect of my life. Now he isn't there, painful reminders wait to ambush me wherever I turn.

The kitchen is the temptation to peer out of the window to find a new message or catch a glimpse of him. The living room the place I went to wait out the time until he replied. The bathroom where I thought of him as I was doing Noah's bath every evening, excited by the prospect of his goodnight messages; the bedroom where I went to sleep smiling because I had a friend and woke up having dreamed of beautiful words curling around a beautiful arm and that smile that could stop my heart at fifty paces. Driving to work is thinking of Lachie; being at work is building the project his words inspired.

I can't escape him. My heart doesn't want to.

I have to find a way out of this or I will lose my mind.

'So serious this morning.' Connie takes off her gardening gloves and rests on the handle of her spade. 'Everything okay?'

I force a smile into my voice. 'I'm good. Thinking of everything we have to do here.'

'Forgive me, but that didn't look like an *I'm so busy* face.' She flaps at a fly with her glove. 'Does he have a name?'

'The fly? No, we don't have pets here,' I reply.

Connie gives a knowing nod. 'I see. I will mind my own beeswax. But here's my two penn'orth first: if you find one worth bothering your head over as much as he is making you, he's probably worth keeping. Less to wonder over if he's right next door.'

Right next door.

She doesn't know about Lachie. It's an expression I've heard a thousand times since I moved here. But it feels like she's just peeked into my soul. It's too much.

I make my excuses and leave.

Darren is sitting at his desk in the small plant section office when I arrive, frowning at a little booklet he's reading.

'Rounds are done, A-to-Z restocked and Eric will be ready for us to move the new saplings in an hour,' I say, surprised by the amount we've done already this morning. At least I have this:

working in this section feels like second nature already and the addition of the Legacy beds has made every day at work fulfilling.

'*Hmph.*'

'Sorry, didn't catch that?'

He doesn't even look up, the words on the small pages summoning his attention. 'Know anything about mobile phones?'

Okay, I wasn't expecting that. 'Not a lot, I'm afraid. I've had mine for eons.'

'iPhone, is it?'

'No.'

He harrumphs and turns the page.

'I think Patrick has one? No point asking Murray, he's more of a Neanderthal than me when it comes to mobiles. Or you could ask Eric – he's the undisputed Tech Champion around here. He's got a higher-spec phone than all of us.'

Nothing. Not a flicker. Not even an exasperated sigh.

'Darren?' I peer around the filing cabinet and catch sight of a bright white cardboard box, a sheet of ripped cellophane covering the little clear space on Darren's desk like a sheen of morning dew.

'Yeah.'

'New phone?'

He closes the leaflet and pushes it to one side. 'Said I'd set it up for a friend.'

'Lucky friend.'

'Yeah, well some of us have them, Bethan.'

'Nice. What do you want me to do now?'

'You might as well keep an eye on the Legacy till lunch. The mothers and sprogs are back up there and we don't want a repeat of the other week.'

His tone grates on me but I say nothing. It's better being here than at home. I need to keep busy.

A third of the beds are being worked on today – Connie, Thelma and Dot, half of the mums-and-toddlers club and two of the retired business club members. The Year 6 kids from the school are arriving at 2 p.m. and I'm expecting the lawyers for an hour before closing – Darren and Patrick are going to make sure they're okay. Murray's new, hopefully toddler-proof enclosures seem to be doing the trick so at least their mothers are more relaxed today.

Using mature plants has had a dramatic effect on the Legacy – it's a riot of green and some of the earlier flowering species are beginning to bloom. Next year when we start from seed the change will take longer to happen but I think all the volunteer gardeners will find it fulfilling. That's if we get a second year. I'm thinking about suggesting a four-year option to our sponsors if this year is a success. Securing five years of income in total would have much more of an impact on the nursery's turnover.

I'm getting ahead of myself but it helps today. Seeing past the problem, planning a future to aim for – that's what I've learned to do with my life.

Maybe that's what I need to do with Lachie.

He might not even stay where he is. It can't be easy living on the first floor with his injury. Not that I can imagine anything stopping him if he puts his mind to it. I loved his determination: but now I'm on its flipside it's impossible to contend with. Maybe he'll go back to his family in the Cotswolds and then the problem will vanish with him.

I catch sight of my reflection in the glass door of Eric's shed. No wonder Connie guessed about me. My face reads like a book. I stare at my hollow eyes, the smile that doesn't quite reach them. I look pale – paler than normal, which is a feat in itself, given my unmistakable Celtic colouring. Mam used to say it was a good job we all had dark hair and blue eyes in the family or else we'd disappear if we stood by magnolia walls.

It will get better, I tell my reflection. It has to.

Three days later, I'm no further on with getting over Lachlan Wallace, but navigating yet another new territory with my son is proving a useful distraction. Noah had a visit from the Animal Lady at preschool today and is now officially a fan of goats. They fed some young goat kids with bottles, apparently, which my son thinks is the best thing ever.

'Do you like goats, Mummy?' he asks, sitting up at the kitchen counter. His legs are swinging underneath; little stripy pirate socks floppy at the toes.

'I – um – they're okay, I guess,' I reply, ladling gravy on our chicken dinners. I wasn't going to do a big tea tonight but I reckon we both need a bit of joy.

'But do you *love* them?'

'Not sure I'd say love…'

'Because *I* love them. And it's my birthday in 'vember…'

Nice try, kiddo. 'Maybe the goats will send you a card.'

A wrinkle appears between his brows. Clearly he didn't see that deflection until it was too late. 'They wouldn't have to if they lived here.'

I pick up our plates and stare at him. 'And where would the goats live, hmm?'

'In my room!'

'Oh, right.' I put his plate in front of him, straightening the plastic placemat beneath and handing him cutlery. 'Just out of interest, how many goats are we talking about?'

'Three. Big one, middle-sized one, baby one.'

So many times as a mum I am torn between being the voice of measured adult authority and bursting out laughing like a naughty kid. I just about hold off the latter reaction as I sit next to him. 'Would they be called Gruff, by any chance? Fond of bridges, not so fond of trolls?'

His eyes widen. Mind reading Maestro Mam wins *again*. 'How did you know?'

'Noah Gwynne, don't ever change.'

He frowns at me, but the call of his roast dinner and the animal stories he's yet to share are too strong to pursue the goat conversation any longer. I eat and listen, the joy radiating from my lovely boy exactly what I need tonight.

Later, when he's curled up next to me on the sofa watching *Bedtime Stories* on CBeebies, I reach for my phone, which I've neglected since I came home. I'm surprised to find three missed calls from Hattie. That's odd.

When I check my voicemail, there's one message:

'Bethan, call me the moment you get this. Tonight, please.'

That's it: no chatter, no apology for calling me at home. Just two sentences and no sign-off. Leaving Noah content with his story, I duck into my room and call Hattie.

She answers on the third ring. 'Bethan. I appreciate you calling me back.'

'I got your message – is everything okay?'

'No. It isn't.' There's an edge to her voice I've never heard before. 'I need you to come in earlier tomorrow.'

I glance at the clock on my bedside table. It's almost 7 p.m. – that's cutting it fine to check if Michelle can have Noah early. 'How early?'

'Seven a.m.'

'What?' I rush, then back-pedal. 'Sorry, I mean I have to take Noah to his childminder for eight before I come in...'

'Seven a.m. Sharp. I'm sure the childminder will accommodate.'

That's a bit presumptuous. 'I'll need to check.'

'I want you here at 7 a.m. This won't wait, I'm afraid.'

'What won't?'

'I'm not discussing it over the phone. Call your childminder and arrange it.'

And then she hangs up.

I stare at my phone.

She bloody hung up on me! Hattie Rowse, who never even shouts at anybody let alone abandons a call to her staff.

'Mu-*uu*-um!'

I'm shaking.

'One minute, *bach*.'

My hands bead with moisture, the phone sliding against my palm. She's never spoken to me like that before. Cold, rude, abrupt. She sounded more like a headmistress than an employer.

'Mummy, I *need* you.'

I stand up but my legs are numb. I don't even notice how I get from my room to my son, panic building as I call Michelle's number and hear a busy signal. I end the call and dial again.

'I need pudding,' Noah beams.

'Not now,' I say, ending the second unsuccessful call and stabbing out a text message instead.

'Can I have cake?'

'No, *bach*, it's your bedtime.'

'O-*o-o-o*-ohh…' His whine is too much. It sears through my nerves.

'I said *no*!' I roar back, instantly kicked by guilt as his face crumples. 'I'm sorry, Noah. I didn't mean… Come here, baby…' I move to pull him to me but he bats my hand away, a furious scowl firmly in place.

I bite my lip, on the verge of tears now.

What the hell is going on?

Chapter Forty-Five

LACHLAN

It's raining when I enter the gates of Catterick garrison, my once-familiar route through the site cloaked in uncertain greyness. Arriving in a taxi feels wrong. I think of my car, unmoved from the parking space behind my building for four months now, and wonder if I will ever be comfortable behind the wheel again.

I got the call from Archer yesterday. The inquiry team have agreed to hear my amended statement. I wanted to text Kim to say thank you, but I didn't. She's risked far too much for me already.

'Just by this building is fine, mate,' I say to the driver. It's not outside the door of our unit but the short walk from here will help to clear my head before I face the panel.

The taxi driver nods and pulls to the side underneath a lime tree. Its branches bow in the rain, large drops of water slapping the roof of the taxi like gunshots. My stomach knots. Eight years since my final tour of duty but this feels like preparing for combat.

Without my request, he climbs out of the car and opens my door, discreetly offering his arm to help me out. I don't want to accept but the gesture is so kind it renders any protest void. 'Cheers,' I say.

He glances down at my leg and the stick I pull from the back seat, then back at me. 'Best of luck, soldier.'

I don't trust myself to reply beyond a nod, but I stand on guard until he reverses away.

Soldier.

Some soldier I turned out to be.

The kerb and dark tarmac of the road are plastered with waterlogged lime-green and gold fallen leaves. They glisten in the dappled light from the canopy above as I begin the slow walk up the hill. Rain anywhere can be ominous, but North Yorkshire rain has a particular weight of foreboding to it. Today, it feels like the downpour itself has already condemned me.

I wish I'd seen Adam Riggs for who he was. I'm an idiot for being the last in the garrison to work it out. I put his self-serving nature down to the scant details he disclosed of an unhappy childhood – the absent father, the barely present mother, roundabout years in and out of care. Was any of that real? For all I know it could have been yet another convenient lie to hook me in.

When he'd found me cowering in the ruins of that building in Iraq I remember being surprised it was him who'd come looking for me. I thought I'd seen a new side of the mouthy joker I'd met at basic training – a privileged view few others were ever granted. The kind of rare glimpse of truth only friends share. Was he genuine in that moment? I try to square Riggsy the guy who rescued me with Adam Riggs the opportunist liar and the two won't reconcile.

I hate him for what he's done to me. Every time I walk, every move my body makes, reminds me of his utter betrayal. And if he takes my career, too?

No.

I am not going to let that happen.

I draw fury into my bones, white-hot and incandescent, powering my spine and pushing my legs against the steepening incline.

He is not going to win this time.

I have tortured myself for too long over this, guilty first that I blamed him but couldn't vocalise it, blaming myself for the decision to take the car. But Riggs fed me that lie, didn't he? Because it suited him to have me regret putting us on the road that night. It kept me compliant and ready to lie to save his skin.

I did nothing wrong: I have to keep coming back to that. I made him drive away from the garrison to stop an attack on Byrne; I grabbed the wheel to save the people in the oncoming car; everything I did was to protect someone else. At no point did I think of myself, or the danger I might be heading for. I acted with integrity in the moment, using my judgement to find the safest route forward. I was a good soldier, a compassionate human being, a life-saver.

This is my truth. My colleagues respect me. Kim wouldn't have taken such an enormous professional risk to warn me of Riggsy's statement if she hadn't believed in me. Archer, for all his barking, afforded me so many opportunities to do the right thing.

This is my battle now. My chance to win.

Kim meets me as I enter the building, horror painting her expression when she sees the state of me.

'You're soaked, Wallace! Why didn't your taxi drop you off at the door? We gave the gate clearance for you.'

'I needed a walk.' I smile, only now noticing the water dripping from my hair.

'Idiot.' She shakes her head and ducks into the staff kitchen, emerging with a tea towel. 'Here. Dry your big thick head.'

'Cheers.'

Her smile fades. 'You ready?'

I nod. It's only us in the entrance lobby but I daren't risk any mention of what she did for me. I hope she knows.

'Come into the office. Archer asked you to wait in there. Want a coffee?'

'No. I need a clear head.'

'It'll be full of rainwater now,' she grins. 'You great saft bat.'

Allies are my advantage, I think, following her through the coded entry door. I count them: Kim, Archer if I'm lucky, other soldiers who trust me – a tiny but strong battalion at my back. Riggs only had me and now he's a one-man band. I have no qualms about throwing him under a bus. I have more than paid my dues to Adam Riggs.

It's a full ten minutes before Major Archer strides in.

I stand as quickly as I can.

'At ease.' He doesn't smile. 'I should say this is a pleasant surprise, however, given the solemnity of the occasion...'

'I know, sir.'

He observes me with an irritated sigh. 'Would that it were better circumstances, Wallace. But I am glad you're here.'

I nod. 'Thank you, sir.'

'Oh, sit down, for heaven's sake. That leg must be giving you hell.' He pulls a chair from behind one of the desks and sits, too. I keep my back straight, and maintain eye contact. I have nothing to hide and I want him to see it. 'How is it now?'

'Still hurts but it's getting stronger.'

'Ah. Good. The SIB officers will be here shortly. Are you certain you have all the necessary information?'

'I am, sir. I hope I will be given a chance to explain my position?'

Archer dismisses my question. 'You can hope. I have to say, Wallace, this could have been avoided. I'm disappointed that you chose not to.'

'I had my reasons sir—' I begin, seeing his frustration and changing tack. I need him to believe I'm putting things right. '—which, in hindsight, were wrong.'

'Hmm. I don't know how this will go. I stuck my neck out to get you this extra hearing: beyond that I can't help you.'

'Thank you for your faith in me, sir.'

He rolls his eyes. 'Don't give me that penitent bollocks, Wallace. Just go in there and tell the bloody truth.'

It's the same three investigating officers as last time. None of them have mastered the art of smiling yet, but I suppose in their job they get very little to smile about. We take identical positions, me alone at a desk facing the three of them at a longer table. I made notes last night, detailing every correction I need to make to my original statement. They are folded up in my pocket, but this time I'm going to speak from the heart. Be as direct as Bethan used to be.

My heart contracts.

Bethan, my friend who couldn't cope with me. It still doesn't make sense. I thought she liked me for who I am – I dared to believe she could love me. So many wrong assumptions in my life and all of them my fault.

I check myself.

This is not the time. I can't do anything about her. But *this* situation is something I have the power to change.

I stand as the investigating officers enter, each one clutching a buff cardboard file. Doctors, military police, the army, all of them carrying my life around on thin pieces of paper in cardboard folders; my existence measured, recorded and summarised in words I'll never see.

'You may be seated.'

'Ma'am.' I do as I'm told.

Willoughby folds her hands on the table and stares at me as Saunders makes a show of spreading out my files and Jenkins sets up the recorder.

'So, Captain Wallace, for the purposes of the tape, could you state your name and your reason for requesting this extraordinary hearing?'

'My name is Captain Lachlan Wallace. I wish to amend my previous statement.'

They make notes, even though they are well aware of why we are here.

'And you are willing to swear, on oath, that the information you give us is correct to the best of your knowledge?'

'I am, ma'am.'

More writing. A whispered exchange between Jenkins and Willoughby. A nod. Saunders looks up from her notes and fixes me with a stare.

'Right. When you're ready.'

'Do you wish me to stand, ma'am?'

As one their eyes drift to my leg.

'That won't be necessary, thank you. Please, proceed.'

I take a sip from the glass on my desk, setting it back down in the ring of condensation it made there. 'First I would like to thank you for this opportunity to clarify matters. I realise that in granting my request, you have afforded me unusual grace.'

Three approving nods. Better than I'd hoped.

'In my previous statement, I said that on the night in question I suggested Lance-Corporal Adam Riggs and I take a car and drive from the garrison. I stated that it was his car and that in my opinion he was of sound mind and therefore safe to drive. This was incorrect. That night, Lance-Corporal Riggs met me at the door to the mess building in a highly charged, volatile state. He said he believed a fellow soldier had made credible threats against him and was intent on causing him harm in revenge.'

Silence. All three are watching me.

I continue. 'He had a knife. A flick-style weapon, with a blade around five inches long. He was threatening to assault the other man.'

'Can you tell us who Lance-Corporal Riggs was threatening to harm?'

'Sergeant Cathal Byrne.'

Three lots of notes taken. My throat burns and I drink more water while they write.

'Continue, please.'

'I couldn't calm him down. I'd seen him in similar states before but never holding a weapon. I knew that if I let him inside the mess, he would attack Sergeant Byrne.' I stop, force air into my lungs and summon the words I rehearsed all day to appear. 'I was scared, for my friend first and our colleague second. I had little time to think, so I chose a course of action that would remove Riggs from the situation immediately. I told him we needed to go for a drive. He resisted at first, but I persuaded him. That's when he told me he had a car.'

'The car you stated belonged to him?'

'Yes. I wish to clarify that Riggs told me his car was having major repairs and this was a rental car he'd hired in the meantime.' I remember Kim's words from that night in the pub in the middle of nowhere; how her revelation had shattered any trust I had in Adam Riggs. I feel the fury of it burning my gut, but I push it back. I have to be calm and clear – I can't let anger derail my statement. 'However, I now know that the car was stolen from the garrison pool and that Lance-Corporal Riggs was responsible. I must state that I was not aware of this on that night.'

There's a shared look between my three superiors. I keep myself as straight and still as possible, ignoring the pain in my leg and hip. Willoughby leans a little towards me.

'How did you become aware of this?'

'Lance-Corporal Riggs told me, when I was in hospital.'

'And why didn't you report this to your superiors as soon as you were able?'

'Because Riggs was concerned he would lose his position if the truth about the car was revealed. He made me question my reason for persuading him to drive that night. I – I have had difficulty processing my emotional response to the accident. I have struggled with guilt, shame, anger...' I hate that I'm saying this out loud, but even as I voice the truth I can see how easily Riggs jumped on those emotions to make me ignore my better judgement and lie. I was a sitting duck. I can't believe how stupid I've been. 'I started to doubt that I'd done the right thing. That doubt made me agree to not mention about the car. I know now that was wrong.'

They ask more about the knife, about the volatile history between Riggs and Byrne, about why I withheld information on their escalating vendetta that could have seen the inquiry concluded weeks ago. I clarify and apologise and do what I should have done from the beginning – what my gut told me, as Bethan would say.

I should have listened to her. Despite her dismissing me, I should have listened back then.

We move to the moment on the road – the part I've been dreading. Because the story version we concocted was safer than the truth. It didn't happen that way, so I could fool my emotions into disengaging with the memory. Now, I have to push myself mentally back into that car again, feel the force of impact, the rush of terror, the sensation of being thrown over and over, convinced I was going to die.

And that's when I realise, my sister was right. I can't move on until I face it, head on; a full-body collision with the stark reality of why I'm here. Bethan once told me honesty heals. Ignoring her lack of honesty about having a son, she's right about this, isn't she?

The only way I will ever walk from the ghost of that crash is to relive every detail, removing its power to control me.

So I face the investigation panel and get into the passenger seat of that car once more, heading out onto a rain-soaked midnight road with Adam Riggs at the wheel...

'He seemed to calm a little, at first. We had the radio on and I remember him singing. But soon he was ranting again, swinging the car all over the road. I grabbed the steering wheel and got us back on our carriageway but next thing I knew he had the knife, blade open, waving it at the windscreen. I didn't realise he still had it. I panicked, made a grab for it, wound the window down and threw it out onto the grass verge at the side of the road. Riggs tried to punch me but I forced him back. And that's when I saw the headlights approaching on the opposite carriageway...'

A ball of acid knots in my stomach, a cold chill passing from my forehead to my gut. I reach for the glass and force water down my throat, trying to swallow the bile and the panic and the pain that rush me.

'Take your time, please.'

'Ma'am.' I breathe, forcing power into my spine. I'm not just fighting for my job now: this is the battle I should have faced with Adam Riggs years ago.

'Are you able to proceed?' Saunders asks, a note of concern in her question.

I nod. 'Ma'am.'

'Then please, continue.'

'He just steered straight into their path. He was screaming at me, spitting obscenities and threatening to kill us both. I wrenched the wheel back once, but he forced us back into the wrong lane. The other vehicle was flashing its lights, its horn blaring... We were seconds away from hitting it... I... I jammed my elbow hard into his left ribs. It winded him and he let go of the steering wheel. That's when I pulled the wheel as hard as I could and swerved the car out of the path of the oncoming vehicle. But...'

The screech as brakes meet water in the dip...

'... We were going too fast. We didn't see the water...'

The crack as the front left tyre catches the kerb…

'… The force pushed us around to face the way we'd come, and…'

That moment before the end: the sensation of gliding, of sound fading, of everything happening so slowly I can take in colours and movement… That breath before the second impact that seems almost serene…

Emotion grips my throat but I don't stop. I can't stop. Because now I'm seeing these things again, knowing what I know, every moment is redefined. All this time I've felt guilty about the raging anger that's consumed my memory of the crash. I thought it was disloyal to my friend to resent him walking away from the wreck of the car unscathed. But I was right to be angry. My stupid loyalty to Adam Riggs put me in that car; my belief that still I owed him strapped me into the seat and forced my body to shatter. None of it was my fault. I shouldn't ever have been there.

And now he expects me to accept the blame like a penance. I will not let him win.

I channel my fury like molten steel into every word. 'We hit the kerb again and then we were rolling. Noise all around me. Riggs yelling obscenities at me. Metal buckling and cracking. Explosions as the airbags deployed. Burns on my face and glass flying everywhere… The last thing I remember before blacking out was a hard force against my head and the sensation of being crushed… The pressure was unbearable… My lungs were on fire… I couldn't breathe… I – I thought I was going to die…'

Jenkins is out of his seat, a box of tissues in his hand. It's only then that I realise my face is soaked with tears. As I pull several from the box, his hand rests briefly on my shoulder. Then he is back in his seat.

I want to close my eyes, exhaustion slamming into my body like the remains of the car.

But I am not finished yet.

'I'm sorry.'

'Do you need to take a break?'

'No, ma'am, thank you, I'm good.' I have another sip of water, stuffing the damp, screwed-up tissues into my pocket. 'When I regained consciousness in the hospital, Lance-Corporal Riggs visited me. He told me he would lose his livelihood if the whole truth came out – that he had a knife, was threatening Sergeant Byrne and had stolen a car from the garrison. He made me feel responsible for protecting him. So, I corroborated his story and omitted key information that might have incriminated him. I chose friendship over truth – and that is a decision I will always regret. I would like to apologise to you and to this inquiry for wasting your time. I hope that what I've told you today goes some way towards making amends for my lack of judgement. I thought I was doing the right thing: I hope now I have.'

Willoughby looks to Saunders, then Jenkins. When her eyes fall on me again, I see the smallest hint of softness.

'We appreciate your candidness, Captain Wallace. Your statement will be amended and we will inform you of our decision in due course.' She looks down at my leg. 'I wish you all the best for your recovery. Your actions saved lives, at cost to your own. That will be taken into consideration. You should consider that, too.'

I wasn't expecting that. 'I will,' I reply, knowing I've yet to understand just what those words will mean for me.

*

I'm hardly aware of the journey home. I'm dog-tired, every reserve of energy drained. I did the right thing, even if it was too late.

In my flat I dare to glance across at Bethan's window. There's a new blind hanging there, bright yellow like the striped T-shirt she was wearing the first time we saw each other. It's pulled halfway down, a sunny happy, slammed door.

Some things can't be fixed by honesty, however late you tell the truth.

I turn away, utterly alone.

Chapter Forty-Six

BETHAN

I have no idea why Hattie wanted me in so early today. I can't stop thinking about her voice when I called last night. Cold. Brisk. She's never spoken to me like that before.

Michelle was great about it – she heard the state of me on the phone and volunteered to have Noah at six before I'd finished asking. She didn't demand details, thankfully. I couldn't have held it together long enough to tell her.

And the worst thing – worse than not knowing what I'm waiting to face now – is that I want Lachie to be here. Despite everything. I want to hear his laugh and his soft voice telling me it's all going to be fine. Because when he said it, I could believe it would be.

I'm a mess already, without a new problem to contend with.

Why do problems hunt in packs? If they spread themselves out evenly over time you'd have a hope in hell of dealing with them. But it's never just one, is it? A problem turns up and beckons all its snarling, sharp-toothed mates – and the next thing you know you're in the centre of a feeding frenzy.

I stare at the opposite wall of the narrow corridor outside Hattie's office, every possibility racing through my mind.

What's happened?

Has the project taken too long to save Bright Hill?

Are we too late?

If I'm about to lose my job, I need to start planning. Perhaps it's best if I look for somewhere else for Noah and me. It breaks my heart, but I couldn't afford the flat. And at least I wouldn't have to see *his* window every bloody day, knowing how close we came to something wonderful. But finding somewhere cheaper means a place like that godforsaken bedsit I fought so hard to get us out of. I can't let that happen again.

It's such a mess and Lachlan Wallace stands right in the middle of it.

A sob tries to escape but I bite it back. I am *not* going to cry over that man. Even though I want him here. Not when he showed himself to be as judgemental as the rest of the world. He's probably not even thinking of me today, let alone breaking his heart over us.

Everything was going too well, wasn't it? I should have seen what was coming. But I was too busy imagining a future we were never going to be allowed into.

I jump as the door opens.

Hattie is standing there – but she isn't the Hattie I know.

'Come in.' Her eyes don't meet mine as she turns to walk back inside.

Numb, I follow.

'Take a seat.' Still no eye contact. She has a small pile of papers on Hector's old oak desk and she spreads them out like a slow-motion croupier dealing cards. When she places her hands on them, I notice her nail varnish is chipped in tiny pieces at the tips, as if some small creature has been gnawing at them.

I say nothing. I should be thinking ahead, planning strategies to meet every possible outcome. But the fight is gone. I have nothing left. Instead, I fold my hands softly in my lap, making my spine as straight as I can, planting my feet on the floor. And I breathe.

Wait. Give yourself air. Find your footing. Stand your ground.

After an age, Hattie looks at me. I don't think she's slept much, either.

'I wish this wasn't happening,' she states. 'But it is. I've always tried to do my best by you, Bethan. I've supported you, invested in you, encouraged you to achieve more. Maybe that was my mistake…' The end of her sentence cracks and she lifts one hand to rub her forehead.

I've heard this tone before, only never from her. From police, from my bank manager, from the legal aid solicitor, from the magistrate – but not from Hattie Rowse. Whatever I'm here for, it's as bad as I feared. The air thickens around us, heavy with foreboding. But I keep my head high, my back straight and my mouth shut.

Come on, then, Hattie. Say your piece.

I stare directly at her. Eyeball her. Her gaze jumps between my shoulder and the wall behind me, then back to her own hands on the desk. But I'm not moving.

'I had a phone call from my bank yesterday. They were querying several anomalous transactions that have taken place in the company account. Small amounts at first: fifty pounds here, thirty there. But then, last Thursday, a withdrawal of six and a half thousand pounds.'

What is this about? I say nothing.

She looks up at me. 'So?'

Is she saying I stole the money? The unspoken accusation hits me like a rock. 'What are you asking?'

Her eyebrows rise like I've sworn at her. I notice her hands shake as she folds them on the bank statement printouts. 'I hoped you would tell me.'

'I don't know anything about that money.'

'Well, you should. Because the only people with access to the community fund are the two of us. And I haven't taken any money out since I set it up, weeks ago.'

'And neither have I.' I can feel fury beginning to build, demolishing my tiredness; pushing past every defence I have to keep it in place. I cannot believe she is accusing me of stealing; that after everything she's said about helping me and believing in me she thinks I would do that to her.

'But the money's gone.' She shakes her head, her mind clearly made up. 'So how do you explain it?'

'I can't explain it because there is nothing to explain.' Every word fires like shots, staccato beats laced with molten anger.

'I don't want to believe it, Bethan. I thought you were better than that. But then I started to investigate…'

'*Investigate?*' The room darkens around us.

'I ran a credit history check on you. Couldn't believe what I found. Debts. Unsecured loans. Multiple credit cards. A court ruling. The amount you owe is frankly frightening. So, having sudden unchecked access to an account where you can gain money…'

'*No…*' My heart is hammering, blood pumping at my wrists.

'It must be hard, in your *situation*—' She enunciates the word and every syllable is a physical slap to my face. 'Single mum, small child to take care of alone with bills to pay, and that mountain of debt towering over you...'

'How *dare* you!'

Of all the people who might use that hackneyed old accusation against me, I never believed it would be Hattie. I don't even know where to begin with this – that she could suspect me of lying to her and stealing from the project I've worked so hard to establish; or that she saw fit to pry into my personal finances and jump to every possible wrong conclusion.

I'm out of my chair now.

I won't sit there and be called a thief.

Nobody knows the truth about that debt because I have hidden it for almost three years, bearing every consequence alone. It is my business and nobody has the right to know except me.

This is too much. Why did I ever think good things were coming?

I start to pace the tiny amount of floor space around me because standing by my chair, hands balling into fists, is no longer an option.

I shouldn't have to tell anyone anything.

But in the red mist clouding my view, I suddenly picture Lachie outside his building. I hate that Noah horrified him. I hate that he boxed and labelled me the moment he met my son. But I had so many chances to tell him and I balked every time. I may have had my reasons, but how else was he to know?

I didn't speak when I should have. Maybe if I had, he could have been prepared – or could have walked away quietly. Anything but what happened. Anything but Noah having to see that horror aimed at him.

Hattie has shrunk a little in her seat, watching me with wide eyes. I'm not going to hit her. But how would she know that? To discover all those details must have made her question everything she knew about me.

Lachie was wrong. But did I lose him because I was too scared to speak?

Hattie is wrong. But she needs to know why what she's accusing me of is impossible. She needs to understand the insult she's just dealt.

So, I stop pacing.

I don't sit – I need to feel the sure ground beneath my feet and the strength in my spine now. I place my hand on the back of the chair for support because I don't know what effect saying this aloud will have on me.

And then, I speak.

'The debt is not mine. I didn't take out the loans, the credit cards, the expensive remortgage. My former fiancé did.'

Hattie stares.

I push on. 'We'd moved from South Wales to North Yorkshire for his job. Kai was earning good money and I found work as a teaching assistant in a local school. We bought a house, got engaged and started planning for a family. After a year, I found out I was expecting Noah. Kai was supportive at first but then he started staying late at work. Weeknights to begin with, then, as I was getting nearer my due date, he'd go for weekends, too. I assumed his employer was going through a tough time – as everyone else seemed to be back then. I had Noah, and Kai was different for the first few months – more attentive, more present. But then the late nights and the weekend conferences started again. And one night, the week before Noah's first birthday, he disappeared.'

I can see my employer squirm a little in her chair. 'This isn't the point, Bethan...'

You don't want to hear it, more like.

You've convicted me already.

'Well, I'm not finished, Miss Rowse. Do you know how I found out what had really been going on?' I don't give her time to reply. 'When the bailiffs arrived at my door, demanding ten thousand pounds. They threatened me, my baby – with prison and social workers and care orders, the lot. A neighbour intervened and got them to leave, but I was terrified. So I went to the bank. That's when they told me. About the credit cards he'd taken out in my name. The signatures he'd forged. The list of payday loans and stupidly high interest moneylender agreements *Bethan Gwynne* had signed. I went to the police and reported him missing. Then I found a legal aid lawyer, who told me that unless Kai was found, I would be liable for the debt because it was my name on the agreements, my signature on everything...'

'The debt must have been dreadful. But the temptation that access to our account must have given you...'

'I didn't steal from you! I'm trying to explain...'

'And I'm sorry, I really am. But the fact remains only you had access...'

'You're not listening to me!'

Hattie falls silent, her hands gripping the arms of her chair.

'*Not my fault.* My house sold to pay off one tiny corner of debt. Everything I owned seized or sold. The police said Kai was out of the country: still is, in case you were wondering. It went to court, they considered me a victim of fraud but without Kai there, I was liable. The credit card companies agreed to lower my debt; the loan sharks didn't. So yes, Hattie, I have debt I may never pay off. Not my fault. Not my doing. But it's my life now... And yes, I am a single mother and I am bloody proud of that. I've kept my son safe, kept us alive, when his father couldn't care if we made it or not. And I'm pulling us out of the mess he left.'

'Bethan, I...'

'And if you had one ounce of compassion and knew me at all you would know what working here has meant to me...' I don't stop the tears now. She needs to see them. 'You would understand that the very last thing I would do would be to jeopardise what I have here. If I lose this job, Hattie, I lose the means to pay for my home, for Noah's keep, for the weekly repayments that take every penny I can afford to get that man out of our lives for good. And frankly, the money you say I stole? It wouldn't even cover a tenth of my debt. It's not worth losing everything else for.'

'Then who...?'

'I don't know!'

I look at Hattie and I realise: it doesn't matter what I say. I'm glad I said it, but I can't stay here. I'll find another job, several, if I have to. I'll work twice as hard to keep us safe. I don't want to start again, but I will.

I take my jacket from the back of the chair and open the office door. Slowly, I turn back and speak, my voice low, my words a jabbed finger back at her.

'Trace the account the withdrawals were transferred to. Get the bank to do it. That's how they traced the money Kai stole from us. I only have one bank account now, a debit account with no overdraft facility. The cash office will have it on my record because it's where my wages are paid. Check the account numbers. And then find someone to take my job, Hattie, because I quit.'

I don't look back. I don't run. I walk away from Bright Hill with my head high, past Darren, past my open-mouthed colleagues who heard the shouting from the end of the corridor, past the sixty-year-old rickety glass walls, out to my car – and drive away for the last time.

A mile down the road, in a grassy lay-by at the entrance to a poppy-stabbed cornfield, I finally let go. Screaming out the injustice, sobbing my fury, gasping against my fear.

What have I done?

Chapter Forty-Seven

LACHLAN

There's still no word from Archer about the inquiry.

What's taking them so long?

I have seven messages on my phone from Riggsy I haven't answered. I have nothing to say to him. Judging by their content, I don't think he knows any more than I do yet. When the time comes – if my statement has implications for him – I'm prepared for the fallout.

But the waiting is the worst.

There are more unanswered texts on my phone – from Sal, who hasn't called since our row but clearly has more to say. I can't read them, not yet. They can all wait.

I settle back into my seat in the taxi and watch the North Yorkshire countryside speed past the window. It rained heavily this morning but now the sun has split the granite-grey clouds, light catching the wet leaves of trees and hedges that line the road. When I first came to Catterick I expected rolling dales like I'd seen on *Last of the Summer Wine*, but here the fields are mostly wide and flat, the sky a broad dome above it. I was expecting towering moors on all sides but fell in love with the vastness of this landscape.

I remember Bethan talking about where she grew up, the presence of mountains always in her peripheral vision. I wish I'd asked how she came to be in North Yorkshire. There are so many things I wish I'd asked her, back when we took our Thursdays together for granted. Planting those flowers, putting the world to rights, back then I was convinced we'd have forever. We didn't need to find out everything in the first few weeks.

I was wrong about that, wasn't I?

I miss her.

I wish I didn't.

What would I tell her about today? That I'm on my way to talk to my consultant at the hospital in Darlington. That Tanya suggested it should happen, earlier than I'd expected. That I don't know what to hope for anymore.

Things have slowed but I always knew that was possible. I've worked hard and I feel stronger, some of the movement has reluctantly returned. But since that day with Bethan – and the silence that's followed – it hasn't felt the same. I wanted to push through to be able to see her face to face. To tell her what she means to me. *Meant* to me.

Maybe I'll look back and see meeting her as a thing that happened when I needed it. Ultimately, she isn't responsible for my recovery. I'd just lost sight of what I wanted before I posted the first message in my window. Bethan arrived when I was slipping into a dark place. I can't wish it hadn't happened. I won't: but knowing she's still in the world when I can't be with her hurts more than any injury.

I move from blood test to X-ray to physio automatically, used now to the stop-start journey along endless corridors. The New York con-artist-turned-lawyer is still with me – the fifth adventure I've accompanied him on almost complete in the book I brought in my bag. But today I let Eddie Flynn rest from his life-or-death pursuit of killers. I owe his final chapters my full attention and I can't give that today.

Waiting for the consultant, I scroll through social media on my phone, but nothing catches my attention. I chuck it in my bag with the resting book hero and rub my hand over my left forearm. When my fingers meet Maya Angelou's ivy-strewn words a sudden, uninvited memory of Bethan's cool fingers passing across them almost stops my heart.

Will I ever be able to forget her?

Annoyed, I shove the question aside. *This* is my life now. I have dealt with far worse. Focus on getting back on my feet, regaining my strength and – God willing – returning to work.

The inquiry is taking as long as it needs. The delay is a good thing, I tell myself. If they'd decided to punish me I would have heard sooner. They are doing their job: mine is to trust them and wait.

'Lachlan Wallace?'

It's the physio I saw before. He's not as chatty today but the waiting room is twice as busy as usual. He looks stressed, his smile warm but brief, his progress down the corridor a little wearier than before. I keep up with him, resisting the urge to press ahead, just to prove I can.

I expect to see the consultant first as I always have, but instead the three physiotherapists tell me she's asked them to put me through my paces before she arrives.

I complete each task, reining in my thoughts as best I can. I'm here to work, so I do, each movement, stretch, push and lift a confirmation of how far I've come. I let myself celebrate the completion of each test. It's time I felt good about the work I've put in to get where I am. The team are encouraging but focused. The room has a determined stillness as we work. The detachment takes me back to how I operate in my job – where it might concern some people, to me it's a comfort. Do the task at hand, do it well, move on to the next. That sense of quiet purpose and accepted order has been the framework of my life for eighteen years and I realise that's why I've struggled at home. I need to return to the order of my life. Too much time without it has been dangerous for my mind.

Dr Fairbairn arrives as I'm resting after the final round of resistance lifts, her smile broad as she greets me.

'Apologies for the delay, Mr Wallace. It's crazy in here today.'

'I noticed.' One of the physios hands me a cup of water and pats my shoulder as she does so. 'Thanks.'

'Right, when you're ready?' The consultant beckons to her desk.

As I'm collecting my bag and stick I notice the three physios leave, the quiet *schhlup-schhlup* of their shoes passing out of the room and the squeak as the door closes in their wake.

'Got a good sweat there, soldier,' she says.

'Thanks, ma'am,' I grin back.

She nods and turns to her file, her smile fading as she reads. 'So, I've reviewed the latest information from Tanya and your most recent X-rays.'

I drink my water and wait, my pulse still not returned to resting rate.

Dr Fairbairn folds her hands on the open file for a moment and I see her distinct intake of breath before she turns to me.

'Your strength is good. We're seeing good progress in your leg musculature and the skin around the surgery wounds is healing well.' Her eyes dip. 'But I know you are keen to return to work and there are considerations you should be aware of.'

'Such as?'

'The damage to your pelvis and hip is, regrettably, more complex than we estimated.'

The sweat on my brow becomes ice cold as blood drains from my head. 'In what way?'

'It is unlikely to heal any more than it has.' Her expression becomes still, solemn eyes in a becalmed sea.

And suddenly everything is in freefall.

I tune her out as she quietly lays out the grounds for her prognosis, her promise that physiotherapy will continue, the shift of their focus now to supporting my leg when I walk, talk of shoe inserts and straps and retraining my leg as it is to do the best job that it can...

The room becomes the garden by my building, a small boy chasing a ball through the border I'd planted by the hedge, the most beautiful face I've ever seen contorted by horror when she saw me.

It's worse than losing her.

It's worse than any of it.

And then I'm sobbing, any hope of maintaining my composure gone. My consultant is shocked into silence. I won't be the first grown man she's seen devastated in this chair but I wonder if she'd expected this response from me. I can't stop it engulfing me. It's all-consuming and breath-stealing and impossible to withstand. With no other course of action, I let everything go – my hurt, my fear, my utter frustration with my useless body I'd expected so much more from.

But this isn't about my leg. It's not even about my own self-image. It's the unfairness of it all. I was doing the right thing. I was saving the people in the oncoming car – and Adam Riggs, for all the thanks he ever gave me. And I trusted Bethan to see beyond the physical me, to see my heart that I'd thrown open for her.

Dr Fairbairn's hand is soft when it rests on mine, her fingers squeezing the top of my fist.

'I am so sorry it's not the news you'd hoped for,' she says, her voice gentle and low. 'But there's no reason why you can't return to work, live independently, carry on with your life as much as you did before.'

I shake my head as if trying to dislodge a swarm of flies. I don't need kind words or reassurances. Nothing will be the same.

'I know this is hard…' I glare at her through tears but she holds my stare. 'I watched my husband go through it.'

That pulls me up short. 'Through this?'

'Similar. He was injured in a training exercise. His right leg was crushed. I watched the towering man I'd loved for years crumble. The body is everything in the army. Physical strength, pushing your limits, establishing your place in the pecking order – I understand, Lachlan, more than you know. But *you* need to understand that life is not about can-do and can't-do, it's about *living*. You could have died in that crash. You didn't. Your body is healing in its own way, not in the way you've decided is best.' She gives a sigh and her hand squeezes mine again. 'I shouldn't say this, it's beyond my professional responsibility to you, but *live* your life. Discover what's possible, forget what isn't. You have worth beyond what you can see. So that's what you prove – to yourself and the world. That's your focus.'

I'm numb as the taxi takes me home. I don't see the light or the vastness of the skies, the tiny villages huddling against the road, the towering trees standing sentry at their boundaries. The taxi driver senses my mood and turns the radio up. I'm not crying now – Dr Fairbairn gave me time to recover before I left – but my eyes are red-rimmed and haunted when I catch sight of them in the rear-view mirror.

I don't want to think of Bethan, but what my consultant said has sparked a memory that refuses to leave.

It's tough on your own, especially if you don't have family nearby. So many times I think I could just give up, but that's when I look for positives.

I remember her words about collecting small signs of positivity in her day, and how the act of looking for them keeps her spirits from dropping. I reach into my bag and pull out my wallet, unzipping the small coin section in the back of the old scratched leather. It's empty save for one thing: a small, smooth, round quartz pebble. The memory of Bethan's fingers meeting mine as she passed it to me through the hedge is broken glass to my heart. I don't know why I kept it. But it sits in my palm as the colours of the countryside fly past the window. Small, unremarkable, but oddly reassuring.

It's just a pebble.

It doesn't change anything.

But it helps.

I may not have Bethan Gwynne in my life now. But I have *this*.

Chapter Forty-Eight

BETHAN

The text arrives at 8 a.m., in the middle of my attempt to cook pancakes. I woke this morning determined to make the most of everything and making Noah's favourite weekend treat seemed the perfect place to start.

I almost drop my phone in the batter bowl when I open the message, my flour-smeared hands skidding against the smooth plastic of its case. Noah looks up from his dragon battalion who are doing manoeuvres across the coffee table, and giggles at the sight of his mam phone-juggling in the kitchen. I wipe it on my T-shirt, which needs a wash anyway, and grin back at him.

'My act needs work,' I say.

'Flip it like a pancake!' he beams back.

At least I have this. Him and me. Mighty Team of Two. Everything else can be worked on.

I look down at the message and smile again. Patrick, bless his heart. He sent so many texts yesterday after I left Bright Hill and told me he wanted to quit in solidarity. I told him he was daft for considering it and that I'd take it as a personal insult if he did. He's sweet, but this isn't his battle.

HEY, B – CAN I COME VISIT TODAY? P x

The flat is a state. I just about got Noah fed, bathed and into bed before I crashed myself. Last night's pots are stacked in the sink, Noah's preschool things dumped by the door where he left them yesterday, his toys everywhere because I want him to be happy here, for as long as we can stay. I fought hard for us to live in this flat – I'm going to squeeze every last drop of joy out of it before we have to leave.

I quickly reply:

HEY, P – NOT UP TO VISITORS TODAY. HOW ABOUT TOMORROW? B xx

Seconds after I hit 'send', a reply pings back. *Man*, that kid types fast...

NOT A QUESTION. I'LL BE WITH YOU AT 10 A.M. TEXT YOUR ADDRESS, K? BRINGING CAKE ☺ P x

I don't need this today. But maybe if I see Patrick now it will draw a line under everything. I stare at the piles of job listings I printed off before Noah woke, and the stacks of washing that need doing. I'll shove it all in my bedroom and shut the door.

But first, my boy needs pancakes...

At 10 a.m. the buzzer sounds and Noah gives a delighted scream. Visitors are such a rare thing here it's akin to Santa turning up, and he's got so much sugar running through his system after his special breakfast that Patrick is likely to be dog-piled the minute he sets foot through the door.

'Calm down,' I say. 'It's Patrick.'

'Is he going to play with me?'

Like he'd have a choice. 'I reckon so. Let's just let him get in and have a cup of tea first, okay?'

'Okay,' Noah beams, but I can tell from his cheeky smile that the chances of Patrick getting to sit at all are slim to non-existent.

'Come on up,' I say, buzzing the entrance door open. 'We're Flat 3, up the stairs and turn right.'

I wait in the open doorway and feel the warm nudge of a little head under my hand, two arms wrapping around my leg. 'He's coming,' I say, stroking his hair.

My son's feet dance on the doormat. He's always done that – little tapping feet of joy, as if the excitement wriggles out of his body through his toes. It all helps this morning. Positives are returning after the darkness of yesterday. I feel lighter, too, having told someone about Kai. Like shrugging off a too-big waterlogged coat and feeling it leave my shoulders.

Patrick's sunny smile appears at the top of the stairwell and I wave. He lifts his hand, too and then turns back to look down the stairs. What is he doing?

'Over here,' I laugh, wondering if maybe he didn't see me after all – and then I see why.

'Two people!' Noah yells, as the smile slips from my face.

Hattie raises her hand. Patrick looks at me and shrugs.

I should tell them both to take a running jump.

'Come and see my dragons!' Noah says, breaking free from me and dashing over to Patrick. He grabs Pat's hand, pulling him past me into the flat.

Shaken, I step into the corridor, pulling the door closed behind me.

'Bethan, can we talk, please?' Hattie asks, the smallest quiver in her voice.

'I don't think we have anything to say.'

'I disagree.' She shifts awkwardly on the top step. 'I'm not leaving until we do…'

You picked your moment to be steely, Hattie Rowse.

I don't know what she thinks she's going to achieve, jumping me like this. Frankly, I don't care. The damage was done yesterday – there's no coming back from what she said.

I open my mouth to say this but the door whips open and Noah bumps into my legs – one of his favourite games.

'Stop jabbering!' he demands. A word he learned from my mam last Christmas and thinks is the most hilarious thing. I feel the tug of his hands on my arm, the kind of pull that won't be mollified by a gentle refusal. Stuck between a rock and a hard place, I stare at Hattie and nod in the direction of my flat. Not saying the words *please come in* makes it easier somehow. I'm going back inside: if she wants to follow that's her business.

Pat already looks like he's done ten rounds with Anthony Joshua, half-sprawled on my sofa with the dragon army advancing across his lap. Five minutes with my son at his most excited will do that to you. *Welcome to the world of Noah Gwynne, my friend.*

'Noah, let Patrick sit for a bit, okay?'

'But he likes the dragons.'

'I'm fine,' Pat replies, looking anything but.

Behind me, Hattie slips into an armchair, her handbag on her knees in case of dragon (or small boy) attack.

I could laugh, seeing them both like that, if I wasn't engaged in a battle of my own. I'm angry they planned this ambush and frustrated that there's no way I can say what I want with my son in the room – which was probably their scheme all along.

I make tea without asking if anyone wants one, more to give myself a moment to regroup than a desperate need to be hospitable.

'This place is proper cool,' Patrick says, eyebrows raised at Hattie as her cue to reply.

'It's nice. The light is… particularly lovely.' She stares back at her handbag, embarrassed by her own weak words.

'I bet you like it here,' Patrick says to Noah, handing him a green-and-pink dragon with a '*raaar*'.

'I've got my own big bed now in my own big bedroom,' my son beams back – and I have to bite my lip hard because *this* is what I'm going to take away from him soon. All the promises I made him about living here, about the things we would do and the life we would have, snatched away by the visitor currently shifting guiltily in my chair.

The slowly boiling kettle acts as a subtle barrier to Hattie and Patrick's polite small talk that's supposed to include me. I zone out their voices and summon my strength. Actually, Hattie *should* be here. She should see what she's going to make us lose because of her actions.

Last night I dreamed we were back in the mould and damp of the bedsit. I woke up unable to breathe, my pillow soaked with sweat. Wherever we go next, it won't be back there, or anywhere like it. I'd rather curl up and die than drag my son back to that stinking hole.

I'm going to call Emrys tonight. I know there's no room for

us at his place or at Mam's but he might know of something close by. I haven't been back to Wales for months but it might be time to make the move home, before Noah has to start his Reception year. I'm not ready to deal with that possibility but it wouldn't hurt to ask.

The kettle clicks and the sound recedes. Noah is explaining his dragon-guarding-pirate-treasure theory to Patrick, who looks lost. Hattie is staring at her hands.

I hope they don't hang about long.

I make tea and deliver mugs to them, pointedly placing coasters out of Noah's reach.

When I step back, I glance over at the window. I do it without thinking.

I wish we were still talking. I wish I still had my friend. The worst part of waking from my nightmare this morning was knowing there wouldn't be a message in Lachie's window wishing me goodnight, or cracking some lame joke about biscuits. When it was all happening, it felt as if every minute of our games stretched out, like shadows in the late-afternoon sun. Already I'm forgetting what it felt like to store things up in my days to share with him by the hedge.

What would I tell Lachie now? That I walked out of the job I told him I loved, away from the project he sparked the idea for?

That the loss of the project is easier to bear because it won't remind me of him every day?

I put that new blind in the window in a bid to stop me looking out. Instead, I just stare at it, a hundred times a day. It doesn't help, despite being made of the sunniest yellow fabric.

When I can put the moment off no longer, I perch on the

farthest edge of the sofa, pulling one of Noah's dragons onto my lap like a shield. Patrick glances at me, then Hattie. I see his completely unsubtle nod at her. It all feels so contrived.

'Why are you here?' I ask, before she tries to speak. I'm keen to get whatever this is over with as soon as possible so Noah and I can have our flat to ourselves.

Hattie dares to look me in the eye at last. 'I owe you an apology. You were right: I checked the account number the money had been transferred to and – it wasn't yours.'

Stung but justified, I stare back.

Patrick nods again, the way Noah's preschool teachers do when coaxing a child to speak in an end-of-term presentation. Hattie's gaze drops to her palms as if the words she needs might be written along the lines in her skin.

'I should have done that first before accusing you.'

'Yes, you should,' Patrick agrees. I hold my hand up to stop him saying more, but he ignores it. 'And maybe you should have asked me.'

Hattie's head sinks further.

That makes no sense. 'Why?'

He sighs. 'Because I worked it out. Who the other person was that had access to the accounts.'

I look at Hattie. 'Which other person?'

Patrick waits for Hattie to respond; when no reply comes, he turns to me. 'Darren.'

What?

'But he didn't...'

'Not officially. But remember that time you asked me to take the account file to Hattie's office for you? When the kid from the Legacy went missing?'

At first none of what he says makes any sense. I push through the lanes of questions dashing both ways in my mind until a dim recollection arrives. 'You said you'd given it to Hattie.'

'I had – well, I knew she was going to get it.'

'I don't understand.'

He sighs. 'I didn't want to worry you after you'd found the kid and were so happy... I was taking the file to Hattie's office but I met Darren on the way. He said he'd take it for me. When I said no, he insisted, telling me to get back out to help look for the kid. I didn't think to question it; I mean, I just thought it was Darren being an *arse*...' He looks at Hattie and I see that it isn't to check whether she approves of his opinion, but to make sure she hears it. 'But after you left yesterday he was like a chuffin' crowing cockerel. Emphasis on the *cock*...'

Hattie winces at that.

I'm still struggling to find the thread of his story. 'So he was glad to be rid of me. That's not a shock.'

'Nah, see, when he took that file he sent me packing. I don't know whether he went straight to Hattie's office or not because I was out of there.'

'He had time to gain access to the passwords. More than enough time.' Hattie's voice strengthens as she speaks. 'The account the money went to wasn't one we recognised but when our bank checked with the online bank it belonged to, they confirmed the holder was a Mr D Gifford.'

'Darren was stealing from Bright Hill?'

Hattie nods. 'Has been for some time, it transpires.'

'But the community fund was only set up recently...' I begin.

'Yeah, but the ordering account wasn't,' Pat grins. 'Tell her, Hattie.'

Hattie shakes her head. 'I'm such a fool, Bethan. I let Darren have control of plant orders and I didn't check the delivery notes from the plant wholesaler against what he told me he'd ordered. Turns out he's been taking money from us for years.'

I can't believe what I'm hearing. I know Darren was always very protective of the delivery chits on Tuesdays when the trucks came in, but I assumed it was just him playing the Big Boss and throwing his weight around as usual. 'How did you find out about the rest?'

'He confessed everything,' Patrick says, scowling at the dragon in his hands as if Darren's face has appeared there. 'Like the weasel he is. Hattie threatened to call the police and he cried like a baby.'

'Where's the baby?' Noah asks, looking around in case the new visitors have stashed one out of view. Several of his preschool friends have recently become big sisters and big brothers and a deep suspicion about new babies is the current hot topic of conversation.

'There's no baby, *bach*. Show Patrick Tân Dragon.'

Concern forgotten, Noah grabs the black-and-rainbow-spotted dragon and wiggles it in Pat's face. It's the break in the tension between us I needed, but I'm still reeling. I knew Darren disliked me, but to set me up like that is just evil. I turn to Hattie. 'So, I'm guessing it was Darren you told first about the withdrawals and he pointed the finger at me?'

Bingo. Hattie looks like she wants to throw up. 'I made a massive error of judgement. I know that now.'

'You should have known it *then*,' I snap, pulling back my anger because I don't want Noah to hear. 'You should have believed me, not Darren.'

'He took me in. He could always argue his way out of it. He...'

'Save it, Hattie. That's all bollocks. He was the last guy your dad hired before he passed away. To get rid of him would be undoing Hector's work.'

Her mouth drops open. For a split second I think I've gone too far. But you know what? She needs to be told. It's high time she knew the truth. 'Everyone knows that. It's why we all put up with him. Not for his sake. Or Hector's memory. But because we loved you.'

Her eyes swim. Patrick is watching me now, too.

I should be kicking off and yelling at her, but right now kindness will achieve more. It annoys the crap out of me that I understand that, but I have to speak from my gut. Be direct, say what I feel. Recriminations will only eat away at me and I have been through enough. 'You should have believed me. And you should have stood up for yourself. But you've worked so hard to make Bright Hill worthy of your dad's legacy and we all saw that. We know what you've sacrificed to keep his name alive. But it isn't his now: it's yours. *Your* life. *Your* legacy to leave. It shouldn't have had to come to this, but it's necessary.'

She pulls a tissue from her sleeve and I look away to give her the time she needs. I feel better for saying it, even if it all came out too late to change anything.

'I want you to have his job,' she says.

'What?'

'I did you a great disservice, Bethan, and I want to put it right. That's why I asked Patrick to help me, because I didn't think you'd see me on my own.'

I'm floundering now. 'I'm not sure I could...'

'Wait, please. There's more. I have a friend – a good friend – he specialises in family law and financial mediation. I think he might be able to help you with…' she glances at Patrick, who is too busy having a roar-off with Noah to notice, '… the *other* situation.'

'No, I…'

'I will pay for it. I want to pay for it,' she says, a defiance in her tone I've not heard before. 'Perhaps if the person in question is tracked down, or the original agreements re-examined, there may be ways to reduce or cancel… certain *figures*.'

'I can't ask you to do that.'

'I insist.'

'Hattie, you have to understand, this isn't something you throw money at to make it go away. The worst thing anyone could ever do to me is to judge me for my son.' I think of Lachie and kick against the burn. 'Thinking I would jeopardise everything in his life to steal poxy amounts of money from you makes you no better than Darren. All that crap he threw at me, every day I worked with him, I could put that down to his ignorance. But not you. I expected better of you.'

The urge to pull back is overwhelming, to accept the offer and stuff it all under the carpet again where it can't hurt me. But I need to speak up, like I did when she accused me yesterday.

Wait. Give yourself air. Find your footing. Stand your ground.

'I am worth more than that,' I say. I don't recognise the calm strength in my voice, but I know it's me saying the words. 'I am not my past, or Kai, or the debt, or my son. I am so much more than that.'

And suddenly, I am.

I have fought this for so long. But here's my truth: I am my own person. I deserve to be seen for everything that I am. For who I am.

I won't accept anything less again.

Chapter Forty-Nine

LACHLAN

It's been a week since the consultant told me the news. I'm not reconciled to it yet, but every day I've held Bethan's pebble and searched for positives. I'm glad the only witnesses to this are Ernie and Bert. Once they worked out it wasn't food, they let me get on with it.

That's a positive in itself.

Now they flank me either side, an uneasy truce called between them. I think they know my shit is greater than theirs and are observing a ceasefire while I deal with it. Bert has even surrendered Sock to my safekeeping. It's currently placed across my knee, inches away from his nose where he keeps guard. The jury is out on whether he's guarding Sock or me. I wouldn't like to call it, either way.

Bert and Ernie's heads lift as one when my phone rings. I recognise the number immediately and my thumb is clumsy as it swipes the screen to answer.

'Hello, Wallace.'

'Sir.'

'The report is in.'

343

'When shall I come in?'

'This afternoon, if possible.'

My mind races as I factor in getting ready, calling a taxi and the journey over to Catterick, my rising nerves complicating the calculations. 'I could be there for two o'clock?'

'Better make it three, give you time to get here.'

'Of course, sir.'

'Excellent. Three it is.'

At 2.50 p.m. I thank the driver and get out of the taxi, right by the entrance to the Educational and Training Service building. No skulking up the hill in the rain for me this time. I walk, keeping my head high, through the entrance doors, owning every step in my new, permanent gait. It still doesn't feel like me, but I am not going to be defined by it. As I wait for someone to let me into the offices, my hand goes to the breast pocket of my shirt. The tiny round shape within the fabric reassures me.

Time to hunt for positives.

Kim appears and grins at me through the doors. I owe even being here to her bravery. I try to communicate that with my smile, but I reckon she knows.

'Hey, Wallace, how goes it?'

'Good,' I say, willing myself to feel it with as much confidence as I say it.

She holds the door open for me to pass through, then follows me down the corridor. 'So, the report came back.'

'And?'

'Archer seems okay with it.' Her eyes narrow. 'Don't suppose you've heard from Riggs lately?'

'Should I have?'

She brightens. 'No.' That's all she says but *not* all she means and I don't know whether that's a positive or not.

Instead of waiting where I did before, Kim ushers me straight towards Archer's office. At least it isn't the room where I met the investigating team. Archer is a stickler for regularity so I'd half-wondered if all conversations pertaining to the inquiry would be conducted there.

I thank Kim and knock on Archer's door.

'Come.'

He stands as I enter. 'Wallace, take a seat. Journey over okay?'

'Yes, sir.'

'Still raining out there, I suppose.'

'No, nice bit of sun now.'

This is surreal. It's not like my superior to engage in discussions about the weather. Is he nervous?

No. Archer only gets nervous if his shift runs over. I have to calm down. This is the news I've been waiting for. I can move on after this meeting.

Archer pats a closed file on his desk. 'So, we've had the report from the inquiry team and there are several developments you should be aware of.'

I straighten in my chair. 'Sir.'

'Firstly, I have to tell you that arrests have been made this morning, disciplinary action to follow.'

'Arrests, sir?'

'Lance-Corporal Adam Riggs was arrested at 0800 hours in his quarters, on charges of theft of a vehicle, possession of a weapon and attempting to pervert the course of justice. And Sergeant Cathal Byrne was arrested an hour later in barracks, charged with intimidation, racketeering and attempted assault.'

It takes a moment to sink in. I'd assumed Riggsy would face some disciplinary action for stealing the pool car, but the rest?

Archer observes me over steepled fingers. 'I hope now you understand the serious nature of this inquiry. And how close you came to joining them in the cells.'

'Sir.' My voice falters. 'What will happen to them?'

'Trial in a military court. Possible involvement of civilian police, it's too early to say. I have no truck with rumours, but the indications are that the case against Byrne particularly may become larger if more witnesses emerge.'

If what I know already about Cathal Byrne comes to light, I don't doubt the military police will have much to deal with. That's if people come forward. But that isn't my problem.

I should ask about Riggsy's fate but my days of bailing him out are over. He wasn't my friend all the time I thought he was: not the friend I needed, anyhow. At least in custody he can't come after me. Not that I think he would. He's always been stronger in the gob than in his fists, talking a good game but rarely seeing it through. I'll block his number from my phone, which I should have done weeks ago and, then I can draw a line under his involvement in my life.

It still stings. But walking away from him – and the crash that changed my life – is a positive I'll hold close.

'Thank you for telling me, sir.'

'Hmm. How's the leg?'

'I met with my consultant last week. The damage is irreversible, but they are confident they can strengthen my posture and work on supporting my body to accommodate the change. It means I can consider a return to work, when appropriate.'

He acknowledges this with a nod. But he wears a strange expression.

'Wallace, do you know how many opportunities I gave you to tell the truth?'

'Sir?'

'You think I wasn't aware of the inconsistencies in your version of events?'

The silence in the office becomes deafening, crushing against my ears. I can't reply, blinking helplessly back at him.

'Do you think I didn't realise you were protecting your friend?'

'He's not my friend, sir...'

Archer's hand slams against the desk and I jump. 'Damn it, Wallace! Pedantics! He was enough of a friend for you to lie, willingly, in collusion, to a military investigation. On *my* watch.'

'I thought I was helping him...'

'By risking your career? Must have been some friendship to jeopardise that for.'

'He thought he'd lose his job. And on the night of the crash I didn't know the car wasn't his.'

'We knew, Wallace. The car was reported stolen a week after the crash. It was kept in-house when Byrne's allegation of Riggs's threat against him came to light. Better not to involve the civilian police when Command deemed our own inquiry necessary.'

No... The revelation slams headlong into my body. 'But he said nobody knew.'

'He was also more than happy to tell the inquiry that it was you who'd taken it. That you had a score to settle with Byrne and roped him into it.'

I was planning to feign surprise when Archer said about Riggsy blaming me for stealing the car, but my shock is real when I hear the rest. I can't believe he was ready to see me face charges – was the damage to my body not enough? Did he hate me that much?

I'm reeling, the truth of it all too much to comprehend.

Archer shakes his head. 'You are cleared on all accounts. The inquiry noted your bravery in averting a greater crash. You saved lives at personal cost to you. That is commendable, Wallace. *That* is the soldier I know.' I search his face for any hint of compassion but the flatness of his tone scares me. 'But the fact remains that you chose to lie for your friend over your loyalty and responsibility to the army.'

'Sir, I made a huge error of judgement. But I wasn't in a place to think clearly after the crash...'

'Agreed. However, in the weeks following, you had ample time to formulate the correct response. I'm disappointed in you. And, as such, your position in this unit is untenable.'

'No, sir...'

He raises his hand to silence me. 'You have two options. You can apply for a desk position to see out the remainder of your career, or you can opt to leave. You have more than served your time and would be free to go. Do you understand?'

No. I don't understand. I did the right thing. I did what I thought was best. And when I realised my mistake, I corrected it. What more does Archer want from me?

I clear my desk in stunned silence, watched by Kim and my colleagues, who have no words either. Archer accompanies me to the waiting taxi and salutes me. His handshake and regretful nod mean nothing. I return the salute and get into the car.

I don't look back as we drive away.

Outside my building I pause by the entrance as the taxi leaves. I'm not going in yet. There's something I have to do first. I stow my pointless cardboard box of belongings I'll never use again in the doorway of my building, turn and walk back down the path, along the pavement to the building next door.

Bethan is home, I know she is. Thursdays are her work-from-home days.

I stab my stick against the paving slabs leading to her building, my mind set. I may have lost my job, I may be facing life in this new body, but I won't apologise for who I am. Bethan should have seen the real me and I need to say that to her. It's the only thing left in my life I have the power to change.

I find the button on the intercom panel for Flat 3 and press it, blood crashing in my ears. After a moment there's a click – and she answers.

'He-llo?' That singsong greeting of hers – that sounds so much brighter and happier in the lilt of her accent – grazes my heart. I have missed that voice. I open my mouth to speak…

… but then I falter.

What will I say to her? Why should I let her hurt me again? If she can't accept me for who I am, why should I even bother?

'Hello?' A note of irritation now.

I don't even know I'm going to be here. I'm sure as hell not going to be relegated to a desk job in that place, going in to work every day with everybody on the site knowing what happened to me. I decided that much already. Why try to talk to Bethan if I don't know what I'm going to be doing? I might not have the luxury of staying around here if jobs aren't available. I'm only here because of the garrison being at Catterick, after all.

'Look, either answer or I'm hanging up.'

I step back from the intercom, turn on my heel and walk away.

At the end of the path to her building, I reach into my pocket, pull out the pebble and throw it as far away from me as I can. I don't see where it lands.

I hold it together long enough to get inside my flat. But the rush of love from Bert and Ernie breaks me. I sink to the floor, the anger and pain and sheer bloody injustice overwhelming. Bert's increasingly frantic attempts to lick my face become blows to my leg and head as I cower beneath them, battling for breath. I am hollowed out, a shell of someone I thought I knew. I can't even feel my heart anymore. Just pain.

It's too much.

I tried to fight for positives and what did it get me?

Everything that mattered to me, lost.

I don't know how long I remain there, my leg and hip screaming at me to move, my dog and cat resorting to just lying against me. Shadows shift and lengthen across the floor, the dying afternoon giving up its final ghosts through the window I no longer want to look out from.

I breathe, bruised in the aftermath. My fingers find the warm fur and immediate lick of my dog. My cat stretches and sits, facing me, his eyes questioning.

What are you going to do?

I can't feel my injured leg. It passed through pins and needles to total numbness long ago. It's time to move.

Slowly, I coax life into my body – this body I have to own because it's mine and it's all I have – and steadily move upright, using the kitchen counter as a support. I fetch Bert and Ernie's food from the cupboard and prepare it. The regular act is comforting, the relief of my housemates palpable. Maybe this is how you move on: linking small acts of normality together. Maybe it's not in the heroic efforts, the milestone moments, but the unremarkable tasks that constitute ordinariness. I've been so obsessed with smashing expectations, pushing myself and proving my worth to the world that I forgot what made my life what it was before. The boring bits. The regular things so automatic I couldn't remember doing them. The Monday mornings, the midweek slumps. I've lost sight of that.

I've been thinking I don't have anyone on my side, but I do, don't I? I have a family who have been trying to care for me for months. I pull my phone from my back pocket and open the messages. Ten texts from my sister. All of them reaching out, all of them ignored until now:

Call whenever you want x

Just checking in. Call back if you want to x

Lachie, I'm thinking of you. Always x

The girls send their love. Would be great to chat x

Hoping this week is better. Hang in there, little brother x

Forget what Mum wants. We just want you to be happy x

A reminder you are loved. Even if you don't want to be x

Hope it goes well at the hospital today. Thinking of you x

Any news from the inquiry? Crossing everything x

I'm going nowhere, Lachie. We love you x

I hit the 'call' button as soon as I read the final text. How can I have ignored these for so long?

Sal answers on the second ring. 'Lachie?'

'Hey, sis,' I begin, emotion balling in my throat. 'I'm so sorry...'

'What happened? Are you okay?'

'I'm not okay,' I manage, before it engulfs me again. I'm sobbing down the line, my words like the words of a small boy, not the man I've spent so long proving I can be. 'My job is gone... My leg won't get better... I don't know what to do... It hurts so much...'

My sister's shock is palpable as she replies. 'No, Lachie... Oh my lovely man... It's okay, *shh*, it's okay...'

'... And *she* doesn't want me... I wanted her to want me but she doesn't...'

'Who doesn't want you? What's going on?'

And then I can't speak anymore. So my sister speaks for me, as she did when I was little and shy of my own voice, panic and passion beating through her words this time.

'Come home, my lovely. Let us be there for you. You're not on your own, Lachie, you never were... Oh my love... Listen to me, okay? I can't imagine how much you're going through, but you need to understand, it's not about us wanting to control you. It's not about forcing you to get better, or you proving to us

352

that you can cope. We *know* you can cope. That was never the issue.' I hear her choke back a sob, a strange sound at odds with the strong woman famous for keeping her emotions in check. 'We nearly lost you... I paced that bloody hospital corridor for three days solid, terrified you were going to die. As far as we are concerned, you've already achieved more than we dared to hope for. Because you survived.'

'I – I didn't know...'

'You think Mum doesn't care, that she has her own agenda. But she didn't sleep for weeks. Even now, she's up until the early hours and wakes at 5 a.m. Something broke in her when she almost lost you. You have nothing to prove. Just come home and let us celebrate still having you.'

In that moment, it all becomes clear. There's nothing for me here anymore. I need to go where I'm loved – and where I can rebuild my life.

'Okay,' I say. My final act of surrender. My last letting go.

It's time to go home.

Chapter Fifty

BETHAN

It's done. I can hardly believe it.

For the last two weeks I've given everything I can to the Legacy project. I accepted Hattie's job offer and will soon be starting as head of the plant section, but Hattie wants me to focus on the Legacy first. In the meantime, Murray has handled everything so well that I don't think anyone at Bright Hill has noticed the changes.

I've made countless phone calls, had meetings in person with local business owners and potential sponsors, repeating the same pitch over and over until I was reciting it in my sleep:

You would be investing in a five-year community initiative to bring all sectors together – old and young, unemployed, retired, community interest groups. You can be a founder of the Bright Hill Legacy, planting seeds in the community that can develop and grow...

I signed the final sponsorship agreement yesterday morning. It feels like I've scaled several mountains. But we're here and I am so proud of it.

All the beds sponsored for five years. Every one dedicated to the community groups who have given so much to it. The school, the excluded kids charity, the agriculture students, the mums-and-toddlers club and the other community groups – they can all continue to use the Legacy, so the wonderful crowd I've seen come together since we started will be able to continue.

Hattie phoned everyone last night and here we are today, gathered by the Bright Hill Legacy, surrounded by our gardeners, to make the announcement.

'You've all worked so hard and the beds look incredible,' Hattie beams. 'Our forthcoming produce show is going to be amazing. I just want to thank you – all of you – for being part of our great, impossible idea. I hope those of you who never gardened before will be inspired to continue and share the love of growing things with your family and friends.'

'I'll have to – they keep nicking my rhubarb!' Thelma yells, eliciting laughter from our band of intrepid volunteers.

'Your rhubarb is legendary, though, Thelma,' I grin.

She winks back. 'Nobody's disputing that.'

'I want to take this opportunity to thank Bethan, too,' Hattie says, laughing when Patrick woop-woops from the crowd. 'Without her tenacity and, let's face it, sheer bloody-mindedness, this wouldn't have been possible. Which is how I'm able to announce that Bethan has secured sponsorship for the Legacy garden for the next five years.'

An enormous cheer erupts and suddenly I'm being hugged on all sides.

But in the heart of the celebration, there's a nagging gap where *something* should be.

I push it away, as I have been doing every day lately. I'm probably just exhausted. Now we're out of the woods, I can start to process everything. It's like the time when Emrys snapped his big toe while out mountain biking – he cycled twenty miles and only realised what he'd done when he got home and took off his shoe. 'It didn't hurt until I stopped.' Bit of an extreme example, I know, but I think I finally understand what he meant. You don't deal with the emotions and the exhaustion when you're going through something, only when it ends.

I have a lot to process.

We're a month away from the Autumn Show that will be the culmination of the project, but the garden plots are teeming with life. Some only have flowers, some vegetables and fruit, some a mixture of both. Even the most experienced gardeners here have grown something new – and watching their joy and surprise at the fruits of their labours is wonderful.

As I was getting the Legacy ready for their arrival this morning, I thought about how far I've come. From a three-shift-a-week gift shop assistant to Head of Plants in this old, cranky, bloody lovely place. Getting a job here was the first glimpse of hope after Kai left us. Those three shifts were solid gold to me. I'm proud of everything I've achieved. I'm excited about the future now. Noah and I can stay in our flat, he can grow and flourish there, like the verdant life that surrounds me as I walk between the raised beds.

I just wish…

No, Bethan, don't go there. It's done. He wasn't right.

But I miss him.

A nudge against my elbow makes me turn.

'You are amazing, B,' Patrick says. I don't think he's stopped smiling all morning. 'Look at what you did.'

'What everyone did.'

'And sponsorship! That's phenomenal.'

'Phenomenal? That's a big word for you, Pat.' I ruffle his hair, laughing when he pushes me back.

'Get stuffed.'

'Sorry. I see your fan club are strong today.'

'Who can blame them?' He waves at Thelma, Connie and Dot, who blow him kisses. 'I'm the younger, sexier Monty Don, apparently. Connie reckons I should do a calendar for my fans.'

'I bet. Knowing Connie, she means one of those naked ones.'

He shrugs the joke off, but I notice his steps quicken as we walk back to the main building. 'So we have our jobs for the foreseeable?'

I look back at the happy crowd still celebrating with Hattie. 'For now. But we're not out of the woods yet. Hattie still needs to find a major investor.'

'Now she's discovered her business balls, I reckon she'll do it,' he says, pulling a face. 'Not sure how I feel about saying that sentence out loud.'

'Well, you helped her find them.' I grimace back. 'Okay, that sounds worse...'

'*Eww*, B! I do not want to claim responsibility for that.'

We've reached the yard now, the chatter from the Legacy barely audible from here. In the field next to the nursery a skylark is circling, its sweet song spinning up and up as it soars into the summer blue.

We slip into the stillness, perching on the stacks of compost bags in the outside bins.

'So, what about the guy?' Patrick's question is velvet-lined but it still stings.

'Nothing to tell.'

'Nah, forget him, B. Look at all the good stuff around you.

Like this...' He reaches into his pocket and produces a small, perfectly white quartz pebble. It shimmers in the sunshine. 'Found that this morning when I was raking the gravel by the café beds. It's what you always say, isn't it? Picking up *tiny shiny* bits of *good*.'

His attempt at a Welsh accent is pathetic, but I love him for it. He taps my hand with the pebble until I unfurl my fingers for him to lay it on my palm.

'Cheers, Pat.'

'Be happy, yeah? If anyone's earned the right for good stuff, it's you.'

He doesn't expect the hug – and accepts it like Noah does when he's on his way somewhere else but grudgingly humours his mam – but I give it to him anyway. I owe him so much and he's become a true friend lately. The one thing I've always missed.

He flushes when we part. 'Er, thanks?'

I can't help giggling at his embarrassment. 'Can I be in your fan club now?'

'Stop it.'

'Can I see your muscles? Connie says they're *delicious*...'

'Argh! Enough!' He shakes his head, but he's laughing, too.

'... And then the Great Rainbow Dragon gathered all the pirate treasure and promised to keep it safe. The pirates said thank you and sorry for trying to fight the dragon army. They had fish and chips for tea and lived happily ever after...'

'That's not how it happens, Mum.'

I stare at my son in his dragon-bedecked bed, the duvet tucked under his chin. 'Hang on, it's my story. I say what happens.'

He gives me a look about fifty years older than his almost-four years. 'It's *my* bedtime story about my dragons. And I know.'

The cheek! 'Er, my story, my rules, thank you very much.'

'Pirates don't say sorry, though.'

'They do if they want fish and chips.'

'*Mu-u-um.*' My son will not be moved. Clearly, I am an amateur in the world of dragon-pirate relations. 'If they said sorry, they wouldn't be pirates.'

How do you argue with that logic?

'Okay, Pirate King, what happens then?'

He rolls his eyes because I should know that. 'They say thank you 'cos that's polite. And the dragons give them fish and chips because they are nice. But really the pirates are waiting until the dragons forget and then they'll just steal the treasure again.'

'Oh really?'

'Yes really. Because *that's* what pirates *do.*'

Why do I think I've just been schooled in Noah's forward plan of action?

I'd promised myself a quiet one tonight, the after-effects of the day making themselves felt. I bought a bottle of wine on the way home because I deserve it, so I fetch it from the fridge where it's been chilling through Noah's teatime, bathtime and bedtime story. It smells like summer when I pour a glass – herbs and apples and freshly mown grass. I laugh at myself for thinking such bollocks, but who cares? There's only me to hear it and I don't mind.

I curl up on the sofa, my aching body succumbing to its cosiness. Time to breathe it in. I find an old Nora Ephron movie on Film4 and settle in for my well-deserved night.

But after a glass, I'm restless again.

Typical. Finally get the chance to relax and my head is playing racetracks.

I push off the sofa and go to get a refill of wine. It's the weekend tomorrow, so a sore head won't be the end of the world.

But a second glass only makes it worse.

Who am I trying to kid? I know what the problem is.

I should feel proud of everything that's happened. I should celebrate every last drop of it because, my life, I worked hard enough to make it happen. And I will celebrate. I will.

But the missing something remains.

It won't budge.

I stare at the drawn yellow blind.

He had no right to judge me. I thought he liked me for who I was. And yes, maybe I should have told him about Noah, but that wasn't his decision to make – or mine to be judged for.

Lachie Wallace should have seen *me*.

Just me.

I should have been enough.

And I'm *furious* with him for missing that. I never got the chance to challenge him on it, because his face told me everything I needed to know. But how dare he react that way, after everything we shared? After all the hope he'd built? And how dare he show that to my son?

The moment he did it, he ripped my heart from out of me.

In front of Noah.

And he needs to know.

Two glasses of wine are enough to kick my reservations to the kerb. I find one remaining sheet of paper in Noah's craft box and the only blue felt-tip that still works. And I write what I should have said to Lachie on that day. I don't hold back. I've found my voice and he needs to hear it.

> I HAVE A KID. HE'S MY HEART.
> BUT I AM MORE THAN JUST HIS MUM.
> I WISH YOU'D SEEN THAT.

I wrench the blind up to its highest setting, grab tape from the kitchen drawer and stick the message in the window. As I do, I glance across at Lachie's building. Ernie is on the windowsill, watching me.

'Tell him to read this, Ern,' I say.

He keeps staring.

Well, fine. I've said it now. Too late to change anything, but it's the line I needed to draw.

Now I can move on.

Chapter Fifty-One

LACHLAN

'Great light... Kitchen's a good size... Are these appliances staying?'

I force a smile at the estate agent, who is far too chirpy for this hour. Eight a.m. is fine to be up and about, but nobody should be this happy about it. He'd last two minutes in the army before someone whacked him with that clipboard he's clutching.

'Yes, all of them. Carpets and curtains, too.'

That pleases him. 'Are you willing to negotiate on light fixtures?'

'Sure, why not,' I reply, casting Bert a warning look as he growls again from his guard post safely beneath the dining table, Sock by his side for backup.

'Your dog's – *okay* – isn't he?' It's the first flicker I've seen from him since he breezed in.

I look at Bert and then back to the estate agent – whose name I've already forgotten – as if to emphasise the point that my dog is about as scary as a grumpy hearth rug. 'He's cool. Just don't try to touch that sock.'

'Is that what it is?'

Yeah, okay, he has a point. Sock is pretty unrecognisable now, just a mass of acrylic knit and drool. 'Once upon a time.' Like me, I think. Once upon a time I was a different person. But like Sock, I'm not finished with yet.

I probably smell better, though…

I stifle a smile as I follow the guy down the corridor to my room and the guest room. Probably best he doesn't know his new client is comparing himself to a stinky dog toy.

In the two weeks since I made the decision to move back to Bourton, I've formally resigned from the army, had my notice period transmuted to an extended gardening leave and started to think about what my options might be for this new life I'm slowly accepting is mine. The estate agent is the last link in a chain of events that began with my call with Sal. I don't know that I feel happier about it all, just calmer. And that's a change I can live with. Life has been too full of mountains and valleys lately. When I move back to the Cotswolds I'll take some time to be quiet at last, to let it all sink in.

Until then, I'm keen to get things wrapped up here as soon as possible.

'Excellent-sized bedrooms, bathroom is great. Not often you find a walk-in shower and separate bath in this age of apartment.' He turns to me with that manic grin of his that makes my own face ache just looking at it. 'I can see you've done a significant deal of work here.'

Jenny did, but he doesn't need to know that. In the six months she lived here she practically rebuilt the place, room by room. I sometimes wonder if she left because she ran out of things to change. Or if all the changes were because she couldn't change me.

Either way, it will make it easier to leave. I've felt like I've been squatting in someone else's show home for a while now.

'So you think buyers will bite?'

'I think you'll be fighting them off. This sized apartment, this quality of finish, close to schools and local amenities – they'll be eating out of your hand. Set the asking price at an optimum level and this could be a nice little earner.'

Do estate agents talk like this about everything in real life? Like an off-duty policeman is still a policeman because of the language they speak? Or are they like those dreadful DJs you see at weddings that assume a completely different voice the moment they take the microphone? I bet this guy is a bundle of fun at parties...

This is the kind of observation that would make Bethan laugh... I catch myself as the old familiar pain hits. I have to stop letting her sneak into my thoughts. It achieves nothing.

It's good news about the flat, though. I want this sorted as soon as possible. I might not even wait until it sells before I leave. I haven't decided yet. I'm hoping for a quick sale and completion and then I can go with every loose end tied. If it takes too long, I'll move and conduct the sales negotiations from my parents' farm.

I've seen the cottage. Sal video-called last week and gave me a live tour. It's nice, pleasant enough. Plenty of room for Bert, Ernie and me. A large open-plan kitchen and living room, similar to what I have here, a bedroom that looks over fields, a decent-sized bathroom and loads of safe outdoor space for my pets to explore. Mum's made some subtle changes, I noticed. No sign of a hoist anywhere and the bed's been changed from an adjustable mattress to a regular one. According to my sister, Dad has snaffled the riser recliner armchair for his study.

It could work. To begin with, at least. The money this place will make, together with what I've saved over the years, and no bills to pay at the farm while I'm living there will mean I can sort out somewhere of my own as soon as I'm back on my feet. Not sure how long me working for the holiday let business will last, if at all. I haven't told Sal or Mum that yet. But my plan is to get down there and then find a job.

It's been strange to consider a career beyond the army. It's been all I've known for eighteen years and I assumed I would remain employed there in some capacity for the majority of my working life. I have some qualifications I earned during my service, including a PGCE, which would mean I could apply for graduate teacher schemes. That's only a possibility for now, but it never hurts to plan ahead.

I have a lot to consider. It helps, though.

'Did you never consider a blind for this window?'

My too-chippy friend has somehow passed me and is standing by the window I haven't looked out of for two weeks.

'No,' I reply, annoyed at the defensive edge to the word.

He pulls a face that would *definitely* earn him a punch in the army. 'Shame, that. Window opposite completely overlooks your property. Only downside with apartment buildings of this age.'

It wasn't a downside to me. 'I'm sure the new owners will rectify that.'

'Hmm.' He peers out of the window and I hear Bert's low growl inches from his feet. 'Odd neighbours, too.'

Why would he say that? 'Sorry?'

He's frowning now. 'See, you might want to think about putting a blind up before the viewings start. And keeping it drawn.'

'Why?'

'That protest banner in your neighbour's window, over the way. Not good at all. That kind of thing can scare buyers right off. I mean, nobody wants to be living next door to a nutter...'

He carries on, skirting Bert's under-table command post and the sofa, where Ernie is sending him the evil eye. But I don't hear a word he says.

Protest banner.

Does that mean what I think?

'Actually, do you mind if we wrap this up?' I say quickly, cutting across his chatter. 'My physio will be arriving any minute and I have to get things ready.' He begins to object, so I lean heavily on my stick and wince. That does it. Horrified, he shoves his camera and clipboard into a shiny briefcase his mum clearly bought him for Christmas and heads to the door. It's too easy, but the first thing I've thanked my injury for since the crash.

'Yes, of course, my apologies. I'll get the details drawn up, guide price, contract and—'

'Yes, that will all be great,' I rush, herding him out.

He teeters on the doorstep, hand outstretched. 'And if you have any questions, Mr Wallace – anything at all – you have my card...'

'I do. I'll be in touch.'

'Oh, and have you thought whether you'd prefer a staked sign at the front of the property or a wall-mounted...?'

'I'll leave that up to you...' I'm already closing the door. 'Thanks so much, er...'

'I'm the area sales manager, Clough and Hall Estates. Tim Ma—'

Nope, still didn't catch it.

Door closed at last, I face the window, forcing breath into my lungs.

A new sign. When I thought she'd forgotten me...

I approach the window, heart in my mouth. And I look out to hers:

> I HAVE A KID. HE'S MY HEART.
> BUT I AM MORE THAN JUST HIS MUM.
> I WISH YOU'D SEEN THAT.

What?

What is that supposed to mean? I *did* see that. It was impossible not to: the kid trampled half of the border my side of the hedge to get his football. She was there; she saw it, too. Shouldn't she be apologising for the way she looked at me?

> BUT I AM MORE THAN JUST HIS MUM.
> I WISH YOU'D SEEN THAT.

Oh...

No.

Did Bethan think I was judging her?

My irritation gives way to a cold, slow realisation.

She wasn't horrified by me. She thought I was horrified by her boy.

I lean against the windowsill and read her words again, imagining Bethan's fury at the one person she thought was her friend judging her for having a son.

I am such an idiot.

All this time I've railed against her for not seeing me when she saw my injury, but that was what she thought I was doing to her when I saw her child. I was so blinkered by my own battle that I never realised it wasn't about me.

No wonder she hates me. I hate the Lachie she thinks she saw. How could I have missed it?

This is all wrong. I can't leave with Bethan thinking I judged her son.

Why on earth would her having a child change how I feel about her? I love her. Everything else comes with the territory. In the brief moment I saw the kid he looked as full as life as she did. He was the spit of her, too. I bet she's the greatest mum. All that fun and positivity and that laugh of hers that makes you believe everything is okay in the world. What kid wouldn't want a mum like that?

I have to talk to her. Now. It can't wait...

I'm on my way to the door, ready to go straight round to her building and make her listen to me. But then I stop.

No. This has to be done properly. I *love* her. I want her in my life. I need to apologise and show her I'm worth the risk. Injury or not. Job or not. If she feels the same for me, I want to be worthy of that.

I have to make a plan.

But first, her sign needs a reply...

Chapter Fifty-Two

BETHAN

Man, I shouldn't have had those extra glasses of wine last night. My head feels like I've a herd of elephants stampeding inside it.

Noah decided 6 a.m. was a fabulous time to wake up this morning, which hasn't helped. So instead of the little lie-in and long hot shower I'd promised myself, I just about managed a two-minute duck under the water before he summoned me.

Coffee's not helping, either. Or the tablets I necked with it. *Ugh.*

It's all Lachie's fault.

I glance over at my window sign and wonder if he's looked over here today. We haven't exchanged messages for so long, he probably didn't even think to. In the cold, *painful* light of day, my sign is pathetic. I should have said something before, shouldn't I?

Pointless, *pointless* exercise.

I should probably take it down.

'Mu-*u-u-u*-um...'

Oh, that's just what I need. Noah's learned this from pre-school – my name sung like a comedy trombone slide, all the way down and up again. I dread to think what else my boy will learn from his little chums. I mean, I'm all for him going off and exploring the world, but it's the horrible kids he's going to meet on the way I worry about.

'What's up, *bach*?'

He hefts a sigh bigger than mine, which is impressive. 'I *said* I want sausage. And beans. And dippy egg.'

My stomach churns. 'Maybe for lunch, yeah? How about some lovely toast?'

He harrumphs into Tân Dragon. 'Ryan's mum makes him sausage and beans and dippy egg every day.'

Well, bully for her. 'Does she now?'

His bottom lip juts out. '*And* chips.'

'Oh, right. Well, good for Ryan's mum. *We* have bunny toast and lovely jam.'

'Bunnies are for sissies.'

I stare incredulously at him. '*Sissies* is not a nice word. And anyway, these aren't just any old bunnies…'

His eyes narrow. 'What are they?'

Think, brain, I need you… I give a long blink. 'They're Golden Crunchy *Space Bunnies*. From the planet… *Toast-Warren*…'

I can't tell if he's persuaded or if I've just confused the hell out of him. 'How do you know?'

Search me, kid.

'I know because I have Mam Vision. And that means I can see things you can't…' Two of everything this morning, with my eyes as blurry as they are. '… And if you listen carefully before you eat them, you might hear them whispering in Secret Space Bunny Language.'

I've lost the plot. Thankfully, Noah is sold on the idea,

so I down the last of my coffee and gingerly approach the bread bin.

Through an act of sheer grit and determination I successfully navigate the toasting of bread and slathering of butter and jam, thanking my lucky stars I picked up a set of bunny biscuit cutters in Bright Hill's post-Easter sale. Covered in strawberry jam they look more like horrific outtakes from *Watership Down* than a fleet of intergalactic rabbits, but Noah seems to like them. I leave him in front of the television, bending his scruffy little head to listen out for whispers.

I love that boy.

Making more coffee and daring to nibble one crust of toast, I tiptoe into my room to get dressed. My bed beckons me but I daren't lie down, even for a second. I pull a brush through my hair and risk a glance at my reflection, surprised that I look fresher than I feel.

First positive of the day.

Actually, that's not true. Another, potentially huge positive is waiting in my phone voicemail for me to reply to:

'Hello, Ms Gwynne, my name is David Ellis and I'm a family law specialist at Stewart & Hogarth Solicitors in York. Hattie Rowse gave me your number. From what she's told me of your case I think I can help. Could you give me a call on this number at your earliest convenience, please?'

I wasn't expecting to hear back so soon. When I returned to Bright Hill after Patrick and Hattie's visit, we started talking about Kai and I gave her a brief outline to share with her friend.

It might turn out to be nothing, or it might be the biggest break we've had. I'll wait until later this morning before I call him back, but knowing there's even a possibility it could help us is the best feeling.

I settle on the sofa and, seeing Noah happily watching CBeebies, I risk laying my head down on a couple of cushions. My aching eyelids begin to droop, the warmth and the peace of the flat wrapping around me like the softest blanket…

'Mummy…'

'I'm just having a rest, Noah.'

Two little hands frame my face. 'Mummy, come and see…'

'One minute, *bach*. Mummy's got a poorly head.' I keep my eyes closed, hoping he takes the hint.

'It's the cat!'

Five minutes. That's all I need. 'In a bit.'

'The cat is back!'

I wince as the light seeps back into my vision. 'What cat?'

Noah's big blue eyes merge into focus, inches from my face. 'Ernie, Mum. Ernie's back.'

My heart sinks to the cushions beneath me. He's pulling at my hand, trying to dislodge it from under my head. I can't look at the window. I can't do it today.

'Go and wave at him,' I say, an idea occurring. 'See if he waves back.'

That works. He skips away to the window. I close my eyes, a tear escaping down my cheek. I knew he'd love that cat from the first time I saw it. I just didn't know I was going to fall for its owner…

'Mum! He twitched his tail!'

'Oh, great. That's great, Noah.'

I didn't just fall for Lachie. I'm in love with him, aren't I? That's why the ache won't leave. First man I've loved since I fell for Kai. Right now the heartbreak feels worse with Lachlan than it did with the man who abandoned us, but I know that isn't real. It just seems that way because the wound is raw. Lachie didn't destroy our lives. I just need time to let it all heal. In time I'll remember the lovely stuff and the way it ended will fade to a sad regret.

'Ernie's done a picture!'

'What? No, he's probably just breathed on the glass, like you do in the car when it's cold.'

My son's footsteps approach again and I silence the groan I want to make. Forcing my eyes back open, I manage a smile when he reaches my side.

'Not a *huffy picture*, Mummy. A wordy one.'

A wordy picture.

A message.

I forget my thundering headache, struggling off the sofa and half-tripping, half-sprinting to the window. Reaching the glass, I hold the windowsill to get my balance, blinking away sleep and saltwater to read the words.

Lachie's words.

For me.

I'M SORRY, BETHAN.
MEET ME BY THE HEDGE AT 11?

'See?' Noah says, his hand on my arm. 'Ernie's a clever cat.'

'Yes… yes, he is…'

I can't think. I can't move. I don't know what to do with this. It's an apology – I think – but is it enough? He really hurt me. He could have really affected my son.

All this time, I've battled with the words I should have said to him. He used to say he admired my directness: yet when I had the chance to pull him up on his reaction, I didn't. I just picked up my son and fled. I thought I could move on from it and get over him.

But I'm nowhere close to that, am I?

So much has happened since that last day. I've fought so many battles, faced losing everything, held my ground. And I should feel it's all enough. It's not enough. Not until I say to his face the words I've carried with me.

I glance at the kitchen clock. Peter Andre confirms it's 10.45 a.m.

There's time.

But we have to hurry.

'Come on,' I say to Noah, taking his hand. 'Let's go outside.'

'Can I bring my ball?'

'No. Not today. But we need to get your coat and nip to the loo and...' Tears swim in my eyes.

'I can wear my wellies!'

'Wellies are a great idea,' I laugh, tears escaping. I wipe them away with my hand as I hurry to grab my shoes.

I don't know if the words will come out right, or if I'll stumble over them. But I need to let them go so they will finally leave me alone.

It's time.

Chapter Fifty-Three

LACHLAN

It's past eleven.

Only two minutes past, but still.

Bert looks up at me, head tilting to one side.

'I don't know, either,' I say, looking down. 'How long should I give it?'

He *oofs*, whiskery cheeks puffing out.

'Yeah. Another few minutes, you're right.'

I feel like a total prat, standing here with my dog and my stick and a large bunch of flowers. They don't smell, it turns out, which is disappointing, but probably just as well seeing as they're inches away from my nose. A sneezing fit would not add favourably to my image when she comes out.

If she comes out...

Ray-nun-*cu-lus*. Is that right? I can't remember what I asked for in the florists or how she repeated the word. I just wanted to buy them and get back here as soon as possible.

Who gives flowers these crazy names, anyway?

'*Rah*-nun-*ci-lis*. Ra-noon-culus?' Bert's tail thumps against my leg. 'I'll just give her the flowers. No need to tell her what they are, is there? I mean, she knows.'

Great. I'm jabbering to my dog. This isn't how I'd planned it.

What if she hasn't seen the sign? She might still be in bed, or have taken her son out for the day. How long am I prepared to wait?

This is insane.

I check my watch again. Right, I'll give it until ten past. Then I'll sack this off and get on with my life.

It just took so much to get out here. The walk to the florist at the end of the road – who, thankfully, had the right flowers. Then the long trek home. All the time aware of people passing; of my uneven steps against their effortlessly perfect ones. Except, I didn't see anyone looking at me. Apart from an old lady on the way back, who smiled at the flowers and said, 'Aw, bless it,' like I was a kid taking them home for my mum.

And then the tricky manoeuvre of getting Bert out of the door while keeping Ernie inside. Because, of course, Ernie chose today to break the habit of a lifetime and try to come out with us.

Should I have brought Bert? It seemed like a good idea at the time. Largely because I wouldn't be alone – and if she didn't show, I could pretend I was just taking him for a walk all along...

... with an enormous bunch of flowers.

Thank heaven I never tried for the SAS. With skills like these I'd be sunk.

If I have to walk back to my building without her, after finally being ready for Bethan to see me as I am, it will be the *worst*...

Bert barks.

I look up and – she's there. Walking from the front door of her building, head bowed as she chats to her son.

And then, she looks up – and freezes.

She is the most beautiful woman I have ever seen.

I wait for her to say something, but she just stares at me. Not at my leg, or the stick, the flowers or my dog. Just straight at me.

'I thought you weren't coming,' I say.

'I nearly didn't.'

My heart contracts.

She flushes a little. 'Also, Noah needed the loo.'

Her son beams proudly by her side. 'I did a *big* poo.'

'Did you?' It's so unexpected, I let out a laugh before stuffing it away behind the flowers – because Bethan isn't laughing.

I fix my eyes on her. 'I want to explain.'

'You don't have to.'

'I do. When you saw me, I thought…'

'Can I pat the doggy?' Bethan's son is tugging at her sleeve.

'Just – wait, okay?' Impatiently, she strokes his head, casting a glance at me. 'He might not want to…'

'No, it's okay,' I rush, my decision to bring Bert suddenly a blinder. 'He can – if he wants to.' I correct myself. 'If *you* want him to.'

Bethan rolls her eyes heavenwards. 'Fine. Be gentle, yeah?'

Noah dashes from his mum to me, stopping at my feet and gazing up at me like I'm a skyscraper. 'I'm Noah.'

'Um, hi. I'm Lachie. And this is Bert.'

Bethan and I watch dumbly as her small boy and my stumpy-limbed dog proceed to become instant buddies. It's remarkable, especially for Bert, considering it took him a week to trust me enough and almost a month to like Jenny.

I look back at Bethan, and my body aches for her. 'I made a mistake, the last time I saw you. I thought you were horrified to see me—' I nod at my leg and the stick supporting me, '—to see *this*.'

'What?'

'It's why I suggested the hedge meetings instead of doing what I wanted to and walking round to see you. I wanted it to be better before that happened. I was working so hard, but… The way I walk now – this is it, permanently. I had an accident, almost four months ago. I was crushed in a car. I should have told you but I didn't because – I liked you liking me without knowing the rest.'

Her eyes are very still as she listens.

'I've lost so much because of it. For months it's been all I can see. But I didn't want you to see it, not before you knew me. You are the only person in my life who doesn't see my injury first. That meant the world. I felt like I could be anyone when I was with you.'

She shakes her head. 'You didn't have to tell me – about your leg. It wouldn't have made a difference. I just liked you…' She stares at the long grass beneath her red sneakers. 'I thought you were shocked I had a kid. I thought you were judging me. I get that all the time, Lachie, from everywhere. Well-meaning or just rude. I hoped you were different.'

'I am different. I care about you, Bethan. I could never judge you. It was a shock because I didn't know you had a kid, not because you do.'

'I was going to tell you, the day you saw us. I know I should have told you before, but I wanted to keep you just for me. I haven't had someone of my own for a long time. I thought you might be the one that changed that. But when I saw your face…'

'I know – I know that now. I'm so sorry. I want to be the one who changes things for you. Both of you. Why would I ever judge you for having a son? He's part of you and…' I have to say it. This might be the last time we speak, but I can't leave until she knows, '… and I love you.'

So there we stand, her and me, not really knowing what to do next. We're feet apart – closer than a hedge width – and I want to close the gap. But I can't read her expression. I've said everything I came here to say. It's her turn now.

'You should have told me *that*,' she says.

'Mummy, look at Bert's paws when I tickle his tummy!'

Her eyes flicker, but don't leave mine. 'That's great, *bach*.'

'They go *boingy-boingy-boing*!'

'Do they? That's funny.' The smallest smile dances on her lips. It's all I can look at. 'I am not ashamed of my son,' she begins, her voice low. 'But you were the first person I've met who was interested in just me. Not someone's mum. Not my job. I loved that.' Her eyes glisten. 'I loved *you*.'

'Could you love me again?' I ask before I can think better of it – because my heart is threatening to knock me over and I need to know.

She doesn't reply.

What does that mean? If you love someone wouldn't you say it immediately?

Bright yellow, red and orange blooms dance in my hand, but there's no breeze moving them.

I can't tell what she's thinking. There is so much at stake and I could kick myself that all this time I've thought I had the most to lose by telling the truth. But I was wrong: the risk for Bethan was always going to eclipse mine.

If it's a *no* – if the damage is too much and we've left it too late to repair – at least we will have had this. I watch her arms fold across her body and her eyes drift towards her son and my dog.

Face to face, far too late, I see Bethan for everything she is. Proud, fearless, tenacious, beautiful and strong. And, coincidentally, a mother whose son is her world. But most of all, I see her. And I hate that I kept this moment away for so long.

Cars pass and chatter drifts up from the street. The sun moves between our buildings, casting two block shadows framing a bright bridge of light. We stand on its periphery, on the edge of possibility. And I don't dare breathe for fear of breaking this moment...

'I don't know...' she says.

It isn't the answer I wanted. I lean against my stick, which is beginning to sink into the soft ground. What do I do now? Throw the flowers at her and run?

'... it depends.'

'On what?'

Her blue eyes flick to mine. 'On whether those flowers are for me.'

I stare back – is that a *yes*? Is she joking? 'They are – sorry.'

I hold them out to her and she moves to accept them, sunlight washing her dark hair a burnished red as she steps into the light. 'I recognise these.'

The spark I have missed so much returns, dancing between us. Feeling brave, I reply, 'A beautiful woman once told me they were called *ray*-noon-*cullis*.'

There's a second where our eyes meet – and then she's laughing – that laugh of hers that summons the sunshine. 'Come again? Not *ray*-noon-*cullis*, you crazy man. *Ran-un*-cu-lus.'

I laugh, too, because that's the most obvious pronunciation

and I completely missed it. I've missed a lot, it seems. 'Oh. *Bollocks.*' Too late, I remember the small child kneeling inches away from us. 'Sorry. *Shit.* I didn't mean...'

'Lachie...'

Great. I'm at the moment it's all supposed to come good for us and the first thing I do is teach Bethan's son two new words he *definitely* doesn't need to learn. 'Seriously, I – I don't even know where that came from. I hardly ever swear these days and...'

'Oi, Lachie.' She's right next to me now, her eyes alive.

'What?'

Bethan's smile returns as she reaches up to stroke my face. 'I love you.'

And then there are no more words.

Just our kiss.

Chapter Fifty-Four

BETHAN

I never had myself pegged as a cat person.

Mind you, Ernie and I have had a connection from the start.

He's purring in my lap now, curled into a perfect circle, a great big grey fluffy lump of contentment.

I know how he feels.

The room is filled with lazy Sunday light and Lachie's sofa is warm around me. I smile as Noah throws a soggy-looking tennis ball for the hundredth time and Bert dashes after it, his cute little legs skidding across the wooden floor. My son claps his hands and gives a screech of delight any dragon would be proud of. He turns his face towards his new best friend – after Bert, of course.

'Did you see that one?'

'Good shot. Awesome, mate.'

I see Noah's little hand rest for just a moment on Lachie's knee and then he's off, chasing after an ecstatic dog. It's that small snapshot that means the world. There have been more of them lately, never expected but always a gift. I don't think Lachie really knows what to do when they happen, but I see his eyes glisten and his smile become that bit broader. Turns out I wasn't the only one ready to love for him for who he is.

'Quick,' I say, 'get up before he comes back.'

'Nah, I'm okay,' he insists.

Honestly, he's been sitting on the floor for over an hour, his back against the dining table and both legs stretched out. His leg won't be happy with him later, but he doesn't seem to mind. He reaches up and grabs a mug from the table, taking a sip of what, by now, will be stone-cold tea, grinning at me when he catches me watching.

'Like what you see, ma'am?'

'It's not bad.' I grin back; feeling my heart swelling so big it might push Ernie right off my lap.

Four weeks feels like a lifetime and the blink of an eye at once. We came so close to *not* having this. It was only after we got together I discovered Lachie was putting this place on the market the day he saw my sign. If he hadn't looked, if he'd already left – I don't want to think what life would have been like without him.

He shifts a little on the floor, his left arm steadying him. I see the twist of his forearm and Maya Angelou's wise words curling around it. That tattoo started this trouble. I blush now, remembering the effect it had on me – before I'd seen his face or knew anything about him. And the shock of touching the words on his skin for the first time, when we met by the hedge. Strange, how a memory can be that powerful still. Even when I have lots of new ones now – and can tell you *exactly* how many inks Lachlan Wallace possesses...

'What?'

'Just admiring the goods,' I reply, grimacing at how bad that sounds.

'Typical. She only wants me for my body.'

'No, not just your body...'

His smile softens. That man is too gorgeous for his own good.

'... Your cat and your dog, too.'

He shakes his head. 'Oh, so now the truth comes out.'

'And your sofa, your telly, which is way bigger than ours, that shower's pretty special as well ...'

'Like that, is it?'

I shrug. 'Say it like I see it, *cariad...*'

That does it. He's up on his feet, moving over to me and scooping me into his arms, a very disgruntled moggie decidedly evicted.

'Ugh, are you kissing *again*?'

We break apart to meet the frown of a flushed-face kid accompanied by his wagging-tailed sidekick.

'Yeah, sorry, mate. Do you mind if I kiss your mum?'

The Noah Gwynne Sigh could win Oscars. '*O-kay*. But if the pirates sneak in, you have to tell the dragons *straight away*.'

'Yes, sir!'

I love this man. I love that he reached out at his lowest ebb and found me at my loneliest. I've never believed in fate, really. I think you make the most of what you find. But I lucked out when I found this one.

I'm so proud of him. Leaving the army has been tough and I don't think he'll be over it for a long time. I know his family weren't happy when he cancelled plans to move back, although I've met them on a video call and they seemed lovely. I think when they see how well he's doing they'll come round. Time is what makes the difference – and I'm not going anywhere.

He's just been accepted on a Graduate Teacher scheme at a school across town, starting in September. It's a fraction of what he was earning at Catterick, but he has some savings and I'm earning a bit more now I'm Head of Plants at Bright Hill, so we'll manage. Lachie keeps joking with Noah that they'll both start Big School on the same day. I don't think I'll ever be used to having a primary school kid, but at least both my boys will be starting their next adventures together.

My boys.

Look at you, Bethan.

I snuggle into Lachie, his arms strong around me. From here, I can see his window and ours out beyond it. There are identical vases of ranunculus in both. He still can't really say it right, but I'm persevering. Just wait till I start teaching him to say Llanfairpwllgwyngyllgogerychwyrndrobwllllantysiliogogogoch...

There's a long way ahead for us and nothing is set in stone.

But this is working. And it's wonderful.

Life isn't perfect, is it? You'd be nuts to think it should be. It's messy and frustrating, beautiful and unjust. Kai will never be in Noah's life, but Lachie just might be. I may never see any money from the counter-proceedings Hattie's friend David is pursuing against the loan company, but I'll get there somehow. Lachie wants to punch Kai's lights out if he ever comes back to the country, which I secretly love. He won't do it, of course, but having him on my side makes all the difference.

I am content with my beautiful mess of a life. With all its unknowns and unseen obstacles that might jump me at any moment. I have more than enough shiny pebbles in my path to keep moving forward.

I don't care what anyone thinks of me. I know who I am and I bloody love her. Lachie loves her too. Which is just as well, really, because I adore the skin off him.

We're okay, all of us.

We're going to be fine.

THE END

Acknowledgements

It takes an army to nurture, grow and support a book. My thanks to:

Head Gardener (My fab editor)
MANPREET GREWAL

Chief of Staff (My amazing agent)
HANNAH FERGUSON

Topiary Specialist (Copy editor)
JON APPLETON

Special Observer (Proofreader)
JANE SELLEY

Expert Plant Team (HQ Production Team)
MELANIE HAYES   LILY CAPEWELL
MELISSA KELLY   DAWN BURNETT
HALEMA BEGUM   ANGIE DOBBS
TOM KEANE

Artist Corps (Production Design)
CHARLOTTE PHILLIPS
STEPHANIE HEATHCOTE

Concessions (Rights & Legal)
HARDMAN SWAINSON

Battalion Support Unit (Fab friends)

AG SMITH	CLAIRE SMITH
RACHAEL LUCAS	CALLY TAYLOR
TAMSYN MURRAY	KATE HARRISON
ROWAN COLEMAN	JULIE COHEN
KIM CURRAN	THE MINTS
THE DREAMERS	WHITES & DICKINSONS

MY FAB SOCIAL MEDIA FOLLOWERS

Bright Hill Nurseries Team (Book cameos)
BHUPINDER BROWN and KERRY-ANN MCDADE
(gift shop assistants)
JENN MCKEAN and JUDITH GRAHAM
(weekend café assistants)
CLAIRE WHITLOCK
(outdoor clothing concession manager)
HARRIET COOKE and CHARLOTTE BENNETT
(farmers' collective gardeners)

HONOURABLE MENTIONS

Lachie's favourite books starring Eddie Flynn are written by STEVE CAVANAGH and are awesome. Sneakily mentioned with love!

Noah's teacher, Mrs Guest, inspired by RAEGON GUEST, with thanks for being awesome. x

Noah's dragons kindly loaned by FLO, who also named Bert & Ernie.

Lockdown buddies, constant entertainers, caterers, hug-suppliers, huge dreamers and the undisputed loves of my life: BOB and FLO, you are my everything. Love you to the moon and back and twice around the stars xx

This book wouldn't have happened without a global pandemic. It's proof to me that good things still happen, even in the darkest times. Dear reader, I send huge love to you for reading this book. Keep looking for shiny pebbles of hope and glimpses of light. Better days are coming xx

The Start of Something:
Miranda's book soundtrack

These are the songs that inspired me as I wrote Bethan and Lachie's story. Music has been a huge comfort to me through the pandemic and many of the artists below saw their livelihoods disappear when live music ceased. Please follow these amazing musicians and buy their music to support them.

Bethan & Lachie's theme:
REAL LOVE – Tom Odell – Real Love (single)

The Start of Something inspired by:
FLOWERS IN THE WINDOW – Travis – *The Invisible Band*
WORLD SPINS MADLY ON – The Weepies – *Say I Am You*
CLOUDS – Newton Faulkner – *Write It On Your Skin* (Deluxe Edition)
CUP OF TEA – Kacey Musgraves – *Pageant Material*
THIS TOWN – Niall Horan – *Flicker*
FIXED – Mary Bragg – *Violets as Camouflage*
BRIGHT LIGHTS – Haevn – *Eyes Closed*
IMPOSSIBLE – James Arthur – Impossible (single)
TIMES LIKE THESE – Live Lounge Allstars – BBC Radio 1 Stay Home Live Lounge

FALLING OFF THE FACE OF THE EARTH – Matt Wertz – *Twenty Three Places*

DIAMONDS – Josef Salvat – Recover 2017 – *Ministry of Sound*

OUTNUMBERED – Dermot Kennedy – *Without Fear*

DON'T GET MAD GET EVEN – The Little Kicks – *Shake Off Your Troubles*

WALK ALONE – Rudimental (feat. Tom Walker) – *Toast to Our Differences*

GLORIOUS – Måns Zelmerlöw – *Chameleon*

GRACE – Lewis Capaldi – *Divinely Uninspired to a Hellish Extent*

KINGS & QUEENS – Ava Max – *Heaven & Hell*

SOMETHING BEAUTIFUL – Tim Halperin – Something Beautiful (single)

**Turn the page to read an exclusive extract
from *Our Story*, the gorgeous love story of
Otty and Joe, from Miranda Dickinson**

Available to buy now!

Chapter One

OTTY

It's my last day.

I repeat it in my mind like a mantra as I go through the motions of the job I've done since I was twenty-one. Even though I have longed for this day to arrive, it's surreal to be living it.

Dad keeps glancing over when he thinks I'm not looking. I know what he's thinking. It's two hours until my final shift ends and I haven't had *the talk*. Yet. But I feel it in the air, the low rumble of approaching thunder.

'It won't be the same without you, bab,' Sheila says, setting another mug of tea next to my workbench. Where other people use words, Sheila Wright uses tea. This is easily the thirteenth mug she's brought me today, although, to be honest, I stopped counting around lunchtime.

'In a few weeks you won't even notice I'm not here,' I smile back, reaching for her hand when her eyes glisten. 'And I'll still scc you at the cricket.'

She nods, dabbing her nose with a tissue she produces from her sleeve. When I was little, I used to imagine the inside of Sheila Wright's cardigan sleeves as endless winter landscapes of white.

She's as close to a real auntie as I've ever had. I'm going to miss her chats every day.

But it's time to go.

I turn my attention back to the bike frame propped up on the bench. There's something dodgy with its suspension and I'm determined to sort it before I hand in my RoadTrail staff badge. A clean slate for my next big adventure to begin.

An hour later, the inevitable happens.

'It's a good job, this.'

I smile but keep my attention on the suspension unit. 'It is, Dad.'

'I'm not looking for anyone else.'

'Well, you should. Steve and Jarvis can't manage the workshop on their own.'

'Oi,' Jarvis says, his head popping up from the bench on the other side of the workshop. One thing I definitely *won't* miss is never being able to conduct a private conversation in this place.

'I'm just saying you need an extra pair of hands here, Jarv.'

'If they come without a gob it'll be an improvement.' His grin is a balm to his barb. For Jarvis and Steve mickey-taking is a badge of belonging. If they mock you, you're in.

'You hope,' I grin back.

'This is a *proper* job,' Dad says. And there it is.

'So is my new one.'

'I mean a steady job. One you can rely on. People are always going to need their bikes fixing…'

'And they're always going to watch TV.'

'*Writing*,' Dad says, spitting the word out like a fly in his tea. 'That in't safe, bab. Six months and then what? You'll be out on your ear with moths in your wallet.'

I meet his frown. 'I'll be fine.'

I'll be more than fine. Writing is my dream. I've done the sensible thing for years, my full-time shifts in Dad's bike shop nothing compared with the endless unseen hours spent wrangling words onto the page. Tomorrow *that me* gets to step out into the light. I'm still expecting to arrive and find it's all a prank. I'm terrified of failing. But I can't wait to try.

'You can still change your mind.'

'I can't.' I glance over at my colleagues, lowering my voice. 'Russell Styles is expecting me.' *He wants me*, I want to add, but I don't. Dad doesn't understand what that sentence means to me. Out of the fifteen hundred scriptwriters who applied, a famous showrunner chose *me*. Even though it's my first experience as a staff writer, my first in a writers' room. My first of *anything*. Russell read my script and wanted me on his team.

'If you work with Jodie Comer tell her she needs a hunky bike mechanic in her life,' Steve says.

'Hunky? More like *chunky*, mate,' Jarvis shoots back.

Dad doesn't smile with them. 'Just think about it, our Otts. It's risky to rest your bills on a pipe dream.'

Nothing I say will change his mind. So I just hug him.

At the end of the day, we gather by the back door of the workshop. The sun is just beginning to dip over the warehouse roofs of the trading estate and starlings are bickering in the ash trees over the road. I fill my lungs for the last time with the scent of oil and metal, sawdust and leather. It's strange to think I won't smell it again, won't be followed home by it clinging to my clothes and hair.

Sheila is in tears, Steve has his arm around her and even Jarvis isn't cracking jokes. Dad stands beside me, a silent sentinel. For a moment, everything is calm. It only lasts as long as a slow intake of breath, but I feel more expressed by the silence than by anything words could say.

'Right then,' I say, surprised to feel tears arriving. I hand Dad my badge and door pass and he takes it as solemnly as a war widow accepting colours from an officer. 'Thanks, guys. For everything.'

Jarvis gives my arm his usual punch, and then scoops me into an enormous hug. 'Knock 'em dead, Otty. You show 'em.'

I smile against his chest, the pull of Past Me suddenly strong. 'I will.'

Steve shakes my hand, which is the most physical contact I've had with him in all the years we've worked together. 'We'll be watching for your name on them telly credits.'

'Cheers, mate.'

I hug Sheila and Dad. 'See you soon, yeah?'

They nod and stand together as I walk from them across the car park to my car. When I open the driver's door, I turn back and take one last look. As one, the RoadTrail team raise their hands in salute.

I don't let myself cry until I've driven off the estate.

Tonight, I'm going to have a quiet one. Let it all finally sink in. I plan a takeaway from Diamond Balti across the street from my flat with one of their enormous Peshwari naans and a bottle of Chang beer, followed by a night of classic drama repeats on telly. Perfect. I'd say an early night, too, but I know my brain. It rarely switches off before midnight and tonight my nerves will probably push that much later. I'll sleep when it comes.

Monty, my yellow Fiat 500, creaks into the car park and when I kill the engine I sit in the stillness for a moment. Last time I'll make that journey. Last time I'll get home with the itch of not having written all day. Tomorrow, everything changes.

I consider going straight to Diamond Balti, but decide on a shower first. Leaving my car, I punch the entry number into the door lock and head inside. The three flights of stairs seem to take longer to climb this evening but everything feels significant today. I'm on the cusp of the next season of my life, my toes inching towards the edge, ready to leap...

Hang on. What's that?

There's an envelope drawing-pinned to my front door. That's odd. Why wasn't it posted through the letterbox? I pull the pin out, which takes more effort than I expect. Someone bashed it into the painted wood with considerable force. When I look at the brass dome of its head, I can see the pin is dented from whatever implement whoever put it there used. Poor thing. I pocket the pin and the envelope and unlock my front door.

It's not Birmingham's most spacious home, but I love my flat. I've rented it for seven years and it might as well be a palace for the security and comfort it gives me. That was another battle with Dad I stuck out and won. He wanted me to stay at home with him, but I needed my own space and somewhere I could write without having to justify it. I love Dad and I know he loves me, but I wish he wouldn't think he has to protect me from the world. I've stopped trying to argue the toss and instead just go with it, trusting that he'll see I made the right choice in time. This flat was the right choice for me: the first night I lived here, I wrote all night, going into the workshop the next day dizzy with exhaustion but buzzing.

I drop my rucksack by the kitchen counter and pull the envelope from my pocket. Inside is a single sheet of paper, typed.

Dear Miss Perry

NOTICE OF EVICTION
As landlord of Flat 6, Princess Building, West Park Road,
I hereby give notice of the termination of your tenancy
agreement, effective immediately. You must vacate the
property, including all furniture and personal effects, by
10 a.m. tomorrow. Failure to do this will result in legal
action being pursued against you.

Yours sincerely
Barrington Theopolis (Mr)
Landlord

What?

I stare at the paper as if the words might relent and rearrange
themselves into something else. The letter creases as my fingers
curl into fists around it. Eviction? Why? I have always paid my
rent on time, never missing a payment in seven years. I haven't
had any warning of this. He can't just evict me!

Shaking, I reach for my phone and dial Barry's number. I
swallow my panic and tears as I wait for him to answer. I won't
cry on the phone. I *won't*.

'Yes?'

'Barry – Mr Theopolis – it's Ottilie Perry. I just got your letter.'
You utter bastard, I add in my head, sucking in a lungful of air to
keep myself from screaming at him or bursting into tears.

'And?'

'You can't evict me. I've always paid my bills, I've never had a
complaint from you or anyone else in the building…'

'I have another tenant.'

'*I'm* your tenant, Barry. I've been your tenant for seven years.'

'She needs the flat tomorrow.'

I can't believe what I'm hearing. This can't happen, not tonight. My life is supposed to change tomorrow. And not like this. It can't be *this*.

'I need the flat *now*.' Deafening silence on the other end of the line sets my blood boiling. 'And anyway, you can't just evict me. I have rights.'

'That's not my problem.' There's no emotion in his voice, not even a hint of remorse or embarrassment at what he's doing. 'I will collect the keys at 10 a.m. tomorrow.'

'No you bloody won't,' I growl back, any pretence of calm abandoned now. He doesn't deserve civility. And I'm not going to beg him. If he wants me gone, it will be on my terms. 'I'm starting a new job tomorrow. So if you want the keys *you* will be here at 6 a.m. And I will require my deposit in full, in cash.'

'*Six?*'

'Six. Or else it will have to be late tomorrow evening. Your choice.'

A beat. I can hear his breathing rasp a little. 'Fine. 6 a.m., sharp.'

I hang up before he has the chance to do it first.

Anger fires through my body, tears and shock chasing its heels. My legs give way and now I'm on the floor, shaking, sobbing, gasping for breath. I should fight this, get legal advice, refuse to leave. But there's no time. I have a new job tomorrow and that's all that matters. I will not give Barry Theopolis the satisfaction of a fight. I will take my business elsewhere.

I just have no idea where.

I allow myself one moment to look around my home – now *not* my home for much longer – taking in the features so familiar

I don't see them anymore. The faded curtains, the stacks of books rising around the walls like the skyscrapers of the city because I've never had space for bookshelves, the sagging sofa that came with the flat and will be left here tomorrow when I'm no longer its tenant.

I can't believe I have to leave.

I sit up, drag my sleeves across my eyes to rid them of tears, will strength into my spine. I need to start packing. I'll work out the rest later.

Chapter Two

JOE

'Come over.'

'I can't.'

'Why not?'

'I have to work tonight.'

Her frustrated sigh slaps my ear where I hold my phone to it. 'Why don't you just shag Russell Styles and get it over with?'

'It's my job, Vic.'

'Yeah, right.'

'It *is*.'

'You know what, Joe? Forget it. You're not the only person I'm seeing.'

Wow.

I blink at the empty room. There's direct and then there's Victoria. I mean, I never imagined I was the only bloke in her life but I kind of thought she'd keep that to herself. 'Right, well. Have fun.'

I end the call.

'You off out, Joe?' Matt, my housemate, bobs his head around the door from the hall.

'Apparently not.' When Matt's expression clouds, I hold up my phone. 'I think I just got dumped.'

'You *think*? Who by?'

'Victoria.'

He chuckles and scratches his hair, which always looks like he's just rolled out of bed. Which he probably has. 'I thought you'd given up on her months ago.'

I grimace back. I should have, but I've been busy. And she has a habit of reappearing when I need distraction from work. 'Turns out she beat me to it.'

'Bummer, mate.' I expect him to mosey off to whatever it is he does most evenings, but he remains by the doorway. 'So – you're not out tonight?'

'Nope. Doesn't matter anyway. I have these sample episodes to get done and the agency sent over a script clean-up they want for the end of the week.'

'Man in demand, Joe.'

'Lucky me. You off out?'

A flicker of something passes across his face. 'Yeah. No. Not sure yet.'

He's working on a feature film script at the moment and is lost in his head most of the time. At least, that's what he *says* it is. Judging by the contents of the ashtray he regularly leaves in the kitchen – never quite making the bin – something else might be calling him to dreamland. 'Hey, but you should totally go out anyway.'

'Too busy. Like I said.'

'Joe. Stop wallowing.'

'I – er – I'm not?'

'That's what Victoria expects you to do, right? Hole yourself away, crying into your beer.'

Since when has Matt Evans ever worried about me? 'Actually, she expected me to be going out tonight. She dumped me because I wasn't.'

'Right.' He nods but his brow is still knotted. 'Even still, you should go out. At least get food or – something. I mean, when was the last time you ate?'

I'm about to dismiss this when I realise he's made a good point. I haven't eaten since a hastily grabbed bacon roll before my meeting with Russell this morning. On cue, my stomach protests its emptiness. I could go to that all-you-can-eat multi-ethnic buffet place in town where my friend works. I could eat enough so I don't have to worry about food again tonight and then work through till three or four-ish. Rumour is we have eight new writers arriving tomorrow and I need to be head and shoulders above them when Russell walks in.

'I might just dash out for food, actually,' I say, snapping my laptop shut and grabbing my keys from the kitchen counter. 'Do you want anything?'

'Nah, I'm good,' Matt says, noticeably brighter than a minute ago. 'Go. A break might be just what your brain needs.'

When he nods at my laptop I have a horrible feeling he saw the tellingly blank page on it before I closed the lid. I'm *not* stuck. I'm just… in a bit of an inspiration lull. Food will help.

Food *does* help. I don't want to admit Matt's right, but being away from the house does wonders for the script. It helps that my old schoolmate Nish works at the buffet place and doesn't care if I work while I eat. An hour turns into two and before I know it, it's almost one in the morning. Nish grins at me as I apologise on my way out.

By the time I get back to the house, sleep and a full belly are conspiring against me. Heading to bed with every intention of working there till the birds start singing, I crash out as soon as I get in.

Which is why, when I jump awake in brave sunlight and grab my phone, I'm sick to discover it's 6 a.m. I'd planned to get into Ensign Media early this morning to be there before the new intake arrives. Cursing, I throw on fresh clothes and drag my fingers through my hair in a lame attempt to tame it before I dash downstairs.

It's only when I'm waiting for my grumpy old filter coffee machine to do its stuff that I notice the note.

A bright pink sticky note, its edges curling, weighed down with a butter knife in the sea of crumbs on the breadboard.

Sorry, mate.
Moved out.
Matt

What?

I snatch the note from its crumby resting place and blink hard to clear sleep from my eyes. *Moved out?* When?

And then I let my gaze travel through the open kitchen door to the hallway. No shoes. No horrible shoe rack. *Matt's* wretched shoe rack he insisted on having there, stinking out the space. I walk through to the empty hall, turn left into the living room and see more evidence: the four empty shelves in the large bookcase where Matt's games and terrible sports biographies always lived. By the TV, no jumble of games console wires and controllers, no Xbox and Wii. I don't have to check his room to work out that the books and his desk will be missing from there, too.

He bloody moved out. A week before the rent is due.

Slowly, it hits me.

He owes me three weeks' rent. Money I don't have.

I can feel panic rising and make myself breathe against the assault. I still have a week. I need to regroup, work out a plan. Matt is an utter dick for doing this to me but I have more important things to do than waste any brain-time on it today – like making sure my boss sees me before everyone else.

Everything else can wait.

ONE PLACE. MANY STORIES

Bold, innovative and
empowering publishing.

FOLLOW US ON:

@HQStories